PRIME TIME TRAVELERS

PRIME TIME TRAVELERS

JARED PLUMMER VS. THE ANCIENT WORLD

NEIL LAIRD

Neillaird.com

CHAPTER 1

Jared was in such a mad dash across Seville that it was only after he arrived at his ex-boyfriend's office that he saw himself in the window.

Dear God, this is how I look when I beg him to take me back?

A tattered T-shirt hung from his shoulders, splattered with serpent guts, embalming fluid, and a huge tear where one of the jackal-headed boatmen held on before getting eaten by Apep, Devourer of Souls.

Jared Plummer had traveled too far into the past and discovered too much about himself to turn back now. He quickly ran his fingers through his unkempt hair, flicked it free of a dead scarab beetle, and burst into the busy office.

It had been two years, with little more than a few terse texts between them, so Jared wasn't even sure if his ex still worked there. Carlos had taken the job at the Seville Tourist Bureau to supplement his income as a local fixer for TV shows. That's where they had met. For all Jared knew, Carlos could be off on a shoot or home making love to his new boyfriend. Jared had considered calling as soon as he landed, but decided it was better to surprise him. If Carlos no longer wanted him, it would be evident in his eyes.

Jared entered the office and glanced around. Carlos' desk used to be in the back, but another man now occupied it. He bit the inside of his mouth as a troublesome feeling started creeping in, the one that almost caused his death in Egypt.

Jared stiffened his back and approached the front desk, knowing he wouldn't succumb again. A receptionist was blandly arranging tourist pamphlets, and when she caught Jared's stare. A look of disgust spread across her face. Jared wasn't sure why until he straightened his jumbled shirt, and a bit of gray matter fell to the floor, probably from the old lady Omm. Only then did it dawn on him why so many people, from the airline stewardess to the customs official and the Uber driver, had treated him like a leper.

Thinking back now, he could barely remember any of it.

Had he really traveled so far in such a short time? Was he truly, finally, there? If so, only one goal remained—to kiss Carlos, apologize, take his hand, and make love to him for all eternity—there in this damn office if need be.

The receptionist said something in Spanish, which Jared, born and raised in rural Kansas, didn't understand.

"Sorry?" he said. "I don't—"

She slipped mid-sentence into English, no doubt a requirement for someone who worked at an international tourist center.

"May I help you… Sir?"

"Yes, yes, you may!" Jared replied with a bit too much enthusiasm. "Carlos!"

A pause. "Yes, Carlos? Is that your name?"

He waved his arms around the crowded room. "No, no. Carlos, is Carlos here?"

"You're in Spain, Sir. There are many men called Carlos."

"Carlos Cortez. He works here." Jared looked around. "Or did."

"Oh, *our* Carlos."

Now the woman appeared truly worried, perhaps afraid to share employee information with someone she suspected of living in a dumpster.

"And you are?"

Jared looked around again—the room was full of people, many of whom now had eyes on him. "I'm his boyfriend, Jared Plummer." He said this loudly, for the first time outing himself to a group of strangers. Doing it in the *Duat* with his friends and crew members was triumph enough, but saying it in public, for all to hear… well, it felt amazing.

"Oh, you are? I can look for him, but he might be… busy." She moved sideways from the desk, clutching a map of Tourist Seville in front of her like Andalusian armor. "Do you have a message?"

"Yes, yes, I do. Tell him—"

Jared stopped mid-sentence, for there in the back, staring at him with all the others, was Carlos, a stack of brochures in his hand.

"That I love him."

Jared's breath halted. Carlos was as beautiful as he remembered: long black hair reaching broad shoulders, wide brown eyes staring back through thick lashes. *How could I have ever walked away from such a man?* Jared wanted to run to him and hold him tight, but fear gripped him and he waited for Carlos to make the first move.

Instead of running to him, Carlos walked to Jared and took his hand, not for a hug but to guide him away from the others. There was no smile, no double kiss. Jared tried to read his eyes, but they were downcast, avoiding all contact.

"Not here," is all Carlos said, his grip limp and light.

The two men exited the street and walked to a bus stop bench a few feet away.

"Sit," Carlos said in a voice not as warm as Jared had hoped.

And why would it be? The way I dumped him, crushed his love, and never looked back. It's a wonder he didn't just push me into an oncoming bus.

They sat in silence for a few seconds. There would be no small talk. It was time for Jared to explain himself.

"I'm sorry," he began. "For all of it. For the way I treated you, for my fear, for my inability to see your side of things. I love you, and I—"

The squeak of a bus cut him off, and after the few waiting passengers boarded, Jared was ready to go on. But Carlos held up a hand.

"You show up at my office," he snapped. "What? Fourteen months after breaking up with me in a goddamn cab to the airport, to tell me this. Loudly. In front of my co-workers. And looking like... I don't know what you look like." He glanced at Jared's feet. "Are those gold slippers?"

"Oh yeah, got them from Ramses the Great's High Priest."

"Gave them to you personally, did he?"

"Oh no, he was already dead from an arrow to the neck."

"Your arrow?"

"A friend's." Jared thought for a moment and sighed wistfully. "A Nubian warrior, actually."

Carlos studied Jared's face more closely. "You still have all your teeth, so it's not meth." A realization seemed to creep over Carlos, and the vaguest of smiles crossed his lips. "At least it seems you've found yourself—in a big way. I congratulate you on that." He scanned Jared's toned, tanned body. "Lost some weight, too, I see."

Jared smiled, knowing how hard he had worked to transform himself. "I guess I dropped a few pounds, packed on some muscle. Like it?"

"Not really. Your old physique was more to my liking. All this," Carlos said with a shrug. "Isn't the Jared I once loved."

Jared's resolve crumbled. Of course, it was arrogant to barge in like this, puffed up and proud. That happened at the end of Hollywood movies, not real life. Carlos, no doubt, had written him off fourteen months ago and was now seeing his ex-lover as the opposite of all that had first attracted him to the naive kid from Kansas. Where Jared Plummer was once sweet-natured and went out of his way—to a fault, it must be said—to offend no one, now he was some self-absorbed jerk peacocking himself at the expense of others.

Jared could do little more than look Carlos in the eyes—the ones he had thought about and yearned for every day since their parting. Carlos finally held his gaze, and only then did Jared notice that his eyes were rimmed with tears. He had wounded Carlos badly, but maybe there was still a chance to make it right. Yet, still no words came out. He had reverted to the lost soul he had thought he left behind in 1200 BC.

"Okay," Carlos said at last. "Go on."

"Those weird dreams of mine… the past... all of it… was real." He stumbled again. There was simply too much to explain. "I came here to see you because I've been to hell and back."

"Hell and back, huh?"

Carlos' voice took on an edge. It was clear he wouldn't be fooled a second time by Jared's flowery words.

"A bit dramatic for the documentary filmmaker, always clinging to the truth."

"That's why I said it, baby. It's *literally* true. And the only thing that got me through was the hope of seeing you alive again."

Carlos sat his tourist brochures on the bench, next to a dung beetle that had crawled from Jared's pants and seemed to be sunning itself in the midday heat. "Umm, maybe you should start at the beginning?"

"When I said those things in the cab, I wasn't myself yet," Jared started. "I was only thinking about—"

"Not *that* far back," Carlos interrupted. "Sadly, I already know what you were thinking that day." He waved his hand over Jared's blood-splattered jeans and the dung beetle that was now busy rolling up bus stop filth into a ball. "Just go far back enough to explain this "new you." How getting dipped in guts and insects and acquiring pharaonic footwear led you back to me. Let's start there."

CHAPTER 2

FIVE DAYS EARLIER

Jared dug his feet into the rain-sodden Egyptian desert and pleaded with the man in the fedora.

"It's three little lines, Derek. Get them on tape, and we head to the hotel to wait out the storm."

"It's three *lousy* lines in what's gotta be the worst episode of the season."

The host of TV's top prime time adventure series checked his reflection in the monitor and flicked a clump of sand from his boxy chin. "Here we are getting drenched in front of an ancient temple, and what do you want the great explorer Derek Dees to talk about? Some old British biddy who claims she can travel through time and was the pharaoh's love child."

Jared bit the inside of his cheek, where a loose chunk of flesh had been taking the brunt of his stress. His first shot at directing, and halfway through day one, the show's star already hated him.

Ancient Encounters with Derek Dees was no *Frontline*, and it often rested on hoary stereotypes and cliches as a substitute for facts. But Jared had to admit this story was flimsier than most, and if his true reason for being there was exposed.... All he knew was that he'd be flying home to New York on his own dime.

Jared nervously tugged on the bottom of his T-shirt, an old habit for someone always pudgier than his clothes. No longer the heavy-set teen raised on Midwestern mall food and soda, he was still chubby enough to feel ten pounds heavier every time his insecurities swelled. Now, standing in a shirt so wet his belly button resembled a whale's blowhole, he was back in gym class, snickering eyes on him as he dodged balls and insults. He turned to Kara, his camerawoman, for support, but she only wiped her lens and shook her head.

Her message was clear: *you're the director, kiddo. What did I tell you about letting this TV hack step all over you?*

"She's right," Jared muttered. "It's *my* story. *I* developed it. Stick to your guns."

He tugged on his shirt one more time, willing it to grow larger, to hide all that was underneath. But then fear took hold.

Who am I to tell this big-time star what to say? A dweeb from the sticks who only got the job because someone insisted?

"Well?" Derek slid his fedora over his glistening locks. "We gonna use my new lines? I get electrocuted in some freak Egyptian typhoon. You got no series." Derek's eyes drifted back to the monitor. "And you know how my hair looks when it's wet."

Jared Plummer's meticulously crafted script went limp in the deluge as he debated the first executive decision of his career. Listen to his best friend Kara, who's done nothing but tell him he's smart and capable, or the self-absorbed prick who once called him *The Joke From Junction City* and cared only about himself? The choice couldn't be more obvious.

"Yeah, sure. Let's try it your way, Derek."

A spider's web of lightning illuminated a nearby temple, where statues of a long-dead king stood watch. Even he looked disappointed by Jared's craven decision.

Kara flicked on the camera and groaned. "And… action!"

Derek took a final glance at the script and smiled:

NARRATION: A MYSTICAL LADY WITH MAGICAL LINKS TO ANCIENT PAST…

IS OMM REALLY A TRAVELER FROM THE TIME OF THE PHARAOHS? AND IF SO, WHAT CAN SHE TELL US ABOUT THE MIGHTY PYRAMIDS. WERE THEY REALLY BUILT BY A LONG-LOST RACE FROM BEYOND OUR GALAXY?

JOIN ME IN THE FORGOTTEN DESERTS OF EGYPT TO FIND OUT!

(Transition to general series open)

Series open/ pre-recorded. Hero Shots of Derek climbing mountains, rappelling into a tomb, crawling over a ruin.

THE WORLD IS FILLED WITH BURIED SECRETS AND HIDDEN HISTORIES… ALL JUST WAITING TO BE REDISCOVERED.

FORGET ABOUT HOLLYWOOD FAKERS. DEREK DEES IS THE REAL THING, A CLASSIC ADVENTURER FOR THE MODERN AGE…

JOIN ME ON THE ADVENTURE OF A LIFETIME!

"Cut!"

Jared swallowed a mouthful of blood. The new lines were awful and demeaning. Everything he tried to avoid when writing his episode.

"Yeah, sure, that works. Let's get out of here before the rain sweeps us away."

"How does that freakin' work?" Kara asked, first to Jared, who was avoiding all eye contact, then Derek, as he dashed to the van. "What's the new shit about aliens?"

"No one cares about some old lady's *Outlander* fantasy," Derek said. "It's soft and doughy, like our director here. *Ancient Encounters* is a guys' show."

Jared stayed quiet. He kind of loved the *Outlander* series, a fact best kept to himself.

"I agree women are smarter than men, but pyramid builders are from outer space?" Kara's voice grew harsh. "That's too lowbrow for even you, Derek."

"Only lovesick women are into a romance with dead kings and queens."

Derek tossed his lavalier onto the dashboard and returned Kara's glare. His insult was obvious. Kara's endless mourning about her long-gone girlfriend had become a drag.

"Real men dig aliens," he added, this time to Jared.

The car door slammed.

"Asshat," Kara shouted. "Let's show him what two angry queens can do…"

"Kara, c'mon, don't…." Jared spoke in a bashful whisper, even though Derek was out of earshot. "It's his show, not ours. No telling what he'll do."

The thought of losing Kara terrified Jared. Without her protection, he wouldn't last the day. But if he didn't quiet her down, he'd have another ugly fight on his hands.

Jared placed his hand on hers, knowing that except for her girlfriend, no one dared get so close—no one was allowed.

He held it gently.

As always, it worked, and Kara mellowed.

"Don't sweat it, baby," she said. "No way he's getting rid of me. I know which angles make him look macho and…" her voice rose, "which make him look like a third-rate clown."

Kara slid the camera off the tripod and, with the help of Ali, the local soundman, began packing up the gear.

"You worked on this script for months, Jared. Talked to this old lady like a dozen times, saying she knows things normal people shouldn't. Don't let him piss all over it."

The inside of Jared's mouth was now raw and painful. So much could go wrong about this shoot. If Derek found out he was gay, it would only add fuel to his conviction that Jared was too much of a lovelorn romantic to lead, that the episode was driven not by fact but fantasy. He'd already come too close with Carlos when Derek banged on their Seville hotel room during some headboard-banging lovemaking.

"We have two other takes," Jared said softly. "I'll just use one of those in the editing room."

"That's not the point." Kara's face softened. "How many times do I gotta tell you? You gotta lead."

"No matter what version you use, this show is still *kalam fadi,* bullshit," Ali interrupted as he collapsed his boom pole.

His voice was smoothly baritone, the Egyptian accent thick and authoritative.

It wasn't the first time Jared had heard this assessment. "Every episode starts like this," he told Ali lightly as if sharing a private joke. "A big Cold Open that promises fantasy stuff for viewers who don't get out much. No harm in it."

"No harm?" Ali scratched his bushy beard as his voice grew sharp. "Why is this desert forgotten? Egypt has a population of a hundred million. *We* never lost track of it. And ancient aliens built the pyramids because, of course, we couldn't possibly do it ourselves. We have a word for people who believe that. Pyramidiots." He chucked his case into the back of the van. "Oh, and the only one you could find to talk about our glorious past is a senile woman from London who claims she has been reincarnated a billion times? I can call several experts at Cairo University right now who know a great deal more and from only one life. It's not only bullshit. It's demeaning."

Jared started munching on the other cheek. Two hours as Episode Director and his crew were already turning on each other.

"It's just a dramatic hook for folks who need their history sugar-coated, larger than life. Once we're in the show, we reveal the truth."

Jared had promised this many times over the phone when pre-interviewing historians or other experts who found the series preposterous. In almost all cases, it was a lie, but just as often, it worked.

Not this time.

"Every producer from America and Europe says that," Ali grumbled. "It's just for fun, they assure me. We don't believe a word. So, if you agree this is *kalam fadi,* why say it at all?"

What Jared couldn't say, wouldn't dare, was that, in this case, he desperately wanted to believe what the crazy old lady was claiming. It was the reason he fought so hard for this story, even after Derek rejected it. He'd been waiting his whole life for something like this, a chance to finally discover the truth. He glanced at Kara and gave her that all too common "help me" face, that pathetic but ever-reliable look he knew he should have long outgrown.

Kara Hawkins welcomed confrontation as much as Jared shirked it. Her green commando cap, cargo pants and utility belt dangling with pliers, pen knife, and gaffer tape telegraphed it well enough as if she could have you bound and gagged in the back of an unmarked van in two minutes. She also exuded an unmistakable aura that she would not be pigeonholed in any way, shape, or form. It was one of the main factors for her meteoric rise in an industry driven by old, straight white men. It was difficult to maintain archaic traditions when a thirty-three-year-old Black lesbian dressed like a Sandinista rebel repeatedly confronted you on it. On this point, she sided with Ali. The series was a dusty relic of another time, where all history's mysteries could only be laid bare by the arrival of a good-looking white dude wearing fancy travel pants and talking as if his four days in the field would solve riddles the locals had failed to crack for thousands of years.

But right now, her friend needed protection. And this trip meant as much to her as it did to him. If he could prove his dreams were real, there was also hope for Kara.

Kara cradled her camera like a newborn baby and slid into the back seat. "C'mon, Ali, leave the kid alone. He's starry-eyed, still learning the ropes. You and I have suffered greater insults."

"True enough." Ali had often worked with Kara and knew she wouldn't befriend a buffoon. "I can tell you mean well, Jared, and you're just giving them what they asked for back home. Just know you're not in Kansas anymore."

High above, an angry clap of thunder made the needles on Ali's sound mixer peak. He ripped his headphones off and massaged his ears.

"Is this common?" Jared asked.

Ali glanced at the sky and shook his head.

"Lived in Egypt my whole life and never saw a storm like this. *That* should be your story. It's far weirder than anything in your script."

From somewhere nearby, the driver honked his horn, telling them to hurry.

On the way back to the main road, the van swerved to avoid ravines quickly becoming waterfalls. They skirted the contours of some ruined city so impossibly old it was difficult to tell where the walls ended, and dunes began. Ahead, a chunk of mud brick that had held fast since the days of god-kings gave way, and the driver swerved hard to avoid the collapse. Jared buried his face in his hands, not out of fear, but an aching feeling of loss and longing, as if something precious and eternal was being gutted. He thought back to the tornado that once ravaged his hometown when he was a child, taking with its lifetimes of keepsakes and security in an instant.

Then, his memories shifted from his Kansas town to something far older but more immediate and vital. He had anticipated its arrival, almost craved it, despite the terror that accompanied it. Usually, it left him exhausted and hyperventilating, often for hours. And now, so close to the source, he could only imagine it'd be far worse.

Jared shifted from his colleagues in the van as his body trembled. He slipped on his sunglasses, hoping it might mask what was to follow. He couldn't let anyone, especially Derek, see him in this state.

He closed his eyes and let it take hold.

A towering palace, shimmering in purple and gold, rises before him. Forked flags snap above a mammoth cedar gate. On either side loom statues of a smirking pharaoh resting on his throne. People shuffle in and out, and Jared finds himself in the center of the crowd. The tang of dust and dung stings his nostrils.

Unlike the others, he's in a rush, and he darts hurriedly between people, eyes fixed on the ground to evade detection. His white tunic is splashed in blood. A dagger, glistening from a recent kill, hangs from a sash. But if anyone recognizes him, they're wise enough to quietly step aside and let him pass. An alley ends at a wooden door manned by two warriors, tattooed and scarred. Together they dash up a rickety set of stairs. At the top, another warrior anxiously awaits. He dips his eyes to the corner, where a young man, head violently cut open, is propped against the wall. A puddle of blood spreads beneath him and a woman desperately waves flies away from the wounds. Between her knees lies the royal crown of Upper and Lower Egypt, shattered down the center.

"There's little time. Act fast," commands the warrior. But instead of treating the injury, the new arrival takes his dagger and rips the king's chest wide open, from rib cage to belly. As the woman cries out, he plunges his hand deep inside.

A sudden dip in the road, and Jared was transported back to the van, his breath lingering in the ancient past. He could still feel the anxious heartbeat that gripped the man wielding the knife, his grim determination to ravage the body of the wounded king. Coming here, he now knew, was a mistake. Rather than answer his questions, it would drive him to madness. He wasn't strong enough for what he might unearth. Jared peered out the window to avoid detection and recognized a shadow through the pounding rain. The battered statues of an angry pharaoh flanking the vestiges of a mammoth cedar gate.

"Move away," someone, or something, told him. "Quickly."

Jared repeated this loudly to the driver, a local who knew the roads far better than any of the crew. He politely raised a palm.

"No worries, Mr. Plummer. We must stick to the road or get stuck in sand."

"But the Ramses statue," Jared said with a voice more assertive than he had used all day. "Move now!"

The driver did. More to placate Jared than out of any real danger.

Derek glanced up from his phone, surprised by Jared's severe tone.

"Stop being such a putz. The dude knows his own roads. There's nothing out there but rain and ruins."

He returned to his text and failed to see the colossi of a towering pharaoh tumble down the hill, just missing the van.

But nothing escaped the eyes of cable TV's sharpest camerawoman: Kara "Hawk-Eye" Hawkins.

"Wha da-fa?" she shouted before noticing the terror in Jared's eyes.

Kara reached out and grabbed his hand, as he had done a few minutes earlier. She lowered her voice.

"What did you see this time?"

Jared's voice cracked. "Something dark, something I was told to see."

Derek turned around, rolled his eyes, and was about to say something snide, but Kara pulled a pair of wire cutters from her belt and snipped at the air before he could open his mouth.

"Go back to your *Hollywood Reporter* and butt out."

"You two weirdos. Freakin' made for each other." Derek shook his head and returned to his phone.

"This is all wrong," Jared whispered. "I shouldn't be here. I can't do this."

"Yes, you can. We'll do it together."

After the van entered the concrete streets of the town, Kara peered through the zoom lens she had been polishing and trained it on the hotel ahead.

"Yo, Ali, please tell me the Horus Eye Guest House has a cocktail lounge. I'd kill Derek for a dry martini."

CHAPTER 3

In her countless lives and jaunts into the past, Omm couldn't recall weather quite this unsettling. She remembered those awful drought years, sometimes during the Mamluk era, when every tree withered, and the wind was so harsh it reduced mud-brick towers to ant hills. But rarely a monsoon, and certainly never one that didn't pass by in a matter of minutes. Something else was going on, something sinister.

The TV crew was to arrive in a bit, but for the moment, Omm was alone among the grand temples of Abydos, her cobalt blue house dress and fuzzy green slippers standing out against bleached ruins. The only feature that blended in was her flyaway mound of gray hair, which mimicked the sandstone pillars behind her. Nearby, a pacing dog watched her every move and seemed too nervous to seek shelter. Brown and scrawny, it moped across the flooded courtyard, begging her to follow. Halfway across, it was nearly struck by lightning and darted under a broken chunk of limestone for protection. Beyond the ruins rose the modern village of El Araba El Madfuna, "the Buried Cart," which the storm had so far strangely spared.

Good. The town would never withstand the deluge.

Not like the original city, built so powerfully of granite and marble. More and more, Omm was unfavorably comparing the now with the then. Something about this current life distressed her. Her dreams had grown hazy, and she couldn't see what was coming next. She knew her time here was coming to an end.

An old telephone pole snapped in the wind, and the dog dashed into the temple for protection. Its anxious yelps snapped Omm out of her gloom.

"Stop being so grim," she told herself out loud, and to the cats watching from the shadows. "You're not dead yet. It's just an old lady's nostalgia for better times."

Ah, but she remembered when this dusty desert outpost really was special—the pharaohs' most sacred site. Mile after mile of colonnades and sphinxes and fabulous shrines melting into the mist. It wasn't really a city at all in the beginning, but a place of worship opened only to the elite and people like Omm, who traveled with them. That was all long before the invading Persians barged in, followed by the overly analytical Greeks, the humorless Romans, the puffed-up British, and finally, the swarms of rattling tour buses. By then, the gods had seen the writing on the wall, and Abydos had tumbled into obscurity. But as long as she still walked among the living, the prince's chapel and tomb would be preserved. It remained her eternal vow to her eternal lover.

That day, she feared, was fast approaching. She no longer took joy in keeping a watchful eye on the temple, and, though loath to admit it, she was eager to finally be released. She had more than done her part.

Thank god that young man arrives today. I do hope he agrees. It's time.

Her mind raced back again, not to her trips to the ancient world, but to the day her father took her to the British Museum. That's when she saw the temple for the first time and was shocked by its deplorable state: a fuzzy black-and-white picture of Abydos covered one wall, and all she could do was cry out: "There it is! My home! But where have all the fig trees gone, daddy?"

Poor dad, a lower-class Irish tailor who moved to London to escape a worse life back home, hadn't a clue what little Dorothy was on about. She had rarely been outside of Blackheath, let alone to Egypt. But someone else was inside her then, and she instinctively knew what she was staring at. She raced from statue to statue, kissing toes and calling them out by name. "Tepi, so good to see you again, even if they do make you look thinner than you were." And: "Oh my, darling Khepy. Mauled by a hippo and never became the queen you hoped, but look at you now!"

A modern intrusion returned her to the present day. The squeak of brakes, the crackle of an intercom. The only tour bus of the day, conducted by Said. She'd known Said nearly all his life, watched him grow up in El Araba, and adored him. Like the other guides, Said knew who she was: the barmy old Brit who thinks she was chosen by the pharaoh Seti to watch over the place. But unlike the others, who clutched hoary history books and a certificate from a six-month tourism course, Said treated her with respect. She watched him exit the bus and dash over to say hello.

From beneath a clipboard running with ink, he gently scolded her. "Omm, grab a hold of your senses and get indoors."

"Just a passing storm, probably coming from the western oases."

"Not according to the news. Only seems to be here, right above the ruins. The town is cloudless and bone dry. Very strange." Behind him, a sea of faces stared back from behind weeping windows. "Depressing group of Swedes. Yesterday they complained it was so hot they were sure they were melting. Like snowballs on fire. Today, it's this crazy rain they're all moaning about."

A rumble of thunder sent the dog under Omm's skirt and she gently scratched its head. Immediately, it stopped shaking. "Will you even bother with your lovely speech?"

"Play it by ear. They're already complaining about the leaking bus, how they should have stayed at the hotel."

Said handed her a slip of paper.

"And for you, it'll only get worse. Your TV people just checked in. This is the number for Jared, the director, who says he's 'most excited to meet you and will now come by after the storm.'"

As Omm took the paper, she wobbled. Said retrieved her cane and wiped the handle dry.

"You need to be resting, not climbing rubble, followed by a camera crew a quarter of your age."

He took a towel from his bag and dabbed her arms and face. Behind him, the group of tourists emerged under bending umbrellas, eager to move.

"Better get this over with," Said sighed and ushered them inside.

Lightning illuminated the desert somewhere behind the temple, and it was then that Omm fully registered what Said had said. It was only raining above the ruins.

That means it's happening at last. He's found the tomb.

Omm grabbed her cane and hobbled into the deluge. The rain was now so intense it came at her sideways, and she could no longer see what was ahead. Pottery shards floated along the path and sliced her bare feet. From the temple, the dog begged for her to come back. But Omm only picked up the pace and made her way behind the Temple of Seti, where the royal graveyard and chapel of Osiris, God of the Dead, lay buried in the desert. A final bolt of lightning lit up the courtyard, and when it disappeared, so had Omm.

CHAPTER 4

By the time Jared awoke the next morning, the storm had passed and a bubble of blue domed the desert. He gazed down from his hotel balcony and rubbed his eyes. Exhausted from both the long flight over and the visions of the day before, he had slept through the night and felt refreshed. Now he took in the landscape he couldn't see when they arrived. The street below was fine, but just beyond, where the modern village met the ancient ruins, a watery wasteland spread beyond sight. Titanic columns had collapsed, brick walls had melded into mud, and the few palm trees that had dotted the horizon were driftwood. A family of goats had climbed the highest dune to avoid the deluge and were now stranded on an island. Noah would have been shocked at the sight.

On the adjacent patio stood Kara, smoking a cigarette and slurping coffee.

"What the hell happened?" Jared asked.

She took a drag and a sip almost simultaneously. "The seven plagues of Egypt, it seems."

Jared squinted into the sun. He could see the colossi of Ramses, his nose and lips poking above water as if relaxing in a salt bath, but Abydos, where they were to do all their filming, was too far off to be seen. "What does this mean for our day?" He realized that as director, he should be answering this question, not posing it.

"Fuck if I know. Ali says the road to the temple is flooded." She laughed. "You promised me an exotic week of fun under the sun, Mr. Plummer, and now this."

Jared laughed back. "Like hell I did. You've mistaken me for someone who doesn't work on *Ancient Encounters with Derek Dees*."

"Touché." She scrutinized her friend and sipped her coffee. "So. Wanna tell me what you saw out there yesterday?"

Jared hadn't yet figured it out for himself. He just knew this one felt more intimate than the others. And much closer. "Sorry, I freaked. We were in a crazy flood. Everyone was shouting."

"It's me you're talkin' to, not Derek. I've seen you go through your visions before, but nothing like that. And then someone 'told you' to look out for a falling statue. Did I get that right?"

Hearing the words repeated out loud, Jared realized how insane they were. "Forget what I said. You know I love research. Studied maps for ruins for months."

"Stop it. They're getting worse?"

Kara was the only person Jared had ever confided in. She discovered his secret on a shoot in Cuzco, Peru, when the ancient, cobbled streets set off an intense reaction in him. At a nearby bar, after a half dozen Pisco Sours loosened his tongue, Jared told her everything, implicitly trusting that she wouldn't tell a soul. It didn't take an ancient Egyptian image to set him off, he explained. It could be a peculiar aroma or sound, or in this case, the touch of a wall smoothed by time. Jared's confession was a rare act of bravery. All his life, he had gone out of his way to dismiss his visions not as flashbacks but as some cognitive impairment that was best ignored. And Kara, seeing how detailed and emotional his images were, agreed there must be more to it. While she didn't follow any organized religion ("just another way for rich men to shackle the poor"), she did believe in a higher being, or at least another realm that had to be a hell of a lot better than the one they were currently enduring. To her, reincarnation made perfect sense.

"I could *feel* the panic of the man I was," Jared admitted. "He was troubled and hellbent on getting to some dying man, a king maybe. But instead of helping him, I, I mean he, sliced him open with a knife."

"You, a killer?" A long slurp. "Cool. It's like *Assassin's Creed* for real." She said this lightly, but Jared knew she wasn't poking fun, only trying to calm him down.

"Yeah, right, Jared Plummer, trained killer." He shook his head. "Just the stress of this show getting to me." He pointed to his forehead. "It's like I'm back in high school with a zit the size of Vesuvius. I never should have let you talk me into this."

Kara blew a puff of smoke his way. "Yo, don't blame me. I encouraged you, yeah, but it was that old lady that made you say yes."

"Who's probably another fraud, just like Derek said."

"Did someone call my name?" On the opposite balcony, Derek appeared with a toothbrush in his mouth. The host was dressed in silk pajamas with DD emblazoned on the right breast pocket, a gift from network executives when his show became a hit. "You do any more rewrites on that gay-ass script, Plummer?" He spat a minty mouthful of toothpaste off the balcony. It just missed sound man Ali, who was chatting on his phone below.

"I'll do it over coffee."

"Let me see the new copy before we shoot. I'll need time for tweaks."

The glass door shut behind him.

"I hate it when he uses that word," Jared whispered. "You think he knows about me?"

"That self-absorbed asshat? He only thinks about himself. Who gives a crap?"

"He'd only use it against me—claim it makes me weaker. A gay guy doing a drippy love story about a pharaoh and his time-traveling mistress. How 'typical'..."

"He stays off my gay ass, right? Mostly 'cause he knows his homophobic rants would only get him punched. Then sued. Wouldn't the *Hollywood Reporter* love that?" She peered off the edge. "If he comes out, I got a huge Bronx hocker waiting."

The thought of a huge wad of phlegm meeting Derek's fedora brought Jared unbridled joy. Only then did he notice a lacquered jewelry box resting on Kara's balcony. "Isn't that the one you bought for...?" He let the word remain unsaid. "What'd you bring that for?"

Kara lit another cigarette, forgetting one was already burning on the railing. "I dunno. Keep shit in it."

"Like?"

"Lighter, smokes, gummies, the head of Derek Dees... never you mind."

"Pretty fancy box for a pack of—"

"Drop it. We got bigger shit to deal with." She gestured over the sunken desert beyond. "Like finding Atlantis."

Jared nodded. "All right. Shall we go down and survey the wrath of the gods?"

On the hotel steps, Ali was still on his cell and fiddling with his sound gear. Reading glasses were perched on the bridge of his nose and attached to his neck by a cheap-looking cord of beads. A birthday gift from his two boys, he had proudly told the crew more than once. He was talking to them now, for at least the fifth time since the shoot began a day ago. Jared had never seen a man more homesick for his family.

"Nothing at all in Cairo?" Ali asked someone on the other end. He nodded good morning to Kara and Jared. "Look, I have to work now.

I'll see you for lamb couscous on Thursday. Kiss your mother for me." He hung up and raised eyebrows as bushy as his beard. "Big mystery. It rained only in Abydos. Not a drop in the town or anywhere else."

"So, how long until we can get out there?" Jared asked.

Ali shrugged. "Since nothing about this is normal, no one knows." He considered the cloudless sky. "But in this heat it shouldn't be long."

Breakfast was ordered and Kara marveled at Ali's fancy sound gear—two electronic nerds bonding. Jared's mind drifted. Technology was not his jam—words and reasoning were. He pulled out his multi-colored binder and a book Omm had sent him when they began conversing a few months ago. At that time he was still just "Jared Plummer, Junior Associate Producer," the lowest man on the *Ancient Encounters* totem pole. His job was to research stories for season three of the popular cable series, with an eye toward 'paranormal themes that could be woven into lightly historical adventures.' Everyone agreed he was perfect for the job, and for once, he didn't talk himself out of it. It seems he had been moving towards this encounter for years—maybe much, much longer.

Born and raised in rural Kansas by parents who thought of little more than the farm and Evangelical services every Saturday and Sunday, Jared had few friends and fewer interests until he saw an ad in the newspaper for the King Tut exhibit coming to Chicago. A strange charge rippled through him when he gazed at the pharaoh's death mask, hazy but familiar as if he was greeting an uncle he'd last seen as a toddler. He begged his parents to take him. Dad, a farmer who barely cared who the current president was ("unless he can drive a tractor, I got no use for him!"), remained unconvinced that traveling 800 miles to look at 'some weird heathen nonsense' was worth the gas money. But eventually, after a sympathetic school teacher intervened ("your boy needs interests beyond Happy Meals and caring for injured farm animals"), they relented.

When he finally came face to face with the Boy King, Jared was, like Omm before him at the British Museum, moved to tears. But unlike Omm, he buried his wonderment, more so after the first visions appeared. No one wanted to hear about some lonely kid's dreams of dead religions and places they'd never visit. And for a while, this worked: as long as nothing triggered Jared's memory, the visions were few and far between. But when they did come—like the time he saw *The Prince of Egypt* in Sunday school—he was a quivering mess on the floor, reeling from sights and sounds seen nowhere in the film. When he opened his eyes, lying between two overturned chairs, he could still smell the sweet fragrance of lotus and the oppressive heat of the African sun. The Sunday school teacher, who read Jared's breakdown as a 'Come To Jesus' moment, lavished him with praise, but the other kids slunk further away. But it wasn't until 9th grade Social Studies class, when a 'World History' book revealed images of pyramids and scrolls that he grew concerned. Not only did he recognize exactly where the pyramid was located, he could read what was written on the scrolls: parts of the *Book of Gates,* a collection of spells recited to survive the Egyptian underworld. Nothing and nowhere in his narrow world of shopping centers, fair grounds and country roads could have taught him that. But terrified of being seen as even weirder than he already was (only a few days earlier, he was caught staring at classmate Tony Kirkpatrick in the high school shower and was the butt of a thousand cruel jokes), he kept his discovery to himself.

College was out of the question—his parents couldn't afford it, or more likely, didn't believe in it—but a chance classroom project offered him the escape he had been seeking. If Jared Plummer had one unique gift, it was being able to talk to anyone and put them at ease. He probably learned this by spending too much time with his parents and their perpetually malcontent friends. He recognized early in life that everyone had a secret, a special story to tell, and was just waiting for the opportunity to tell it. Through his gentle, caring demeanor, Jared could coax the most intimate confessions out of even the grumpiest of souls. And, as an added bonus, avoid talking about himself at the same time.

So when the teacher assigned roles for the project—a documentary that highlighted the student's hometown—she picked Jared to direct, to the collective groans of his classmates, who never sat with him long enough to witness his gifts. The story he chose alienated him even further from his peers: a profile about the local funeral parlor, cemetery and morgue. Why he was drawn to this, Jared couldn't articulate, but something about the immediacy of grief and his fascination with how people cared for the dead, often with a tenderness that they never afforded the living, fascinated him. The finished film was so raw that even the bullies teared up. It won Jared first place and a summer internship at a New York production company, all expenses paid. His initial instinct was to decline. *I can barely handle Junction City. How would I survive the Big Apple?* But he also knew that if he stayed in Kansas, he'd never find out who the real Jared Plummer was. So he made the first bold decision of his life. He said goodbye to Mom and Dad with the mutual understanding that he'd never be back. After the internship ended, he was hired by Premiere Productions as Junior Historical Researcher.

Jared had stumbled upon Omm's story in a New Age magazine, and he tracked her down through a local guide named Said Issawi. There were other stories his bosses wanted him to develop—a coven of oracles said to still be practicing on Crete; a haunted junk ship in the bay of Hong Kong; and a particularly inane one concerning a cursed Aztec treasure rumored to be buried under a trailer park outside of Baton Rouge. But he found swift reasons to dismiss them, telling the executives they were all too easily explained. In truth, as soon as he'd talked to Omm, he was shaken by what she had told him. For the first time in his life he realized he was not alone. Someone else had experienced what he had, and was brave enough to talk about it. And that it all would happen in Africa, thousands of miles from his "regular" life meant there would be no change to the world he had created back home. All his denials and lies would remain safe.

It was as if Omm had been expecting his call. Like all good production assistants, Jared recorded his conversation, so the producers would have all the details to write up a treatment. And to hide his personal interests, he resolved to be tougher on her than other interviewees. He wouldn't be "Gentle Jared."

Now, with Kara retreating to the AC of her hotel and Ali awaiting the all-clear from the villagers, he reread the transcript…

Initial research call, Premium Productions

April 11 9 AM EST time/ 3 PM Abydos, Egypt

Subject: **Omm a/k/a Dorothy Kershaw** *(potential episode subject)*

Researcher: **Jared Plummer** *(assistant producer, Ancient Encounters, season 3)*

Jared: You don't mind if I record our call, do you? That way I can talk without having to stop and take notes.

Omm: Not at all, dear. So happy to chat at last.

Jared: Oh, did Said tell you I was going to call?

Omm: No. Should he have?

Jared: So how—?

Omm: You're keen to know about my life, I suspect. What exactly?

Jared: Well, your claims to time travel and reincarnation sound fascinating. But many would discount them both, saying it's just a yearning for escape from a dull present.

Omm: What would you say?

Jared: My opinions are of no concern to the show. Curious what you think.

Omm: And if you're eager to speak to me, I'm curious what you think.

Jared: Well, okay, let's start with your claim that you can travel into the past. I've read up on it and not sure I buy it. It's physically impossible. Time only moves forward, never in reverse. That's what makes it the 'march of time.'

Omm: Where did you read such hogwash? Time wanders off in all directions, dear. One just needs the proper door.

Jared: *Door?* And you have one?

Omm: It's not mine exactly, but, yes.

Jared: Okay, we'll get back to that. On top of that, you also say you've been reincarnated many times. Why need both? If you have a door, why also rebirth?

Omm: Jolly good question. Time travel is only for the chosen few, by invitation only. Even I don't do it often, and never without permission. And my reincarnation is in the humble service of those same people, to safeguard a priceless treasure in the modern world.

Jared: Many would also discount transmigration. I'm eager to see some proof.

Omm: Is that what they're calling it now? And proof, Jared, is everywhere. Why do you think people become obsessed with strangely specific things? A little boy in Malaysia who's fascinated by the English moors. A young girl from Sudan who's mastered the seas without ever seeing even a river. Or, say, a boy from the farmlands of America who recognized the aroma of Nile lotus and can read *the Book of Gates*. Passions are not happenstance, they're traces of past lives we cannot dislodge and often spend lifetimes trying to recapture, for reasons beyond understanding.

Jared: *(pause)* Or, they're just an escape from boredom. An impressionable trip to the botanical gardens as an infant. Or someone sees a movie and is so transported they convince themselves they were once Jack the Ripper or Vlad the Impaler.

Omm: My word, so dark... Why so much resistance? I wonder, Jared, have you had any flashbacks of your own?

Jared: *(shuffling of papers, pause)* Why would you ask that?

Omm: Most who seek me out have.

Jared: I'm just researching a story for cable TV. Personally, I think it's kind of presumptuous to claim someone else's achievements as our own. Another person so unhappy with their own life that they're looking to disappear into some silly fantasy. So they pretend they were once some famous figure to hide the fact their own life has amounted to nothing. How many Nefertitis have you met?

Omm: Besides her? None. You sound like you've memorized that as a defense. Who said we had to "do something" in our previous lives? Not everyone was Saladin or Joan of Arc. Most of us just lived. I wonder, would you mind terribly if we played a little game?

Jared: I'm really just looking to interview you, ma'am. See if you might be a good fit for the show.

Omm: This game might help me decide.

Jared: Fine.

Omm: I'm currently sitting on my rocking chair outside the Temple of Seti. A researcher like you certainly knows what it looks like.

Jared: Of course. It's beautiful.

Omm: So it is. As you enter, there's a long corridor to the far left. Can you picture it?

Jared: I can. Long and sloping upwards, ends with another corridor to the right that goes out back.

Omm: Correct. Now enter the corridor and turn around. What do you see above the door?

Jared: *(pause)* Well, on the right side is the famous King's List.

Omm: Everyone knows that. It's on the postcards. What's on the wall *behind you*?

Jared: Um, a huge painting of the pharaoh Seti and the gods?

Omm: Describe the scene to the far right.

Jared: Seti is reaching out, offering a bowl to Osiris, who stands holding a scepter.

Omm: Very good. And what's in the bowl, love?

Jared: C'mon. I couldn't possibly know that.

Omm: Don't reason, recall. Then toss out the first thing that comes to you.

Jared: *(short pause)* It's natron. Embalming salt.

Omm: Very impressive.

Jared: I'm a documentarian. I'm sure I saw it in an old film or book.

Omm: Not that old. That relief disappeared hundreds of years ago. Today it's only a block of modern cement holding up the roof. No expert knows about it, and it certainly hasn't appeared on the telly.

Jared: *(breathing only)*

Omm: Hello, love. Still there?

Jared: I am.

Omm: Good. You know I was just talking to two of my friends about you the other day. Khnumhotep and Niankhkhnum .... Ever hear of them?

Jared: No.

Omm: Well, love, they've heard of you. Look them up when you can. Their tombs are in Sakkara.

Jared: Tombs?

Omm: Oh yes, they've been dead for 4,000 years. But one step at a time.

Jared: So what are you trying to tell me?

Omm: That you're quite special, Jared Plummer and should visit me straight away. And when you arrive, I'll show you things you've only dreamt about. If you fancy what you see, we'll chat about how we can make them last forever.

Jared didn't put the receiver back on the phone for ten minutes. Only after the sound of the dial tone annoyed his colleague in the adjacent cubicle did he return to his senses. What was the woman saying, and how did she know all those things about him? The lotus, the *Book of the Gates?* Get a grip, he told himself: if he had learned anything as a researcher for a lame-ass paranormal show, it was that charlatans were everywhere, people who knew how to pick up on words and signals and make someone believe anything. Like the guy he talked to last week who claimed to be a prophet but was really an out-of-work magician from Coney Island.

He quickly googled 'Khnumhotep and Niankhkhnum' to see if she was making even this up. She wasn't. It seemed they were two men living in the royal court of the Old Kingdom, circa 2500 BC, and although disputed by historians (read: homophobes), they were gay lovers, the walls of their tomb bursting with joyous images of the two of them in an intimate embrace.

But most perplexing was Omm's final comment: "with my help, we can make it last forever." He decided it simply meant that together they would make a film so good it would last forever. A bit lofty for an episode of *Ancient Encounters with Derek Dees,* but her enthusiasm was welcome. Jared called her a few more times—far more than was needed to write up a short treatment—and Omm even sent Jared her unpublished memoir. "I wrote with the help of Tiya, my original self, to tell her story. Anything to keep the prince's name alive," she explained. "If you know any New York literary agents, could you be a dear and share it?" After a month of crafting a treatment and a shooting script that would have dazzled the *60 Minutes* team, Jared passed it on to the senior staff. They loved it. "So romantic and rich," gushed Sarah. "Omm's a nutcase, but it's a fun way into a story about Ramses the Great," countered Ted. But when that producer called to set up a visit, Omm was quite rude.

"Where's Jared?" she snapped. "He's the one I gave permission to."

The producer informed her that Jared was merely an associate producer and not yet ready to direct. "And he's now researching another episode, so the timing doesn't work out for him to come over. Don't worry. I read his report."

"Only he can tell my story," Omm insisted.

"As I said, he's not ready, ma'am."

Omm could hear the producer desperately trying to wrap up the conversation so she could inform her bosses, the real decision-makers. Papers rustled, her voice dipping in and out as she scribbled notes. "We know what we're doing. Last week we almost beat *The Curse of Oak Island* in the ratings."

"My dear, how long have you been doing this exactly?"

"Over a year now," the producer said, with more than a hint of arrogance.

"And that makes you a gatekeeper? A storyteller? You've had your big break, so this is Jared's. He sought me out, and understands me. It's the boy or no one."

The producer went silent and, finding nothing more to add, hung up. Twenty minutes later, Jared called, apologizing for his colleague ("she really wanted to see the Sphinx") but also admitting he hadn't the experience to direct just yet. "I've never written a script or run a crew. As much as I'd like…"

Omm only repeated her threat. "It's you or no one, love. You're being here is vital. Shall I speak to your bosses directly?"

Desperate to wrap up the season, the execs begrudgingly agreed. No one believed Jared was ready, and to hide his true interest, he didn't share the transcripts of his first call to Omm. (After all, she all but outed him as both gay *and* reincarnated.) But they adored the story too much to let it go, and more importantly, the season had gone way over budget. If Jared directed, they could pay him AP rates and save thousands of dollars. Kara, their best Director of Photography, was pulled from another show. "She's your friend, Jared, and no offense, you might need her should things get tough. Working with Derek is no walk in the park, even for veteran producers."

Jared knew he wasn't ready, but with Kara at his side convinced himself he could at least pull it off with minimal damage. The show, he realized, was almost incidental. The true reason he agreed was the chance to meet Omm and ask her about his dreams. Now, two months later, here he was: gazing off the hotel steps of the Horus Eye Guest House in rural Egypt, a bizarre rainstorm washing away his prime location and violent new memories suggesting that whomever he was in the past, he didn't come in peace. He was, in a word, doomed.

CHAPTER 5

Kara caressed her lacquered box and watched Jared from the balcony of her hotel room. Now was her chance before the road to Abydos dried and the shoot began. But first, she needed to find out if the tomb she was looking for was as flooded as the temple. Across the street, Ali was at a coffee shop, smoking a shisha and gabbing away on his phone. While Jared had his head in his laptop and couldn't see her pass, she joined him.

"Yo, Ali, where did you say that cemetery was again?"

He said goodbye to his boys and offered her a seat. "Which cemetery?"

"I forget the name. You know, the real old one." Kara fidgeted in the hot sun, uninterested in joining him in the shade of the cafe.

"This is Egypt," Ali laughed, "everything is real old."

"You know, the one where the first pharaoh was buried."

"Ah, Umm El Qa'ab." He asked one of the locals smoking a shisha nearby and translated. "Just at the edge of town, why? You'd like to go there *now*?"

"Is it flooded?"

"Weirdly, no," he said with a shake of the head.

"Excellent, a good time to get some B roll," Kara announced with perhaps a touch too much excitement. She lowered her voice so as to not give away her true intentions. "Wide shots of the tombs, shit like that."

"It's a furnace out there. It will be a lot cooler later." He looked at the midday sun. "Better shadows too. Now, you'll get no definition."

"It'll be good enough." Kara started to pack up her gear. "Tired of waiting for the fuckin' sand to dry."

Ali swapped his phone with a boom pole. "*Yallah,* wait, I'm coming."

"No, don't need audio. I'll do this alone."

Ali savored a final drag from the water pipe and shook it back and forth at Kara as if making air quotes. "Don't you always tell me that every shot is better with wild sound?" He tossed a few bills on the table and called out *Shukran.*

"Finish your bong. Just gonna grab some quick wide shots and be back in a few minutes."

Ali put his sunglasses on and pointed to her two plastic cases and tripod. "You going to carry the gear by yourself? There's no road. I'm coming."

"I said no, I'm cool!" She didn't mean to answer so sharply, but there was no way he could join her—he'd only tell Jared. But it was true: no way could she carry all that gear that far. Next to the café, she noticed an animal saddled with empty leather bags. "Whose pony is that?"

"Here, we call them donkeys."

Kara swatted at a horse fly the size of an overripe black olive. "I'm from the Bronx. We don't see many donkeys."

"But you got ponies?"

"Oh, for Christ's sake, will this thing carry my gear or no?"

Ali asked. "It belongs to this guy over here." The old man, in dusty gallabiyah and even dustier skull cap, rose from a patch of shade and moved forward.

"May I borrow your pet for a bit?" she asked him in English.

The man understood without translation. Swiftly and expertly, he strapped Kara's tripod, camera and lens case to the saddle. But when he reached for her smaller bag, she grabbed it first. He raised two hands by way of apology and took the reins.

"No, no, I can do it alone." But the man shook his head. His donkey, his guidance.

"He'll show you the necropolis," Ali said. "No way would anyone here be so rude as to let you walk around out there on your own. There are sinkholes." The man added something that Ali translated. "Venomous snakes too." Then more Arabic. "And jackals, apparently. You sure you don't—"

"Tell Jared I'll be back in a few."

"You didn't tell him you were going out there. Don't you—"

Kara's response came fast and loud. "I don't wanna bug him. He's reworking the script. Give me something to do while I wait."

"If you say so." Ali's phone rang, and he answered with a hearty hello. As Kara walked away, he called out. "If you need me, I got my cell phone."

"Yeah, saw that." Kara followed the farmer out of the village and into a vast desert bereft of shadow. To the south, the rain had swallowed up everything in sight, but straight ahead, it remained bone dry. "Freakin' strange," she said to the farmer, who didn't need translation to agree.

In the distance, the landscape erupted into what looked like monstrous anthills. Kara had never seen anything more desolate and uninviting in her life and, for a moment, thought about turning back. *Is this really the best I can do?* But the farmer moved further away, and her gear along with it, so she followed. She had come this far and was not going to chicken out now.

Kara Hawkins had spent her whole life fighting, usually against men who foolishly thought themselves stronger and smarter. Raised by a single mother in the William McKinley Houses (an everyday reminder that white men dominated even places they had no right. Think President McKinley would be caught dead visiting this place?), she learned early that if she was not only to survive but thrive, an unwavering show of dominance was expected. Over the years, it became second nature, and she had grown to enjoy it. At ten, she fought the lazy superintendent who wouldn't fix the sagging ceiling in her bathroom. At twelve, the delinquent boys in the hallway foolishly saw her as a plaything; by fifteen, she was going toe to toe with the jaundiced school board that twice expelled her for not playing by the 'rules.' At twenty, she was shutting down the homophobes who glared at her and her girlfriend the wrong way on the B15 bus. After earning a scholarship for one of the city art schools, she moved out of the South Bronx and into a nice "mixed" neighborhood in Brooklyn. But beyond the faces, little changed. She fought supposedly open-minded neighbors who locked the door as she passed, and challenged narrow-minded teachers who thought she'd make a better nurse than a cameraperson, which, "let's be honest Kara," they'd whisper, "was a man's job." She barnstormed her way to an internship first for public access TV and then cable TV, run by timid men who at first hesitated to hire her because she was now not only Black but a practicing lesbian and were thus worried they'd have to watch what they said and didn't think it worth the risk, and, once she was hired, battled old school union men who didn't like taking orders from women. She proved every last one wrong: in a few short years, Kara was regarded as one the best Directors of Photography in New York and every sensible producer wanted her on their documentary. And when she met Lynette and fell in love, it was Kara who convinced her to plan big, and in the open: a summer house in the Hamptons, a big public wedding, travel to where they wanted, and, when they were ready, as many kids as they damn well pleased. And when Lynette, a sweet Jewish girl from Boston who, like Jared, was wary to "offend" or "make a scene," Kara was always there to nudge her along. Life's what you make it, not what you're told. And for a while, it had all worked perfectly.

That she was doing this now, in secret and with the fear of ridicule, went against all she stood for, the kind of thing she'd deride back home as weak-kneed delusion. Even Jared, her best friend, who confessed everything to her, couldn't know. It would only reveal her weakness, and for him, she needed to stay strong.

But ever since he first mentioned Omm, she couldn't get this idea out of her head. Even if the whole thing was the pile of bullshit she long suspected, it couldn't hurt. Hell, as Jared would say (if he knew what she was up to), "it might give you closure."

Closure. Please.

What's 'closure' but a pretentious word for giving up? And one thing Kara Hawkins of Mott Haven never did was give the fuck up.

Ali was right: the noonday sun was out to kill her, and she was sweating so much it was collecting in her rolled-up sleeves and around her bracelets. She found a new respect for the horse flies back in town. They were smart enough to not follow her into this hellscape. Just ahead, twinkling in the haze like an old VHS video, the donkey owner said something and then started walking respectfully between a carpet of crunching objects. For perhaps the first time on *Ancient Encounters with Derek Dees*, Kara had done some historical research. This was Omm El Qa'ab, or Kab, or something like that. "The Mother of Pots." Thousands, maybe millions of pot shards, purposely broken and scattered by grieving loved ones as offerings. She was in the right place.

Then the anthills were upon her, and up close, she finally saw them for what they once were. Mud brick tombs were more ancient than civilization itself. So old, she remembered Jared saying that we were closer in time to Cleopatra than she was to the people buried here. Now, nothing remained but open, roofless pits, the mummies and their treasures long gone. But there was no denying one fact: even in its forlorn state, the presence of something ageless, maybe even spiritual, still lingered here. She could feel it.

The farmer stopped in front of a pit much larger than the others. But if the owner had been some bigwig back in the day, he was now no better than all his neighbors. His tomb was just as open and gutted, the only thing standing out a ramp wide enough to drive a chariot of treasure down. The farmer tied up his donkey and pointed down the ramp. "U-Jay," he seemed to be saying. The words meant nothing to her.

"Is this the oldest tomb here? The one all the others were built around?"

"U-jay, U- Jay," he repeated, and when this again failed to register, he tried another word. "Scorpion."

Kara smiled. That's the one, the easier name to remember. The Scorpion King, Egypt's first. Like that stupid movie with the Rock. Another reason not to tell anyone what nonsense she was up to. "Good, good." She made a circle with her fingers and placed it over one eye. "I'll shoot here." The man nodded and unloaded her camera and tripod. She clicked it all into place and found her focus. Dear God, Ali was right again: the lighting this time of day sucked donkey ass. She began shooting pans and tilts of the same shapeless mounds until the farmer grew bored. He rolled a cigarette and moved to the shallow wall, where a patch of shade offered the only sliver of hope in this wasteland.

It was the moment she had been waiting for. Kara quickly retrieved the other bag and pulled out the lacquered box. Making sure the clasps were firmly in place, she walked to the bottom of the tomb, where sand and shards drifted halfway up the wall. Making sure she wasn't being watched, she took the pliers from her belt and started digging. Swiftly and frantically. The sand was not only hot but so fine it kept filling up the hole as quickly as she dug it, like water through her fingers. After another "fuck" or two, she began filling up the bag and dumping sand a few feet away. Her arms and neck began to burn.

Why didn't I bring some sunscreen? Jared packed, like, six bottles.

Finally, hard earth. After another few inches, she placed the box inside and covered it back up. By now, her fingertips were beginning to blister, the sand like a flame. She considered saying a prayer or a speech, something formal to mark the occasion, but the only thing that came was tears. Angry tears that she had been holding back for two endless years.

Life is never fair, but this was not how it was supposed to be.

Then, a change of heart overcame her. This place was indeed hell.

What if I just made things worse?

Her tears were now as oppressive as her sweat, and she found herself unable to move, to let go. She had never felt so fucking vulnerable, so fucking alone. All she knew was that Kara Hawkins never failed at anything, yet here she was, babbling in a hole in the ground, pathetically trying to fix the one thing she knew she never could.

She used her commando cap to wipe the sand and sweat from her face and looked at the anonymous lump in front of her.

There must be another solution. Maybe the old lady can help.

She was about to dig it all up, until a voice behind her called her name.

At the top of the ramp, the silhouette of Ali loomed. "What in god's name are you doing down there?" he shouted.

"Makin' a fuckin' TV show, whatya think?" Trying to sound professional, the words instead came out as defensive.

Ali paused, no doubt knowing something more was going on, but respectful enough to not pry. "That's possibly the worst shot I've ever seen you frame."

"You came all the way out here just to tell me that?"

"No, I came out to tell you the road is clear."

"Already? It was a fuckin' ocean twenty minutes ago."

Ali shrugged. "Welcome to the world's oldest necropolis. The dead are thirsty."

CHAPTER 6

As Jared waited for the crew to gather, he sat outside and worked on the rewrite, dropping in random mentions of mystical aliens and levitating pyramids. Then, the long shadow of an Indiana Jones hat darkened his laptop.

Derek took a swig from his chrome-plated water bottle. "What's that?" he said, pointing to the manuscript on the table.

"Omm's memoir. Remember? I sent you a copy."

"Oh yeah, skimmed it."

"And?" Jared set the book down.

"Harlequin romance shit. A prince keeps reincarnating mindless babes so he can bonk his way across time." Derek gulped. "Great for the Ladies' Book Club of Tallahassee but hardly the stuff of an adventure show." Derek sat. "Hope you're not putting any of that slop into the script."

"No, adding other slop…I mean, stuff."

"Don't get too judgy, buddy, like your perpetually pissed-off camerawoman." The hat came off, Derek's way of saying he was no longer 'in character.' "Listen, Plummer. We need to talk."

Here it comes, thought Jared, when Derek schools him on what it means to be a "real adventurer." What Derek didn't know was that, green as he may be, Jared already saw the host for what he was: a failed actor playing the only part he could get. He wondered who was the bigger fraud on this shoot: he for achieving so little, or Derek for pretending that he had.

TV's "Great Explorer" plopped his fancy leather bag on the table, which came with oversized buckles and ready-made imperfections as if he'd just wandered in from the wild. He even had a name for it: 'Bertha,' after a female elephant he claimed to have killed in Africa to procure the hide. The story was untrue of course, something made up on the spot at a Comicon convention. In actuality, it was bought at a fancy luggage store at Dubai Airport during a layover. "I have my reputation and my research to protect." He opened it up and began excavating something deep within.

That Derek studied theater, not archeology, was also never discussed. The closest Derek ever came to discovering a lost tomb was when he played "Brad, Beach Bum Victim #4" in some cheap slasher film shot at ruins near Cancun. He was decapitated by a Mayan goddess as he clutched a handful of stolen jewels. The film failed to find a distributor, and Derek's agent instead explored TV possibilities. He got the *Ancient Encounters* gig after he showed up in a leather vest, his teeth whitened, designer stubble outlining his boxy jawline. For added verisimilitude, he claimed he patterned his look not on Indiana Jones ("too obvious") but Giovanni Belzoni, the notorious Italian explorer who raided Egypt's grandest tombs in the 19th century, long before it was cool. That obscure touch landed him the job.

"It's your first episode, so let me show you all you got wrong." Derek began placing items on the table as he searched for the script. If he was a true adventurer in the mold of Belzoni, out would come compasses, mangled maps, and a dagger to ward off angry tribesmen. Instead, he presented his tattered *Hollywood Reporter* (an old one, from last year, with him on the cover), something that *looked* like a compass but was actually a compact with mirror and make-up; nail clippers with a built-in flashlight: then, finally, the script. It was pocked with fiery red marks, like Jared's forehead. "I know you did your research. But this is nothing but flighty schoolboy nonsense."

Jared wanted to counter that it was a good script, certainly no worse than past episodes, and adding aliens wouldn't help. But he didn't.

"For a start, it's dull as dirt," Derek began. "No one gives a shit that..." he found the correct graph.

SCENE 2, ACT 1: ABYDOS, EXTERIOR, DAY

VIDEO: *Walk and talk: Derek Dees looks down at the sunken temple*

NARRATION: AS I APPROACH THE EDGE OF THE ANCIENT TEMPLE OF THE DEAD, I FINALLY UNDERSTAND ITS DEEP SIGNIFICANCE.

Derek on camera: *Seti created the Osireion temple complex so he could emulate the ancestral lands and achieve ma'at, or balance, with the deities of the underworld.*

FURTHER ALONG THE TEMPLE, I MEET...

"What words you tryin' to shove in my mouth?" Derek asked after reading the script aloud. "What does that even mean?"

"It means the pharaoh built Abydos as a place of pilgrimage for those who wished to commune with the dead. A way to honor their memory."

"No, it means that instead of me going on an exotic escapade, you have me asking questions about post and lintels, and cladding stones. We're making a mystery show, not an episode of *House Hunters.*"

"We can add a few lines to make it more… mysterious if you like."

"You bet we can." Derek flipped through the script to reveal that his river of red ink never dried. "And here, this is the stuff that's really gay."

VIDEO: *SIT DOWN INTERVIEW with Sanjay Traveti, Eastern Religion Scholar*

NARRATION:

I MEET WITH DR TRAVETI IN HIS OFFICE AT PENN UNIVERSITY. I WANT TO BETTER UNDERSTAND THE CONCEPT OF REINCARNATION.

Derek: Thanks for seeing me, Dr. So, what exactly did rebirth mean to the ancient people of the Nile?

Traveti: Reincarnation is not an ancient Egyptian belief per se. Like Western religions—Judaism, Islam, Christianity—they believed in a heaven, where souls went for eternity.

Derek: Does that prove Omm's claim is false? That she could never have been a pharaonic priestess simply because the ancient Egyptians did not believe in rebirth?

Traveti: We know very little about their early religious thoughts. But we do know they believe in something called the *ba* and the *ka*. The *ka* is like our soul and it finds everlasting life in the Field of Reeds, their heaven. But the *ba* is trickier to understand. It remains attached to the body and likes to stay close to the land above. This could be for any reason, from keeping an eye on family or loved ones, or the desire to fulfill something they never could in their last form.

"Blah, blah, *ba* and *ka*..." Derek surmised. "Two minutes of screen time conducting a bookshelf interview back in Philly when I could be discovering a lost tomb in the desert."

"Isn't the idea to investigate Omm's claims, see if they hold up to scrutiny?"

"Of course. There's nothing I'd love more than exposing a phony." This was a line Derek had used many times before, but rarely when the cameras, and his hat, were off. Without all that attention, his voice lacked conviction.

"Well then, this suggests that Omm's beliefs are not completely unfounded," Jared said with a bit too much enthusiasm.

Derek's eyes went wide. "Wait a minute! You believe this crap?"

"Of course not," Jared chewed on a flap of skin inside his mouth. "Just trying to educate viewers a little while we give them the fun stuff."

A plate of fava beans and pita arrived, and Derek gave it a wary frown. "You're only here because this nut job demanded it, and my worry is that she's using you because she knows you'll fall for anything. Your loyalty is to the show, never the subject. How many episodes of my show have you worked on?"

"Ten, three in the field."

"All as an assistant, and every time, all you did was read books and suggest historical tweaks in the middle of the shoot. Like telling me the Greeks came before the Romans, or the Great Belzoni didn't wear a fedora like me since they weren't invented yet… Hell, then there was that time in Seville. You were barely around, off sightseeing with that fixer instead of arranging lunches and transportation. Almost fired you for that. Kara talked me out of it."

Jared's face burned. It was true. On that shoot, he spent more time with Carlos, the local historian. It was Jared's first trip to the Old World, and a great passion was triggered, one that Carlos happily fed. What started as a spirited tour of the Alhambra and Mesquite quickly evolved into something deeper, and for the first time in his life, Jared had fallen in love. For a start, Carlos was drop-dead gorgeous: fit, charming, and bursting with confidence. Although masculine, with muscles and a beard, his skin was soft as silk, and when he held Jared and, after the first night, made love to him on the balcony of their hotel, under a sliver of a moon, Jared realized that any fantasy of his would never equal what he just experienced. Like someone who had tasted a new drug and was instantly hooked, Jared couldn't get enough of Carlos. He raced through his work, was late to set or claimed he was researching the next scene, when in reality, the two of them were entwined in his hotel bed, under blaring AC and saying things to each other that would make a romcom writer cringe. He was madly, uncontrollably in love, and miracle of miracles, Carlos felt the same way.

Only once, when Derek needed something in a hurry and banged on his door, did Jared realize how serious it had become. Carlos snuck from balcony to balcony before Jared opened the door—leaving behind a pair of sexy thongs on the floor. Derek saw them—how could he not? They were hot pink, for Christ's sake. Yet he surely knew what Jared did: no way did they belong to the 'Craven Clown from Kansas.'

Nothing more was said, but it changed Derek's opinion of his new AP. Yet in the end, who cared? It was the best few weeks of Jared's life and could have gone much further if, true to form, he didn't wimp out at the end and ruin everything. "Enough of the past," Jared told himself.

He looked across the patio, where the rest of the crew had appeared with the gear.

Unexpectedly, it was Ali and not Kara who came to Jared's rescue. "I read the script last night and think there's some good stuff in there. A lot of bullshit too. But at least you showed respect for our history."

Behind him was Kara, sweating profusely and looking strangely out of sorts. "You okay?" Jared asked as he packed up his laptop. "Ali said you were out there shooting? In this light?"

"My God, is everyone a camera person these days? I was bored. Let's hurry. I wanna meet this 'Mystical Mistress of the Nile' already. Hear what she's gotta say."

Jared knew why he was so anxious to see Omm, but not Kara. Especially since the accident, she rarely cared about the story or the subject, only that they looked great. But before he could ask her what she meant, Derek plopped the fedora on his head and soured the moment.

"I'm keen to meet this old biddy, too," he said. "For your sake, Plummer, let's hope she's better than your gay-ass script."

CHAPTER 7

El Araba El Madfuna village was nestled among Biblical-looking dwellings and shaded courtyards and rimmed by errant sand dunes. The crew was to meet Said at the village's only coffee shop: a single room with plastic chairs and a smattering of men smoking sheeshas and watching football on a tiny TV. On a nearby terrace, half finished with rusted rebar poking up where there should have been a roof, a donkey stared down, munching hay.

"Hello, Mr. Plummer!" a voice called out.

Said beckoned them into the coffee shop with a warm smile. After handshakes, Jared apologized for being late and said that he had tried to call several times. He gave Said a longer-than-needed glance and hoped he wasn't discovered. The guide was handsome and casually masculine—but very clearly straight. Growing up in rural America sharpens a closeted man's gaydar. He looked away before being noticed.

"No problem. Reception here is never great," Said responded with a casual wave. "Must be a downed tower. I was out looking for Omm."

"She's to meet us here, right?"

"*Inshallah*. But now I can't find her." Said had bright, thoughtful eyes and a casual manner. Jared instantly liked him. He noticed residents picking up fallen palm fronds blown in from the desert. "Could it have been the storm?" Ali asked.

"Most possibly. Her house has been damaged. But no sign of Omm." Said squinted at the mountains beyond the town. "I can only guess she considered the rain a message from the gods. She does this sometimes when odd things happen. We had a terrible sandstorm a few years back, and she went off to pray to Re, the sun god."

"And?"

"The sandstorm stopped."

Jared studied Said's face to glean if he believed in Omm's claims but could detect nothing. "Where would she go?"

"See those cliffs?" Said pointed down an alleyway that afforded a view of the desert beyond. "There is a pharaonic altar of some kind halfway up."

It looked far away and hot, but if Omm could make it, Jared was determined. How hard can it be? He may not look like a rugged adventurer, but neither was he Jabba the Hutt. He pulled his T-shirt over his sticky belly. "Let's go find her."

"Oh no, if she's communing with Re, she'll hate to be disturbed. Give them their time together."

The rim of Derek's hat was already fringed with sweat. "How long that gonna be, you reckon? Not gonna stand here all day."

"Depends on how much they have to talk about."

Jared suppressed a smile. So he was not the only one who found something in Omm that was genuine. Jared had expected the locals to treat Omm as a harmless old kook, not support her story. He hit upon an idea. "Listen, I know we were supposed to start with Omm's master interview, but can we ask you a few questions first?"

"*La shukran.* No thank you, I'm not your story. Omm is. Let her tell it."

To make this story work, and to keep Derek off his back, Jared needed a believer beyond Omm and himself. Truth be told, he needed it for himself. If anyone suspected her of being a fraud, it would be a local. "Some people call her crazy, an ignorant foreigner who has invaded other people's land for selfish reasons."

"It's a fair charge. So many of you have, but not Omm. She's as much a part of this village as anyone else."

"That needs to be said."

Said peered into the barren hills. "I'll say nothing to disparage anyone's beliefs, mine, hers or anyone else's, so don't ask."

Whatever had given Kara concern earlier in the day seemed to have passed. She was now firmly in "Director of Photography" mode. Her eyes had already settled on a suitably exotic backdrop: a stone well, a palm tree, and the donkey, noisily moved from the terrace. "Put that pony thing over there, Ali, and let's set up two chairs from the cafe here."

As this was a standard talking head interview and not a conversation with Derek, he wasn't needed on camera. But he lingered in the nearby shade like a rattlesnake.

Said tucked in his T-shirt, slipped on his Wayfarers and sat.

"Is that all you have to wear?" Derek asked with disappointment.

"I can put on a dress shirt if you like. But in this heat, like you, I'd sweat like an ox."

Derek glanced around and pointed to an old man in the coffee shop. "Do you have anything like the robe that guy is wearing? Looks cool."

Said turned his head. "A gallabiyah? That's the traditional garb of the *fellahin*, the farmers. I'm not one of them."

"It's just that we're trying to capture the spirit of this place, the timelessness of Egypt. T-shirts and sunglasses don't cut it."

"Perhaps a fancy turban too? A flute to charm snakes? Curled slippers?"

"Yeah, all that works."

"What you want is an image that suits your antiquated vision. I respect those who wear the gallabiyah, but I'm not dressing like Aladdin so you can wallow in Orientalism."

Derek rolled his eyes. "C'mon man, it's just a TV interview. No need to get all preachy." He went silent, and Jared wondered if the penny had finally dropped and Derek had seen himself for the fool he was. "But no, seriously," the host said at last, "an Orientalist turban would be super cool." It was patently clear that Derek had no idea what the term meant.

Said removed his lavalier microphone and handed it to Ali. "I'll go look for Omm. She'll give you what they want back in America." He looked to Ali and smiled. "I'll use my flying carpet, it's faster."

Ali bust up laughing.

"No, you're absolutely right," Jared said before Derek could make things worse. "Said is fine as is." He turned to Kara, who was tying the donkey tighter to stop it from wandering out of the shot. "Let the damn donkey be. We shoot everything exactly as it appears."

Kara nodded in approval. "And action."

Interview transcript

Location: the village of **El Araba El Madfuna, Egypt**

Subject: **Said Issawi** *(Local resident/Tour Guide)*

Interviewer: **Jared Plummer, et al.**

(inaudible female and male voices)

Jared: Let's start at the beginning: when did you first meet Omm?

Said: For me, she was always here, always looking after the place. That's why we call her Omm. It means 'mother' in Arabic, you know.

Jared: Why mother? Did you lose your own?

Said: No, no, the whole village calls her that. She didn't want to use her old name, and then when we saw how the animals here treated her, someone called her Omm and it stuck.

Jared: The animals? I don't follow.

Said: All the creatures here, from wild dogs to the scorpions, seem to understand her, love her. She says it is because she can communicate with the ancient deities she claims still live here, which of course are all half-animal. Sekhmet, Anubis… Once Omm came to my house to get a rabid jackal out of the barn.

Jared: What exactly did she say to the jackal?

Said: No idea. Something in the ancient language.

Jared: And?

Said: It licked her hand, walked out my door and now lives with her.

Unidentified male voice: *(off mic)*: Just some ancient mumbo jumbo that frightened the creature and scared the locals, right?

Said: Who are you again?

Male voice: I'm Derek Dees, the host of the program.

Said: What's with the Halloween costume? The Indiana Jones get-up?

Derek: It's what adventurers wear.

Said: And you're suggesting Egypt's stuck in the past? *(laughs)* So, you think that with a few old words, we're all on our knees trembling, like we've never seen an eclipse, or a white woman, before? You've been reading too much Kipling. *(mic noise)*

Jared: No, no, please sit. Derek, let me conduct the interview. If you have any questions, you can ask them at the end.

Derek: You're wasting our time. We need one bite that says Omm is off her head, and we can wrap this up. Go hunt for aliens, lost treasures, something that rates.

Said: That's the purpose of your coming all this way? So some second-rate actor dressed like an old movie character can determine it's all a fantasy? Then create his own?

Unknown female voice: *(louder now)* Derek, stop being a fuckin' prick. Jared is the director. Let him fuckin' direct.

Derek: Stop defending him, Hawkins. That's not your job.

(off mic arguing: only snippets audible: only here … he's your friend… what happened, you used to not be so full of yourself… inaudible…why are you always so damn angry?…inaudible)

Kara: Go ahead, Jared.

Jared: I want to hear your story. Forget what Derek said. Please, sit back down. Ali, will you get his lavalier back in place? *(microphone scratches)*

Ali: Sure, just sit back, Said, I need to run it under your shirt again.

Said: Aliens? From Egyptian to Egyptian, wouldn't it be nice if someone from the States actually let us tell our own stories for once?

Ali: *(untranslated Arabic, followed by two men laughing) Yallah*, we're good.

Jared: Kara, we rolling?

Kara: Speed.

Jared: Said, help me believe Omm is not just some kook, so I can tell the world. What other strange things have you seen her do?

Said: Well, there was one story that happened when I was young, but I don't want to get anyone in trouble. *(long pause)* But father is gone, and Omm and I have laughed about it many times since, so, it's probably fine.

Jared: Please go on. I'll only interrupt if I need to.

Said: Growing up here—

Jared: Sorry, could you put my question in your answer?

Said: Pardon?

Jared: My question won't appear in the film, so we need context.

Said: It's like talking to my parents with you all, can't get words in edgewise. *(scratching sound, maybe beard or shirt)* I've seen Omm do some strange things. Growing up here, next to the temple of Seti, the ruins were mostly something for me and the other children to play in. By the time I was perhaps eight, I knew every hiding place, every secret passage. One day my father called me and my brother Adly with a task. He had just bought two donkeys and said, 'get the wagon, you have a job to do'.

Derek: *(low audio, off mic)* And did it involve Omm?

Said: But of course. Why is everyone from America so impatient? Don't you know how to tell a good story?

Kara: *(low audio, off mic)* Derek, sit in the van. Call your agent. Or jerk off to your *Hollywood Reporter* pic.

Said: Is he always like that? I've seen more seasoned explorers in *The Goonies.*

Kara: Love that film...

Jared: Please, continue.

Said: At first, I figured we were to till the garden. But Father waved us into the shadows and lowered his voice. 'What you must do, sons, you must do at night, so no one sees, especially the antiquities inspector. Sneak into the temple, find loose boulders, the bigger the better. Bring them to the back of the house, chisel off any hieroglyphs and I'll build a new barn.'

(unknown noise, maybe shuffling of feet in sand) Shall I continue? Indy here seems to be getting restless.

Jared: Please, take all the time you need. I'm very intrigued to hear your story.

Said: Thank you… Even as a child, I knew the request was wrong. But we were excited to be doing something dangerous, and, more importantly, making my father happy, which was not an easy task. So, that night, when the night watchman had gone home we wheeled the cart past the gate. *(Said laughs)* The wagon squeaked so loudly I feared the chief inspector in Luxor fifty kilometers away would hear it.

Kara: What a minute, the freakin' pony is moving out of shot. Okay, rolling.

Said: Without exchanging a word, we knew where to go—the rear of the temple where restoration had stopped. That summer, the scaffolding had given way and revealed a new opening. So, we entered. *(laughter, followed by pause)*

Jared: What's so funny?

Said: Sorry, I was just thinking about the trail in the sand we left in our wake. Any inspector would know in an instant who made it: 'two kids with a barrel, probably the no-good Issawi boys.' *(more laughter, now Jared too)* But they were all too big to pick up when we got there. That meant going deeper into the Holy of Holies, where thin limestone once covered the walls to make them easier to carve.

My flashlight guided us to an area roped off since a tremor shook the foundations many years before. The wall had recently given way, revealing a set of stairs I had never seen. It plunged into the bedrock, and down below, something was giving off a dim light. I'd played in this temple my whole life, and never before had I felt any fear of being here… but that evening, everything seemed odd, and these new stairs made things worse.

Derek: Dear God, it's one interview in an hour-long show—forty-three minutes actually, with commercials. We don't need all this.

Jared: Derek, enough already! Show some goddamn respect for once.

Kara: Attaboy!

Jared: I'm sorry, I shouldn't have…

Kara: Shhhhh….

Jared: *(pause)* Said, please go on.

Said: All around were scattered stones that would suit my purpose, but instead, I was drawn to the light. I clicked off my flashlight and slipped out of my sandals. Adly wouldn't budge. So I went alone. The stairway was choked with fallen stones, some so recent that I feared the walls would cave in. Below, human voices. On the ceiling above, the flicker of candlelight. I crawled up the rubble and peered over.

Ali: *Ya salam!* What did you see?

Kara: Ali! You know the rules. Sound guys are never heard.

Ali: Sorry.

Kara: It is a good story, though. What did you see?

Jared: Can everyone just let me ask the questions? Said, please continue.

Said: There were two people facing away from me, holding hands and kissing. One I recognized: Omm. The other, a man I'd never met. From behind all I could notice was how weirdly dressed he was. Naked from the waist up, except for a band of beads around his neck. A white cloth of some kind was pinned around his body, and his head was bald, shining in the candle light. Very fit. He looked like one of the wall drawings come to life.

Jared: What were they saying?

Said: Mostly nothing. They were making love. Rather passionately.

Derek: Eww. An old broad like her?

Said: Older people don't make love? You're as shallow as the dust on my sandals.

Jared: Then what? They never spoke?

Said: Oh, yes, eventually. Strange, monotonous words, like the ones she used on our jackal. None of it was Arabic.

(inaudible screams from new male voices, all off microphone)

Said: My friends in the coffee shop have heard this tale before, so they know where it's going.

Jared: So, what are they shouting?

Said: 'It's the prince, the prince!' *(Said speaks in Arabic)* I told them to get out of my story. Shall I?

Jared: Please.

Said: I kept watching. At one point they grew closer and kissed, and I could see his face. Kohl on his eyes, a flowery fragrance I had never smelled before, and a band of fancy jewels around his head that rattled when he moved.

Derek: Wait. You're saying Omm was talking to an ancient Egyptian?

Said: I'm telling you what I saw. I did not say who he was or where he was from.

Derek: *(inaudible, something about 'bullshit.')*

Said: I thought the same, so I crept closer to the rock pile. As I put my eye to the hole, a stone tumbled down. I was terrified and froze. Beside my breathing, everything had gone quiet. I figured they either fled, or I was just seeing things. I returned my eye to the hole—and saw another eye staring back at me. It blinked.

Ali: *Ya!*

Kara: Ali!

Said: I screamed and tumbled down the rubble. When I looked up, Omm was towering over me. 'What are you doing in Horus's chapel?' she asked in broken Arabic. I wanted to shout that she was nothing but an imposter but couldn't bring myself to. I rose and looked behind her for the man, worried he'd do me harm. But he was gone. "Where is that man, I asked, the bald priest?"

"You saw that?" I remember she seemed surprised. "All of it, I imagine." She seemed understandably embarrassed. As I said, they were really going at it. 'Take me, my prince,' and all that good stuff.

She looked me in the eye. "And you want to drag these sacred stones away to a donkey den, is that right?"

I asked how she could possibly know that.

"It's all over your face, poor child. Plus, you're not the first to do so. Hundreds have done so over the centuries. But not on my watch." She sat on one of the rocks and rubbed it like it was a pet. "You know it's wrong. I can see that in your face, too. They belong here, where Seti intends them to be."

Jared: So, you're saying that was the pharaoh Seti she was talking to?

Said: Not at all. I'm saying it was his son Mehy, the crown prince. *(louder)* Like my friends in the coffee shop already gave away.

(Arabic chatter, laughter)

Jared: Wow, okay. What did you do then?

Said: The only thing that came to me: I ran and hid in my bedroom until daylight. *(more unknown male voices off mic)* Yes, yes, now you can shout it: the prince! And... that's my story. Sorry if it was so long, keeping Dr. Jones over here from finding the Ark.

Jared: No, at all, thanks, that was brilliant. So. Where do you think Omm is?

Said: Your best question yet. It's been way too long. Let's go find out. Ali, can you get this damn wire off me, please? *Shukran.*

CHAPTER 8

Hidden deep below the ruins of Abydos, there long existed a tomb, richly decorated and stacked with treasure. For over three thousand years, it lay undisturbed, preserving the mummy of an otherwise forgotten prince. The vaulted ceiling burst with frescos so vivid it was if the artist had just laid down his brush. Sacred spells shepherding the deceased through the twelve gates of the underworld covered every inch of the wall. Each of these gates presented a deadly challenge to overcome: a fiery lake, a cave of spikes, and a hungry snake, all keen to devour Prince Mehy before he reached the heavenly Field of Reeds. But as long as these spells remained intact, it would be possible for him to not only arrive in paradise but safely return to the world above at any time of his choosing.

Then, on an otherwise ordinary April evening, dark clouds appeared over the necropolis. Prince Mehy's tomb, concealed in a secret chamber with no way in or out, should have been protected. But this flood was otherworldly and found flaws in the rock. A dark stain appeared on the face of the night goddess Nut as she hovered over the ceiling. Her cobalt cheeks billowed, and her charcoal eyes wept. Chunks of plaster came free, and she crumbled into the tomb.

Soon Mehy's favorite earthly goods, those worthy enough to pack for the afterlife—his golden war chariot, priceless statues of the gods, his glittering silver throne—began to move about in the rising water. The statues became an invading army, the chariot a battering ram, all marching down the sloping corridor towards Mehy's coffin. Mixed in was artillery picked up as it advanced: silver-tipped arrows once used to hunt fowl in the Great Swamp, glass goblets long ago filled with the sweetest wine from Canaan, sublime alabaster jars containing the prince's four mummified organs.

As Mehy's prized possessions advanced, spells and incantations that allowed him to survive the afterlife and move between worlds were scrubbed from the walls. Yet the invaders were not yet satisfied. They next advanced and attacked the burial chamber, where the prince's gilded sarcophagus was pushed over and snapped in two. The body of Mehy, carefully wrapped and sealed for eternity, spun round and round like a bug in a whirlpool, the body melting to muck within a linen cocoon. Protective amulets on the prince's neck, chest and heart were of no help. His head snapped free and cascaded to one side of the tomb, his torso to another, and his lower body was ground up beyond recognition. After thirty-three centuries of peace, hidden away from those who wished him harm, the body and the soul of Prince Mehy were destroyed in less than ten minutes.

The tumble into the abyss wasn't far, and the pool of water helped cushion the blow, but Omm took the brunt of the impact on her head. Yet she felt strangely alert, heard her heart thumping, and retained the wits to move a fist under her face to raise it above the waterline.

Would a dead person bother to do that?

Omm tried to piece together what had happened. She recalled running to Mehy's hidden chapel to secure it from the storm. But this was not where she was now; it was dark and flooded with debris. Alabaster shards were strewn about, a chariot wheel floated against her cheek, and tightly wrapped items the size of a fist bobbed up and down. Omm knew what these were: embalmed organs that had broken free from Canopic jars. She was in a tomb, but whose? The walls had been scrubbed away so completely there was little to read. An image of Apep, the evil serpent of the underworld, was all that remained. She peered up and saw, far beyond reach, a broken ceiling. She must have fallen right through the face of the night goddess Nut, her outstretched arm failing to catch her on the way down.

Further along the wall, a royal visage stared back from sandstone, eyes painted white and lips thick and full. She recognized him immediately, and her heart sank.

Oh, my prince. What have they done to you?

Omm had never been in Mehy's actual tomb before, just the chapel above it. But she always knew its location, as Seti and Tiya had secretly built a modest altar above it so she could visit every day to keep incense burning. Omm found the strength to push a broken statue of Hathor off her chest and rise. The tomb was L-shaped and ended in a flat wall where Mehy's sarcophagus lay in pieces. But his body was nowhere to be found. A jumble of mummy fabric had been pushed against the wall and Omm tried to pick it up. Oddly, it had fully unraveled and was now somehow stuck where the wall met the floor. No amount of yanking would set it free. She examined the space between the floor and wall. There wasn't any.

After another useless tug, a thought occurred, and she pushed instead of pulled this time. The wall crept forward slightly as if on polished tracks. She pushed again, a bit harder, and it slid several feet. Omm loosened her grip; the ten-foot-high wall seemed to be moving forward by itself. At her feet, the unrolled mummy linen continued like a glowing pathway. Shelves stacked with crisp papyrus scrolls came into view. Many bore the marks of a royal seal. The shelves were not solid in the back, and she could see oil lamps burning and a solitary woman sitting at a table in front of a stack of scrolls. The linen made a trail directly to her feet.

Omm knew now where she was: deep within the Hall of Records, a place she had never been as it existed within the hazy space between her world and the realm of the gods.

Why now?

Omm drew closer to the woman and knew she'd soon find out. Tiya beckoned her closer still, two silver bowls of wine already poured.

Omm took a delicate sip. "Fermented pomegranate. His favorite."

Tiya nodded. "You still remember? The last time we drank this was in the Levant. Near the end..." They both lapsed into silence as they conjured up mirror memories of Mehy moldering on his deathbed, his hand reaching out for one final embrace.

Fear snapped Omm back to the present. "But if we're together, our *ka* is intertwined, and everything gets messy. It's been a law since the beginning: you must always be there, I must be here, or the bond breaks down."

Tiya brushed away a tear with her palm. "I know, it's a great risk. Which is why I chose the outskirts of both our worlds. Even so, we must talk fast in case the gods catch on." Her last few words were choked. "You've seen his tomb?"

"I have. Who did this?"

"I can only imagine Ramses, in union with someone in the underworld. Such forces don't reach the surface until someone from below sanctions it."

Omm drank again, this time less delicately. "But Ramses got all he wanted."

"Not everything," Tiya said with a shake of her head. "He never forgave me and his father for burying Mehy in secret. Never stopped hunting for his brother's tomb. And as you see, it appears he's found it at last."

"But as long as I keep the chants going, Mehy will never be completely forgotten."

"What you and your predecessors have done is devotion beyond dreams. You've kept my vow and his *ka*, alive for thousands of years. But you know as well as I, that it only illuminates what was hidden below. On its own, it's not enough. And..." Tiya looked Omm over and saw the elderly lady slumped before her. "How much time have you got? We can keep maladies at bay, but even the gods have not vanquished old age."

No use hiding it. "The nagging village doctor tells me not long. Says my heart can't take much more of me rambling through ruins and clambering up cliffs."

Tiya took an old parchment from the table and wrapped it around Omm's wrist, which was bleeding from the fall. "Any candidates?"

"Perhaps. A lost boy from America. He's up there now. Has traveled through our world before but remains inert. Lost. My hope is that he'll welcome the opportunity to forfeit his body in exchange for a life free of conflict and choice." She watched Tiya bandage her wound. "As I did."

"A man? We've not had one of those in some time." Tiya tied the parchment tight and ripped off the end. Then she smiled at another memory, more personal. "But we both know Mehy wasn't particular. He fancied anyone young and pretty, regardless of sex. You've not yet asked him?"

Omm sighed and lifted her bowl but didn't drink. "It's not as easy as it used to be. Up above, our gods have retreated, and few want to spend their lives in an abandoned temple, keeping what they see as a dead culture alive. I'll need to butter him up first."

It appeared Tiya was no longer listening. She rolled up a scroll and hastily replaced it with another from the basket. "We have more immediate problems. If we don't solve them first, we won't need a replacement."

Omm took in the vast Hall of Records. "What do you hope to find here?"

"A mention of Mehy's name in the royal edicts. Something he did that was grand and lasting." Tiya angrily tossed the papyrus to the floor and retrieved another. "Ramses was obsessed with blotting his brother out, making sure none of his deeds remained."

Omm was afraid to ask the next question. "And Mehy himself?"

Tiya's eyes were fixed on the scroll, but it was clear she was not seeing anything. She attempted to speak, but nothing emerged. Instead, she rose. "It's best if I just show you."

The pair followed the cord of linen into another room, where several men in white robes were huddled over a quartzite slab.

"I've brought a few of Seti's best embalmers with me to see what they can do."

When they saw Tiya, they bowed and stepped aside, except for one at the head of the table. He was holding several body parts, trying desperately to make them look like a complete human.

"There is simply not enough, my lady," he said defeatedly. "I fear we've failed you and that you've brought us through the door in vain."

Mehy's skull was intact, but his flesh had melted away. Only a patch of skin over the forehead and left cheek suggested who he once was. Part of his rib cage and hip remained, but the tendons were mostly gone. The left foot survived, and here the skin remained relatively crisp. A lonely finger lay nearby, pointing into the dark.

Omm approached and like Tiya, began to sob. The man they had both venerated and made love to and knew every inch of his body, from the mole on his neck to the cleft in his cheek, the man who had given their lives purpose for so long, was an incomprehensible puzzle, swollen and misshapen. A mummy was created expressly so the deceased's spirit would have a place to live should it want to return to the land above. There was no place here for Mehy to enter.

"What does this mean?" Omm asked, knowing full well the answer.

"It means from this moment, he ceases to be, and everything we built comes to an end. Unless we find another way for his name to live."

The notion of Mehy disappearing after all she had done made Omm dizzy. Thirty-three hundred centuries and over five hundred devotees, and it was under her eye where it all fell apart. There must be a solution. A way to capture his *ka* that didn't involve a physical body. It took her another moment for something to snap into view.

Is that why the American is here? If so, Mehy must be behind this, using the dreams to summon him.

She laughed at his ingenuity.

Always one step ahead, our prince.

Tiya studied her face. "You have a solution?"

"Not mine, I suspect, but Mehy's."

Omm ushered Tiya further away from the embalmers, who were listening to their every word.

Who knows who's working for Ramses?

When she finished whispering, Tiya shook her head slowly. "If that's my prince's plan, it's a foolish one."

"Can you not reach him to ask?"

"I've been trying since the storm. He's gone completely silent."

Omm lowered her voice as the embalmers crept closer. "Maybe it's only the boy he wants to talk to."

Tiya saw them too and moved Omm farther down the corridor. "We've no idea who this child was in the past, and if he's as weak as you claim, he'll only fail. Put our faith in a timid boy from America? Mehy will wander the gates forever."

"Do nothing, and he'll surely disappear. Which is worse?"

Tiya's eyes traveled down the hall, her gaze resting on her lover, lying in unidentifiable pieces. An embalmer picked up an ankle bone and tried to attach it to a foot. It fell away immediately. She could bear no more. "It's a tremendous task. But you and I have accomplished more. Would he even do it?"

Omm shrugged and wiped at the blood trickling down her neck. "I haven't a clue, but I must get back straightaway to find out."

CHAPTER 9

Jared called out to Kara, who was capping the camera and tenderly putting it back in its case. The precious child she and Lynette never had. "Don't power down just yet. We need to find Omm."

Said raised a palm. "Let's be sure she is okay first. Afterward, you can make your film."

"Fair enough. Kara, wanna stay here with the crew?"

"You kidding? I want to meet Omm." She packed her camera away. "But gotcha, no shooting for now."

Part of being a good producer, Jared had learned through observation, was ensuring that his crew felt included. He took stock. Ali was back on his phone recounting Said's story to his children, and Derek had finally retreated to the van. He had headphones on, proudly watching an older episode of himself on his laptop: muscles flexed, he was canoeing up a jungle river and consulting a compass. Every few seconds, he'd nod approvingly.

"Fine, let's go." The three of them walked towards the Temple of Seti, looming at the end of a long, cobbled causeway.

"You okay?" Jared asked Kara as they went. "You seem a little grumpy today, even for you." He asked this with a smile that wasn't returned.

"Totally fine." Her response came quickly and defensively.

"Doesn't sound like it." His mind went to the only place it ever drifted. "Did I do something wrong?"

She mellowed. "You're doing great. It's just 120 degrees in the shade and every time I stop moving the fuckin' horse flies bite me." To prove her point, she swatted at one that had landed on her forearm. She grimaced in pain at the sunburn that bubbled her skin. "Next episode, pick someplace cold. They gotta have weird shit in Iceland. Viking ghosts or something?"

Jared smiled. He knew the desert was not Kara's cup of tea. She was a city girl who had enough of rough living, so the urban ruins of Rome or Mexico City suited her just fine. Better hotels, bars and restaurants. She only agreed to do this episode because of Jared's precarious situation. But then, to his great surprise, she threw herself into research, asking Jared obscure questions about the *Book of the Dead* or mummification practices that even he couldn't answer. ("How long after death can you wait to embalm a heart?" or "Can non-believers make it the underworld or must one be a follower of Osiris?") He chalked it up to one selfless reason: she wanted to help him get to the bottom of his weird dreams.

Their first stop was Omm's shack, tucked just behind the temple. A knock went unanswered. The house was never locked—what was worth stealing?—and Said let himself in. It had been violently rearranged by the storm, furniture askew, teacups on the floor, wet clothes clogging corners. A jackal slept on the window sill, and several dogs and cats were hoovering up a split bag of lentils, but no Omm.

"Think she got cold feet?" Kara asked, dipping her hands in the cool water.

"Omm never gets cold feet about anything, and she was excited about your visit. She trusted you all to tell her story, was even going to do a spiritual cleanse of a special place she wanted to show you." He looked out the window at the Osireion, the grand sunken temple dedicated to Osiris in the rear of Seti's palace. "Let's check there."

Jared knew about this site from his research, but nothing prepared him for its sheer otherworldliness. Twelve roofless columns, impossibly large and cut from rose-colored granite, decorated with obscure, badly eroded reliefs no one could translate. Resting in a trench at least thirty feet deep, the Osireion resembled a prehistoric Stonehenge being reclaimed by the earth. As Jared drew close, his chest tightened. He was about to enter his first ancient Egyptian site. Something he had been dreaming about, and dreading, for god knows how long. Would the visions return, and how bad would they be? He halted at the edge of the site, his feet burrowed in the sand.

"It's an easy climb," Said announced casually, oblivious to Jared's fear. He shimmied down and began looking around. As he did, a mark of worry crossed his face. "There's always a couple inches of water down here. From the Nile maybe, or an aquifer no one's ever figured it out, but the level's much higher today."

Only then he noticed Jared and Kara hadn't followed. "It seems safe. Unless you're afraid of water?"

Kara took Jared by the hand and led him to the ladder. "You didn't fly halfway around the world to look at temples from the outside only, did you?"

"No, I didn't," he said as he inched forward.

"One step at a time, you'll be fine."

The ladder creaked as he made his way down and found himself in knee-high water. It was warm and murky. Happily, no visions surfaced.

"You good?" Kara asked as she joined him.

He sighed with relief. "I am."

At the far end of the temple stood a truncated column. On it, in a shallow bowl, rested a few cones of spent incense. "Omm often climbs up there to pray," Said remarked, rubbing the dry incense between his fingers, "but hasn't been here recently. Let's check the cliffs." He turned back to the ladder.

Jared noticed a pair of green slippers floating nearby. "Are those hers?"

"Damn." For the first time, Said looked concerned. "She's probably down there." He pointed to an open doorway poking out from the water.

"You're kidding me?" Kara said. "It's, like, completely submerged."

"It's always like that," Said noted. "The tunnel ascends again after a meter or two, then the inside is dry. But today, the water seems more agitated than normal." He sloshed his way into the opening, then took out his mobile phone, wallet and keys and set them on the pillar. "We can make it. Just leave your stuff here and stay close to me."

A litany of rational reasons to go no further flashed in front of Jared. His clothes would be wet, and then how would he direct? Derek would be angry he left the set for so long. Someone would steal his wallet, and the company credit card was inside. He once got swimmers' ears that hurt all summer. If he and Kara both died, that's half the crew at once, much harder to replace. But he knew the real reason to turn back was sheer terror of what awaited him down there and if he could handle it.

Then a voice behind him chimed in. "Stop now, and you'll regret it for eternity."

He turned around, suspecting it was Kara, but she was ahead of him, checking out the passageway. No one was behind him except a few wild dogs watching from above.

"Ready?" Said asked as Jared joined them.

"You go after Said," Kara said. "I'll be right behind you."

A deep breath, and they descended. Jared was determined not to open his eyes, assuming that without a trigger, nothing would materialize. Still, after a moment, his hands struck a wall and panic set in.

Which way do I swim? Where was Kara?

After his forehead banged into a rock, he opened his eyes and was happy to see the soles of Said's sneakers. Two glowing white footprints to follow. Look only at them, and all will be fine. But then he turned a corner, and a sunken chamber came into view. Carved into it were little alcoves, like shelves, each exactly the same size. This was all it took.

He's in a chamber similar to this one, but dry, the walls glittering with images of Osiris, Lord of the Dead. Oil lamps flicker as a group gathers in a circle. Everyone wears jackal-headed masks and shiny tunics. Above them, a thick cloud of incense clings to the ceiling. Chants echo from some place that can't be seen, as if others are just out of view and watching. The alcoves along the wall are no longer empty but are filled with recently used instruments of torture. Clamps and knives and a long thin rod hooked at the end. One of the jackal-headed men reaches for it. From its tip, blood dribbles to the floor.

A scream brought Jared back to reality, followed by a mouthful of sandy water. His arm flailed as he struggled to rise, but he banged against something hard before he could. More water flooded into his lungs, this time deeper. His body began to mellow, and he could feel himself letting go, almost willingly drifting to a place of safety and warmth. Faces drifted in front of him: Kara, Carlos, and his parents back in Kansas. Then, a cloaked figure he didn't recognize. Unlike the others, who were all still very much alive, this one seemed to be beckoning him forward to join him in the afterlife.

But before that meeting could occur, Jared was tossed onto a dry surface. Kara tucked both arms under Jared's and squeezed. Turbid water billowed out, followed by an aching cough that brought up more. He could taste sand in his mouth, mixed with an odd sweetness he recognized. Jared raised a hand to say he was okay. But he was not okay and wasn't sure what frightened him more: the fact that this time a vision almost killed him or that he was almost at peace to say goodbye to all those people and let it happen.

Kara moved him to a nearby bench. "Just breathe."

"I'm fine, I'm fine…"

"Another vision?"

He spat out the last of the water. "Yeah, a bad one. Something that happened in here a long time ago."

Said gazed at Jared and slowly nodded. "So Omm was right about you. Can you rise?"

Jared was surprised that he could. He looked around in wonder.

"My God, where are we?" Kara asked. "It's creepy as hell. Like an East New York train station late at night."

"No one knows," Said answered. "But, best guess is that it was a cenotaph, a symbolic tomb meant to represent a gateway to the underworld. Probably never used as anything."

Jared wanted to correct him, add a few details that were not quite right, but instead wiped snot from his face. He did feel compelled to answer one question, however. "The water comes from the Nile, not an aquifer."

"How do you know?"

"I could taste it."

"But no Omm, it seems," Kara said. "Does it go on?"

Said pointed to another corridor. "One more chamber." He walked towards it. "It's narrow but navigable, but maybe you'd rather stay here?"

Kara looked at Jared. "You wanna? I can check it out."

Jared motioned them both forward. "We go together." The second corridor was no more than two feet wide and two feet high, clearly not designed for easy access. But after a short crab-like crawl, it opened into a tiny domed chapel. It, too, was empty, except for incense cones glowing from a well-used altar.

"Frankincense," Jared said, more to himself.

But still they were alone.

Fresh worry marked Said's face.

"If the altar is burning, she's been here recently."

As he approached it, the crunch of fresh stones echoed underfoot. He glanced down to see a spider's web of cracks.

"These are new."

Jared instinctively retreated to the wall where he felt more secure. As Said moved forward, rubble scattered until a louder sound halted their advance: rocks meeting water. Ahead, a ragged hole plunged into places unknown. It wasn't difficult to figure out what happened. The floor had given way and took Omm with it.

Said retrieved a lighter from the altar and lowered it into the abyss. At first, all they could see was their broken reflection in a pool of water, some six or so feet down. Then, objects came into focus. A pile of shattered crystal, floating wood, and off to the side, the bare foot of a woman, toes gnarled and still. "I warned her this might happen, but she never listened." By the tone in Said's voice, Jared could see how close the two must be and how worried he was. No wonder he became so offended when Derek called her crazy. These two were friends.

"Is she... moving?" Kara asked. "That's a long way down."

Said called her name several times and got no response. With the flickering light, he traced Omm's body from heel to head, where her gray hair rested on a shallow pool of blood. Silently, they watched her face for signs of breathing, neither keen to make a medical diagnosis. The only breathing they heard was their own, and the only motion in the tomb was the dripping of water onto Omm's frozen face.

CHAPTER 10

Ten minutes after they found Omm, the entire village of El Araba had raced to the Osireion to bring her to the surface. A human chain stretched across the ruins and into Omm's shack. She was still breathing, but little beyond. A nasty gash ran down the back of her head and neck where she had landed in Mehy's tomb. Over 80 years old and weak of heart, the prognosis was bleak, and as she was carried to her house, not a word was said. One villager began to wail. It was as if the funeral procession had already begun.

Jared followed behind, in no rush to join the others. Everything had fallen to pieces. Not only had he almost died in the Osireion, unable to handle his visions, the one person who could help was dying in front of his eyes. The show was over, his career was over, and, most tragically, all his questions about himself would remain unanswered.

After laying her on her cot, Said turned to the anxious throng crowding into the hut. "Give her space. Someone fetch Nile water, fast."

"There's water all over the shack from the rain."

Jared dipped a cup in and filled it up.

"It must be from the river. Like you, she knows Nile water when she tastes it."

The village doctor soon arrived, an oversized stethoscope dangling from his neck like a prop.

"I warned her about this kind of activity," was the best he could offer.

He shook his head sadly, and Jared was touched by how fully these people accepted an outsider as an equal. He wondered if his hometown would do the same if the situation reversed. If an old Arab woman appeared out of nowhere one day and started living in the abandoned train station, how would she be treated? Would the locals race to her aid should she fall ill? Would he?

Kara retrieved her camera. "You can't let her die," she snapped. "Too much we got to know."

She looked at Jared. "Tell them she can't die."

Jared thought it was a strangely emotional reaction from a woman who trusted no one.

Ali held the boom pole high while Derek lingered in the back, not bothering to clip his microphone to his lapel.

"Don't see why you're shooting. If she croaks, stupid episode's over and we go home."

Jared moved forward but didn't try to direct.

Instead, he turned to Said. "What do you think?"

"I think there are too many people in here, and we need to give her space," he answered sharply, waving to the crew to step back.

They did but kept rolling. About a dozen villagers returned with buckets of Nile water and Said splashed Omm's face and lips. At first, it did nothing, but then, slowly, her nose began to twitch.

A moment later, she opened her eyes and looked around, "Cleopatra," she whispered.

There was a collective sigh and claps from the villagers.

"See, they all think they were great queens in past lives," Derek said, this time to the camera, and he stepped into view. "Fantasy book club stuff."

"No," Said explained. "She wants her favorite cat."

A boy went to the yard to find her. Several other animals followed him into the room. Two dogs trailed behind, then the timid jackal. A nervous-looking scorpion watched from the windowsill.

Omm spoke slowly, first in Arabic, but when she saw Jared, she shifted, mid-word, into English.

"I've seen such wonderful things."

"What were you doing going down there?" Said asked. "Especially after that flood? How many times have I told you—"

"As many as there are stars in the sky." Omm shrugged. "But I knew you'd find me." She reached out her hand. "Seti assured me you would. He helped bring me back to the land above."

"So, it was Seti you were talking to this time?" Said spoke softly, as a son would to a muddled parent. "And what did you speak of?"

"A great deal. All of the utmost importance." Only then did Omm notice the film crew hovering nearby, and it took a moment for things to snap into place. "Put that camera down for a moment, love," she said to Kara. When she did, Omm offered her a warm smile. "Poor dear, why so sad? It can't be that bad." Before Kara could defend herself, Omm shifted back to Jared as she searched for something hidden in his face. "First, I must speak to this young man alone if you're the director."

"Nice to finally meet, but not in these circumstances."

"No, the circumstances, it turns out, couldn't be better suited." She rose with a start. "Must be swift. The pharaoh is waiting for an answer."

Jared guided Omm to a flower garden that commanded a sprawling view of the temple complex framed between palm and sand. It felt like one of those old David Roberts etchings from the mid-1800s, where decay and destruction had been rendered exotic. Jared scanned the temple of Seti as he visualized every twist and turn within. He could even see a little alcove where votive statues once stood, smooth and shiny from veneration.

Omm, rocking quietly in her wicker chair, was watching. "Have you ever dreamt about this place?"

Jared thought again of his recent visions. A cabal of torturers huddled in a hidden crypt and, worse, killing an injured man in cold blood. Neither were images he had seen back at home. The nearer he got to the source, the darker and more violent they had become. What if, in ancient times, he was some deranged cult leader who murdered a prince or pharaoh? Does Omm know? Is that why he was beckoned? Could the real reason be revenge? If so, he needed to be on guard.

"No," he said flatly. "No memories of the place."

"I see." Omm tottered forward, and Jared attempted to help. "I can manage. Fetch me my cane over there." He retrieved it. An old wooden thing splintered in the middle and worn at the top. "Would you fancy a private tour of the temple?" she asked.

"No. You need to rest."

Truth be told, he wasn't sure if he could handle another ancient temple.

"Rubbish. We need to speak, and it's better we do it there. So Seti can listen in."

Before Jared could argue, Omm was walking across the desert, followed by her army of worried pets. The sun was scorching, the ground like concrete, and anyone not in town the day before would be forgiven for imagining it hadn't rained in centuries. A cobra emerged from hiding and wiggled its tongue as if saying hello. Big black beetles stopped pushing balls of dung to let her pass. One crawled up Jared's pant leg, perhaps to tag along.

At the temple, Omm threw a light headdress over her disheveled hair. Jared thought this odd, as it would have served better use in the bright sun, not as they were about to escape it.

"The headdress is not for me," she explained. "But for respect to the gods. This remains a holy site, as alive as a mosque, synagogue, or church."

Rare for pharaonic temples, this one retained a roof, not only preserving it from the elements but making it much easier to imagine what it looked like when in use Jared halted at the door before Omm took his hand.

"Come, love, you're with me. You'll be fine."

He took a deep breath as if, like the previous ruin, he was about to submerge himself into a deadly current.

Jared walked no more than five feet before he had to shut his eyes and clutch a column for support. A chalky taste clogged the back of his mouth. A cocktail of ochre and malachite blended with lime plaster. His fingers caressed cool, pink granite and a round carving he recognized as the cartouche of Ramses the Great. And from above, a chorus of gentle chirps made him grin. Were speckled sparrows still nesting in the rafters?

Unlike the Osireion, a place of death, this space was calming and peaceful. He knew its energy and could relax. Omm was right. There was nothing to fear here. Whoever he was or did in the past, it didn't involve this sacred place. Jared exhaled and opened his eyes.

Omm had been watching.

"Welcome back," she said as she plunged deeper into the temple.

The only light came from small squares left open to the sky. This created slabs of sun that streamed down at canted angles. Framed against black, the light was harsh, swirling with dust and obscuring all that lay behind it. Omm dipped into one of them. She continued chatting, but Jared couldn't pinpoint her location. Her voice was disembodied, ricocheting across the sacred site.

"Sublime, isn't it? Took twenty-three years for Seti to build it. His youngest son Ramses finished it for him." For the first time since they met, she sounded sad. "And before you thank him, he erased most mentions of his dad and chiseled his own name in instead."

Omm was now standing many yards off, next to a wall draped in hieroglyphs.

"Surely, in your line of work, you've seen this engraving."

She pointed to a relief high up between two columns. It began with a giant wasp or bug and, next to it, a very curious image.

"So that's it?" Jared asked, relieved that he could enjoy the site purely on its own merit. "The infamous "Abydos Helicopter." A million cheesy books and shows have been written about this."

"Each worse than the last," she laughed. "What's your assessment?"

Logic was something Jared had easily mastered, so he was ready for this question.

"Pareidolia. An optical illusion, just like Egyptologists say. Ramses plastered over Seti's name but in time, parts fell out, leaving a rim that looked like a helicopter blade. Still, people see what they want to see."

"A good theory and another fancy word. And, of course, pharaohs could have never had a helicopter in New Kingdom Egypt."

"So, you agree?" Jared wished Kara was here to film Omm's answer.

"Oh, most certainly," she nodded. "Empty propaganda from Ramses. He tried to reverse engineer one but could never get it into the air. Didn't have the proper metals. They didn't call it the Bronze Age for nothing, you see."

"Wait, you're saying it *is* a helicopter?"

"Of course, just a rather dodgy one. Look at it again. Trust your eyes."

"How could Ramses know about helicopters?"

"I'm getting to that."

She vanished into a ray of dust.

A moment later, Jared found her sitting on a limestone bench at least thirty feet away. A small chunk of the roof had fallen away, and light beamed down.

"There used to be an adorable little chapel here, absolutely slathered in hieroglyphs, one of them featuring Prince Mehy. But see it now. The plaster is gone, and the rains last night washed it away even more." She invited Jared to join her. "Tell me, big-time TV man. Why exactly have you decided to come here from Manhattan to interview dotty ol' Dorothy of Blackheath?"

Jared sat. As he did, he noticed her head was no longer bleeding, and the scars nearly healed.

"The network and I," he said, careful to not let her think it was all about him. "Are fascinated by your claims to this place, its history."

"I've watched your shows, you know. Said had to drive me to a cyber cafe in Luxor to view them." She lowered her voice. "In the main, they're not particularly good, are they?"

This woman was far less gullible than she appeared. He needed to be honest but wary. "Some episodes are stronger than others. It's true."

"And I'm to be this week's sideshow freak. Rather like Big Foot and the episode you did regarding that large prehistoric dog killing livestock in Mexico. What was it called?"

Jared laughed at what was certainly one of *Ancient Encounters* most inane episodes. "That would be the Chupacabra."

"Lovely word, loathsome show. So, I'm to be this week's Chupacabra?"

"I'm not here to make fun of you or judge what you claim. Just record what you say and show me. The truth will come out."

"On that, we can agree." Omm walked toward the rear of the temple. "Come, I want to show you something few have had the privilege to see." When they arrived at a roped-off section and a partially collapsed hallway, Jared realized she was taking him to the same area Said had told him about, where he claimed to have seen her making love to the prince. Omm clamored over a pile of rubble and into a small opening, beyond, the hallway ended abruptly, the solid wall chiseled to resemble a huge door without a knob.

"You know what this is, correct?"

Jared has seen many, at least in books. The carving was in low relief. Two linear columns and what looked like a field of wheat overhead. In the center, a simple solid square about two feet across corbelled on the edges but otherwise empty.

"A false door. A mock gateway where the dead person's *ka* can pass through should they want to visit the land above."

"Mostly correct, except for the 'mock' bit. The door was added by Seti late in the temple's construction."

"For what?"

"That's what I'm about to show you. On the other side of this wall is the hypostyle hall, where most visitors enter, with all those lovely columns and such."

Omm handed Jared her cane, closed her eyes, and remained still. One minute became three. Had the old woman drifted off? Jared studied her to make sure she was still breathing and that the cut on her head had not opened back up. Swirling light behind her on the wall made him gaze beyond her. The false door was no longer solid but a window into the main hall. What's more, people were shuffling back and forth.

Her eyes fluttered open.

"Come closer, Jared. It's time to stop living in the shadows."

The hypostyle hall appeared much different from when they walked through it a few minutes prior. It was now bursting with bright colors, paint glistening. On either side of the gateway, massive cauldrons belched emerald-green smoke. Two men draped in leopard skins walked by carrying silver boxes. High priests presented daily offerings to the gods. Nearby, a man dressed in a simple tunic stood on a wooden pedestal, chiseling an image into what appeared to be fresh stone.

"What's all this?"

Jared rubbed his eyes, turning briefly around to locate the glare of a film projector. Nothing but rock and wall.

"It can't be."

"Oh, but it can," Omm said, pointing to a young girl standing by one of the cauldrons, adding cones of incense.

She was tall and shapely, with luminous skin and hair.

"That's me. Or rather, Tiya, my original *ka.* I was much prettier in my first incarnation than in this one." She sighed. "You can see now why Mehy fancied her."

Jared drew closer. It all seemed real except for two telltale omissions. No sound or smell. A silent movie, no more real than an episode of *Ancient Encounters.* He reached out, but Omm tapped his hand with her cane.

"Do that, and the portal closes. It's like an image in the river—you're permitted to see it, but the other senses are not yet allowed. Touch it, and it ripples away."

"Well?"

Tiya seemed to be anxiously asking from the other side.

"A bit more time, a bit more time… he's still sussing it out," Omm responded with raised palms.

The image, rather than frightening him, gave Jared an expected burst of relief. It was the answer he had hoped for all along, disappointingly true, but easier to handle.

It's all been smoke and mirrors.

I was no ancient killer, and there's no such thing as reincarnation. I was and remain a complete nobody. Everything has been the delusion of a lonely kid with a desperate need to escape. What he saw now was so patently phony, so clearly designed to bamboozle him, that he could finally walk away. Derek was right all along. This was all planned in advance. Some Pyramidiots in costumes out to hoodwink a naïve producer.

She didn't invite me here because of some mumbo jumbo about past lives. She picked the kid so green and full of desire to be anyone but himself he'd believe anything. Even my own silly dreams.

He turned on Omm, his eyes red.

"You got the wrong person. I've seen no visions of the past. No one does. And I'm certainly not just some fool who will fall for anything."

"You think I arranged all of this just to have a laugh at the young producer of *Awkward Encounters*, or whatever it's called? As if that's all I have to do with my time. We've greater things to discuss." She thought for a moment. "Let's play another game like we did on the phone. Pick a time period, anything post-pharaonic."

"I'm sick of games," he snapped, and he meant it.

"Oh, you've come this far. Will ten more minutes of an open mind kill you?"

Jared wanted out of this place, wanted to crawl back to Derek, admit he'd been duped, and accept his fate. Let the strong lead. It had been his M.O. all his life and had preserved him well. But then he caught himself. Not this time. This time, do your job. If she's a fraud, confront her. That's what documentary filmmakers do.

"Humor an old lady."

"Fine. Ancient Rome."

"Ghastly folk. Pompeii was jolly good fun, though. Now *that* would make a thrilling episode."

Omm went silent again and this time Jared realized she was deep in some trance. After a moment, she nodded.

"*Gratias tibi*," she said at last.

"Come again?"

"It's thank you in Latin. I wasn't speaking to you, love."

Lights flickered, and Jared could again see movement through the solid wall. It was like the sun was swiftly rising and falling, days and years zipping by. Flashes and figures appeared and then were gone; a column collapsed and remained there for a while. Then it rose again, different from before, as all the other columns changed color and décor. Omm raised a hand, and the flickering slowed and stopped like an old Nickelodeon. A regal-looking woman approached. She was dressed in the height of Imperial fashion: a mountain of curls, ringlets, and a silver band topped her head, while a chunky golden necklace towered over a bright blue toga. Smiles were exchanged.

"That's Drusilla, another of my predecessors. She honored Mehy's name for many decades after he cured her cancer. He can do that, you know. Keep maladies at bay as long as you maintain your vows. I myself had a dreadful glaucoma and was nearly blind. Now, at eighty-one, I can still see like a newborn."

Some Latin was exchanged, and Drusilla stepped aside so Jared could fully take in the view.

The main hall had been transformed. A few stern-faced men in Centurion garb pushed around some priests. Above the door, replacing the image of Seti with one of a pharaoh was more animated than the original: you could see muscle and tendon, and the perspective was not a complete profile.

"Not an ounce of subtlety in their art." Omm sighed. "And it's supposed to be Emperor Nero, can you believe it? Whom we all know was a fat toad of a man."

Jared rolled his eyes, relieved to confirm it was all a ruse. "Just a bunch of cardboard sets from *I Claudius*."

He rubbed his nose and halted a sneeze.

"What do you smell?"

The answer came to him before he could censor himself.

"Talinum and... rose water."

"You recognize Talinum, which, mind you, has not been used in centuries, yet you doubt reincarnation. Now, like Claudius, who's playing the fool, Mr. Plummer?"

Keep poking holes, that's my job.

"Aha. I thought you said we could only use our eyes here. No other senses."

"Drusilla was kind enough to open the door a bit wider, so you could sample the scene in full." Omm sniffed the air and winced. "She did tend to overdress for the part as if she was still a vestal virgin back on Palatine Hill."

Jared moved closer to the wall and inhaled but stayed clear of touching it. As much as he decided it was all an act, the last thing he wanted was for the door, open to him for the first time, to close. His senses were inflamed; the images conjured up more feelings deep within that had been buried for ages. A moment of pride washed over him. Trip Omm up with a time period so obscure she couldn't possibly conjure it up. That's the one thing, Jared Plummer, ace researcher, was good at.

"With all due respect, I'm still not buying it. How about one more?"

"If you insist. I know scholars only trust evidence when it comes in threes."

"Early 1800s. The Age of Exploration."

Derek would like that. It might even win him a rare compliment when he told the crew about all this later.

"Tres bien."

Omm lowered her eyes. Years whizzed by, columns collapsed, and this time stayed that way. Seti's temple decayed and became a ruin. Half the roof caved in, and sand dunes obscured much of the interior. In the corner, a woman hidden under a thick headdress tended her herd of goats and was cooking something in a little fire. She saw Omm but did not approach.

"There's Farah. Originally from a desert tribe, she was quite reserved and mostly kept to herself. But a beautiful soul. Watched over Abydos for nearly fifty years in exchange for a place to live and pray after Napoleon's army opened Egypt to European thieves."

The women exchanged silent greetings. Outside, a few men arrived on camels. They squatted down and entered the sand-choked doorway. Two appeared to be Egyptians, but the other was brashly, almost comically, Western. He was broad and red-headed and donned a large felt hat and leather vest. In one hand, he clutched a rifle. In the other, something that resembled a crowbar. After scanning the walls, he called to the others. Together they began tearing the painting off the wall.

Jared recognized the man but wanted to hear Omm say it. "Who is that?"

"Giovanni Belzoni," Omm said with disdain. "The Great Belzoni, I believe you foolishly call him back in the West. Odious man not only ripped this place apart but carted Seti's sarcophagus back to Europe, where it molders to this day."

They watched as Belzoni tore a panel off the wall and handed it to his men, who tied it to a camel.

Jared moved closer. There were paintings and drawings of Belzoni, the same ones Derek used to fashion his on-camera persona, and this man surely looked like him. But if Derek could ape him, so could Omm. Still, Jared had to admit Omm had done a better job of it.

Omm smiled wistfully.

"At least Belzoni died young. Killed by bandits in the Niger, I was told, then stripped clean down to his leather boots and stained undies. Just rewards for a life of cultural theft. I do loathe the modern era. So primitive."

The images faded to sandstone.

Despite his protests that it was all theatrics, this last one seemed a bit too real to dismiss out of hand. But instead of growing more intrigued, the opposite began to happen. When confronted with something new, best to shut down, avoid anything that would make him look over-eager. So he remained on defense.

"Nice costumes, but why are you showing me all this?"

"This portal allows Prince Mehy to pass back and forth, preserve his name, and see me or any of the other gatekeepers when he's in the mood. It can also be used on special occasions to invite people into his world. We've all been hand-picked by Mehy and Tiya to keep this gate open and guarded. It's all in my memoir. Have you not even read it?"

"Yes, but…"

"I told you on the phone I could offer you access to eternity. I still can, but it turns out the gods seem to have another offer, even greater, for you."

Here we go. The shell game begins.

"My only job is to make a great film for my bosses. If you can't do that, in all due respect, we need to cancel the shoot."

"I can help you make the greatest documentary ever made. One far better than your *Asinine Dilemmas with Derek Do-hicky* or whatever nonsense you call it."

"And how could you do that?"

"Isn't it obvious? By taking you and your camera crew to the other side, to your deep past, and letting you film all you like of ancient Egypt. But in return, you must do something for Mehy. Something no one else can."

Jared reached for the false door, and this time, Omm let him touch it. It was solid. He felt around the edges, and it too felt like part of the boulders around it. However she faked it, she had done it well.

"And how could I, a junior cable TV producer from America, possibly help a crown prince of Ancient Egypt?"

Omm glanced around the room to ensure they were alone. To be safe, she beckoned Jared closer.

"We must be careful. Ramses won't like what I have to say. Lend me your ear."

After she finished, Jared rose with a start.

"That's insane. *You're* insane."

He knew it. He had been used since their first conversation when he confessed an interest in reincarnation.

"I went out on a limb to listen to your story, even pitched you to the network to convince them that you're not the flake they all suspected." He stepped back from the false door. "What an idiot I was."

Omm sighed.

"That's what Tiya feared you would say. A perpetual follower and never a leader. The kind who glides in and out of life. But I believe you have it within you. All you must do is prove yourself to the gods."

"That's it, huh? The gods of Egypt want my help?"

"Not the gods themselves. We must keep it from them for now, lest they find out and grow angry."

Jared wouldn't let her finish. He dashed down the corridor, away from not only Omm but the eyes of the deities on the wall, who, if real, would surely mock him for thinking he could outwit them. Ahead of him was a relief of the Ninth Gate of the underworld, where a soul's heart had been placed on a scale and weighed against a feather. If it was lighter, if the soul had performed noble deeds in his current life, he would be allowed to live again. If not, a hungry demon, equal parts hippo, crocodile, and leopard, was anxiously waiting.

The goddess Ammit, "The Gobbler."

That, Jared knew, would be his fate. If he had any gifts to offer the world, he had squandered them through a lifetime of diffidence and inaction. And if Omm hadn't picked up on that right away, she was as big a fraud as he was.

"I'm telling the crew you sustained an injury and can't do the show," Jared announced. "I'm tired of always being played and laughed at."

He continued walking to the end of the hall, only to discover it was a dead-end and had to retrace his steps past her.

Omm stopped him with her cane.

"I wonder, Jared, how long will you continue to bury your true self? Don't tell me you came all this way for this naff TV program? You're seeking something, and if you can only open your eyes, you'll realize it's right before you. The pharaoh has offered you something extraordinary. He could have chosen anyone. He chose you."

Jared turned away again to see Ammit salivating in front of a tipping scale. He felt pitiful and small and didn't know where to turn. All he knew was that his time here was over.

"I need to get back. Tell the crew the show is off."

Omm sadly shook her head.

"If all you desire is for me to be your Chupacabra, fair enough. It's the least I can do to hear me out. Let's do your interview, and if after ruminating on it for a bit—but not too long, mind you—you have a change of heart, I'll open doors you assumed were long closed."

But Jared hadn't heard her. He was halfway to the exit, once again trying to outrun himself.

CHAPTER 11

When they returned to the village, the scene was already set for a master 'walk and talk' with Derek and Omm. As Ali clipped the microphone on her, Derek pulled Jared aside.

"Is the old broad gonna survive, or is the show off?" he asked.

"She'll live and is up for the interview," Jared said, his mind still reeling from what she asked of him in the temple. "But..."

"What?"

He lowered his voice. Even after his harsh words to her, public manners came first.

"You might be right about her. She's up to something. Wants to use me—us—for some bullshit game."

Derek's voice didn't afford her the same respect.

"Of course she does," he shouted. "Don't worry. No one gaslights my crew and gets away with it. I'm gonna make mincemeat of her. You sit in the shade and watch and learn."

Before action was called, Derek glanced at the script one last time and rolled his eyes.

Frame in from the temple of Seti. Begin as a shaking of hands, then walk along outside of the temple as Omm shows Derek a few choice features. (TBD)

MASTER INTERVIEW: DEREK DEES AND OMM:

THRU LINE. DEREK IS INTRIGUED BY HER STORIES AND PLANS TO INVESTIGATE FURTHER TO FIND THE TRUTH, STARTING WITH EXPLORING A LOST TOMB AND RAPPELLING UP A CLIFF.

DEREK: This place is amazing, thanks for giving us a tour. Now share with me how you came to Egypt.

OMM: I was called by the gods as a very young girl in London. They promised me a long and safe life, free of worry and fear, as long as I kept their prince alive. I was their chosen one, I suppose you might say.

DEREK: Fascinating. And how did it feel to think that of all the people alive, it was only you the ancient gods wanted? Pretty special, I guess?

OMM: If I was the only one who could achieve this, then I must sacrifice myself to the cause.

DEREK: Please tell me how this wondrous adventure of yours began

OMM: Well quite by chance, actually. I was only seven and had...

"Got it." Derek checked his hat on the monitor, got the thumbs-up sign from Kara, and tossed the script on the ground.

"So tell me, Miss Dorothy Kershaw, of London, England, just who on God's green earth are you tryin' to fool? Even Jared thinks you're a fraud. That takes some doing."

Interview transcript

Location: the village of **El Araba, Egypt**

April 11

Subject: Omm, a/k/a Dorothy Kershaw

Interviewer: Derek Dees, et al.

Omm: Beg your pardon, dear.

Derek: I asked, who in the hell do you think you're fooling with all this crap?

Omm: I'm Omm, the current guardian of Abydos.

Derek: And what makes an old white lady from England come to the middle of Africa and claim she knows it better than everyone who's lived here for thousands of years?

Ali: Finally, a good question.

Derek: Thanks, I got it from you. Thought it might be fun. Anything to throw the old biddy off.

Jared *(off mic)*: Derek, I'm fine with the tough questions, but can you at least be civil?

Omm: No, love, I agree. It's actually a fair question. I may look like a European white lady now, but inside this current shell of mine, I've been every color, age, and nationality under the sun. Gender too. Never judge a *ka*, a spirit, by its cover. Very narrow-minded of you.

Derek: And what's a *ka* again for the folks at home who might not live in an ancient graveyard?

Omm: A *ka* is a bit like a soul. It survives the death of a body and lives inside a mummy, another person, or even a picture or statue.

Derek: And you got some old Egyptian soul living in you, kinda like a tapeworm?

Omm: Before I answer, one query of my own: I know Jared, but who exactly are you?

Derek: For Christ's Sake! Does no one have cable over here? I'm the host, Derek Dees. My name's on the freakin' title.

Omm: Right, now I recall. *Derek Do-hicky.* I fast-forwarded those bits. Why ever are you dressed like that? The leather vest and puffy trousers and fancy boots and whatnot? You look like Zorba, the Greek, and an Ottoman waiter, meets... Said, what's the name of that old movie?

Said: *(off mic, inaudible)*

Omm: That's it. Meets Indiana Jones. It simply makes no historical sense.

Derek: You said one question. That was two. I'm interviewing you.

Omm: So you are. I'm merely one of the many women, and sometimes men, who've answered the call to keep Prince Mehy alive by forfeiting my body, and my original *ka*, for a greater good. I certainly don't pretend to have ownership of this place any more than those who live here and whom I adore.

(indistinct chatter from group off mic)

Ah, how sweet. It appears they love me back. Now, what's your next question, Mr. Dees?

Derek: *(rustling of paper)* Okay, let's have a peek. What am I supposed to ask? "This place is amazing..." Probing questions, Plummer. Watergate level. Ah, here's where it gets interesting. "Why are you the Chosen One?" So, to rephrase, the spirit inside you was a bunch of other people from all over the world before your present one. So, who told you to keep coming back in the first place?

Omm: The pharaoh Seti. In concert with the gods, of course.

Derek: Seti, who died in.... Jared?

Jared: 1279 BC.

Derek: Quite some time ago.

Omm: Actually, it was more like 1296. Julian's calendar mucked a few things up. Those ghastly Romans, again.

Derek: Either way, well over 3,000 years ago. And you say you two were chummy?

Omm: Oh yes. A fine pharaoh.

Derek: Right. Let's go back to the top of the script since none of this makes much sense. *Tell me how your journey here began,* I'm to ask.

Omm: With a bang on the head.

Derek: Now, that fits. Okay, just sit back and tell me about that day.

Omm: My father was a tailor, a good man, but not an educated one. He raised us well enough in London, but I'm afraid an incident when I was seven caused him a greater headache than he could ever imagine. I was playing in the kitchen, and the door to the cellar had been left open—my parents bitterly argued for years after who had done it—and I suppose I got too close. I don't remember the details, but I do recall falling, racking my head on the stairs as I went. Things went black. Am I rambling?

Derek: No more than usual.

Kara: Why are you being a hard-ass? On most shows, you just smile dimly and say, "Wow, is that when you saw the Loch Ness Monster?" Why pretend to be a journalist now?

Derek: Because this time, she's out to use on my crew members, who also think she's a menace. And why are you, of all people defending her?

Kara: It's just another episode of *Ancient Encounters.* Just ask her about reincarnation and the afterlife. How it works.

Derek: Why? You're directing now?

Kara: It's why we're here. To find out if it's all real.

Omm: It's very real, love. After the shoot, come to me, and we can talk more about what you really want to know.

Derek: Kara, for once, do your job and let me do mine. *(pause)* Now Dorothy, please, go on.

Omm: Apparently, when they found me an hour or so later, I wasn't breathing. They called the local doctor. All of this, mind you, I was told later—I remember nothing. When I woke, I was on a slab in the morgue, being washed down.

Derek: So, you were declared dead?

Omm: Quite inconveniently. The funeral arrangements had already begun. My parents blamed the doctor, saying he drank and that he almost condemned a seven-year-old to her grave while still alive.

Derek: And were there any lasting effects of the fall? I mean, beyond what we're seeing now.

Omm: You're quite sure of yourself for a man of such *(pause)* modest talents. I do wonder why? Anyway, as soon as I woke, I began wailing that I wanted to go home.

Derek: I'm sure of myself because I've traveled the world and know a few things, seen real things and fake things. People with an agenda. But I understand your desire to go home. I was once laid up in a remote Honduran hospital after being bitten by a scorpion, searching for the fabled *Ciudad Blanca*. When in pain, all one wants is the comforts of home.

Omm: Did you find it?

Derek: Find what?

Omm: The White City.

Derek: Not yet.

Omm: Shocking. No, I wasn't saying that at hospital. I was saying it when they took me back to our flat.

Derek: You lost me again, Dorothy.

Omm: I meant here, this home. I didn't fully understand it at the time, either. It wasn't until a while later, after seeing the art in the British Museum, that I realized what 'home' was.

Derek: Abydos, I suspect.

Omm: I know what you are thinking, Mr. Deeks, as my parents thought the same. I was somehow damaged from the tumble down the stairs. But truth be told, Dorothy *did* die that day, and someone else, an ancient presence, took her place. A presence that had already entered many other host bodies in the past and needed a new one. I retain the memories and personality traits of Dorothy, but you might say she's stepped aside and let me lead.

Derek: And how exactly does that work?

Omm: It was explained to me years later by Prince Mehy. He said a *ka* returns in two ways. Most are simply reincarnated. One life ends, so you begin again, at birth, in another body, without any obvious connection to your past lives. Like Jared, it appears.

Derek: Wait, our young director here is also from the past? That isn't in the script.

Jared: I'm not, don't listen to her. We were just chatting.

Derek: So you too are in cahoots, is that it? Two lost souls reincarnated to keep Egypt alive? Is that why we're here, Plummer? And I thought it was for 'entertainment and education.'

Jared: It is. Finish the interview, and we can talk.

Derek: We will. Okay, Dorothy.

Omm: I prefer Omm.

Derek: I prefer Dorothy. So, you say there are two kinds of reincarnation. Jared of Junction City, Kansas, is one, it appears. What's the other?

Omm: Well, Dr. Jones, there are also what I like to call the "interventions," when you take over a host's body after that life has already begun. This is rare and can only happen with the help of the gods. These souls are usually sent into a body closely resembling their own and enter at the time of death or deep anguish.

Kara: So, not really reincarnation, but one soul swapping places with another? That's possible?

Omm: Very much so. Happens all the time.

Kara: How exactly?

Derek: Kara, stop it. And what happened to little Dorothy, Dorothy?

Omm: For reasons that were her own, she didn't want the life she had, so she swapped it to go directly to the Duat.

Derek: The what?

Omm: The Egyptian Land of the Dead.

Derek: How sweet. So you took advantage of a little girl, stole her body and sent her to the underworld. *(rustling of paper)* Now, I read here that you did it all for a mission. And what is that mission?

Omm: To keep Mehy's own *ka* alive for all time, of course.

Derek: How's that goin' for you?

Omm: Well, here we are talking about him thirty-three centuries after he died. So rather well, I think.

Derek: Right. So all of us have had past lives, you say?

Omm: Surely.

Derek: Me too?

Omm: Most assuredly.

Derek: Okay, where else did I live?

Omm: Oh, I'm merely a gatekeeper, not a god. I can't read people's minds or know where they've lived. But there are always traces that can help narrow it down.

Derek: Traces. Wonderful. Where else has the Great Derek Dees explored?

Omm: If you're asking, were you some dashing adventurer like your hero, the Great Belzoni? It's difficult to say. But judging by your bearing, how you dress and comport yourself, I'd say it's quite unlikely. Belzoni never bothered to shave or cared about how he looked when off plundering. He was a foul human being, mind you, but not a troubadour. I suspect you were. A traveling minstrel of some ilk, rattling a tambourine to collect a few dirty coins from peasants before they run you out of town. Any memories along those lines, love?

Derek: And. Cut.

CHAPTER 12

"Wha da fa?" Kara flicked one cigarette onto the cobblestone and immediately lit another. On Jared's suggestion, the two had wandered down to the souk, where they could speak freely, away from the rest of the crew. The bazaar was a single-twisting alleyway near the Nile, covered by a dusty tarp and lined with an endless string of trinket shops. Their words, Jared hoped, would be safeguarded by sonorous shopkeepers selling Ramses T-shirts or plaster busts of King Tut that looked more like Michael Jackson than the Boy King.

"Slow down and tell me that all again," she pleaded.

Jared's voice was hurried and high-pitched, a habit when he was nervous. He explained again all that he had witnessed in the temple. If it was anyone else, he would have been halted by a derisive laugh. But no one knew him like Kara.

"Anyway, it's all a bunch of bull," he concluded. "She saw the target on my back the moment I called her."

Kara shooed away an assertive perfume merchant.

"How long have we been friends? How many weeks have we spent together on planes, in shitty hotels, under awnings waiting for the monsoon to stop? One thing I learned about you is that while you let yourself be easily led, you're no idiot. What you're telling me doesn't jive with how you're saying it."

These words alone gave Jared a measure of comfort. There was no one he trusted with his feelings more than Kara. The two had met on his first show at Premiere Productions, and though different as chalk and cheese, they immediately hit it off. Jared loved bold, funny, assertive women, and Kara adored geeky, smart men—and the fact that they were both gay eliminated any awkward sexual tension. On location, while the rest of the crew hit the hotel bar or cheated on their spouses back home, they also found escape in shopping, especially in out-of-the-way local markets. Back in Brooklyn, their respective apartments resembled the gift shop at the UN. So there was no better place to meet than the tourist's souk.

"As much as I want to, I can't dismiss it completely," Jared confessed.

"I wouldn't write her off so fast. Maybe it's all true."

Kara had made it her mission to protect Jared and to help him rise through the ranks. That meant stopping him before he did something to sabotage his career. So he was surprised by this easy acceptance.

"You, of all people, are ready to give her the benefit of the doubt?"

A shrug. "Why not? What's the harm in it?"

"You did hear what she's asking us to do?"

"Something about saving Mehy's name by going to the land of the dead, right?"

"Even if it was true, why on earth should I, should you, agree to that?"

Jared timidly informed a young boy selling tiny packs of facial tissues that he wasn't interested, but the boy only repeated his pitch at a higher volume. After the third plea, Jared searched his pocket for something to get rid of him.

"Yo, kid, you see him sneezin'?" Kara said, her firmness sending the boy down the street.

"See, I can't even deflect a kid hawkin' Kleenex. And you're telling me it's okay to contemplate a trip to Egyptian hell?"

"I'd be there to help. But explain to me again how all this works. I mean, I watched *Moon Knight*, but probably shouldn't base all I know on that."

"In ancient Egypt, people had two lives," Jared explained. "The first above ground, the second beneath, in the Field of Reeds. Basically, our heaven. You only truly die if your tomb is forgotten and your mummy, name, and accomplishments are erased. Then you'll never be accepted into the Field."

"Does that mean she's just asking us to die?"

"*Just?* I think you got heat stroke, Kara. No, she said we won't have to die, merely travel the twelves gates of night to find him."

"And that's what that weird-ass flood did? Close the gates for Mehy?"

A Nefertiti rug briefly floated between them.

"Apparently. Since nothing's left, he can no longer travel them, stuck in some hellscape along the way. Omm is asking me—us—to go into the Duat, find him, use the camera to capture his likeness, and bring it back to the land of the living. Does that make a lick of sense?"

"That's how someone lives forever? Appear in an episode of *Ancient Encounters*? Why do we gotta go to hell to do that? Why not just film it up here? Talk to experts, visit a museum, and do some cheesy recreations. I once played Harriet Tubman. You played Marc Anthony *and* Genghis Khan. No one's forgotten them."

Jared slipped behind her to avoid another hawker. "Prince Mehy wants more. As long as he had a mummy or a tomb in the current world, he was able to visit the land of the living through his false door. See Omm or whoever else he wanted."

"Nice to be a prince."

Kara moved away to let Jared lead. She seemed in no mood to shield him from the world. "But now his tomb and mummy are useless."

"Exactly. The video images give him a shell he can return to and inhabit. It allows him to be ever-present. Like King Tut."

Kara stopped and scanned the marketplace and the sea of all-male faces. "Wait, now you're sayin' King Tut walks among us?"

"If he wants to, sure. We still have his face mask, his mummy, his tomb. But even if you buy her story, there are some plot holes. Not sure how a two-dimensional image is the same as an actual body. Omm said Tiya and Seti would explain it better when we got there."

Kara stopped in front of a rack of royal plaster faces. "Seti? The pharaoh?"

"Correct."

"Pharaoh?" A nearby merchant's ears pricked up, and he offered them a Ramses-headed piggy bank. "Which do you like? I have many."

Kara and Jared moved on.

A scarf shop appeared ahead, and Kara's face lit up.

"Oh, real Egyptian cotton. I want one—great for the heat. Come."

She walked in and said hello to an old man sitting beneath a tower of colored cloth. Kara pointed to a bright red one, and he wrapped it over her head.

"Way I see it, it's either bullshit or real. If the first, no harm done. If it's real… isn't this what you want? What you've been dreaming about?"

Jared was slow to answer, knowing his voice would betray him. "Truth is, I'd love nothing more than to know who I once was."

"So?"

"C'mon, isn't it clear? I'm just not up for it."

"Jesus, Jared, I'm sick of you always putting yourself down. If you want to do this, then do it." She considered a paisley scarf.

"I'm a coward—you know it better than anyone. It's why those dreams have meant so much to me. When I'm there, I'm somebody else, someone who's confident, in charge."

"You're no coward. You're shy, a thinker. Not everyone needs to be as obnoxious as me." As if to prove her point, she asked the merchant the price of the scarf and laughed at the answer. "A joke, right, my friend? Bet this is not even real Egyptian cotton. Can buy this at Bay Plaza Mall in the Bronx. How about half?" The man countered that it was not only genuine but impossible to lower the price lest his five children starve. "Bring 'em round. I'll buy them dinner. But this scarf is crap."

The merchant ignored Kara and moved closer to Jared.

"One thousand Egyptian pounds, top quality."

Instinctively, Jared reached into his pocket and pulled out a wad of cash.

"Know what they called me in school?" he told Kara as he counted it out. "'Jared the Gerbil,' since I was always running away. Did I ever tell you about the school bus stop incident?"

"Many times, yes, bu—"

"A bunch of kids two grades behind me started picking on my sister. They pushed her down and laughed at me. I only moved when one threw her *Free Willy* lunchbox at me. The entire school, and my sister, never forgot."

"Like I say every time you tell me that story, you were a kid."

"I've barely changed," The merchant handed him the purchased scarf he never wanted but was too afraid to refuse. "Not once have I ever been brave enough to go against the grain for something I believed in?" He thought of the Seville airport, the tears in Carlos's eyes as Jared wheeled his luggage away. "Or loved."

Kara ushered Jared out of the souk and into the main plaza. "Okay, let's say this is all true—the dreams, Omm's story, the *du-wap,* or whatever. Does that mean anyone who ever died will be there?"

Jared hadn't considered this until now. "I'm not sure if Egyptian heaven overlaps with Christian. Why do you ask?"

Kara took a drag, taking a beat to answer. "Imagine the famous people we'd meet. It'll be one hell of a film."

"A *film?* I'm worried about dying some horrible death in the underworld, getting judged by the gods, and you're thinking about some damn film? Do you even know what goes on between the gates?"

Kara blew a bit of smoke and smiled. "You just gave me a clue."

Jared was in no mood to smile back. All he saw was The Gobbler waiting to rid the Duat of vermin. "Each gate is guarded by a goddess whose sole job is to make sure travelers don't pass unless they're worthy. Even if all of history's heroes were having tea in the Field of Reeds, we wouldn't live long enough to meet them."

"But just imagine if we did. You'd be a hero. 'Man Braves Hell to Make Greatest Film of All Time!'"

She moved to the exit of the marketplace.

Jared couldn't deny it. He fantasized about nothing more than being a genuine leader, someone others look to for security and knowledge. But for the moment, he was still just Jared and was in no rush to return to the troubles awaiting him at the hotel. He thought it odd that Kara was so swiftly on board. It had been her M.O. the last few years, to question everything and do it harshly. Yet tonight, she seemed to feel differently, accepting everything he had told her at face value. She raced ahead, where an eager crowd of taxi drivers was waiting. On past trips abroad, it had become a running joke to let Jared haggle a fare; another way, she claimed, of toughening him up. He expected the same tonight. But instead, she opened the door to the first cab she saw and didn't negotiate.

"To the Horus Guest House, fast. We got shit to do."

CHAPTER 13

Locating a pustule of sand in an otherwise shapeless desert was no easy task, especially in the dead of night. But Kara had a good sense of direction, and the moon was nearly full. Being midnight rather than noon also meant it was cooler. She moved much faster than on her first trip here. Her feet crunched broken pottery, and she knew she was close.

However, finding the Scorpion King's tomb proved more difficult, one mound as shapeless as the next. Round and round, she went, shining her light into empty pits, one time into the sparkling eyes of a hyena, but none of them had the ramp she was looking for. Panic started to take over. Now that there was another option, there was no way she would let Lynette's ashes lie in this hellscape for eternity. If only Omm had told Jared of her offer sooner, she never would have brought her here. And even if Jared chickened out, Kara would talk to Omm personally, say she'd do anything to swap places with Lynette, like little Dorothy Kershaw had done with Omm. It was the least she could do for failing her.

Kara had promised to keep Lynette safe no matter the obstacles, but she never saw this one coming. A month before their wedding, a driver on the Palisades Parkway texting his wife that he was on his way home never made it because he jumped the median and landed in Lynette's car. His corpse was only gently banged up, but Lynette's was too mangled for an open casket. So Kara had her cremated and placed on her mantlepiece, between gifts she had bought in places Lynette would never see. Jared and a few other friends had urged her to seek closure with a funeral as a way to move on. But she didn't want to move on. She wanted Lynette. Beautiful, freckled Lynette with a curvy torso and tiny sexy tattoos between each thigh that only Kara knew about. Beautiful, freckled Lynette who, while only ninety-seven pounds, could pick Kara up and toss her anywhere around the bed or sofa she damn well pleased. Beautiful Lynette, who had more kindness in her pinky than all of five fuckin' boroughs of New York City ever did since the cheating Dutch stole it from the locals for a sack of beads.

Kara had spent her life fighting villains. Racists, sexists, homophobes and haters, and always came out on top. Only the Grim Reaper, who treated everyone with equal contempt (a trait she greatly admired), was the single foe she couldn't overcome. And it had made her, she knew, short-tempered and angry at pretty much anything that got in her way, big or small. Until, perhaps now.

But where the fuck was the Scorpion King's goddamn tomb?

Then another light appeared, shining down on her from above. Perhaps a ghost who lingered here had emerged from the sand to help her along?

"That's not the one. I know where it is." Jared wiggled the flashlight in front of her so she could scramble out of the pit she had all but fallen into. Kara said nothing, her tears mixed with relief. When push came to shove, she knew Jared would be there for her. He looked after her as closely as she did for him.

"You followed me?"

She wanted to sound offended, but it came out as grateful.

"I wondered why you kept asking questions about the Mother of Jars and the Scorpion King," he said as she returned to the surface. "When did you ever give a shit about history? Come, it's over here."

He walked to her another mud brick pustule and traced the ramp.

"When did you figure it out?"

"Should have when I saw you clutching that box on the balcony as if sharing the view with a friend."

The two of them moved down the ramp, and he let Kara lead him to the burial site.

"But tonight at the souk. First, you paid way too much for that taxi. But the giveaway was how quickly you believed Omm story. You challenge waiters who suggest you try the soup of the day. Why would you agree to something so crazy?"

"Out of better options, I guess." She recognized the mound ahead. "I feel like a traitor for out-living her, for surviving."

"Her death was not your fault, and you know it."

Kara said nothing, only stumbled forward in the dark.

Jared beamed his light on the Scorpion King's tomb. "Well, I could have told you this wouldn't work. The Egyptians didn't cremate their dead. Went against the whole idea of eternity. Without a body, there's nowhere for the soul to live."

"Yeah, I learned that from you tonight." She moved down the ramp. "I should have told you from the start, sorry."

"Why didn't you? After everything I've confessed to you."

Jared sounded genuinely hurt.

"This trip is about you, not me. Didn't wanna add to your worry."

Kara hated displays of vulnerability and was keen to change the subject. In matters of love, both of them were losers.

"Did you talk to her?"

Luckily, Jared didn't dwell on her betrayal.

"Yes. She was waiting for me at the hotel. Said she knew I'd come around."

"And did you?"

She approached the spot where she had buried Lynette.

Jared sat on a mound of sand.

"If I let this slip by," he confessed. "I'd spend the rest of my days wondering, regretting it."

"Get up. You're sitting on my girlfriend."

Jared moved, and Kara started excavating.

"But it *is* crazy, isn't it? What she's asking of us."

"It is. But what I saw, how I felt when I did. It can't be faked."

Kara stopped digging and watched as the hole filled back up with sand.

"You think that if we go, I might see her again?"

Jared helped her by moving the sand away.

"I don't know anything anymore. If I said no, would you stay behind?"

"No. We both got to discover what we lost. If we fail, well, guess it's better than the half-assed lives we're dealing with now, right?"

Kara pulled the lacquered box back into the moonlight and kissed the lid.

"I'm so sorry, love. We have another idea now. Jared's going to help."

They climbed the ramp and started back to town.

"Only one demon can stop us now."

Jared groaned.

"It'll be a good test. If I can't win a battle with the man in the fedora, how do I ever expect to outwit the monsters of hell?"

They made their way toward the lights of El Madfuna as the hyena and other darkened shapes watched them go.

CHAPTER 14

The next day the crew gathered for a traditional Egyptian feast. The setting, arranged by Jared so the crew was in a relaxed place to hear his offer, was evocative: an abandoned 4th-century church known as the Red Monastery. The domed roof was half exposed to the glittering sky and torches encircled a curved nave. Thinking like a producer, Jared even hired a local oud player to add a calming soundtrack. But changing Derek's mind wouldn't be easy: the host was eager to not only skip dinner but cancel the entire shoot. Without a crew, there'd be no film, and that's what Omm needed to bring Mehy back. So Jared had spent the day crafting a bullet-pointed checklist that would convince Derek and Ali to join them. Now, as drinks arrived, he opened his mouth to begin. And nothing came out.

"Cool space," Kara said, giving him a moment to collect his thoughts. "First time I've ever drunk in a medieval ruin."

Ali grinned mischievously. "If it wasn't for old buildings, Egyptian boys would never have any place to party."

Bullet point one: relax the crew.

"Another round, then," Jared said to the waiter, who, with no other customers, was lingering about ten inches away.

Derek caught Jared's blank gaze, and instead of offering his usual putdown, a half-smile crept across his face.

He shook his head. "Got to say, you finally impressed me, Plummer."

"How's that?" Jared asked, hopeful that Derek had seen some value in the story at last.

"You figured out, all by your lonesome, that Omm is a fraud and that the episode should be scrapped. Bravo." After asking the confused waiter for a frosted glass, he went on. "Had we made it, it would definitely be the worst show of the series."

Jared mentally returned to his checklist.

Next: build a relationship through a shared experience.

"Oh, I'm not sure about that," Jared said with a smile. "Don't forget the episode we did at Rosslyn Chapel in Scotland, where some guy said the Knights Templar had hidden the head of Christ under the altar."

"Right you are," Derek remembered with a laugh. "And it turned out to be a broom closet."

Jared held his glass high. "All hail the sacred mop and bucket."

"Fair enough," Derek said, beer bottle raised high. "This is the second worst."

Now, introduce your thesis.

"But... what if it wasn't?"

"Wasn't what?" Derek's hand froze mid-sip, like a watch in need of winding.

"The worst show. What if it was the best?"

"The best *what*? Episode? What's wrong with you, Plummer?"

Be careful not to oversell the show until you've fully pulled your viewers in.

"Or... at least the most special and unique."

"How's that even possible? It's a senile old lady being directed by a naïve kid."

"What if we did the episode but made some big changes?"

Jared paused for Derek to say *such as?* as he did when Jared had rehearsed it in his head.

But as usual, the host went off script.

"Hell no, I'm pulling the plug on this crap tomorrow as soon as New York wakes up."

A plate of lamb kofta arrived, followed by freshly baked pita puffed like a balloon. The waiter popped them with a knife, releasing hot air that deflated them to sand dollars. When no one said anything, Ali ripped off a piece and dipped it into oily hummus.

"Not bad."

Jared mentally scanned his bullet points.

If challenged, build your case through the support of others.

"What do you think about all this, Ali? You believe in reincarnation?"

The sound man double-dipped and nodded.

"Why not? Egypt has been around forever, and we still venerate the past as if it was yesterday. How could that be if we didn't feel some spiritual connection?"

"Don't discount mass tourism," Derek offered. "You guys over here are good at that."

"True, there's money to be made from exploiting our forefathers. We're not the only ones. How many hotels in America promise that "George Washington Slept Here?" And how much you charging these days for 9/11 tours in Lower Manhattan? But reincarnation? That's different. My grandmother, born and raised in Cairo, somehow knew how to write medieval calligraphy when she was a child without ever taking a class. Once, we went on holiday to Alexandria. She was determined to visit this one particular mosque, a place she had never been. As soon as she entered, she started chatting in classic Arabic and insisted we pray in one corner, where she claimed her teacher, Abul Abbas al Mursi's, indentations were."

"Were they?" Jared asked.

"Right where she said they'd be. A smooth broken stone, under a prayer rug and exactly as she described."

Derek wasn't following. "So?"

"Al Mursi died in 1287 AD."

"That means you don't discount Omm's sanity?" Jared asked Ali hopefully.

"Not fully. Not yet."

"Wait a minute," Derek reminded him. "Yesterday, you said she was just another lost Westerner searching for a home."

"True," Ali continued, "she fits all the stereotypes. Westerners are experts at devaluing our culture or believing that only with their participation does it gain meaning. But seeing how the locals respect her, and call her mother, I'm no longer so sure. I spoke to a few, and they all defended her, said what she claimed was, if not true, impossible to dismiss." He wiped his beard of hummus. "Who am I to judge? To discount someone's experiences merely because they don't fit into my own beliefs. Do that. I'm no better than all those arrogant Westerners." He smiled at Derek across the table. "You know, the ones in pith helmets who claim this land for king and country."

Jared leaned forward.

Maintain eye contact and avoid the little voice in the back of your head telling you to bail.

"I'm glad you think that. It took me a while to realize it, but Omm's hiding much more than a broom closet. She showed me things that involve us all."

"Wait." Derek raised a manicured hand. "Yesterday, you came out of that temple screaming that she was a phony. Now, you believe her again?"

"We talked again last night. And I do feel differently about it now."

Derek was about to say something else, surely loud and glib, but Ali cut him off.

"You were white as a sheet when you came out of there. Tell us, slowly, what you saw."

Jared sat up straight, polished off his beer... and found his voice at last. Once he began, he no longer needed a checklist. The words flowed fully and vividly.

Silence descended on the table as suffocating as a sandstorm. For a while, only the loud music could be heard—until Ali put an end to that.

"*Imshi,* be off," he barked as the man set his instrument at his side and took a sip of tea.

As was often the case, Derek was the first to offer commentary.

"First, you believed she was a pharaoh's plaything. Now you're sayin' that dotty ol' Dorothy is inviting us to travel to the past with her to have a look-see around?"

"More than that, it sounds like," Ali added. "She's asking us to help her steal from a sacred underground tomb or something?"

"No, we're not stealing anything," Jared corrected him. "We're not tomb robbers or cultural thieves. We take nothing, change nothing, and only record what we see. Then share it with the world. In short, we make the most amazing film the world has ever created."

"I'm fine with the idea of reincarnation," groaned Ali. "But time travel? *Kalam fadi.* You don't really believe all this, do you?"

"I only know what I saw. And what I saw were guys dressed like high priests and 19th-century explorers. If it was an act, it was a damn elaborate one."

"Don't fall for this," Ali warned him. "There are a million ways to get money from gullible foreigners—no offense—and this is surely one."

"Executive decision." Derek plopped his empty glass down. "We're out of here tomorrow morning. I'm not even waiting for the network to respond. The episode is DOA, and Jared is unfit to direct." He scrutinized the table. "Now, where's my entrée? Quick dinner and back to the hotel. You have flights to book."

Ali sighed and gazed sympathetically at Jared.

"Pretend we're traveling to the ancient world to help a pharaoh out of a jam? Derek's right. We'd be laughed out of the industry. I'd end up spending the rest of my career making industrial videos for the Ministry of Sanitation."

Kara seemed poised to say something but then changed her mind. Instead, she kicked Jared under the table. Her message was painfully evident. *You're losing 'em. Try harder.*

Okay, should evidence and team building not work, move on to Plan B. Appeal to the Derek's ego.

"I have a proposition," Jared met Derek's gaze. "Allow me one more day to prove to you this is legit. If it's not, you can fire me—"

"I already did, ninety seconds ago."

"Let me finish. You can fire me, and I'll leave the business for good. You'll never see my face again."

"Also done. What can you promise me I can't do on my own?"

"You always said you wanted to bring integrity to the series, to flush out fraud. Let your many fans know you're too smart to be fooled."

"Because I am."

He gazed at Ali and Kara for support, but both were peeling labels from their bottles.

"Right," Jared continued. "But we never actually expose the fakers, not fully. Most shows end with you saying, *who knows?*"

Jared knew Derek hated that since it was someone else, not him, drawing conclusions and putting words in his mouth.

The host nodded in agreement. "That's because scaredy-cats execs say we can't alienate the tinfoil nut jobs or we have no audience. They wanted that alien nonsense, not me."

Jared drew a breath. "Exactly, and you want more. You said it yourself. The next chapter of Derek Dees."

"Yeah, so?" Derek laughed mockingly. "I do that by making the shittiest show possible?"

"No, we secretly wire you, and you offer expert commentary as we go beyond what you say to the boom pole and the actors if that's what they are. You're convinced Omm is a fraud. Fine. Prove it. If you discover it's a bunch of actors, you expose them for what they are and get it all on camera. Show the world that Derek Dees has outgrown cable TV and become a true Belzoni, not some corporate creation."

Derek went silent. Jared could almost hear his gears and pistons struggling to fire. Slowly, a thought clicked into position. Derek raised his empty glass, took a sip but failed to notice it was empty. He was too enamored with some image in his head.

"My agent will love this. When this show finally ends, I'll be set up as something more than just a pretty face." He stopped himself. "I mean, I'll still be that, but I'll also be famous for being someone you can't trifle with."

"So," Jared asked loudly, out of bullet points and eager to seal the deal. "That means the show goes on?"

"One day, more only if I sanction it. At any time, I can pull the plug. If and when I do, you're not only off the show, you're immediately out of the business."

"And if it's true?"

Derek laughed. "I forgot that was an option. If it's true, Plummer, I'll never stand in the way of your career, never utter a disparaging thing again."

"Ali?" Jared asked.

Ali polished his readers but didn't put them on.

"Professionally speaking, it's all absurd. I want you, Kara, to record me saying that on tape. Promise to still get back to Cairo by Thursday as scheduled?"

"I do."

"Then it's settled," Kara added, impressed that Jared has achieved the impossible: getting Derek to change his mind, something she could rarely do. "When and where is this all supposed to go down?"

"Tomorrow at dawn. Outside the temple of Seti."

Kara raised her bottle.

"From the second-worst episode of *Ancient Encounters* to the best!"

A clink of glasses followed, and the oud player struck up a new song. Jared's body tingled, and he feared a flashback coming on. But then he realized what it really was. A rare feeling of accomplishment. He had actually won a battle. But how many more lay ahead?

CALL SHEET

ANCIENT ENCOUNTERS WITH DEREK DEES

EPISODE 37: MAGICAL MISTRESS OF THE NILE.

Shoot dates: Egypt April 3-9th

WEATHER: 97 AND SUNNY

SUNRISE 6 AM SUNSET 6 PM

Day 2

SCENE AND LOCATION/ CALL TIME AND ADDITIONAL NOTES

Scene 1: Stand up temple. 5 AM-6 AM. Note: see new cold open script.

Scene 2: Omm opens magical door. 6 AM- 7 AM

Scene 3: Go back to 1279 BC. 730. *Scenes to come.*

Lunch as available. Will have water/granola bars. Avoid local cuisine. Pack cipro.

Scene 4: Save Mehy's mummy. 1230 PM to 3 PM. *Scenes to come.*

Dinner at hotel. Please specify chicken or beef. Note: No alcohol charged to company bill, talk to Jared.

CHAPTER 15

Memoir excerpt: "The Many Lives and Times of Tiya's Ka," by Omm (chapter one)

I put these memories down on paper so all who come after me can see how and why it all began, why hundreds of devoted gatekeepers came after me in my quest to keep Mehy alive for all time. If there is a greater love story in history, I have yet to encounter it.

My first name was Bentreshyt, "Harp of Joy," but no one's called me that in thousands of years. No loss, I suppose. It was always a mouthful. Happily, the temple priest changed that to Tiya, but let me try to remember before then…

I lived in a rough patch of Thebes that no one would visit unless they were up to no good. Today they'd call it the slums. Most of those early years blur together into surges of feeling rather than images, but there was one day I can still see quite vividly as it changed my life—lives, I suppose—forever.

I rose to discover a small plate of food on the floor, no doubt left by Kha, my father. When Mother was around, food was never a problem;

she was a vegetable seller and always saved a few onions or leeks. But then she was carried off by plague, and what little security I had disappeared with her. Father had no income, and I never asked him where the scraps of food came from; I was too afraid to learn the answer, I suspect. Kha tried to find work, but as a lifelong soldier during a time of peace, he was one among thousands seeking the same.

Instead, he drank, and in time our house was taken away; we now lived in a tiny shack along the fetid canals. Funny, I can't recall the shack itself, but I can still smell the rotting fish and the shit from the nearby dump as I write this. One upside: the street blunted my appetite. Father was rarely home these days, instead carousing with his army mates at the "Hippo's Jaw," the terrifying bar nearby where drinks were cheap and all were welcome.

I had no choice but to seek work on my own. Peering up and down my putrid alley, with all the painted women from Thebes to Babylon crowded in doorways, I could see my future.

Perhaps Kha saw it too. One day I rose to find that bowl of food on the floor. I was touched when he thought of me, as by this point, he was usually too drunk to stand. But that day was the third anniversary of Mother's death, a time that hit us both hard. I watched him closely—he was deep in thought, and appeared more troubled than usual. I knew him well enough to know he had made some decisions and was struggling to turn them into words. The ones he chose were, as usual, the coarsest he could find.

"I no longer want you. You need to live somewhere else." Father picked up my bedding, a small gesture that I knew registered his own pain of what had to be done, and we plunged into the wretched alleyways of Thebes. He walked quickly, always ahead, wanting this to be over. A donkey cart separated us, then an old man carrying a clay water jug leaving me further behind. He turned down a back alley so narrow I could touch each side with my elbows, and at last, I knew where he was leading me. The pier. Wherever I was going, it required a boat. Fine, I recall thinking, nothing in Thebes worth missing.

The boatman asked no questions, just stuck his long oar into the water and set off. Traffic was thick, the reeds even thicker, and Father had to help push other boats away until the canal ended and the open Nile appeared. Here, the vessel turned north, following the course of the river. I had never been anywhere beyond the city gates, so everything felt vast and new. Tiny palm wood boats were replaced by larger ones, two or three stories high, casting towering silhouettes over the morning waves. New aromas overpowered me, not of sewage and decay but of lotus and jasmine. On either side of the Nile, mud brick houses became fewer, and an endless expanse of fields stretched beyond sight.

Finally, Father turned to me and held my gaze. "We are heading to Abydos, where you will work in the temple."

"But we know no one there," I said.

"I saved a priest during the wars. He promised to get you a position." Father squinted into the sun. "Whatever he chooses, it will be more than I could offer." He said no more, and I knew better than to betray my worry; soldiers hated that. I dipped my hand in the water, surprised at how much cooler it was than in the murky urban canals. A fish nibbled at my finger and, finding it inedible, disappeared beneath the boat.

The sun had traveled from one side of the Great River to the other before a majestic temple appeared on the western shore, at first obscured by wild papyrus. Tucked back from the river by a web of canals was a gateway guarded by men with spears and scowls. Thebes hosted these types of men too. Medjay warriors from Nubia who safeguarded all royal sites and would think nothing of running someone through with a blade if they didn't belong.

These canals were completely different from the clotted veins back home. These were straight as an arrow, precisely manicured, and flanked by rows of blue lotus in full bloom and buzzing with bees and butterflies.

Beyond, where workers were planting crops, tiny irrigation ditches sparkled in the sun like ribbons. I inhaled. So curious how, three thousand years on, smells linger while my father's face has completely faded.

Before we reached the main temple, a man emerged and waved us ashore. He was clearly a priest, his head and eyebrows shaved, kohl around his eyes, crisp white linen failing to hide a generous belly.

"Hori!" he said with a smile. "Welcome to you both."

"This is Paneb," Father informed me. "You will go with him and do all he commands. He controls your destiny now, not I. May he do a better job of it."

Paneb helped tie the boat and extended me a firm hand. I took it and was soon on land, softer than anything back home. I turned to help my father, but he only held out my bedding.

"Are you not walking me all the way?"

"I could not provide," he said, "so have no right to touch this sacred land." He wanted to say more, but we both knew he would not. I only bowed and watched the ferry retreat. It flickered behind some lotuses and was gone.

Finally, I found the nerve to speak. "Where am I to go?"

"You will work in the temple of Seti as an apprentice. This is no easy job. You must learn hundreds of incantations and spells. Can you read or write?"

"A little."

"That will have to become a lot." He walked along the path, so moist my toes were swallowed by mud.

"We must change your name to sever your identity and give you a new history. What do you think of 'Tiya'?"

I thought it was pretty and told him so.

His answer finally convinced me I was in good hands. "Good, it was my daughter's name, Amun bless her in the Underworld." Paneb stopped and tugged at my ragged tunic. "But first, Tiya, we must get you bathed and outfitted in the proper attire." We walked toward a tiny hamlet where several other boys and girls around my age were gathered. "Those are the other disciples of Seti. They'll teach you how to behave. If you fail, there is little I can do to save you. Once you have been initiated into the mysteries of the temple, you may never live elsewhere. Do you understand?"

"And if I fail?"

Paneb looked over to a large pool where several crocodiles were sunning themselves.

My contribution was befitting of a lowborn. I walked the temple grounds from cauldron to cauldron with cones of incense, making sure fresh ones replaced those burnt to a nub. The fires must never stop. This was a larger task than it at first might sound. There were over one hundred incense vats scattered over Abydos, and they were fast burning. I was in harried motion from sunrise to sunset. But it gave me intimate access to the temple; I soon knew every hallway, every secret chamber.

As the years passed, I grew more and more beautiful, or so they told me, but I had no desire to be some holy man's plaything. So I fixated on my task with a focus so unwavering that no suitors could get anywhere beyond, *hello, pretty one.* Like my father, who gave his life and service to the military, I did the same with the sacred temple of Seti. Over the years, this determination was noticed, and one day dear Paneb, who had always treated me with fatherly kindness, approached. "Your devotion has been reported to the king. Seti arrives from Memphis tomorrow and has demanded to see you."

All of Abydos knew the pharaoh was near long before the ships had even docked. Trumpets and horns, followed by at least six barges, garishly painted and fluttering with flags, preceded him. Orchids were strewn from the pier to the pylon gates, and the temple had been scrubbed, torches freshened, and incense cauldrons stacked high. Paneb brought me a fresh white tunic and thin bracelets made of lapis lazuli to adorn my wrists and ankles. My hair was so lustrous I needed no wig, and the kohl in my eyes brought out the green tint, almost the color of my bracelets. A few years earlier, I had been living next to a cesspool eating old fish. I had never felt more special in my life.

Seti appeared as I expected: firm, grim in countenance, eyes staring at the temple ahead, wholly uninterested in the minions at his feet. The double crown of Upper and Lower Egypt fit snugly on his head, and a glittering breastplate encircled his upper body. Jasmine petals were thrown at the carriers' feet, and as the sedan approached, everyone assumed the role of supplication, head down on the ground, hands stretched ahead, eyes averted at all costs. The pavement burned my forehead, and I remember lifting it slightly, afraid it might leave a lasting mark.

As I kissed the cobble, someone stopped in front of me. All I could see were fancy leather sandals, but I felt his gaze. He said nothing but lingered and cleared his throat, daring me to look up. Amun help me, I did. So many times since then, I wonder how different life would have been if I had continued to stare at the cracks in the pavement. I would be dead, and Prince Mehy would still be alive.

RINNNNNNNNG, RINNNNNG!!!!!

The wake-up call sent Omm's memoir flying from Jared's hand. He was already up—how could he sleep?—but had not realized it was already four AM.

"Yes, shukran. Can you make coffee and toast for the crew? We'll be down in thirty minutes."

Jared had spent most of the night pacing and gnawing at the inside of his cheek. He had scoured his three-ring binder, which contained his research articles, all highlighted in different colors to denote character, act, and historical details. But what only yesterday seemed like the world's most complete producer's package now underscored how deeply out of his depth he was. If what Omm said was true, he would have to rely not on bullet points but on his strength and convictions. Both, he knew, were sorely lacking. But in the end, he recognized that it wasn't fear that had kept him up all night. Forget about pharaoh-slaying assassins and scales of justice and man-eating demons for just a few moments. What he most felt was giddy anticipation.

Am I really going to step back into a time I've been dreaming about for so long?

A copper glow gilded the temple of Seti when the crew gathered outside. But Omm was nowhere to be found.

The team was drowsy but in good spirits. "We got everything?" Kara asked, taking in the small pile of pelican cases and gear stacked in the courtyard.

Ali nodded. "Yes, left the big stuff behind to travel light. Mics checked, batteries charged, and we have a hundred hours of media." He saw the smaller bag, the one Kara never let him touch, curious to ask why it, too, needed to come. But he had been chewed out once or twice already by bringing it up. He silently walked around it and clipped hidden microphones on both Derek and Jared.

"Why me?" Jared asked.

"If this is an undercover shoot, chances are she'll be talking to you too, so everyone needs to be wired." Ali tucked the lavalier under Jared's shirt, creating yet another worry. Would Omm feel betrayed if she found out that Jared was wired? He imagined some mafia sting operation where the FBI rat gets blown away.

Kara noticed Derek's fancy leather satchel, now bursting in size. "What all did you bring?"

"Just a few extra things in case it's a long day." He opened it to reveal his loot.

Kara took stock. "Granola bars, protein shakes, beard trimmer. A sewing kit? What use is that ever gonna be in the gates of hell?"

"I dunno. Might be gone for a thousand years, Jared said. Gotta look my best."

"So, part of you believes this?" Jared was hoping the answer was yes. *Dear god, I could use the support.*

"Hardly, but no way I'm gonna be caught looking shaggy, just in case."

Kara peered deeper into the satchel. Baseball caps and T-shirts emblazoned with *Ancient Encounters with Derek Dees* logos. On the reverse, an image of Derek gliding across Lake Atitlan in a Mayan canoe, one thumb up.

"*Swag*?" Kara groaned. "We're shooting guerilla-style, and you brought swag?"

"Won't it look great after we expose the actors? We give them shirts, and pose for a publicity photo? My agent thinks he can get me on the *Today* show to talk about it."

The comment took Jared by surprise. If all this was true, they would indeed be famous. It was odd how such thoughts never entered his mind. When he was rewriting the script, he found it difficult to focus. Now that he realized that it wasn't 'making the best episode of *Ancient Encounters With Derek Dees*' that drove him forward, he realized that the show was just a front. It had helped him achieve what he wanted—the possibility of answers—and had almost outlived its usefulness. But best not to share that with the crew. "Here's an updated call sheet and Cold Open. The new text is underlined."

Derek searched his bag and retrieved a nail clipper keychain. Before Jared could ask if this was the right time, a light was illuminated, and the host began to read.

"You're still waffling, suggesting it might be true," Derek snorted, "I'll be the judge of that. But fine, it's a freakin' Tease. Let's shoot this thing."

PRETITLE COLD OPEN TEASE:

ANCIENT ENCOUNTERS EPISODE 37: MAGICAL MISTRESS OF THE NILE

VIDEO: Derek Dees standing in front of a temple.

NARRATION:

A MYSTICAL LADY WITH MAGICAL LINKS TO ANCIENT PAST…

Derek turns and takes in the temple, examining a fallen statue.

IS OMM A TIME TRAVELER FROM THE ANCIENT PAST? OR ONE OF THE MODERN WORLD'S GREATEST SWINDLERS?

TOGETHER ON THIS VERY SPECIAL EPISODE OF ANCIENT ENCOUNTERS WE'LL FIND OUT.

OMM HAS OFFERED TO TAKE US ON AN EXCLUSIVE TOUR OF THE ANCIENT PAST, AND WE'RE INVITING YOU TO COME ALONG.

(Derek, revealing hidden microphones) Walk beside me as I separate fact from fantasy. If Omm's story is a fraud, you'll be there the moment we expose her. And if she's the real deal, well then, my friends, we're about to meet real-life pharaohs, queens, and gods together!

Series open/ pre-recorded. Hero shots of Derek climbing mountains, rappelling into a tomb, crawling over a ruin.

THE WORLD IS FILLED WITH FORGOTTEN SECRETS, HIDDEN HISTORIES… ALL JUST WAITING TO BE REDISCOVERED.

FORGET ABOUT HOLLYWOOD FAKERS, DEREK DEES IS THE REAL THING, A CLASSIC ADVENTURER FOR THE MODERN AGE…

JOIN ME ON A SPECIAL UNDERCOVER EPISODE OF ANCIENT ENCOUNTERS WITH DEREK DEES!

"And cut." To everyone's surprise, Derek not only kept to the script but nailed it on the first take.

"We should do all our filming before sunrise," Kara whispered to Jared. "He's too tired to be an asshat."

Half an hour later, after the copper glow had become a burning orb, they were still standing alone in the courtyard.

"Just as I said," Derek grumbled. "The rantings of a demented spinster." He glanced at his watch. "Seems like our time traveler found something more fun to do. Probably dancing all night with Casanova." He sipped coffee from a thermos, one with his own face on it, a leftover from last year's Comic Con. "Five minutes, and we're booking flights home. I want a window seat and the vegan option, remember."

Something black rubbed against Derek's leg. He shook it loose, and it gazed up and hissed.

"It's Cleopatra," Jared said. "Which means Omm is close."

Several more cats paced by the temple door as if afraid to venture any further. An echo reached them from within. Chanting. Jared waved the team closer and, with a spin of his finger, told Kara to start recording.

The hypostyle hall was still eclipsed in darkness, too early for shafts of light to lend their shape. But from the far end, a single candle shimmered where Omm faced the false door, reciting an incantation. A blanket of incense thinned her features, making her appear almost as an aberration. She fell to her knees as another voice, much deeper and not attached to a human form, echoed her words.

Kara turned on the camera and crept forward. Leaning against a pillar, she found a steady angle and gave Jared the thumbs-up sign. Eager to be the center of attention, Derek moved into the frame and righted his hat, ready to add commentary. Jared stopped him. "Stay quiet for now. Give her time to finish."

A noise from behind made them swoop around. Had she summoned the gods? Said stood behind them, still in his pajamas and dipping a tea bag into a mug. "Omm asked me to keep her company until you get back, in case she nods off or has to take a pee."

Kara turned on the camera light, and a boom pole hovered above Said's face. Derek slipped into 'host' mode. "What happens, exactly, if she's not here when we want to return?"

"Uh oh, didn't she tell you?" Said shrugged and slurped his tea. "You're stuck in the past."

"What?"

"Only she can open up this end of the portal. Otherwise, we'd have busloads of tourists asking me if they could have a peek."

"You mean…?" Derek asked, the first tiny hint of worry crossing his face.

Said nodded.

"Should something happen to her while you're over there, there's no getting back. She must be right here at the right time to unlock the door. And someone, Tiya, in your case, needs to be on the other side. Think of it as a phone call. Need someone at both ends, or it doesn't connect."

Whatever internal concern Derek had was quickly dispelled when he remembered the camera was rolling. Instead, he resorted to his patently phony laugh to let the audience know he was too smart for what he was being told, a substitute for thoughtful commentary.

"We'll see who's on the other end soon enough."

"You sure you're up for all this, Mr. Dees?" Said slurped again. "What you're doing comes with great risk. I know Omm goes back every now and again, but I never heard of her taking company." He gave Derek a once-over. "Never been myself. A bit insulted that her first guest is you."

"So, you buy into all this?" Derek asked, more to the camera than Said.

"Of course. You still don't?" He looked to Omm, who had finished her prayers and was lighting more cones. "It's gonna be a hell of a lot easier if you do." Said walked to a truncated pillar, sat down, and yawned. "You'll see."

Omm finally acknowledged the team. She called Jared closer and held up her hand for Kara to turn off the camera. "Not just yet, love. Let me have a private word with your leader."

Derek stepped forward, and Omm brushed him aside with a laugh. "I said your leader."

She waved Jared closer.

"Have you explained all of this to them?" Omm asked Jared when they were a ways off.

"As best I could. I can't promise they all believe."

"Do you?"

Jared had been trying for over a day to poke holes in her story, to pull at loose threads that only he could see. But either he couldn't find them or chose not to. "I do."

Omm smiled.

"Then no bother. As long as you don't waiver, they'll come around."

She dipped her eyes to Derek. "Must we bring the toothy one? We need adventurers, not troubadours."

Behind them, Ali, monitoring all the mics under his headphones, burst out laughing.

"What's so funny? What are they saying?" Derek asked him, but Ali waved him away with another chuckle.

Jared would have wanted nothing more than to send Derek back to the hotel, but Omm's cutting remark offended him more than he expected. Derek was a buffoon, yes, but still part of the crew. And one thing Jared promised himself before agreeing to this was to keep his crew safe and together. Whatever their personal motivations for saying yes, they were here at his behest. That afforded them respect.

"Where we go, so does he."

"Fair enough, no time to argue. But do understand: once you walk through that door, the clock starts ticking, and there's no coming back until the task is complete. In exchange, everything you film is yours forever. Return with nothing but footage." She lowered her voice as if aware the camera was rolling. "And all you need to do is trust your instincts. Over there, you're no longer just Jared Plummer. You're everyone you were before you. Don't fight it, no matter how dark and disturbing. Embrace it and act on it."

"Do you know?" Jared was afraid to ask but desperate for an answer. "Who, or what, I was?"

Omm shook her head, almost sadly. "I don't love. If we had shared a *ka,* I would. But you were someone outside my immediate circle. No one knows except the gods. And you."

"So it wasn't you who called me here?"

"Called you?"

"Someone has been, I dunno, beckoning me here for a long time."

"Wouldn't be able to if I tried, love."

"Then who?"

"I suspect you'll find out on your own." She raised her voice to include the others. "Now, my dear children. Has Jared explained my offer?"

"Not in great detail," Derek said. "There was beer."

Omm pursed her lips. "Drinking the night before time travel upsets the tummy." She walked to the false door. "With this false door, we can travel anywhere we choose." She scanned the faces of the crew. "With me so far?"

Derek turned to the camera and whispered into his chest. "False door. Couldn't come up with a better name myself."

"What's time like on that side? Does it move differently?" Ali asked.

Everything he did seemed based on how soon he could return to his kids. He'd be on the phone with them now if they were awake.

"A minute there is a minute here," Omm explained. "Once you go in, you'll have a bit of a wait until Seti dies—that time is a bit loose in case your arrival causes a slight ripple effect. But very soon, Seti will cross over. The moment that happens, you have exactly twelve hours to complete your task."

"Why twelve hours?" Ali asked.

Jared knew the answer. "Because it takes that long to travel the twelve gates, following the sun god through the hours of the night."

Omm smiled. "Correct."

"This is a bit more than our director here told us last night," Derek said.

"Don't fret. You'll be following Seti's solar boat, and Tiya, my original self, will be there to join you. She is a priestess and knows the chants, spells, and meanings of each gate. Follow her lead, meet Mehy, and capture his *ka* on tape, and you will emerge right back here at dawn on the twelfth hour, just as the sun rises."

"And what will we see in the underworld?" Kara asked, her camera on pause and pointing to the ground.

"Seti will explain all that when you get there."

"I mean, will we see the dead?"

Omm looked at her tenderly. "Yes, dear. Did you have someone specific in mind?"

Kara hoisted the camera back on her shoulder, her face now pinched in a look of cool indifference. "Naw, just wondering if I'll see Prince and Tupac and shit. Make for good TV." She stepped back to frame a wide shot.

No one could formulate a rational follow-up question until Derek stepped forward. "Whatever. Let's do this before Jared buckles again."

"It's you I'm more worried about," Omm said. "Now, if in agreement, I will ask Tiya to open the door so you may cross."

She returned to the portal and spread her arms wide. As before, the door flickered. Sandstone swirled and then settled to reveal a brightly painted temple. Standing eye to eye with Omm was the young woman Jared had seen the first time he peered through the false door. Her lustrous hair was cut into a bob just above the neck, her eyes framed in kohl, and she wore an amber tunic wrapped in a purple sash.

"Wha da fa?" Kara said as she zoomed in. After a moment, she looked over at Jared and raised her eyebrows. "Holy shit!"

Omm turned to the crew.

"I'd like you to meet Tiya, my original *ka*. I can go no further. Now, here's an important bit to remember. Only the owner of the false door can allow you access to return. Without two hosts, you'll be unable to cross back."

"I see. Kind of like a phone call," Derek said to the camera.

"Nice analogy," Said echoed from the shadows.

Noting that the entire crew was wide-eyed from both fear and wonder, Omm softened her tone.

"Don't worry, I won't budge. And remember, Tiya is still me, just much younger and heaps more fun. Trust her."

She motioned them forward.

"Now then, who has a timepiece we can rely on?"

Derek raised a fancy underwater watch he bought on vacation in St. Lucia. A damn silly item to bring to the Sahara, but product placement was important to an expensive show like this.

"5:39 AM," he announced to the camera.

Omm pointed to their shoes.

"Take them off and carry them until you're out of the temple. It is an active holy site you're crossing into."

Jared felt like a jittery kid who couldn't hold in his pee—all he wanted to do was *cross the hell over already,* to find relief at last.

He slipped out of sneakers and dashed forward.

After a deep breath, perhaps the last he ever drew in this world, he put one foot in front of the other… and almost tripped over Derek.

"On-camera talent first, kiddo," Derek reminded him. "Didn't they teach you anything back in New York?"

The star of *Ancient Encounters* smirked for the camera, as if inviting his fans to join him.

"Let's just see what kind of Styrofoam they're using in Pharaonic Egypt these days."

"What an absolute sod," Omm muttered.

Kara laughed. "You don't know the half of it."

The crew lingered a moment to capture his reaction. Ali's boom pole stretched across the threshold and three thousand years into the past.

"Well, I'll be damned," was all Derek could muster as he wandered farther into the temple. "It's a lot better than the mop and bucket we saw in Scotland."

CHAPTER 16

In a single step, everything would change. Whatever happened from here, Jared would soon know if what was promised was true or if he was still in the world he was so eager to flee. If real, would he collapse in a heap, unable to go on? Deliberately, slowly, he lifted his left foot over the door jamb and placed it on the sandy floor. A quiver radiated from his soles to his ears, and he halted, keeping the other foot planted in the modern world for one final moment. Between his left toes, the sand was silky, refined, as if somehow purer for being three thousand years older—or younger. His right foot remained fixed to coarse, common grain, unremarkable, and without history. He knew where he wanted to be and took his final step, digging both feet into the sand on the other side. Playfully, he flicked fine grains over his toes, let them trickle down the sides, then buried each foot further into the warm sand, knowing precisely how deep to go before it cooled and comforted him. That's when he knew for certain. It was as if he had returned to a beloved childhood beach after a lifetime of wintery anticipation. He had entered the world of his flashbacks, and they were real. My god, Omm was right: he had come home.

Then, another step and he lost his balance and fell to the temple floor. He gazed up at the walls from the cool sandstone, at least forty feet high and freshly decorated. He heard the swallows chirping somewhere in the rafters, the ancient ancestors of those who would replace them three thousand years later. The aroma of paint and plaster was no longer a detached memory but as immediate and familiar as the wallpaper back home.

A woman's hand came into view.

"Welcome to 1279 BC," Tiya said in relatively clear English. "Think you can stand?"

"I'm not sure," he confessed.

"It takes some getting used to. I felt it the first time I traveled to my past. Omm, dear thing, still has a time of it, with her wobbling knees."

Jared finally remembered he was not alone. He rose to his feet and took stock. The rest of the crew seemed to have had an easier time with the crossing and were standing around, trying to figure out where they were. That suggested they had no connection to this time and place or, for whatever reason, had forgotten. But that wasn't to say they remained unaffected. Kara was leaning against a statue of Amun for support, unsure where to train her camera, giggling with excitement. Ali and Derek had yet to accept what had happened and were looking to Tiya for answers.

Tiya scrutinized her guests and looked a bit disappointed. "We must get you to Seti's palace at once. Convince him you're up for the task." She handed Derek his hat, which had fallen to the floor. "Must confess. He has his doubts."

"How do you know English?" Kara asked.

Her query helped answer one of his own: at least one other person believed they had traveled back in time.

Tiya continued moving down a corridor. "As I've been given the gift of immediate and constant rebirth, I speak many languages. But most here do not, so I will translate."

Derek and Ali, moving warily, lingering behind. Whatever bravado they had on the other side now eluded them. Ali had completely forgotten to raise his boom pole, and Derek no longer hugged the spotlight. He was off on his own, fingering a column, examining it closely. He pulled out a penknife and was about to scrape at the painting, perhaps to see what was underneath, but Tiya stopped him.

"Do that, and Pharaoh Seti, and the gods, will be most displeased."

Instead of rolling his eyes, he slipped the knife into his pocket.

Tiya gave them another moment to collect themselves, then ushered them up a stone stairway, glossy from centuries of use. She halted in front of a wooden door some fifteen feet high. "Beyond these cedars is the sacred temple complex of Abydos. Prepare yourself, as it has changed since you last saw it." Tiya unwrapped a thick knot of hemp and pushed the doors open. The darkened corridor flooded with harsh light.

The first thing that struck Jared, even before his eyes adjusted, was the fragrance—spicy, verdant, earthy. Everything felt richer, more alive than it did back home. A pebbled trail twisted into a garden, and Tiya led them forward. As a footbridge arched over a bubbling brook, Jared caught his first tantalizing glimpse of a building: the summit of some glorious shrine poking over a field of blue lotus. Then the trail dipped again, and, to his frustration, it was gone.

Voices chattered ahead, and Tiya halted to say something. Before she could, Kara and her camera bumped into her.

"Oops, sorry," Kara said, lowering the lens and rubbing her eyes. "Am I really..."

"So far, just foliage." Derek shrugged. "Which hasn't changed in a thousand years."

But his usual bravado was missing.

"I'm picking up weird sounds I've never heard before," Ali whispered. "Animals breathing and splashing. People talking in languages that are not Arabic. Stuff that wasn't here yesterday."

"An audio library of Nile creatures," Derek whispered to the folks watching from home. "Like on a jungle ride at Six Flags."

They moved down a trail flanked by papyri reeds until it spilled into a small clearing. A few modest houses stood there, framed in carved stones and wide-open windows. Jared noticed people moving about inside. He considered the sight of his crew and panicked for the first time. A bearded man with glasses, clutching what looked like a dangerous spear, a commando-capped woman hiding her face behind a sinister black box, and Derek dressed as… what *would* the Egyptians make of him? Would they attack as soon as they saw this armed group of aliens approach?

The Egyptians looked exactly as they should. White loincloths, naked from the waist up, kohl around the eyes to reduce the sun's glare. But unlike the stiff-backed, slender images on the temple walls, some slumped, bulged in the middle, had hairy chests, big noses, acne, and scars. In short, they seemed like real people. And most strangely, not one of them seemed shocked to see this motley band of outsiders.

Kara giggled as she framed a family who casually sauntered past. "Didn't know the ancient Egyptians came in three dimensions."

Tiya addressed the crew. "In case you're wondering why they're not alarmed, it's because you're not the first. A select few have charmed the gatekeepers enough to walk through these doors. Alexander the Great, naturally, but also Herodotus and Nostradamus, and Rumi. Naguib Mahfouz spent an entire month here writing his novel, *Thebes at War*. Elizabeth Taylor and Richard Burton popped by once, claiming to be researching a film, but all they did was drink palm wine, argue, and go home." Tiya thought some more. "Oh, then of course General Zolchak barged in, but he's still in your future. Good thing, too." She moved on. "No one will delay us if we mind our own business."

Tiya led them along a canal, croaking with bullfrogs and buzzing with dragonflies. At one point, a water buffalo poked out of the reeds and motionlessly watched them pass.

Derek scrutinized it. "A-ha! A mechanical beast, see. Even its eyes don't move." He beckoned the camera closer and reached out to touch it. The animal bellowed and charged. Derek screamed so loud that Ali plucked the headphones from his ears.

A pat on the head from Tiya halted its progress. She pointed to Derek's hat. "It's probably that thing. It's rather large and…unnecessary. What purpose does it serve?" Derek slipped the fedora off his head and smoothed his hair. Behind him, Kara and Ali stifled laughs.

"Watch it. I'm still the star of this show."

Tiya's eyes met the sky. "You're a star?"

Kara kept laughing. "Not that kind. Means super famous, known by everyone."

Tiya tilted her head and considered Derek more closely. A grin escaped.

"It must be very dark where you come from."

They approached the palace, and Jared now understood why they called present-day Abydos a ruin. For what stood before them was nothing like the bleached assemblage of bones they had just left. Dozens of forked banners hung from pylons so garishly painted they almost seemed like a children's pop-up book. A huge palm wood gate prevented Jared from seeing what wonders lay within.

Kara couldn't stop videotaping everything she saw, almost breathlessly. "I don't know where to rest my camera. As soon as I do, something even more amazing appears." She zoomed in on a pair of children. The boy's hair flowed in a pigtail from the left side of the head, the girl's cascading down to her belly as she played with a toy hippo on wheels.

Tethered by an audio cord, Ali danced to keep up with Kara's jerky movements. He stretched his boom pole into the air to capture ambient noise.

"We need to be careful not to film everything that moves," he reminded her. "Once the batteries die, it's over."

Kara tapped her case. "Solar charge."

"Good." Ali looked to the sky. "Whatever this place is, that sun is real."

Tiya called Jared over and began explaining to him how, as a leader, he should address the pharaoh. As she did, Jared noticed that Derek was wandering off on his own. He called out to Kara, who didn't hear him until the third try.

"Mind staying close to him? Give him something to do, a stand-up or something."

She nodded and followed. "Yo, Mr. Presenter. Present!"

OUTSIDE TEMPLE OF SETI

STAND UP: *Derek walks along temple, camera follows, hand-held.*

DEREK: We're outside what our guides are calling the temple of Seti, but not the one we just left. Seems this one has been all gussied up. But not so fast…

Come with me. I'm going to peek around the side, where the plywood ends and the actors change costumes. I see something at the edge that looks like slats, like how they had in old Western movie sets.

Derek moves forward, ducking beyond a mud brick wall and slinks closer to the edge of the palace.

After finishing, Derek continued to explore. But Kara's mind was wandering in different directions, and she failed to follow. For the first time in years, she didn't want to hide behind a camera. She wanted to be part of the world, not see it through a one-inch viewfinder. When she had first started out as Director of Photography, it was her commitment to capturing the truth at all costs that inspired her, be it a bullshit artist who needed to be exposed or an intimate encounter others were too embarrassed to intrude on. But after Lynette was taken from her, things took a darker turn. It became less about the subject or the shot and more about dehumanizing death, to keep it faceless and remote, to rob it of its power. Once, when they were shooting Biblical recreations in Ramallah, an incident broke out between Israeli guards and Palestinian residents. The crew fled to their cars and screamed at her to follow. But she ignored their pleas and followed the action all the way to the border. At one point, she even hopped atop a jeep to get a wide shot. Only afterward, when the angry director chewed her out for endangering herself and the crew, did she react.

"Didn't you hire me to capture what was in front of me? Well, that's what I did."

"We're doing a show about the Holy Grail, not the intifada," he reminded her.

He was so shaken that he wanted to send her home and hire a local DP. Ultimately, Jared came to the rescue, convincing her to apologize and privately reminding her that he'd be heartbroken should anything happen to her.

But now, taking in the serenity around her, the last thing she wanted to do was hide. She put the camera down and absorbed the scene. A family was repairing a thatched roof, and a young boy was tying together palm fronds and handing them to his father. In the shade, a woman and another child were doing the same, while an ostrich kept trying to eat their hard work. Free of drama or agenda, it was a moment simply to be savored. Kara walked up to the woman and nodded hello. After her smile was returned, Kara picked up two fronds and tried to mimic the family's actions. She was unable, and the family laughed lightly. The woman then noticed Kara's arm, the one that had bubbled from too much sun. She reached into a wicker basket and pulled out a bowl filled with something golden and gooey. Only after it had been brushed over her boils did Kara recognize it as honey. The woman smiled and returned to her work, and even when a fly the size of an olive landed on Kara's arm to suck up the sugar, her own smile didn't fade. Being here, a thousand years from her worries, seeing how little everyday life had changed, down to the kind of flies, and the same honey she had in her cabinet back home, gave her an odd sense of security and calm. She never knew how much she missed consistency.

"Hawkins, the show is over here," Derek bellowed. Kara looked over and groaned.

Was there anything more intrusive and less real than reality TV? She jerked the camera back over her shoulder and joined him.

"That hut over there, it looks like some prop house," he said to the folks back home. "Let's check it out. Expose the Not Ready For Prime Time Players of Abydos, Egypt."

The camera crew rejoined Jared a moment later, led by a scowling, dark-skinned warrior. Derek turned to protest, but the point of a spear guided him forward. If he did not yet fully believe, Jared concluded, he was inching closer. For their part, Kara and Ali seemed almost bemused, no doubt worried, but coming to terms with where they really were.

Tiya spoke casually to the warrior, and he stepped aside.

"This is Mentmose, a Medjay guard from Nubia. A trained killer. He's also one of Seti's most trusted men and promises to protect you for as long as you're our guest." She singled out Derek. "Provided you don't go exploring on your own."

Jared studied the warrior closely—not for signs that he was an actor in costume, but because he might have been the most beautiful man he had ever laid eyes on. Cheekbones forged of granite, a broad masculine nose, and a body out of one of his most intimate Gladiator fantasies. The man was literally encased in muscles from neck to calves, but beyond his intimidating appearance, in the eyes and lips, a modest sweetness showed through. This was no stereotypical cold warrior—a real man stood behind the shield, and it was all Jared could do to shut his mouth from drooling. Before he did, he noticed Mentmose staring back.

Tiya pushed the temple door open. Inside, a walkway of torches led the way past fluted columns. And on the far end, sitting on a golden throne, was what could only be a pharaoh. Topped by a double crown of serpent and snake and adorned in a multicolored breastplate, it was evident he was not at his peak. His skin sagged, his body appeared diminished under oversized accouterments, and liver spots mimicking the surface of the moon pocked his forehead. Jared was sure he heard the pharaoh's breath rattle from across the room.

"Do not look the great Seti in the eye," Tiya whispered. "Walk forward slowly, staring only at your feet." When they reached the throne, Tiya bent her face to the floor, and everyone followed. Derek had put his hat back on; a small bald spot had appeared recently, and he made it clear he never wanted the camera to pick it up. Mentmose immediately snatched it off. Jared stared at him again and this time was greeted with a small smile as the warrior scrutinized the odd hat and shook his head in mock bewilderment.

For several minutes, no one dared move. Jared stared at the decorative paving stone in front of him: an image of a hawk, wings raised before it. He could almost taste the paint, sticky and tingling. Then it hit his first vision since crossing over. His body quaked but didn't crumble. Jared inhaled and let it come.

He's sitting on a stone wall, watching a cloudless sky as several birds circle overhead. At first, they look like hawks, similar to the one before him, but they come into sharper relief as they draw close. Vultures circled a pile of human bodies stacked in a courtyard. He rises from a patch of shade and approaches one of the birds as it sinks its claws into the eyes of a corpse. He lets it claim its prize—the eyes are useless now anyway—but chases the creature away before it can do further damage. He drags the body, naked and stiff, into a wooden shed. Several other bodies are already stacked inside. The dead man's mouth falls open as if in protest of his fate, and the door slams shut.

The image faded as quickly and simply as it started, leaving no ill effect. Jared tried to analyze why. The flashback was as gruesome as the others, but for the first time, it wasn't fear that lingered. It was something more benign… almost as if it was sent to remind him of something important. Instead of running, he should embrace these visions. A message was being sent. But what?

But before he could pick it apart, a voice echoed across the hall. "Everyone rise and approach," Tiya announced. "Seti will speak to us now."

Up close, the pharaoh appeared even more infirm than he had from across the room. He smiled warmly at Tiya, then considered Jared and his crew. His face sank to a sour expression, and Jared could only guess what he was thinking.

This is the best you could find to rescue my son from oblivion? Some pudgy kid with a zit the size of a volcano on his forehead and his merry band of mirth makers?

Tiya pointed at Kara and said something to the pharaoh, who nodded in agreement. "Please draw nearer," Tiya said. "Show him your soul catcher."

"Say what?"

Tiya pointed to her camera. "Your ossuary with all those glass eyes. He must know that everything is ready. His time approaches."

Kara held the camera out in two hands like King Arthur might a sword he was presenting to one of his knights. Despite his feeble appearance, the pharaoh snatched it from her hand with unexpected force and spun it around. Pharaoh or not, that wouldn't do. No one was going to break her baby. Do that, and not only no film, but Kara's power would evaporate. She lurched forward just as it slipped out of her hands, catching it before it could hit the floor.

"If this breaks," she informed Tiya, "there's no place for us to capture his kid. Tell him that, will you?"

Seti nodded in understanding and then asked something in return. "And where exactly will Mehy's soul be housed? It's small, and he sees no sacred chamber."

Kara ejected the media drive. "In here."

The king said something harsh. Tiya translated. "Don't insult the pharaoh. Mehy is greater and larger than that, he says. Convince him, fast."

Kara was now in her element. Like Jared loved writing words, she loved crafting images. She called Ali over. "Sticks and sound for a master shot." He slung the mixer over his shoulder and pulled the tripod from the case. The camera whirled to life, a few lights illuminated, and, ever the perfectionist, Kara rearranged the tripod legs three or four times before finding the right frame.

"This is a demo of how a camera works," Ali reminded her. "No need to win an Emmy."

Kara didn't hear. Instead, she asked Mentmose, the spear-wielding Medjay, to move slightly to his left, as his huge frame was blocking the light. He only glared back and planted his feet more firmly—until a scowl from Seti forced him aside. Kara peered through the viewfinder and, meeting Mentmose's eyes, said. "It's like shooting through a Sequoia tree. Tell him another three inches to the left." Mentmose moved completely out of the way, choosing to stand next to Jared. He was now so close that Jared recognized the musk the warrior was wearing: something from a big cat, either a leopard or a cheetah. The scent made parts of his body tingle that should definitely be at rest.

"Rolling." The camera buzzed, but no one did anything. Kara stared at Seti, and he stared back. "Yo, director, wanna help me out here? Ask him something, what he had for breakfast, why pyramids are pointy. I don't care."

Jared stepped closer. He bowed to Seti, and a strange realization overcame him. This was not the first pharaoh he had spoken to. Words came easy, words he had never said as Jared Plummer. "*Ankh, Wedja, Seneb*. Life, Prosperity, Health".

Tiya had no need to translate, and Seti smiled in understanding. Then, other words came, some foreign, some English, garbled enough for Tiya to intervene. "He appreciates the effort but is lost. Speak your language, and I will convey."

Jared asked Seti about his temple, how beautiful it was, and how long it took to complete. The conversation might have gone on longer if Mentmose hadn't intervened. She said something to Tiya that made her eyebrows raise. "That's enough," she said to Jared. "Show him."

Kara gestured that Seti should look into the viewfinder. When he did, he roared with laughter.

"It has captured his very essence," Tiya said. "He's pleased. It's exactly what we need to restore Mehy." Seti pointed to the wall behind him, carved in cartouches of kings, and spoke some more. Like all interview subjects, Jared had put him at ease, and spoke in a way that made him want to go on sharing. His eyes teared up at one point as he caressed a hieroglyph on the wall. That's when Tiya raised a hand to translate. "This is Seti's royal name." Next to it was a blank cartouche. "He had hoped Mehy would follow. He still has not gotten over his untimely death and misses him still. Now his younger son Ramses will fill this space. But even though his ascension is guaranteed, Ramses will erase all mention of his brother once Seti dies. That's the kind of son he is. We've done all we could to keep Mehy's name alive, but now it's been destroyed by forces we don't understand. Unless your soul catcher can bring him back, Seti's favorite will be lost forever."

Derek had heard the same from Jared and figured now was the time to do his job. Kara kept rolling. "Surely his tomb exists in this world," he said. "Why use us? Take his mummy, hide it." It was a good question and well asked.

"His body has been buried where even Ramses cannot find. To move it now would only alert him."

Derek spread his arm wide to remind everywhere where they were. "Build another tomb out in the desert. It's huge. Or zip back further in time to some other country. Stonehenge. Under the Great Wall of China. Has that been built yet?"

"Ramses has men everywhere, watching everything we do. It's too late."

Tiya remained silent, and Derek moved on. "The guy has survived 3,300 years. How long does he need to be remembered?"

Tiya looked at him as if something was lost in translation. "What a ridiculous question. For eternity, of course."

"Media drives break down, disappear." Derek countered, relishing his role as inquisitor. "Nothing lasts forever."

"But it does," Tiya explained. "Consider King Tutankhamun." Seti groaned at the mention and shook his head in disgust. "Yes, we know, my lord. Mehy was a far greater man." She pointed to the Kings List on the wall. "Such a minor boy king. He doesn't even appear here. But even if all his treasures get melted down, and he can never return to the land of the living, he will still be remembered forever. That's from all your films and books and magazines and jigsaw puzzles." She pointed the camera. "That's what you must do for Mehy. You must make him, as you claim to be, an everlasting 'star'."

Seti rose and moved forward, first on his own and then, when he couldn't go on, with the support of Mentmose.

"Come," Tiya said. "He wants to show you how to do it. But we must travel quickly. He hasn't much time." Mentmose again whispered something else into her ear. Whatever sweetness Jared saw before was now obscured by a look of grim purpose. Tiya frowned. "And another reason to hurry. Ramses has been alerted to your arrival. He's racing back from Memphis to see why outsiders have crossed through his father's false door."

"Is that a bad thing?" Derek asked. "Wouldn't mind meeting the Great Ramses."

"Trust me, you don't. Did Omm neglect to tell you? Ramses doesn't yet know why you're here, but if he did, he would surely stop you."

"How?"

"His usual method is to slowly skin someone alive until they die from pain and shock."

Mentmose, who must have understood English well enough to follow along, added something in Egyptian, which Tiya translated. "Right, and feed your body parts to his pet hippos as you watch."

CHAPTER 17

Seti was carted out on his sedan chair, and guards led Jared and the team down a footpath to the river's edge. A small hut used by ferrymen to store oars was commandeered, and the crew ushered inside. "Don't wander," Tiya ordered. "When the boat is ready, I will fetch you."

Kara kept filming, knowing that whatever was unfolding, it was more authentic than any stand-up Derek would have delivered. She only turned it off when the hut door closed, but Ali kept the sound rolling. "You can shut it down," she whispered. "If I turn my light on, they'll only see us."

"No way." Ali laid the boom pole between them. "I'm recording everything we say, just in case."

Kara: In case of what?

Ali: In case something happens to us. At least they'll know.

Derek: Enough is enough. The joke's not funny anymore.

Jared: C'mon, Derek, what makes you still think all this could be staged?

Derek: Because if you believe all this, then you also got to believe Ramses the Great is after us, ready to skin us alive. That's not what I signed up for.

Ali: There's a place in Cairo called the Pharaonic Village, an amusement park for kids to step back in time and see life as it was during ancient times. People building Styrofoam sphinxes and shit. I was dragged there more than once on field trips.

Derek: And? This is just like that?

Ali: No *(pause)* It's much, much better. If this is real, Jared, you had no right leading us here, especially if you knew we'd be in danger.

Derek: No one is in danger, Ali. That's my point. Don't go soft like these two.

Ali: I have a wife and two young boys at home. People I love dearly, people I want to stay alive for. I don't even travel abroad for fear the plane might go down, and they'd be left without a husband and father. If this is real, and something horrible happens...I swear...

Kara: Ok, ok, let's think this through, step by step. First off: this *is* real...right, Jared?

Jared: It's real. I know it.

Derek: Why the hell should we take your word for it? What could you possibly know that we don't?

Jared: Only that I've been here before. Not this place exactly, I don't think, but here, in ancient Egypt.

Derek: Dear fucking god, we're being led by a Pyramidiot!

Ali: Calm down, Derek. Right, suppose this is real. Jared, what do we do? I refuse to give up my life for some crappy American show like *Adventure Time With Derek Dees.*

Kara: We can all agree on that. Surely there are better ways to go.

Ali: And unlike you all, who have no spouses or kids, I work for my family, not for fun. If you've done anything to compromise that…

Jared: Trust me, I didn't know about the dangers. At least not to you. I should have thought that through. I was thinking about myself, and I apologize.

Kara: Don't apologize. Too late for all that. It is what it is.

Derek: Hey, just because you got some death wish, Hawkins, don't write this all off.

Kara: Who says I have a death wish?

Derek: Uh, everyone. Ever since you lost your girlfriend, which I'm sorry about, as I've said, you've checked out. Dangerous and unpredictable on shoots, fighting men with badges, climbing out on cliffs, not ducking when the fucking Israeli police start shooting. Sorry if you're ready to pack it in, but not me.

Kara: You sound a bit worried, Derek. So you *do* believe all this?

Derek: One thing I know for sure, I got a lot more to live for than this show.

Kara: Such as?

Derek: Never you mind.

Kara: Knew it. You have nothing else to live for but this damn stupid-ass show. At least I had someone I loved and loved me back, all you care about is yourself.

Derek: *(pause)* The point is where we are right now. A ferryman's hut along the Nile, rudderless. With no one but you two losers to guide us.

Jared: Can you just shut the hell up and stop criticizing for one damn minute so I can think?

Derek: How dare you?

Kara: You asshat. Listen to you. Look where we are. If you've got nothing constructive to say, then say nothing at all. *(pause)* So, what are you thinking?

Jared: A couple things. One, no matter what happens, we gotta stick together. There's no way we'd all find our way back to the false door at the exact time Omm is opening it if separated.

Two, we have to trust Tiya and Seti. They want us to succeed. They're the only reason we were allowed to come.

Ali: Why should we trust Tiya? She just left us. And she knew Ramses was after us but neglected to tell us until after we got here. Not exactly team-building stuff.

Jared: True, but maybe she didn't know.

Ali: Or maybe she's not who she says she is.

Kara: Ok, what else, Jared?

Jared: One more thing. A big one. I need you to listen to me, even if you don't see me as a leader. I can't explain it, but I know things or am being told things. Stuff that may keep us safe.

Ali: I'm fine with that. You, I trust.

Jared: Derek?

Derek: I'm not. This is still all a game. And if not, there isn't a snowball's chance in hell you'd be the one to lead us to safety.

Kara: Derek, you asshat, I swear to god I'm gonna take this tripod and shove it—

A rustling outside heralded Mentmose's low voice, this time in broken English: "Ready. You follow." He didn't stop to offer more information. Not far off, a royal barge was waiting, dramatically curled on either end like lotus blossoms. The boat sat low in the water. More like a fancy, oversized canoe, with a golden box in its center where the pharaoh was waiting. Curtains were drawn to shield him from onlookers. Mentmose moved to protect the king, a frown keeping the crew at bay.

Kara and Ali captured everything she saw but remembered Jared's words from a safe distance.

Tiya beckoned them forward. As soon as the gangplank was drawn up, a dozen barefooted oarsmen eased the boat out of the tributary and into a small lake where it could turn. On the ridge, two men on horseback appeared, and Mentmose said something that made Tiya nervous. She turned to Jared and was about to say something but swallowed it instead. No matter, Jared knew the words without them being spoken: they had been spotted by Ramses' men.

The boat entered the Nile just as the sun was melting into the western cliffs. On both banks, farmers quitting their fields for the day stopped to watch their god-king pass. A few got on their knees, others touched fingers to their head and held their oxen close to keep them from wandering off. Tiya pointed upriver.

"The Great Bend. When it straightens out again, you'll be greeted with a splendid view of the holy city of Karnak."

Jared closed his eyes and drank it all in. He could smell the rich fertile soil mixed with cattle dung, the sweet fragrance of pink flowered tamarisk peppering the shore, and the sound of Nile water splashing against their palm wood boat. He remembered, nostalgically, walking along the riverbank as a child, collecting nets and counting the fish. "Not too close, Hori," a woman's gentle voice said from behind him. "The crocodiles." But he was transfixed by the wriggling nets, knowing each was bursting with perch. His father would be waiting eagerly at home to take them to market, and he so wanted to impress him. He drew closer to the river's edge until his mother's voice was joined by two hands, warm and firm, around his waist. "Hori, what did I tell you?" she said as she pulled him back to the shore. "Get the baskets. I'll do it."

Jared opened his eyes. "This really is happening, right?"

"Why would we go to all this trouble to fool you?" Tiya answered. She studied his face and pointed to his cheeks. Jared wiped away a tear.

"What have you seen?"

"My mother. I forgot how tender her voice was." He wiped away another tear, wondering how many thousands of springs had passed since that voice went silent.

Tiya looked out at a grand temple on the western shore. Priests were lighting lamps as the evening shadows faded into the dark. "Everyone gets a bit emotional when reunited with something they thought was lost forever."

"I'm not sure what it is I've lost, exactly." As he said this, he knew it was a lie. What he had lost, somewhere along the way, was not simply past lives but faith in himself. The belief that he mattered to both himself and others, and could make a difference. How he yearned to recapture even a tiny piece of that.

"Something you had here has bound you to this place. I hope you'll find it before the sun rises and you return to your world."

On either side of the river, villages of squat mud brick peppered lush fields. As the last of the light faded, farmers guided beasts of burden into grass pens. A donkey brayed. Bonfires flared up from tiny courtyards as families prepared the evening meal. The aroma of roasting meat was so strong it wafted to the middle of the river, making Jared's mouth water. Kara joined him and when she saw his tears gave his hand a light squeeze. Her eyes also glistened but for a different reason.

"Lynette would have adored this. Remember how she always wanted to join me at the end of every shoot? Tack on a few days vacation." She shook her head slowly. "But she never did, did she? I was always too busy at work or never wanted to intrude. She'd hang my gifts on the wall, listen to my stories, tell me how proud she was, and promise me 'next time.' And now, I feel guilty seeing all this without her. While she…" Kara went silent for a long time. "So many memories we'll never share."

After Lynette's death, Kara had tried to keep despair at bay by always being on the road, far from her Fort Greene apartment and the normal life that she decided was no longer possible. When *Ancient Encounters* was between seasons, she would take any job, regardless of the pay, or danger to herself. One time she spent three months shooting a story about Afghan refugees fleeing Kabul over mountain passes. She followed that up with an eight-part series documenting volcano chasers in Indonesia. The closer to danger, and perhaps death, she came, her thinking was, the closer to Lynette.

Although Jared shirked any job that had even the hint of danger—until this one—he shared one trait with her, and that had sealed their friendship. When he was on the road, documenting other people's stories, his own troubles couldn't find him. Even his most intimate moments were dealt with in this way. He thought of his own empty sexual encounters, the beautiful, nameless men who brushed against him in a London bar or a Colombian hotel but were never allowed any closer because 'career was more important.' A patent lie. The show itself meant far less to him than the angst of being called out as a 'fag,' only one of the infinite slurs he had to endure growing up. Being gay, Jared had long ago concluded, was no different from all the other worries in his life. Conflict of any kind was a threat best avoided. Kara had tried many times to get him to come out, as she had done years earlier.

"First of all, Brooklyn ain't Kansas," she assured him. "You have no freaking idea how much happier you'll be."

But like most other 'obstacles' in Jared's life, it was safer to ask questions rather than answer them. They were quite the misfit pair: Jared was afraid to embrace the present, and Kara couldn't escape the past. The only difference was that for he and Carlos there was still time. All Kara had was memories.

A vast, twinkling city appeared on the eastern bank. Obelisks some fifty feet high were brightly illuminated by cauldrons below, like limestone rockets about to take to the sky. Connecting twin temples was a colonnade of ram-headed sphinxes, smoke twisting from cauldrons lined up along the way.

"The holy city of Thebes," Tiya said. "We'll sleep there tonight, but first Seti must show you something across the Nile that will prepare you for your journey."

The boat swerved towards the lush west bank. A heavily guarded canal cut between two mammoth walls, so high Jared couldn't see the top. "Seti's Temple of Millions of Years," Tiya said before Jared could ask. "As soon as he dies, Seti's body will come to this mortuary complex to be readied for the journey through the Twelve Gates."

The boat moored, and Mentmose ushered them ashore, spear drawn as an incentive to move quickly. Chariots were waiting, and the Medjay all but pushed them inside. A rutted road twisted into a desert wasteland flanked by towering cliffs. Every few yards, Jared saw doors carved into barren rock face, each manned by stern-faced warriors. Jared recognized where they were: the Valley of the Kings, where over sixty pharaohs of the New Kingdom had been buried. A vast desert sky arched overhead, and he marveled at the billions of stars—the very stars that would still be there three-thousand years later, when he would be a Kansas kid playing in cornfields, and his mother would call to him from the porch. "Not too far, Jared. The coyotes are out." It dawned on him that if a star went dark right now, its light would still be burning bright when he was in Junction City—it was that distant. His past life and current one weren't so far apart after all.

In the folds of a craggy bluff, a large open tomb came into view, and the sounds of chiseling echoed from within. Men were hurriedly mixing plaster and rushing in and out with great urgency. Tiya explained that Seti's tomb, his vessel to the underworld, remained incomplete. As soon as he died, all work must stop. If something was amiss, be it the smallest incantation or image of a god, it could compromise his pilgrimage across the night sky.

The litter halted, and Seti was moved from the sedan chair and into the chamber. As he passed craftsmen on scaffolding, his gaze betrayed worry—there was still much work to be done and little time to do it.

Kara was shooting all she could, and Ali, tethered by a cord, tried to keep up. "Twist suddenly like that one more time," Ali complained, "and you'll strangle us both."

There were well over a dozen rooms, each with pillars built into the living rock and descending three levels. Seti slowed down when the corridor ended in a final room coated in fantastical images of serpents and mummies. He began to speak, his voice raspy and thin.

"Seti says this room is most important," Tiya translated, "so use your soul catcher to capture all it can hold. Should you lose the pharaoh along the way."

Jared recognized it immediately, and to his surprise, so did Ali. "Isn't this the *Book of the Gates*?"

"Exactly. It lists all the goddesses and great challenges you must face before arriving in paradise."

Derek only snorted. "So why do we need to know all this? More myth and magic." He scanned the walls. "Dog-headed gods fighting snakes, parades of mummies…"

"Is that what you still think," Tiya asked, "even after these same gods have brought you here?"

Seti tapped Kara on the shoulder, pointing to the wall. She understood and began filming.

Jared gazed at a dip in the floor, where a huge alabaster sarcophagus rested. Little of this made sense. Break it down, one step at a time. "So we will stay here, and in the ancient world, until Seti's journey to the underworld begin?"

"Yes," Tiya explained, "as soon as his mummy is interred and the door is sealed, the gate opens to the Duat."

"And what do we do?"

"We follow the pharaoh's night boat at a safe distance."

"We?"

"Yes, I'm coming too."

Jared studied the paintings with a critical eye. Some of the symbols he could easily translate, but many more he could not. They seemed to be written in an archaic form of Egyptian, like reading the *Canterbury Tales* or *Beowulf* in its original form. "Even if we capture it on video, I won't be able to make sense of them." He realized he had used the dreaded "I" word, a distinction he always tried to avoid, as it was not only selfish but set himself up for ridicule. But this time, no one called him on it, not even Derek.

"That's why I am joining you. I'm one of the few who can." Tiya led Jared to the sarcophagus, where more spells were etched into the lid. "This version is an ancient text, older than the first pharaoh. A modern translation is housed in the Holy of Holies in Karnak temple. By comparing this with that, I was able to understand these markings." At the far corner, a painter was studying a slate of stone and painting over something on the wall and starting again. "But I'm not different from him. If we get even one thing wrong, we will never reach the Field of Reeds."

"Then why not borrow the modern version, just in case, you know, you screw up?" Kara asked. "We'll promise to give it back on the way out, cross our hearts."

"Impossible. It's not a lending library. It's surrounded by a churning river of stone and watched over by the High Priests of Karnak. No one, not even a pharaoh, can remove it. It's the only copy." Tiya waved her arms around the room. "So best we can do is capture all we can now in case we need to consult it on the way."

Ali moved closer to the wall. "I had a coloring book as a kid that showed the gods of the underworld. Got it as a gift for *Khitan*, my circumcision ceremony. I remember it was a horror show of hungry demons." He faced his director. "And we're to do battle with them?"

"Not battle, just appease."

Ali studied one image of a giant snake swallowing a man's head. "And if we don't?"

"That's not an option," Tiya said unhelpfully.

"So, we're to follow these cartoons through a bunch of doors guarded by monsters until we get to heaven? Got it." Kara asked. "How exactly?"

Mentmose removed a stone to reveal a small alcove where carpets had been spread out. "As soon as Seti dies and work in the tomb stops," Tiya explained, "we return and hide here while everyone is preoccupied with his funeral. Once the first gate of the underworld opens for him, we simply enter."

Mentmose crawled in to show them where to sit. "Will he be coming too?" Jared asked Tiya, the thought of having the Nubian warrior at his side pleasing in more ways than one.

"No, he must stay behind to cover our tracks."

"Since we're being followed by Ramses," Kara decided, "I'd rather hide there now."

"Workers saw you come in. If you don't leave the same way, it will get back to him, and he may block our escape."

"Wait a minute," Ali said, palms raised. "I'm still getting my head around being in my country thousands of years before I was born. Now I'm also expected to accept that the gods themselves exist? That the underworld was not some state-sponsored religion to keep rich people rich, but a *real place*?"

"And we're to hide in a cupboard and slip past them and a bunch of man-eating goblins on the way to heaven?" Derek ripped the lavalier from his shirt. "That's it, game or not, it's over. I was fine to have a laugh at Omm's expense. But I'm not interested in being eaten by a giant snake."

"If we did do this," Kara asked, still peering into the alcove, "will your heaven be the same as ours?"

"No, I'm afraid not. Omm told me you were seeking someone. I'm sorry, it doesn't work like that. One needs to be invited into the Field of Reeds. It's not open to those of other faiths. You four should consider yourself blessed."

"Blessed is not the word I would use," Ali said. "I'm with Derek. This is madness. Take us home, Tiya."

"Is that even possible?" Jared asked, his own resolve crumbling as he remembered all the challenges of the gates, especially the Ninth. When he would be judged not on who he was at the moment but who he had been until now. Current coward or ancient pharaoh-slayer, he saw no way he'd be allowed to pass.

"Can we still say no?"

Tiya appeared alarmed by the question. "You can, I suppose. Seti will not harm you or force you." Her eyes met Jared. "Omm assured me you were strong enough. That you wanted to be here, to prove yourself. Was she wrong?" When he said nothing, she addressed the group. "But know that danger awaits you in either direction. Ramses' men are close and know we went through the Abydos entry point. They may be at the false door now, barring your exit home."

Jared counted the options. There were three. The first: work their way back to Abydos and hope Ramses and his army had grown tired of waiting. But if he hadn't, what did it mean? Death or eternal imprisonment in some parched cell on this side of the door? He had promised to keep the crew safe, and this seemed no way to do that.

Option two: hide and do absolutely nothing. They might live in ancient times forever, but Mehy would still be forgotten, and they'd spend the rest of their days knowing that they took the coward's way out. Worse, it would be a betrayal to Ali and his family and even Derek's ambitions in their current world.

That left option three. But he had one question for Tiya first. "You will be with us the entire time, correct?"

"Of course, no way could you do this alone. Your job is to merely capture it on your camera."

"So it will be you who face the gods, not me…us?

"Naturally. I have been a priestess of Amun's since I was a child. There will be no delay getting us across."

"I say we do what we promised," Jared announced to his colleagues. "We complete our task, make our film. The only place Ramses won't follow is into the underworld, and as long as Tiya is by our side, we can pull this off." He studied the faces of his crew. He looked to his best friend, hoping she was still on his side.

It took Kara a moment to reply, as Jared feared. Her one reason for coming here had just been dashed. Finally, she spoke. "Ali and Derek are right about one thing. They shouldn't risk their lives just for something you and I want. That means we do this only to keep Mehy alive." She shifted her camera from one shoulder to the other. "Is that worth it? Why does he get eternity when the rest of us disappear without a trace?"

"Because we made a promise," Jared said weakly.

She shook her head and sighed. "I dunno…"

"Can we all sleep on it?" Jared pleaded.

"Nothing to sleep on as far as I'm concerned," Derek said. "But wouldn't mind getting out of here. Where can we do it where we won't get skinned alive?"

Tiya looked hurt that half the crew was ready to give up before they even started. "A few hours of rest might give you strength. I know somewhere that should be safe. A place so wretched and foul even Ramses soldiers are afraid to go there."

CHAPTER 18

An armada of boats lined the shores of the Nile, hovering over a membrane of mist. At this ungodly hour, most of the ferrymen were still asleep, but one old-timer was awake and washing his face. Mentmose shouted something to him, but the man only rubbed his eyes and brushed his few remaining teeth with a gnarled finger. An argument broke out.

"What's the problem?" Jared asked.

"The ferryman doesn't want to take us to that part of town, he says it's cursed," Tiya said. "He's not half wrong."

More words were exchanged, and the man pretended to go back to sleep—until sharper words were exchanged. The man sighed, and Mentmose jumped aboard, his weight nearly capsizing the vessel.

"That worked," Kara observed. "He threatened him with that bad-ass blade?"

"Worse," Tiya said. "Mentmose says he works for the pharaoh and wondered when the last time the ferryman paid his river tax."

"Three thousand years and so little has changed," Ali said as he stepped into the boat. "I had the same conversation about my car with the Ministry of Transportation last week."

Unseen beasts protested as they made their way through broken lotus stalks. The eastern shoreline, shrouded in fog, failed to reveal itself until they were skirting its bank. "Here?" the ferryman must have asked as a ramshackle row of houses came into view.

Mentmose shook his head and pointed further along the river. The oarsman tried to object, but Mentmose placed his hand on his dagger, and the boat picked up speed. Eventually, a row of uninviting mud brick buildings emerged, smoke twirling from patchy domed roofs. And everywhere, a petrifying stench of degradation and decay.

The ferryman's next comment wasn't difficult to translate. "Dear gods, please, not here."

Mentmose nodded as he pointed to the docks. The crew disembarked, but the warrior remained on the boat.

"Is he not coming with us?" Jared asked, having grown fond of the Medjay's close presence.

"He'll join us shortly," Tiya said.

Through the fog, Jared heard a muffled cry and a heavy splash. Mentmose returned, dragging the empty boat onto shore and wiping his dagger of blood. A splash of red covered his left leg, and seeing it, Jared picked up a ragged piece of cloth nearby and handed it to him. Mentmose smiled and wiped it free.

"No one must know we're here," was all Tiya offered.

"And where exactly is 'here'?"

"Embalmers' Row."

"For god's sake, why?" Derek asked, sounding not like a seasoned host but a package tourist who foolishly had wandered off the bus. "Worst episode ever."

"I used to live in the slums nearby. And my uncle is an embalmer. I've sent him lots of work, let's just say. He owes me."

Embalmers Row was a tangle of rotting alleyways and rounded paths that rose and fell like smallpox. Crumbling buildings fragmented to the touch, and the streets were half blocked by eroding brick mounds, as if eager to return to sand. Twice they got lost and had to start all over again.

"Been a while since I've visited," Tiya admitted. "He's not my favorite uncle."

Finally, they arrived at a cul-de-sac where an otherworldly mist hovered above an open courtyard.

"Good," Tiya said. "That means he's awake."

She banged on the door.

A shuffle, a clang of bolts, and two bleached fingers opened the gate a few wary inches. Inside, someone sneezed. The door opened a bit wider, and the crew slid inside. Only then, in the soft light of the courtyard, did they glimpse Ameni's face. Derek screamed. Kara clutched Ali's arm.

A sharp-faced jackal stared back at him, standing on its hind legs, with a long nose and huge pointed ears.

"Don't be alarmed," Tiya explained as Ameni lifted the mask to his forehead and revealed a ruddy, runny human face. "He must do this every time he soaks the bodies in salt. Part of the ritual."

Behind Uncle Ameni stretched a shallow pool of jaundiced liquid, broken by pyramids of powder. A few hands and toes poked through, the last drops of moisture being leached from the flesh. One poor soul had risen too far, and his open mouth and empty eye sockets bobbed up and down. Ameni sneezed again and bolted the door behind him.

"I see you're still allergic to all this," Tiya said first in her native tongue, then translated as Ameni continued.

"Damn natron burns the nose. You're as lovely as ever, but you never visit just to say hello. Last time it was to dispose of Ramses' royal fanbearer."

The two spoke hurriedly for a moment more, and this time, she didn't translate. It soon became apparent that Uncle Ameni was not as welcoming as Tiya had hoped. He kept shaking his head, and she kept adding new details.

Jared took the time to tour his surroundings and, for once, knew it was coming before it washed over him. He welcomed it like a leap into a lake on a hot summer's day.

Hori's sitting on a stone wall, watching a cloudless sky as several birds circle overhead. Before they can attack, he moves a pile of bodies, naked and stiff, through a wooden door. Several other bodies are stacked inside. All of them are immersed in salt, in various states of preservation, and on the other end, a long corridor leads to a stone room lined with slabs. There, several corpses are being carefully washed. The first awaits his attention. Hori picks up a long bronze poker, turns the dead man's face to one side, and shoves it deep up a nostril.

Jared opened his eyes, a smile bisecting his face. He not only felt this place, he *knew* it. He'd been here before. Down the hall, he was certain, were several rooms where corpses were laid out and the organs carefully removed. A small drain ran down its center to wash away blood and viscera. Beyond, in a courtyard open to the elements, the discarded organs would be stacked. The vultures he dreamt about were sleeping now on the cliffs but would return with the sun for a breakfast feast. A quick way to dispose of the waste.

I was no ancient serial killer or assassin. I was an embalmer.

Jared wanted to laugh, to tell everyone how wrong and terrified of the truth he had been. He was not a cruel killer but a man of science, of value. A man who dealt with death, but to bring comfort, not pain. Suddenly it all made sense, from the student film he made about funeral parlors, to his innate desire to listen to people who were hurting, eager to reminisce and share their story for posterity. His gift was helping not only the dead transition to their next chapter, but those they left behind. A bridge between worlds. And, just as Omm had suggested, the perfect candidate to take this journey for Mehy. He was a link, the rare person who could make the process seamless. The discovery hit him like granite: he hadn't changed as much as he imagined, was still a man driven not by brute strength but by empathy and logic. The only thing that happened was somewhere along the way, he lost sight of this gift. He couldn't stop laughing. One thing was now certain: with or without the rest of his team, he was going to finish the job he had been chosen for. He had been chosen not out of happenstance but for a reason. He wanted to tell Kara, tell everyone. But when he looked back at Tiya, she was arguing with Ameni.

At last, Tiya translated.

"He's worried that Ramses' men will find out. I told them it was just for the night. Mentmose wants to do the same to him as the ferryman, but I talked him out of it." She looked to the warrior. "For the moment."

She said a few more things and, Mentmose drawing nearer, Ameni relented. He pointed to a small shed outside.

"We can stay there. It's where new bodies are brought, but empty now. We'll hide the boat and leave before dawn."

Ameni returned to the body on the slab, and Jared inched closer to watch. The embalmer was in the process of removing an old lady's internal organs and stuffing them with fine linen rubbed in myrrh. He picked up a long poker similar to the one Jared had seen while swimming through the Osireion. But now he knew it was a surgical tool. The brain was the only organ the ancients felt was not worth preserving, so they would slide the poker up the nose, mash the brain to a pulp and discard it. Jared wanted to offer suggestions, especially after Ameni seemed too brusque with the poker: he was opening the nostril too widely and risked marring the face. Jared anticipated every move before Ameni made it. His fingers fidgeted as Ameni worked, urging him to slow down, hold it steady. Jared recalled his most terrifying flashback, the one where he sliced open the man's belly.

That's what I was doing, trying to save the slain pharaoh's soul, not kill him.

Jared moved closer as Ameni was doing a botched job of the right nostril. But before he could offer suggestions, Ameni sneezed and huddled closer to the corpse, blocking his view.

Jared understood. The embalmer was uneasy in a spectator's presence, as any craftsman would. Meticulously, Ameni unrolled an immeasurably long cord of linen, fifty feet at least, and began wrapping the woman from head to toe. When complete, he grabbed another roll and repeated the process twice more. Jared moved in for a better view, but Ameni sneezed again and slipped back under his mask, which seemed a polite way to say, get lost. Jared took the hint and joined the others in the hut out back. The space was small but thankfully freshly washed and lined with hay.

He approached Kara, who was clutching her lacquered box, absent-mindedly fiddling with one of the locks.

"I saw something," he said. "Something that helps me make sense of all this."

Kara didn't seem to be listening. Finally, she laid the box down and noticed Jared. "You heard what she said. It's impossible."

"Nothing is impossible. Look where we are."

"I need a break from looking. I'm so tired." She slipped the box under one of her scarves to act as a pillow. "How much time do we have, Tiya?"

"As long as we're gone before sunlight touches the Nile, we're fine. I'll wake you."

Kara crunched up her scarf and only then remembered what Jared had said. "Said you saw something? Tell me…" her eyes closed, and Jared let them stay that way. There would be enough time in the morning. A minute later, Ali, no doubt exhausted from holding a heavy pole aloft all day, was also snoring.

"Mentmose will keep watch by the river," Tiya said. "You should sleep too."

But try as he might, Jared couldn't get comfortable. He was wide-eyed with excitement at what he had learned. He was no outcast in his past life but someone with a honed skill that people relied on. For the first time in what seemed like millennia, Jared was proud of himself. He had value. He looked over at Tiya, who was also wide awake.

"You've discovered who you were," she said.

"I did."

"I can guess what it is."

He shut his eyes again, but sleep wouldn't come. When he sat up, he saw that Derek was staring back at him, equally restless.

"You okay?" Jared asked, a dumb question, but he could think of no other.

"This is all really happening, isn't it?"

"It is."

Derek shook his head, trying to wrap his head around something.

"What?" Jared asked.

"If that's true, then I really am the Great Explorer, Derek Dees."

"I suppose you are."

"Well, I'll be damned."

He went silent, but remained bolt-upright.

"You two want something to help you relax?" Tiya asked, equally wide-eyed. "Down the street is a bar I've often visited. Could use one myself."

"Is it safe?" Jared asked, the lure of a drink overriding logic.

"Patrons come to the Hippo's Jaw for anonymity."

"Why not? No way I'm sleeping. Derek?"

The host glanced at Kara and Ali, who were slobbering over their gear. Beyond them on the wall was a series of blades and pokers, none exactly clean.

"Beats spending the night in a house of horrors."

CHAPTER 19

The Hippo's Jaw was tucked away in an uninviting alley full of rats and shadows. Over a thousand years old and far from the feet of priests and kings, it had seen better days, indeed, better centuries. Instead of a sign, an enormous hippopotamus skull, mouth agape and boasting huge, sawn-off teeth, beckoned in the brave. A babel of languages, all sounding violently drunk, roared through the cracks.

"Dear lord, we're going in *there*?" Derek asked. "I'm actually feeling a bit drowsy now…" His last words were drowned out by Tiya's kick to the door.

Jared expected all conversation to stop, like in some Western film when the new guy shows up in Dodge. But no one batted an eye, and he was grateful for it. Never could he imagine a more frightening cast of cut throats. Men with lightning bolt scars from forehead to chin, thugs dressed in greasy, feathered headdresses, all shouting at one another or slumped over tables. One man covered in a greasy hood took particular interest in them, following them as they worked their way across the room. A faint grin marred his face.

Tiya found a table in the back and, brushing aside something moist and chunky—Jared refrained from asking—offered her guests a seat. As he took his place, Jared stole another glance at the hooded man, to see if he was still watching them.

He was.

A young woman appeared, not to take an order but to plop down three vaguely washed gourds. A string of something limp and grassy clung to one. Jared picked it out just before the woman ladled a mysterious liquid into each bowl.

"No menu, I guess?" Derek asked.

"Those haven't been invented yet," Tiya said. "I think it's the Greeks who do that. So logical and dull." Jared smiled. She sounded just like Omm. Then he realized she was Omm, sort of. In light of all he had seen, it was too much of a brain teaser to get his head around at this hour. But he did have one question he was dying to ask.

"How can you see the future, if—?"

"I live in the past? Remember, all of my future vessels share the same *ka,* but are fractured into several spirits. So, if I want, I can tap into their memories, their times."

"And they yours?"

"Only if I let them. I still lead. But none of us can get inside the other's head or know where we are at any given moment. Only that we are not receiving." She raised her bowl. "This is called 'Seth's Breath,' after the god of destruction. The magic is that it leaves no residue, so no heavy head tomorrow."

They gulped and winced, and within a flash, the woman was back, ladle in hand.

"She's working for a tip tonight," Derek said through a grimace.

"That doesn't come around until Tudor England. Another way for the privileged to feel better about themselves while doing as little as possible." Tiya placed her palms over the empty bowls, and the woman moved on. "Don't rush. Let it take hold." She leaned back. "So, I can assume neither of you believed Omm when she told you about all this."

"I thought she—you—was mad as a hatter," Derek said. "I'm still searching for signs that will reveal this to be a new Epcot Center attraction."

Behind him, someone vomited explosively over another customer, who took out a dagger and pinned the drunk man's hand to the table.

"You're not in Disney World, I assure you."

Tiya laughed, her face flush and her smile wide. The cocktail had smoothed the worry lines on her face, and for the first time, Jared saw how ravishing she was. No wonder a prince had fallen for her.

"This is the real Egypt," she went on. "Not the gilded temples of the elite. Billions of people just like this will come and go before you two are born and never leave a trace. My parents among them."

Jared remembered Omm's diary. "Is your father still alive somewhere?"

"That's why I still come here from time to time. I'm hoping to see him stumble through that door." The door opened, and a few Babylonians barged in. "Never has."

Jared glanced up and noticed that the hooded man was no longer at his table. He scanned the room, but he was gone. But somehow, Jared still felt eyes on him. "Do you think—"

The waitress returned with some loud demand. Sitting with an empty bowl must have meant you were denying a paying customer comfort. Seth's Breath was back in three ladles, even chunkier than the last. Tiya relented.

"Okay, one more, then home to bed. I see your eyes drooping."

Things went from a tingle to a sway.

"What's in here?" Derek muttered as he plucked something unidentifiable from his mouth—either a hard seed or a tooth.

"Trust me..." Tiya began.

"It's best not to know? Another question..."

"The bathroom?" Tiya guessed.

"Please don't tell me they won't be invented until the Crusades."

"We have closets with deep holes in them, but if you fall in like many have, no one will dare help you out." After he stumbled off, Tiya shook her head. "You sure he's up for this? He hasn't the strength of you."

Jared was touched by the comment. He couldn't help comparing everything he did to Derek. He was everything Jared wasn't: confident, cocky, popular, opinionated, and, when he wanted to be, immensely charming. Derek should naturally be leading this expedition, but so far—and much to Jared's surprise—he had failed to rally. "He's kind of a jerk," Jared admitted. "But he's part of the team. He's here because I asked him. So it's my job to keep him safe."

"You're too kind, Jared. Many here would just toss him to the crocodiles." Tiya took another sip. "Now Kara, I like. She's strong. You two a couple?"

Jared laughed. "No, no, just best of friends. I wouldn't have made it this far if it wasn't for her."

"She's grieving."

"A lost love she can't forget."

Tiya smiled sadly. "Good. She should never do that. In the end, our grief may be the only thing that keeps them alive."

She looked Jared over and seemed keen to change the subject.

"I'll talk to her again in the morning," Jared said. "She'll come around. Maybe Ali, too. He wants to help but has too much invested in his current world." He took a tiny sip. "If they don't, you get them safely back to Omm, and we will do it ourselves."

Tiya shook her head. "We need the camera and all those things."

"I know how to work a camera well enough and clip microphones on people. I'll do that. You just translate the *Book of Gates.*"

"We'll discuss it in the morning. I also need a moment's break from it all." Tiya looked Jared over and grinned. "What about you? Like Ali and Kara, is there someone you're living for? A woman back home?"

Jared wanted to talk about his recent discovery but then realized talking about his other secret was more inviting. And to ignore the question was another evasion, and he had come to loathe evasions.

"I'm gay. A few men here and there, but nothing serious."

It felt good to say it until he turned to the far end of the bar, where Derek was working his way through the crowd, hands in the air like touch alone could kill him.

Tiya picked up on Jared's nervousness.

"Why hide it? Especially from a jester like him? No one here does. In fact, there's not even a word for 'gay' yet."

"Certainly it exists?"

"Oh yes," she smiled. "Have you heard of Khnumhotep and Niankhkhnum?"

"As a matter of fact, Omm mentioned them to me on our first call."

"Before you fly home, visit their tomb in Saqqara. It still exists in your time and is beautiful. Two men who were buried together as royal confidantes. Happily arm in arm, in every relief. One panel even shows them kissing. Two of the most powerful men of their day and madly, openly in love." She looked to the door and smiled. "And Mentmose, of course, he's gay. Thinks you're sexy too."

"He is? And he said that? All that… man?"

Tiya laughed. "Only your times link sexual attraction to gender."

"Maybe I should just stay here, not go back," Jared said, only half-joking.

Here he was respected in a land that greatly valued his skills, and he now learned a man who could love whom he desired. He wondered for the first time about Omm's proposition during that same first call.

If you like it here, we can make it last forever.

"Maybe you should. I know a way you can. Visit Mentmose any time you choose. You do like him back, am I right?" But before Jared could answer, an Indiana Jones hat butted in.

"I never felt better," Derek announced through pearly whites. "I love this drink." He sensed they were deep in some private conversation. "So what are we talkin' about?"

"Just that life is short," Tiya said, waving her hand over the bar. "A blink of an eye and all this is over. Every act of love on display tonight, every promise, every promise, and every heartbreak will disappear without leaving a record. In that way, even grief, however painful, is better than not living."

For the first time, and to his great embarrassment, Jared realized Tiya was more than some ancient guide who only existed to help them in their quest. She was as flesh and blood as the rest of them, her feeling over Mehy's death still raw.

"You must love him very much."

"Deeply and eternally."

"How did he die again?" Derek asked, revealing he never bothered to read the memoir.

"Not now, Derek," Jared said. "We need to finish up and get out of here."

Again he scanned the room. The hooded man was back, this time doing a lousy job of ignoring them. Jared watched for a moment until the man made eye contact, held it a beat too long, and nervously walked away. Could this be a gay bar? He shook his head; he had seen how men cruise, and whatever it was, sex was not on the stranger's mind.

Tiya must have noted his worry. "Yes, another minute, and let's go. And it's fine. I like talking about him, especially now, when I don't know where he is. We were in Canaan to quell a rebellion. The campaign was a success, but on the way home, one of Mehy's generals suggested a shorter route. That meant traveling through a narrow pass that only a few months earlier would have been dangerous. The general convinced Mehy it was free of rebels." She swallowed the final word.

"I'm guessing it wasn't?" Jared asked.

"No, it was. But it wasn't free of Ramses' men, who, one night while we rested, overcame us." She shook her head at some horrible memory. "It was a massacre. They flooded down from the hills. Mehy's best soldiers were cut down, and soon the assassins were in our tent. They were dressed like Philistines, but as one came toward us and Mehy sliced his belly, he begged for mercy in Egyptian."

Jared listened but was anxious to leave. He felt something dark was happening out front. He looked at Tiya, wanting to interrupt, but her eyes were lined with tears, and besides, if she wasn't worried, why should he be? For once, live in the moment without fear, he scolded himself.

"It became clear that it wasn't Mehy they were after," Tiya continued. "Ramses knew better than to kill his brother directly. It was me and my baby, they were after. Two more men came at me so fast that Mehy, whose sword was still in the body of the first assassin, jumped unarmed in front of me, not to attack but to shield me."

She went silent.

"What happened?" Derek asked softly, finally interested in Tiya's story.

"He began to rot, and in the end, he was no longer a prince, just a young man who very much did not want to die. I don't think he ever let go of my hand the entire time. I made a promise that I would devote my days to one goal: preserve Mehy's name for all time. And he, in turn, promised to speak to the gods and find a way to safeguard me so I, too, would somehow live on." Her tears flowed easier now. "Even at the end, his last thoughts were of me."

The waitress returned, and Tiya brushed her away.

"With Seti's blessing, I secretly arranged for the creation of a hidden tomb in Abydos, where Ramses never visited. When it came time for the funeral, Mehy's mummy was swapped with that of a commoner, who was buried in the royal crypt. And his real body went to the Osireion."

"That worked?" Derek asked.

"Until a few days ago."

"And the child?"

"A boy. Born in secrecy, and quickly smuggled out of Egypt to Knossos. I hope to see him again after all of this is over." She sighed. "Truth is, Jared, I've grown tired."

A loud bang at the door made them all jump. Mentmose barged in and, with a swift motion, bolted across the room and sliced the neck of the man who had been watching them. No one batted an eye. The Medjay then headed towards Tiya with alarming speed and whispered something in her ear that made her eyes go wide.

"What?" Jared asked.

"My uncle sold us out," Tiya said with genuine alarm. "They've taken Ali and Kara."

"What do you mean 'taken'?"

"Just as I said, everything. The two of them were carried away on boats with their camera gear, everything. Only this was left behind." She handed Jared the lacquered box. "Now they're coming for us." Her attention shifted to the front door, where two soldiers now stood. "Out the back." The four dashed toward the rear of the bar and into a narrow alley that twisted in opposite directions. At either end, the silhouettes of soldiers blocked the way. On the roof rested two others, each with arrows drawn.

One soldier approached and shouted something at Tiya. "Stay back. Let me speak to them," she said. "Seti is still alive, and I'm part of his royal entourage, so they can't harm me." She moved forward, hands up, silently commanding the men to stop. After she smiled and grandly said something that was meant to placate, the soldier moved forward and sliced off her left arm at the wrist. Arrows rained down, and as she fell to her knees, another soldier went for her neck.

Before Jared had a chance to scream, Mentmose plunged his dagger into an advancing soldier and grabbed his shield. He placed it above Jared and Derek and charged with great force into the assailants. One arm held Jared tight. But as he ran, Jared slipped on something wet and nearly fell. Mentmose kicked Tiya's severed head out of the way, and the three continued on.

CALL SHEET

EPISODE 37: MAGICAL MISTRESS OF THE NILE

Shoot dates: Egypt, April 9-16th

Sunrise: 6 AM/ Sunset: 6 PM. Weather: 97 degrees and sunny

DAY 3

Scene 1: Hippo Hunt with Ramses the Great 5AM-6 AM pack light for water travel

Scene 2: Tour of Holy of Holies 6 AM- 8 AM Scout only; cameras not needed

Scene 3: Master interview Ramses the Great 12 PM -2 PM Sit down. Host not needed.

Scene 4: Seti Funeral and burial 5- 6PM Note: Must be in place by 5.45 PM

Scene 5: Enter the underworld 6 PM Details to come

Dinner: TBD

CHAPTER 20

Omm gasped as her knees turned to sand. Said caught her before she struck the temple floor.

"I knew this was too much," he shouted as he moved her to the severed pillar. "I'll get the village doctor. Just breathe."

"No, love, it's not my heart. Help me to the portal. Something's gone wrong."

Said knew better than to ask questions. Carefully, he guided her to the rear of the temple where the wall, solid and dim, revealed no hint of trouble.

"Let's go fetch the doctor. You said yourself that if you're not here to open the gate, they'll be stuck. No good if you're dead."

She leaned on her cane with both hands. "It's not me. It's Tiya. Something's happened to her. Something that shouldn't have until the task is complete."

Said held her upright as she began to sway. "What?"

"I can't reach her to ask. It's a blank. Stand back and mind that I don't fall."

The wall swirled, and the years raced by in reverse. Finally, they sputtered and stopped, and even Said, a few feet back, nearly lost his footing. Where once would be Tiya, guarding the gate as she had always done, now loomed a group of armed soldiers. Their backs were to the false door, which meant they couldn't yet see Omm. But on their knees, several masons were building a sandstone wall over the entrance. Two fitted boulders were in place while two others were swiftly plastered over them. One poor laborer saw Omm and, terrified, pretended he hadn't.

"Who are they?" Said moved closer and gripped Omm by the elbow.

"Ramses' men."

"What does it mean?"

"It means he's onto us. And Tiya and I are no longer connected." Omm's eyebrows dipped in the middle. "I can already feel her protection slipping away. Back to the pillar, must have a think."

The events of the past few days had made Omm feel depressingly mortal. Her gnarled hands and feet ached. Her heart had taken a beating in the fall, and the cut on her head was far from healed. Things were not snapping into view like they used to. But as long as she had Mehy's protection and his love, her aches were always minor, and her one-time maladies, from bad eyesight to a dodgy spine, were kept at bay. Now, with both of them silent, it was as if her entire body was reacting to some new poison. She had lost the love of her life a second time, something no one should endure.

Sitting next to her, Said must have noticed the shift.

"It's you I'm worried about, not Tiya. You look dreadful."

"I've not been kind to this vessel of mine recently, I must confess. I only need it a bit longer." She waved the thought away as if a fly. "But I don't understand. Tiya always dies the same way at exactly the same time. Nothing about it can be, or ever has been, altered, not in three millennia. Mehy's pact with the gods ensured it."

"How is she supposed to die?"

"She's to be killed by Ramses' men upon his coronation, several months after Seti's burial, struck down as she tried to flee the country to be with her son. But only after her first replacement was in place."

Said scrutinized the gray wall before him. "If Seti's not dead yet, there's still hope. I'll tear down the wall so you can summon him. Wait while I get my hammer."

"Without Tiya, it'll be a waste. Everything springs from her. You need someone on the other side to invite you in. And Ramses knows that, which is why he's walling it up."

Said rubbed his thinning hair, confused by all the news. "Which means?"

"He must suspect what Jared is planning and is willing to alter history to stop him. We must seek out another door, and another *ka,* so Jared and his crew have a place they can return through. Before I... "

"Before you *what?*"

A small sparrow flew down from the rafters and sat between them. Omm raised a shaking finger, and it hopped on board.

"No time to discuss it now. We must hurry."

Said rubbed his head again, a beat behind. "Is such a thing even possible, finding another way in?"

"In theory, yes." Omm's voice was weak, and it took her a moment to formulate her words and get them all out. "Egypt is full of false doors. I'm just not sure which are still active or still have someone on the other side willing to help."

What she didn't share with Said was that, without Mehy's protection, her body would swiftly break down as it became fully mortal again. Whatever maladies were held at bay would come roaring back.

Said handed her the bottle again. "Drink. You've gone green." This time she did. "So where do we look?"

The sane answer was that they shouldn't, that it was already too late and sending Jared in was a grave mistake. Without Tiya's protection, he didn't stand a chance. But Omm always dismissed sanity as common and predictable.

"I recall a few doors we can visit. Mehy showed them to me on our trips together. But my lord, it's been a spell."

"Can you at least recall where?"

She polished off the water, and it did her good. "One of the pyramids up north. Not sure which."

Said laughed darkly. "Forget it, then. There are over fifty, they're a hundred miles away, and we have half a day."

"Then we best make a start." Omm reached for her cane but couldn't find it. She looked around and saw only shadows. "Who's taken it?" she snapped at Said, a rare outburst. "I left it right here!"

Said gently fetched it from a few inches away and placed it in her hand. Omm remained quiet, doing her best to raise herself up without Said catching on that she could no longer see a blessed thing.

CHAPTER 21

Rimming the western cliffs, where the tombs of the pharaohs ended and the Great Desert began, rose a series of rock-hewn towers more desolate than the peaks themselves. There were ten in total, all boasting a bird's-eye view of the Valley of the Kings below. In each outpost stood a solitary Medjay warrior, shield and spear in hand. These mercenaries were brought from Nubia, where they had trained since birth to become fearless assassins. Now, they were the last line of defense between a dead king's treasure and those who might want the gold for themselves. Beyond these sentries, the only living things to call this wasteland home were vultures and mountain lions. No one would be foolish enough to visit one of these towers without just cause, so it was the perfect place for Jared and Derek to hold up until they figured out their next move.

Mentmose, who had been chief of the necropolis police for twenty years, brought them here as soon as they escaped Ramses's men. But this place could only be a temporary safe house. It wouldn't be long before they were found: where else would a Medjay hide but in a Medjay guard house? They had a day, maybe two.

From atop the tower, Jared scanned the valley below. From this vantage point, he could see beyond the darkened necropolis and the Nile to the holy city on the eastern shore. At the far northern end, the sacred temple complex of Karnak glowed in the moonlight.

Jared had barely uttered a word since Tiya had been cut down. What could he possibly say? His protector and guide, the only one here who believed in him and the only one who could translate the *Book of the Gates*, had been chopped in two. How was that even possible? Wasn't history fixed? Did Jared's arrival here cause a Butterfly Effect that would change everything that came after? Including his own future life and death? He had no idea.

Far more troubling was the fate of Kara and Ali. They had been taken away and, for all he knew, were already dead. Jared cursed himself for his premature bravado earlier that night when he congratulated himself for being valued and a man of worth. What bullshit. Three thousand years ago, he was a mortician to the elite. How did that solve his problem now?

He had at least regained enough understanding of ancient Egyptian to converse with Mentmose and ask how royally screwed they really were. His first questions were not about himself.

"Could we try to rescue them?" he asked the Medjay, who fixed his stare on the horizon and appeared anxious.

"Impossible," is all the Medjay said. "Ramses."

"Where might he be holding them?"

Mentmose shrugged. "Many palaces dot the Nile, all heavily guarded. They could be in Memphis by now."

It took Jared a moment to brave the next question. "Will he kill them?"

Mentmose nodded. "Certainly. But only after he tortures them to seek our whereabouts."

The absolute worst had happened. Jared had failed to protect Kara after all she had done for him. And deepening his defeat, he could do nothing for Derek, who cowered on the other end of the tower in shock since they fled the Hippo's Jaw. Everything had fallen apart. With Tiya dead, escaping through the underworld was no longer an option. On his own, Jared knew he'd never be able to understand the hieroglyphics. Forget about being judged in the Ninth Gate on the scale of justice. He and Derek would be torn apart by Apep as soon as they crossed into the Duat.

Mentmose shifted his gaze to cliffs on the far side of the tower, seemingly waiting for someone to appear. Not Ramses and his men. They would come from the east, where the town lay. The Medjay hurriedly lit a small cauldron and grabbed a silver shield, polished to a reflective glare. He moved it near the flame and wiggled it back and forth as Jared wondered what form of tribal magic he was trying to conjure up. Maybe he was seeking help from his ancestral gods in Nubia. Nothing happened, so he did it twice more, each time scanning the blackened desert bluffs for something that never came. "So that's it," Jared concluded. Even the gods and their magic never existed. He had traveled back to find that the ancient Egyptians were just as alone and forsaken as he was in Sunday school class back in Kansas. No one was out there.

Then, Mentmose's flash produced a response. Someone, perhaps in another tower, repeated his actions. Two flashes, a pause, then another. So it wasn't magic or mysticism that Mentmose was performing; it was an earthly signal of some kind. When it stopped, Jared asked Mentmose to translate.

"Ramses' men are looking everywhere for us. The necropolis is unsafe."

This at least answered one question–even if Jared wanted to try his luck in the Duat, there was no getting there.

"Abydos?" Jared asked, hoping the false door was still in use, and Omm still waiting on the other side.

"Let me ask."

Mentmose returned to his cauldron and signaled his unseen friends. A long series of bolts and flashes followed. The Medjay shook his head and translated.

"Abydos is guarded, too, since that's where you first appeared." He grew still for a moment before adding, sadly, "Doesn't matter. Without Tiya, there's no one to open this side."

From behind them, Derek began to sob. Whatever strength he had clung to during their escape had vanished, and he was reduced to a terrified man sentenced to die a million years and miles from home. All his dreams and desires were snuffed out without a trace. He was no Great Explorer and never would be.

Jared also wanted to cry, to at last give up and accept his fate. Forever the zero, never the hero. He looked back at Mentmose and asked without hope. "Is there anything we can do?"

Mentmose gestured out to the Great Desert. "We can get you to the Meshwesh."

It was a term Jared had never heard. "The who?"

"Meshwesh nomads. They live in the Great Desert. Beyond the reach of Ramses and his men."

"So, they can get us home?"

Mentmose shook his head.

"Jared, I'm sorry, but there is no going home. But I know them, and they are good people. They invite you both to live out your days as herdsmen until Ramses dies. Then you can return here to the comfort of Thebes."

"And how long is that?" Derek asked from the shadows.

"Only the gods know," Mentmose said.

"Or someone from the future," Jared said to himself. He turned to Derek and sighed. "He rules for the next sixty-six years."

Derek began to weep loudly, and Jared could find nothing to say or do to comfort him. He had failed spectacularly. Two of his crew were either dead or soon to be, and he and Derek cursed to live their lives in tents as Saharan fugitives, always afraid each day could be their last.

He couldn't bear to sit still and watch his colleague sob. He paced for several minutes and stared into the abyss. Finally, he peered down a set of twisting stairs, where a small room was illuminated by flickering light.

"What's down there?" he asked Mentmose.

"My bed. Nothing much to see."

Jared glanced over at Derek, who had somehow managed to fall asleep, his fedora over his head as if offering some protection for the hell he had found himself in. Jared worked his way down the stone staircase to find himself in a modest room with a few blankets on the floor, random shields and weapons hanging on the wall, and a tiny oil lamp casting long shadows. It was a bland space, bereft of the power of a man so accomplished as Mentmose. It also looked very lonely.

He heard a creak on the stairs behind him, and Mentmose appeared. He laid his spear against the wall but struggled to take his breastplate off. Jared imagined he must be exhausted, considering all he had done to get them here. He helped pull the plate over Mentmose's huge shoulders. As he did, he noticed a gash running along the seam—a knife wound that two inches higher would have severed his throat.

"You're still bleeding," Jared said. "Anything to clean the wound?" He looked around, and his instinct for science and anatomy kicked in. A few small cups of lotions were on the wall. Honey and goose fat. Another cup contained puffs of lint, and this he knew would stem the bleeding. "Sit. Let me get the gunk out there."

Mentmose said nothing. He sat cross-legged on the blanket, close to Jared. The wound was long but not deep, and as Jared made his way across it with a wet cloth, he took in Mentmose's body. His shoulders burst with muscle, and his coiled locks, now that he was close, were treated with sesame oil to keep it shiny and clean. So he was aware and proud of his looks, Jared thought with a smile. He moved in closer to pluck some dirt from the wound, and the men were now face to face. Mentmose looked him in the eyes, but it was Jared who made the first move. He kissed the warrior firmly on the lips, knowing Derek could walk in at any time.

"To hell with him," Jared thought. "We may all be dead by dawn."

He ran his hand across Mentmose's chest and pulled him down to the bed, legs now entwined. Jared flipped Mentmose on his back, and his hands moved toward his buckle. The warrior let him—only stopping long enough to extinguish the flame. Should the host on the tower come looking for them, they may at least have time to slide their trousers back on.

As the first crack of light entered the tower, Mentmose was already up. Still naked, he woke Jared with a kiss and rose to slip back into his breastplate.

"I need to send another signal. Then we make a plan."

Jared watched him rise, noticing a scratch on Mentmose's ass that wasn't there last night. Despite all that had happened and was surely about to, he smiled.

At the top of the tower, Derek was still sleeping in the same position as the night before. He gave him a few more minutes of peace while Mentmose scanned the horizon.

"See anything?" Jared asked.

"No, surprisingly. Maybe since I killed all the attackers, there was no one left to identify me." He chuckled. "And to Egyptians, all we Nubian warriors look alike."

"Does that mean we're in the clear?"

"No, it just means we have perhaps another day to hide. Tiya is dead, and someone will connect that with me soon enough."

The men slipped into quiet contemplation. Jared wanted to kiss Mentmose again, but in the glare of the daylight and with Derek nearby, fear had returned.

"Safe for the moment. You can stay here with me. We will go into the Nubian desert together," Mentmose said in Egyptian, which Jared could understand and Derek could not.

"What about Derek?"

Mentmose shrugged. "He is not a good person. He can find his own way." He glanced over and sighed. "I'll see that he is safely taken care of. Get him out of the country, to Babylon. It's full of clowns and charlatans. Fit right in."

"And Kara and Ali?"

"We can look, but I fear it's already too late. Tiya tells me you lived here before. I don't follow the gods of Egypt, so I don't understand all that. My gods abandoned us long ago, which is why I sell my skills to the highest bidder. Right now, that's Egypt. But we could go south to the oasis, beyond the laws, and live without fear."

"Is that where your family is?" Jared realized he didn't know a thing about Mentmose beyond what he had seen in action.

Mentmose shook his head. "No, they are all gone. Either killed by the Egyptians in battle or fled deeper into the desert and disappeared. We Medjay only stay because we have nowhere better to go." He caressed Jared's knee while his other hand cradled his neck.

"If you stayed too, that would change."

Jared had to admit the thought had crossed his mind. Who was he back home but a nobody kid smiling at people who he'd much rather punch in the face? Is this what the dreams were telling him? Come here, find true love from a man who would protect him until the end of time. Forget the future by returning to the past. It was a tantalizing offer, one that would solve all his problems. But then his thoughts turned again, first to his crew, who would not want to spend their final days here, and to the man he truly loved and wanted to hold for eternity. As gorgeous and brave as he was, that man was not Mentmose. That man was a thousand miles away and three thousand years in the future, at a little tourist center in downtown Seville.

Jared turned from the desert and looked in the opposite direction, across the Nile and to the smokey streets of Karnak. It was only then he remembered something Tiya had said. At first, he discounted it, but then realized it was their only hope of returning home to the world he could still change, with or without Kara and Ali.

"Is Seti still pharaoh? Does he still live?"

"He does." The Medjay gestured to the city below. "We will know when he dies. All of Egypt will stop and mourn."

Jared remained still another minute, trying to locate the strength he so had briefly clung to earlier that evening. It was still there, faint and frayed, but close enough where he could snag a slender thread. He gently took the warrior's hand. "Then thank you, Mentmose, for your kind offer. It's very tempting, but I'm sorry, I have another plan."

"Do you?" Mentmose asked, sounding a bit hurt.

He was going to say more, but a noise behind them shut his mouth.

"What are you guys talking about?" Derek said, standing with a stretch. A recollection overcame him. "Dear God, did last night really happen?"

Jared let go of Mentmose's hand and turned to his host. "It did. But don't worry, I got an idea to get us home."

Derek picked up his hat, but before putting it on, he saw something inside and gave it a shake. A scorpion fell out.

"How will you do that?"

His voice was no longer challenging but hopeful and pleading.

"I just need you to follow my lead, regardless of where it goes. And know that it's still more than likely we may die trying. Are you willing to do all that?"

Derek had no follow-up. He only stood and, after a moment's thought, placed his hat on his head.

"I am."

"Mentmose, can you take us back to town?"

"Is not safe. Where? When?"

"After dark." Jared pointed to the holy temples at Karnak. "In the center of that. The Holy of Holies."

CHAPTER 22

"Who are you to boss me around like that?" Kara asked the smug official pressing a spear tip to her face. "We're here at the behest of Seti, son of Re. He invited us as his honored guests. You got issues with that. Take it up with the gods."

"The man in which thou speaks has just crossed over. Tis Ramses who leads." The official somehow spoke English, albeit old English, which made the encounter feel like something out of the Salem Witch Trials. It also suggested it wasn't only Seti who knew about the time slip. Ramses knew about it too. It had just been a while since he used it.

"I am Nehi, the vizier of Lower Egypt, and tis my duty to interrogate and execute thee."

"What the hell's a vizier? I'm not talkin' to some middle management lackey named after a lousy soft drink." Kara had lost everything: Jared, Lynette, her ashes, and, it now seemed, the hope of ever being reunited with any of them. She knew it was only a matter of time before she said or did the wrong thing. If Jared was here, he might step in and calm her down. But he wasn't; she had failed to protect him, and she could only hope that Tiya was taking good care of him.

"A vizier is second in command of all the Nile to do the pharaoh's political duties," Nehi said with pride. "I conduct state affairs while he consults with the deities."

Few things annoyed Kara more than politics. A bunch of privileged jackasses making up stupid titles for themselves. All she knew was that if Seti was dead, that meant the gates were about to open, and that was their only way out of here. She didn't care so much about her own fate, but Ali stood next to her, clearly terrified. And until she heard otherwise, she would assume that Jared and Derek were still alive. Now was not the time to give up.

"Then we must be released," she announced. "Seti brought us here to document his passing. You got no right to delay us."

Kara tried to rise, but Nehi halted her with his weapon. He waved it first towards Kara and then Ali, who was still recovering from a head wound. A raw cut ran down his forehead, the result of a kick he received for shielding Kara from attack when they were captured. Another cut zig-zagged along his hand from the punch he gave the traitorous Uncle Ameni, who sold them out.

Ali clutched his phone, useless since the moment they crossed into the past, but held high as if he'd find full bars at any moment.

Nehi waved his spear over the film gear.

"Thee Son of Re demands explanation."

Kara wasn't sure how much Ramses knew, but a few things soon became obvious. Jared and Derek were still at large, as the vizier kept asking where they might be. Good, Tiya will guide them through the underworld and back home. And their true purpose for being here, to travel the twelve gates and restore Mehy's name, remained a secret. So Kara did something uncharacteristic, if not for her sake, then for Ali. She chose her words carefully.

"You guys lead a sheltered life if you don't recognize these. They're magic boxes from the future, where chosen souls never die. Seti has asked us to capture his final days, so they may be placed in the tomb and his achievements celebrated for all times."

Nehi translated to someone watching from a wooden balcony hidden behind wooden slates. Kara assumed it could only be Ramses himself. At last, the hidden figure spoke, and his minion translated.

"Thee Son of Re demands demonstration."

"To do that, we need to stand up. Your boy here gonna at least let us do that?"

"Should we be talking to them like that?" Ali had slipped his phone away and was now fully present.

"All I know is that weakness never works. To impress them, we gotta act as full of ourselves as they are."

A sharp command from behind the balcony and the two were escorted to the gear.

"Want to do the whole thing again? Wires, sound mixer, boom?" Ali asked, wiping blood from his face. "I'm not sure he cares about sound quality."

Kara tore a page off the call sheet, folded it, and used gaffer tape to adhere it to Ali's forehead.

"You sure you're okay, buddy? Looks nasty."

"A small wound. We have bigger problems."

"Let's use it all. The weirder we seem, the better our story. Like two cheap *Star Trek* villains from some bad-ass planet." Equipment was slung over their shoulders and they powered up. "We need a subject to shoot," Kara said, not to the soldier but to Ramses.

Let Vizier Nehi know she recognizes where the real power rested. After a moment, a door opened, and the figure made his way into the light.

Ramses appeared precisely as Kara expected: proud, bare-chested, and preening, another man wallowing in power he had never earned. He was also extremely short. To overcompensate, he was freshly shaved and oiled, his biceps flexing as if clutching invisible barbells. Ramses reminded Kara of some of the guys at her neighborhood Gold's Gym, grunting loudly and never bothering to re-rack the weights. On closer inspection, she also noted how much he was like Yul Brynner's portrayal of him thirty centuries later. Tiya had mentioned that visitors occasionally came from the present. Could Yul have used Seti's door for research? Or did all ancient assholes act the same?

Ramses pointed to the camera and said something that needed no translation.

"Where we come from," Kara began. "What we put in this box will be seen by billions of people. It replaces the need for tombs and mummies. What I fit in here lives forever in the eyes of the gods."

She was laying it on thick—*Ancient Encounters* ratings had plummeted almost fifty percent in the last year, and more people got their information from TikTok than cable TV—but, as she saw it, it was their only way out of here.

"Future generations will watch this over and over and marvel that such a great man as your father walked the earth."

"Demonstrate," Nehi ordered as he moved closer for a better view.

Kara raised a hand in mock disgust. "Only a god king's *ka* can be preserved within the magic box. Nothing lowborn. It will break the box."

Ramses seemed pleased with this answer. He strutted closer. "Show now me you," he ordered in crucified English.

Soon the same tutorial that Kara conducted for Seti was repeated for his son. Ramses snorted with pride when he saw his image and demanded Kara do it two more times. An idea had come to Kara, one that might not save her and Ali, but possibly the rest of the crew. *Stall.* Give them more time to get to the tomb before the gates open. Without the camera, Jared wouldn't be able to make a film, but he might live.

"Let us do for you what we did for your father. Capture your great deeds so that they may be venerated for all time."

She spoke haughtily as if she was in one of those crappy old Biblical movies her mother used to watch. (Like *Ben Hur,* maybe, which she always thought would be a great name for a drag queen.)

She wasn't sure if that made it more authentic, but it seemed to get her in the spirit. A brief discussion in ancient Egyptian followed, and it was clear her efforts had paid off.

"We do it here, now," Nehi barked. "Put thy pharaoh in ye magic box."

"Here? You insult your lord. We must show him in his glory."

"There be no time. Seti has died, and Ramses must be present to assume the crook and flail. Even now, his body is being readied for the tomb."

"Then we got no time for even this," Kara said, turning from Nehi and bowing before Ramses. "The box will only work if it's placed in Seti's tomb before he travels to the du wop, as it was he who conjured it up."

It was a lame-ass lie *and dear god were those even the right words?*

Jared knew the history, not her. She had little interest in remembering the past—it was littered with people who tried to judge and bully her and, in one case, love her. And see how that turned out.

"We'll gladly do for you what we did for your father, but certainly not here, and only if the magic box is placed in his tomb afterwards."

"Impossible," Nehi concluded.

"Then Ramses' images will fade forever, as will his holy fathers. Is that how he wants to treat the man who passed on his cook and flair?"

"Crook and Flail," Ali whispered.

"Flail. Both are too great for such an end," Kara said this with the same confidence she displayed in her hallway of the McKinley Homes when the Ryan twins tried to shake her down for cash.

After some back and forth between minion and master, it was decided the funeral could be delayed a few hours so they could make a film befitting a god king. Seti would certainly not mind; after all, it was his final wish.

"Ramses decrees that you will follow him, watch him battle the great enemies of Egypt with his bare hands, so that all may see his eternal strength. Gather thy magic boxes."

The two hurriedly packed up their gear and whispered while Ramses berated his minion for ineptitude.

Kara moved closer to Ali, who had his phone back out. "You gotta let go of the phone. No one's on the other end. Sorry man, but it's just me and you."

"I know, I know." He seemed to be fighting back tears. "It just dawned on me that my entire relationship with my family has been through this tiny device. That's probably how they'll picture long after I'm gone. When I was at home, there wasn't one call I wouldn't immediately take, not one text I ignored until later. The only time I really talked to them was when I was on the road. Now, all I want to do is say goodbye, and it's been taken from me."

"Hey, don't give up. There's always a chance. Omm and Tiya are still out there, and so is Jared. They may come for us yet."

"You're right. Anything is possible."

Ali slipped on his headphones as a slight smile crossed his face.

"It dazzles me that Ramses bought your story. There's more bullshit in it than a matador's ring."

CHAPTER 23

Jared crept silently along the Avenue of the Sphinxes. Most commoners would be drawn and quartered for approaching the outer gates of Karnak temple, where only high priests were worthy to tread. But Jared's plan went much further: his mission, with Mentmose's reluctant help, was simple. They must breach the temple's innermost chamber, the Holy of Holies, where they kept the *Book of Gates*. As a Medjay policeman for Seti, Mentmose knew about a secret passage that existed halfway down the wall that allowed dignitaries to slip into the temple quickly in times of trouble. He agreed to take Jared and Derek there, but no further. This was the home of the gods, after all, who might strike him down the moment he entered their domain. Jared felt terrible asking even this of him: he knew Mentmose was a lonely, kind man, who seemed hurt by Jared's rejection to stay with him as his lover. If Jared didn't already have a future, he could easily imagine a blissful life here. Make love under the shade of an oasis palm with the most gorgeous man he had ever laid eyes on, wrapped in his protective arms. Mentmose was a fantasy come true. Trouble was, Jared was tired of living in fantasy worlds.

He instead focused only on the task ahead. His discovery of his past had allowed more memories to resurface, and he could visualize the layout inside the temple. As a royal embalmer, he must have spent time there. What it didn't promise was the courage to see it through. Embalmers worked with those already dead and were known for their skill and precision. Bravery was not required.

The legion of ram-headed sphinxes halted beneath a colossus of Amun-Re, the sun god who ruled over Thebes. Jared slung his backpack, empty except for the lacquered box, over his shoulder and averted his gaze. What would the Great Creator make of these lowly commoners befouling Egypt's most sacred site to steal its most holy relic? No time to dwell.

Ahead rose an imposing cedar door, corbelled in lapis lazuli and protected by four guards, javelins in hand. The three intruders slipped into the twilight and worked their way around the side of the temple. Jared heard the gentle gurgle of a nearby canal as it joined the Nile and, further off, the chant of a crazed prophet ranting along the riverbank, but otherwise the place seemed forsaken. Perhaps priests assumed that no one would be foolish enough to venture this close, and certainly not someone hoping to penetrate the Holy of Holies.

"There are guards everywhere," Derek whimpered. "We'll be dead before we find the passage."

Jared did his best not to shout. "Got a better idea? Got one *single* better idea?"

"No."

"Then stay quiet and follow me."

Since Tiya's death, Derek had become useless. Whatever resolve he had walking through the door was now eclipsed by fear and worry. Without the spotlight, Derek was more a hindrance than a host. It wasn't as if Jared wasn't afraid. As he inched forward, he kept reminding himself to breathe. But it was almost as if, without Kara's camera, the two men's personae had swapped.

Mentmose kept halting, scrutinizing the wall, searching for the secret passage. He pointed to the night sky and shrugged, pantomime for, "I've never done this in the dark."

They moved forward, scurrying around cauldrons of glowing frankincense that left quivering shadows along the wall. Mentmose stopped again and scratched his chin.

"Anything? Jared asked.

The Medjay gazed up and down, then behind him. He was obviously disoriented.

"What are we looking for exactly?"

Jared pantomimed, pointing from his eyes to the wall and shrugging.

Mentmose cupped a hand over his crotch and then made a cutting motion with his dagger.

"Dear God, what the hell does that mean?" Derek said. "We're getting castrated if we go inside?"

"No, it means to look for images of severed penises."

"Plummer. What the hell?"

"It was a common relief in Seti's day. After a battle was won, the victors would slice off the penises of the vanquished to count the dead."

"Penises?" was all Derek could respond. He gazed at the long wall stretching ahead of him. "What the hell do ancient Egyptian dicks look like?"

Having just seen one, Jared was about the offer details, then caught himself.

"I suspect a lot like ours."

Mentmose shot them a harsh glare to stay quiet. He moved ahead, beyond a panel of charioteers and horses, until the mammoth pile appeared.

"That? They look more like writhing worms than penises," Derek said after moving closer for a better view.

Mentmose said nothing, knowing words would only get them caught. Instead, he felt along the seams of two boulders, seeking a break. Nothing. He moved beneath a carving of some long-dead king discharging arrows and still no secret door.

Far ahead, where a guard post was built into the temple, another sentry emerged. Jared dipped behind a fallen chunk of limestone and hid from the moon, which had emerged from clouds and seemed to light up all of Karnak. The guard moved no further than the nearest cauldron. After a furtive glance around, he leaned his spear along the wall, lit a basalt pipe, and raised it to his mouth. A brief glow illuminated a foul face, war paint splattered across a ravaged forehead. One eye had been erased by a diagonal scar that snarled at the lip. His remaining eye appeared more troubled than fierce as he took a long, satisfying drag and relaxed. Jared relaxed as well. However cruel he might be, the fog of opium would prevent him from moving any further.

Mentmose ran a finger along a boulder and slid his pinky into a cavity along the seam. A false capstone, its thickness no more than an inch, and with Jared's help, it came loose without struggle. Beyond stretched a long uninviting corridor, a giant spider's web blocking the entrance.

"No freakin' way," Derek whispered.

With the tip of his dagger, Mentmose flicked a spider to the ground and gave it a good stomp. Satisfied that his duty was complete, he waved them in, and pantomimed that he would keep an eye on the guards.

"I should stay with him," Derek said. "Make sure he doesn't rat us out, like that embalmer guy."

Already Derek was returning to his old self and needed to be put in his place. Jared thought about how Kara would say it.

"Why the freakin' hell would he do that at this stage? He saved your ass last night, or have you forgotten? You're coming with me. This is a two-man job."

Jared turned to Mentmose, well aware they may never see each other again, especially if their plans failed. After pushing Derek into the dark, he gave Mentmose a long kiss and ran his hand across his head, caressing his neck.

"Thank you, if I don't—"

Mentmose cut him off. "You will. I'll be waiting right here. Now go."

The tunnel was no more than a foot wide and high and eclipsed in darkness. Jared crawled forward like a crab until his palms made unexpected contact with a sharp object on the desert floor. Cobras, he suddenly recalled, loved the cool recesses of the temple walls. Carefully, he raised his hands. Pieces stuck to sweaty palms: thin, jagged chips of bone, probably the skull of someone else who didn't have permission to use this passage.

A pinprick of light glimmered through a crack ahead. Two jowly priests lumbered into view. They checked to make sure oil lamps along the wall were burning brightly and went on their way. Jared recognized the aroma of duck wafting from the cones of fat attached to their heads. As the cones melted, it kept them cool in the summer heat.

When it grew quiet, Jared tipped his head towards the capstone. Derek grabbed one end and nodded back. Again, the door came easily loose—*too* easily, and Jared had to grab it before it shattered to the temple floor. There were infinite ways he could get killed tonight. And he hadn't even reached the inner courtyard. His well-honed desire to flee had never been stronger. Instead, he moved forward and stood up.

The pair found themselves in a titanic stone forest. Jared gazed up in awe: over one hundred columns ascending eighty feet high, each carved to resemble lotus stems in full bloom and nurtured by flickering lamplight. The primeval swamp where all life began.

"Which way?" Derek asked as if Jared was a regular visitor.

"Give me a minute." Jared closed his eyes. For the first time, he tried to summon a specific place, and it worked.

Hori trails behind a litany of priests as they hoist a royal mummy high above their heads. The scarred and tattooed general, who Jared remembers from his earlier flashback, stands next to him. The man now seems at peace and looks at Jared with what could only be appreciation and relief. Jared had embalmed the great pharaoh before it was too late, and his funeral could commence from the hallowed courtyard of Amun, deep within Karnak.

"That way, towards the Sacred Lake."

They slunk forward, keeping a watchful eye out for priests, but the place now seemed abandoned, as if the two holy men were doing final rounds before bed. At the end of a long alleyway, he saw it. A tiny chapel trimmed in gold. Like the tombs in the Valley of the Kings, it featured a single door that plunged deep into the bedrock, the descending walls smooth and plastered. Fresh oil lamps led the way down a sloped corridor, which meant that priests came here regularly. At the bottom, the passage ended with a statue of Amun chiseled into living rock. There, one corridor became two. He noticed, with some misplaced amusement, that the floor was plated gold. Another kid from Kansas following a yellow brick road.

When they arrived, both corridors seemed equally terrifying. Jared picked the one closest to him. The corridor twisted in a semi-circle and plunged into darkness. Moving forward was dangerous; anyone could be standing in front of them, and they'd never know.

"Wait, I just remembered something," Derek said. After the sound of his bag being riffled through, a small light flicked on. "My toenail clippers. Told you they'd come in handy."

"Your first contribution involves self-grooming?" Jared wanted to ask but swallowed his words. Instead, he dismissed Derek's inane comment and took a step forward—only to be violently pulled back. "What the hell?"

Derek wiggled the toenail clipper light in front of them, and something shiny and thin reflected back, like a strand of spider's web.

"Holy shit," Derek said as it came into sharper view.

A long wire stretched from side to side at neck level. Derek took a page of the script, still rolled up in his back pocket, and ran it diagonally across the wire. It split cleanly in two.

"Nice work," Jared had to admit as he dipped beneath it and rubbed his neck.

On either side, alcoves appeared, each housing enormous stone coffins. Jared suspected they were probably the tombs of the generations of high priests who had overseen Karnak. Some of them may even showcase his own work as an embalmer. He was dying to take a quick peek, but now was not the time to feed his ego. He needed to find the inner chamber, where the translation of the *Book of the Gates* was kept. Then, all they had to do was steal it without being caught and flailed alive.

The hallway ended at another set of stairs. From below, odd silvery lights glimmered like water against the walls. As they descended, strange sounds echoed, and a sharp tang, metallic and eye-watering, rose to meet them.

Jared and Derek arrived at the bottom and were met with the strangest sight both had ever seen, so surreal it was hard to turn the image into logic. A circular lake spread out before them, made not of water but something highly reflective and chrome-colored. At first, it seemed like just a shiny floor. But drawing closer, it was swirling in a counterclockwise motion as if it was a blender at low power. The ceiling above was domed and painted with reflective stars that radiated in a cobalt sky. From various places, thick hemp ropes hung from the ceiling, each cradling oil lamps that lit the room up like a chandelier. But surely the most dramatic vision came from the little island that rose in the center of the lake. A black basalt podium housed a simple chapel. And cradled inside, in a smoothed-out hollow, a single thick scroll, jaundiced and cracked along the edges. A slender band of silver prevented it from unrolling.

"*The Book of Gates*," Jared said before Derek could ask.

"What's surrounding it?"

Jared moved in closer and grew so woozy Derek had to pull him back before he tumbled in.

"Just as Tiya said: 'a churning river of stone.' Mercury."

"Of all things, *mercury*?"

"Represented the ancestral earth and warded away evil spirits. Like us, I guess."

Jared moved around the side of the lake, searching for a bridge or board to cross. Surely some means of getting to the island existed. Otherwise, how could they have built it? But there seemed no way across. Perhaps priests brought the plank with them when they visited.

Derek tossed a pebble into the lake. It didn't melt but simply hovered on the top.

"Mercury doesn't burn, right?"

"No, it's not hot. But if it touches the skin, we'll go crazy. It's poisonous." Jared put a hand to his mouth. "Even breathing it can make us go mad."

Derek was staring at the ceiling, where the three lamp ropes hung low and made a Tarzan-like trail to the chapel.

"What about them? We can swing from one to the other?"

"Maybe the first, with a good push, but the second won't move enough to reach the next. We'd be stuck."

Derek considered the walls.

"I can rappel. Remember the time I did it in Cappadocia? Climbed right up to that old Christian cave."

Derek had watched his shows so many times he confused reality TV with actual reality.

"We had professional Turkish mountain climbers and harnesses to help us," Jared reminded him. "You went about fifteen feet before you said we had enough footage."

"Right," Derek recalled with a frown. "Then we walked the rest of the way up the concrete path." He went silent. "Shit, we're both total phonies, aren't we?"

While he was happy Derek finally had a moment of self-reflection, his timing was dreadful. He considered the three hemp lamp ropes more closely.

Maybe if we connect them somehow…

"Come, back to the corridor. Let's figure it out where we can breathe."

They retreated to the hall lined with tombs and plopped down on the cool sandy floor. It took a few moments before the room stopped spinning.

"So, that's it then?" Derek removed his fedora and fanned his face. "I ain't dying in a toxic tomb. Let's just sneak back to Seti's chamber. Maybe we can fake our way through the gates. The wall paintings of the gates might be enough."

"They won't be. Without Tiya, we'd be unable to make sense of anything. That scroll in there contains all the incantations and codes to let us cross. We gotta go back in and get it."

Jared took stock of what lay scattered about that might help. A bunch of Canopic jars and a room full of granite coffins. A short list. He closed his eyes, but no vision surfaced. He began to pace, but it too did little to jog his memory. Defeated, he leaned against one of the coffins and realized their journey was indeed over. He had led not only himself, but his crew and best friend to their deaths. He had regained his past only to misuse it. Visions of the elementary school bus stop and his sister's *Free Willy* lunch box tumbled into view.

Then something else popped into his head, not a flashback, but a recent memory. He was back in Uncle Ameni's embalming chamber, watching him wrap a mummy three times over.

"That's how we get across," Jared said as he ran a hand along the top of the coffin, looking for the lid. He tipped it over and out rolled a mummy. "Help me unravel this guy. Fast."

"You wanna unwrap a mummy *now*?" came the response, the old Derek Dees returning. "The mercury's gone to your head, Plummer. I knew it was a mistake to follow your lead."

Jared had no idea if his plan would work, but he had no intention of letting Derek dismiss it before it was even explained.

"If I recall, you made a promise up on that tower. To follow and aid me, no matter what I asked, remember?" Jared moved to one side of the corpse. "So stop whining and start unraveling."

He began by yanking off the mummy's death mask. For a spell, it held fast, then finally plopped off, revealing the cause for its resistance. The face underneath had not been properly embalmed, and fluids had leached into the wrapping, causing it to rot. Half of the poor high priest's face remained stuck to the inside of the mask. A foul odor took hold. But Jared was unbothered; he had smelled worse. But the mangy wrappings, he knew, would slow them down.

"This one is rotten, so we may need to unravel a few more."

Jared said this with such certainty and force that Derek asked no more questions.

A few minutes later, the high priest lay naked on the floor, his puckered body and face no longer casting a supercilious air of superiority. Next to him lay a mound of linen at least thirty feet in length.

"Probably need two more," Jared said, moving on to the next coffin. "Fast." Jared gathered up the mummy wrappings. "But they should be strong enough."

Derek caught on. "Make a bridge of some kind?"

"Not a bridge, a tightrope. If I get within a few inches of that mercury, I'll pass out. Need to come in from higher up."

He handed Derek the set of linens.

A short while later, they reentered the Holy of Holies and took stock. The first lamp hung directly above them. Two others swung not far away, the second directly over the island.

"No way," Derek said, finally catching on. "It won't hold."

"If we double the linen, it *might*. Then, I need you to walk back and swing me from rope to rope so I can lasso the next lamp."

Jared hopped on Derek's back and was lifted to just beneath the light. He tied the linen as tightly as he could and tested it. After climbing from Derek's shoulder to the hanging rope, he doubled the linen and gazed over at the second. It hovered directly above the pool.

"Back up, pull the linen taut, and let go so I can hook it from underneath."

"Why the linens? Can't you just swing from one to one like a vine?"

"I have to get back too. I'll be holding a sacred scroll in one hand and probably be damn dizzy. I'll need to shimmy across."

Derek did as he was instructed.

The first swing was too weak to reach, but Derek got into the spirit of things, climbing halfway up the stairs for another go. This time, Jared was able to loop the linen under the lamp and tie it taut. After a third strip was added, he twisted them together as tightly as he could to form a single strong tightrope. By now, his eyes were red, and his breath erratic. A rash had developed on his exposed face and palms, anything pointing downward. He crawled back down to solid ground.

"We need one more unwrapped mummy."

"It seems strong enough."

"Not for the lamps, for me. You need to cover me head to toe, double-wrapped at the eyes and mouth, so I don't take in the toxins."

"You'll see nothing."

"Not true. You'll be down below to guide me."

"I guess I will."

A vague smile crossed Derek's face.

A few minutes later, every inch of Jared looked no different from one of the mummies he had just exhumed. Derek used his toenail clippers to make little incisions over one nostril, enough for an occasional sniff of air. He then wrapped a piece around his own mouth like a surgical mask but kept his eyes free and remained far enough from the lake to not be affected.

Under gauze, Jared was strangely calm. Against his well-honed habits, he didn't ruminate on all the things that could go wrong, or what others may think of him if he failed. That had long been his undoing, so he only thought about those who would die if he didn't pull this off. "Time's running out. Guide me to the first rope."

"It's above you to the left," Derek shouted up. "Can you at least see the lamp light?"

Jared could, and finding it proved to be easy enough. He gave the rope a tug and seemed confident it would hold. Now the hard part. Weighed down by his body, the next lamp was too far to swing to, so he had to put his faith in the mummy wrappings that hovered between them like holiday tinsel. He tried first to crawl out, but it was too thin to support his entire body.

"I need to cross hanging from my hands and legs," he called down, his voice muffled from the bandages. "Is there enough room?"

A worried voice from behind. "You got maybe two feet to spare."

Jared grabbed on tight and began shimming across. The linen bowed under his weight.

"Now you've got about six inches," Derek informed him. "Keep your ass up high. I'll guide you."

The first few moves supported Jared's weight. He felt the thick linen cutting into his hands, the taste of natron on his lips from where it once covered a dead man. Ever so slowly, he inched forward. He could smell the toxins, and the pinpoint of light began dancing. His nostrils throbbed where the air was seeping in. As he reached forward, his grip loosened, and he almost fell.

"How much room between me and mercury?"

"Shit, like an inch. It's starting to unravel on my side. Hurry!"

Jared tried to focus on the bouncing light a few feet away and quickened his pace. As he did, he felt the linen behind him go slack.

"Up! Up!" Derek shouted.

The wrappings snapped. Now hanging from one strand, Jared scampered up the remaining linen until he felt the thick hemp rope in his hand. The third lamp. He had made it. How much more of this he could take remained a growing concern—as did how he would get back. First, he needed to reach the altar below.

"The scroll is directly beneath you," Derek called. "Just drop straight and don't move your position. If you miss your mark by even a few inches, you fall right into it."

Jared drew a breath, brought his feet together, and let go. He felt solid ground beneath his feet but had no idea where he landed. His feet felt like sponges. A few more minutes, he knew, and he'd be dead.

"Okay, you're standing on either side of the altar. The scroll is right below you. Can you see anything?"

"Nothing." His words were fevered. "Everything's starting to spin."

"Keep your feet planted and squat. It's literally between your legs."

Jared reached down and felt something thin and brittle in his hand.

"Got it!" Silence. "Didn't I?"

Only a muffled noise—maybe Derek stifling a scream?—reached him.

New voices took his place, angry and loud. Then there was a scuffle of some kind that Jared couldn't make sense of from beneath his blindfold. All he knew was that if it was the sound of advancing guards, he had just been caught red-handed stealing the most sacred relic in all of Egypt and had nowhere to hide, nor the strength to do it. He tightened his body, drew a final breath and waited for the arrows to strike.

CHAPTER 24

Kara was a lousy director, and she knew it. It's not that she lacked confidence. Quite the opposite. She had too much. This meant the traits best suited to directing: compromise, placating, and making thin-skinned fools like Derek the Dick or Ramses the Runt feel happy did not come naturally. She'd much rather put them in their place and challenge them as to why the world needed to hear their stories over so many others. But that's not how successful documentaries were made. It was another reason why she and Jared made such a perfect team. He was a pro at buttering people up, making them feel valued and befriended, while Kara stealthily moved in for the close-up and exposed their warts and scars.

But as long as Jared had a fighting chance, wherever he was, all that was required of her was to stall for time. To do that, she must treat Ramses like a petulant rockstar—humor him, tell him he's awesome, and whatever else she does, don't start a fight. All the things she found it revolting to do with Derek Dees.

For fuck's sake, it wouldn't be easy.

She and Ali were led to a canal and pushed onto a flat-bottomed boat.

"I thought we were going to watch him fight in an arena or something?" Ali asked the vizier.

"Too small for such a grand man," Nehi sniffed. "You will witness the great Ramses wrestle the most powerful creatures in the Nile." The boat was unmoored and made its way down the palace canal, where an armada of barges were waiting. Square sails were hoisted, each displaying mythological scenes: Isis collecting Osiris's body from the primordial swamp, or the sun god Re weeping, his tears giving birth to the first human. Taken together, they conveyed twin messages: the mighty pharaoh was out for a day of manly sport. And the gods were watching.

Ramses stood on the bow as they headed toward the Great Swamp. The vizier called Kara and Ali over.

"Ramses shall hunt. Do nothing to interfere."

"May we ask a question or two?" Kara asked, knowing nothing slowed time more than an entitled jerk with a platform to speak about himself.

"No one addresses pharaoh. Ye shall watch and squeeze all his triumphs into your black box."

A few smaller vessels sailed ahead, making a way through a tangle of thicket, swarms of dragonflies scattering as they went. A hummingbird-sized mosquito wouldn't leave Ali's bleeding scar alone until he smashed it with his mixer. Ahead of them, a timeworn wall soared twenty feet high.

"What is this place?" Kara asked Nehi.

"The royal hunting grounds. Used by all pharaohs since Thebes was founded. Here the greatest beasts of the Nile are left to run wild as in the Ancestral Swamp. Ramses shall slay them all."

Kara removed the lens cap and slid it into her back pocket. "And what do we do?"

The vizier seemed surprised by such an inane question. "Try not to get eaten right away."

Kara trained her camera on Ramses, first from the back, as a test to see how he'd react. When he glanced behind him and sucked in his gut, she knew she could move closer.

For a man born thousands of years before the Daguerreotype was invented, Ramses quickly gleaned the power of cinema. He checked Kara's frame in the monitor and, seeing where it ended, walked out and back to make a grand entrance. Then he pointed, quite theatrically, off the bow to something moving in the water. It was like that silent film Jared once dragged her to at the Film Forum, the one that put her to sleep in ten minutes. When Kara couldn't pan fast enough, he happily repeated the action. This time she found her focus: an enormous crocodile poking up from the reeds, its yellow eyes fixed on the boat. It inched forward and revealed itself to be at least fifteen feet long. Ramses reached for a dagger, climbed to the edge of the boat and dived in.

Impressed at last, Kara stepped back to capture the king as he plunged his knife into the deadly beast.

That took guts. Maybe he isn't such a fraud after all?

His aim was so precise that the animal barely put up a struggle as the dagger plunged deep between the eyes. Kara zoomed in for cutaways and saw something peculiar. Behind the animal were two human heads bobbing in the tide. Its last victims?

Ramses gripped the croc and dragged it towards the boat with startling ease. Only then were heads revealed to be not only alive but still attached to two men who seemed to be helping the king push it forward. At one point, they shook the reptile to make it seem like it was fighting back. In truth, it was no doubt dead long before Ramses jumped off the boat.

Kara suppressed a laugh. The mightiest pharaoh of all time, and he resorted to the same sideshow tricks still used on the Coney Island boardwalk.

"Knew it," Ali whispered into the mic. "This *is* the Pharaonic Village, after all." The crocodile was dragged onto the boat, and Ramses climbed on top, hunter and prey posing for a snapshot. He said something to Nehi, who translated. "He asked if you captured all of that. If not, we shall throw it back and repeat the act."

"Nah, we're good."

The boat moved further into the marshlands as the charade continued. First, a tiger, which had no ecological reason to be in the middle of the swamp, was cut down, mostly as it was tied to a tree. Then the royal barge crept into a feral-looking inlet festooned with orchids and papyrus stalks bending at the flower. There, glaring back between reeds, were three massive hippos, each at least ten feet across. Kara could smell them even before they came into view.

"The deadliest beast to ever walk the earth," Vizier Nehi announced.

Kara agreed. As a kid, she watched one in the Bronx Zoo charge a group of nosey tourists. Tranquilizers stopped it, but even then, it trashed its way through a metal fence before collapsing a few feet in front of the Henderson clan of Cuyahoga Falls, Ohio. Now there were three, and unlike the crocodile, they seemed very much alive.

"Ramses shall slay each with bow and arrow," Nehi explained. "Go get on a smaller boat so that he may be captured in full glory." He pointed to a tiny reed skiff no more than four feet across, rounded like a saucer and just as flimsy.

"I don't think we can balance—" Kara's words were cut off by the tip of a spear.

"Do not perish until all be slain. Then, like your two friends have just been, you'll be taken apart, limb by limb." The vizier took great pleasure in saying the words.

Kara froze, her camera halfway to her eye. "They're dead? You killed them?!"

"Not me, unfortunately, by some royal guards. Caught and slaughtered, I'm told, as they deserve." Before Kara could ask another question, they were set adrift and pushed toward the hippos. The beasts' glassy eyes followed them as they drifted closer and clanged into a thick wooden fence.

An irrational thought cloaked Kara's mind. Whether he was lying or not, the vizier and the pharaoh needed to die. Now, while she has the chance. If Jared is really dead, then none of the matters. Only revenge. She looked around and saw a way. "You see what I see?" She pointed to the bend in the fence where a gate appeared.

"Of course there's a fence," Ali said. "Think he's gonna risk even the slightest scratch?" He too was frozen in place. "You think it's true?"

Kara ignored the question. She had only one thing on her mind. "Look further on," Kara muttered. "See the large wooden hook? That's a gate. We wanted to create a distraction, right, slow things down? Help me get closer."

"*La.* That's suicide. They may charge after us instead of Ramses. You'd be crushed in seconds."

"As soon as I open it, push back the other way to avoid the stampede." Ali would survive, she told herself. They'd need him to finish the film. So the decision came easy. She had been dancing with death for two endless years and getting nowhere. Now she could finish the job and take out a few awful people with her. It was time to join Lynette.

"Don't do this, please."

Kara barely heard what Ali had said. Jared was dead, so her promise to keep fighting as a team was null and void. Her thoughts had already drifted to her girlfriend, and what she'd say when they finally met.

Before Ali could stop her, Kara handed him the camera and jumped in the water. She swam to the gate, where a trio of hungry hippos glared at her from the other side. Not far away, the pharaoh had also dived into the water, no doubt to kill the beast from his side of the fence. The two made eye contact, and the pharaoh raised his eyebrows in surprise. Yet before he could react, Kara unlocked the gate and pushed it wide open. All three hippos roared in pent-up fury and barged through. Kara was swallowed up by their advance, and she let go at last.

Would she still be wearing that peacock blue dress I picked out for her funeral, or did the dead get new clothes when they reached the afterlife?

She was so looking forward to finding out.

CHAPTER 25

Said sped north as quickly as traffic would allow, which in Egypt was never fast enough. He honked and swerved between tractors tilting with sugar cane and rickshaws puttering along on three wheels. In the passenger seat, Omm stared out the window at the shrouded landscape, trying to patch together a plan. The blindness didn't worry her as much as it should. It was all coming to an end, one way or another. The only true fear was time—something she always thought she had *too much* of. Omm had not told Said her vision was gone; he'd surely drive her straight to the hospital. Instead, she relied on her memory to talk about things that *should* be passing by as they headed north along the snaking Sohag Agricultural Road. For the moment, Said seemed too preoccupied to notice.

When Omm was younger, she had visited every ruin she could along the Nile, seeking out ancient tombs and derelict temples to say hello to the gods who dwelled there. Some were well-marked and restored, but others she'd find in backyards and gullies, under overpasses, and melded into the foundations of modern banks. One held an abandoned tank from the Six-Day War. Not all who lingered there wanted company, and a few were downright hostile. "Said, dear, keep an eye out for two pyramids on the horizon."

"I see them ahead. But they're dangerous and closed for ages. The locals say they're full of ghosts."

"Perfect," Omm smiled.

"Why these?"

"One of them, Mehy and Tiya, used to visit when we, eh, they were young. Perhaps the occupants will remember."

"You went there to pray?"

"Not quite." She rubbed her sore head and felt blood on her fingers. It had opened back up. "Try the one further north first. It appears a bit more...."

"Ghostly?"

"Indeed."

The two pyramids, denuded and looking like sandcastles after high tide, were framed by a retreating sun, bright enough that Omm could still make out vague silhouettes. Said guided her up the trail, and she used her to cane to feel what was ahead. Her knees quivered and her heart throbbed. Twice she had to stop to catch her breath. Her entire body was in retreat.

Said halted. "They're even worse than they look from the road. Piles of rubble. No one would dare linger here, dead or alive."

But in her mind's eye, Omm was visualizing something quite different. She recalled stories Tiya told here about coming here on a romantic getaway when it was still maintained by priests, polished and gleaming. Mehy would announce her as his 'temple chantress' and insist they visit the old tombs and chapels in private to perform prayers to the great kings of the past. No one believed them, but who could say no to the Crown Prince?

Omm ran her hands along a keystone of granite, the edges still retaining their shape. With her link to Tiya's *ka* severed, she couldn't access her memories, but she remembered the tales well enough. This one belonged to Senusret, one of the most powerful and cruel pharaohs of all time. A warrior who conquered Nubia, he turned on his own people and forced them to build monuments until they dropped. She called out a greeting but got no reply. It's possible he was just playing hard to get, but just as possible, she was still too far away to get his attention. Omm hugged the monument and worked her way to the entrance.

"Is it open?" she asked.

"Yes, but can't you see the huge sign: "Danger, No Entry?""

"Of course I do," she lied. "I need to get down there, see if there's still a false door."

Said peered into the fathomless shaft. "Like hell you will. I'll go."

"And do what, love? Only I know the rituals for joining the two worlds. And if it does, I'll need to talk to whoever is on the other side, convince them to let our friends pass."

"We don't even have a flashlight," Said protested.

Omm dismissed him with a shrug. A flashlight would do her no good now, anyway. She slipped out of her fuzzy green slippers, fell to her knees, and began crawling.

"You just mind the road. If inspectors come round, they'll cart us off for trespassing. Bloody civil servants."

By now Said's face had blended into the landscape, nothing but a worried voice in a smear of beige.

"Anything happens down there, you call me. Allah knows the condition of that thing."

Omm broke through a web and apologized to a jittery spider that dashed across her forehead. Being inside a tomb without sight didn't worry her; she had lived in a pitch-black temple for years and knew how to navigate by touch. At first, it was easygoing, flat stones on a thirty-degree angle straight into bedrock. Her head bumped into an obstacle, probably a huge casing stone that had fallen from the ceiling.

There was a cavity wide enough to slither passed, but as she tried, the boulder protested from above. Omm froze. Ever so gently, she reached out to determine what lay in front of her. Her hand met a large chunk of limestone, but as she held on to it to scoot by, it crumbled like chalk. With the merest brush, she could be crushed under a mountain of stone. And it would serve her right: an eighty-one-year-old blind Londoner poking around places both dangerous and off limits.

Omm quietly called out to pharaoh Senusret, asking for permission to move forward, and at last received a response. The entire ceiling wobbled, and chunks of stone rained down. Pebbles met toes, which suggested that the passage was being sealed from above. Some kings were like that, eternally bitter at how poorly their pyramids had held up, how dimly they were remembered.

"Forgive the intrusion, my Lord," she whispered. "I'll just be on my way."

Delicately, she backed out. Without her hands guiding her, this proved more difficult. Her back grazed the ceiling, and another chunk of boulder came loose. Far below, it struck something hard, and a new rumble reverberated up the tunnel. Senusret's voice was no longer dim. He was informing her, quite angrily, to leave immediately, or she never would.

Omm returned to the surface with a gasp and welcomed the cool evening breeze. She found the edge of a fallen block, her face covered in blood and soot. Unsure where Said was, she picked a general location facing away from the pyramid. "Not very inviting, I fear. Take my hand, love, and let's move on."

Said didn't reply, but Omm could hear strange flickers that reached her from behind. A brief flash of light flared up in front of her and was extinguished like a faraway comet. Then a whiff of gas.

"You can't see a thing," Said all but shouted. "I nearly burned your nose off with my lighter just now, and you didn't blink. What's happening?"

"The greatest gift Mehy gave me was insight. So, it only makes sense my eyes would be the first to fade." She raised her hand for him to grab. "All the more reason why we must try the next one, fast."

"*Ant majnoon.* You're crazy. Also, you're bleeding."

Omm felt soft cotton being wrapped around her head. The checkered scarf Said always wore to keep the heat off his face and neck.

"It's straight to the hospital."

"No, it's not. I shan't waste my remaining hours in some ghastly waiting room staring at a photo of President Sisi. We've come this far, and I can see in the dark as well as you can in the light. I've spent decades in training." She rose. "Now, to the next pyramid and say no more."

There was a sigh as Said guided her to the second pyramid. This tomb was made for Amenemhat, the father of Senusret, who, poor fellow, was assassinated young and more or less forgotten even by Seti's time. "This must have been the one they made love in," Omm recalled, "less haughty priests wandering about. Perhaps because his life had been cut short, Amenemhat might fancy some company." If he did, she recalled, there was an offering hall with a granite altar not far inside where she and Mehy had fooled around. It would be an ideal place to peer into the past.

"I'll come with you this time," Said insisted. "Be your eyes."

"No, stay here and keep watch. And don't go wandering off. I'd be lost without you."

"Where the hell would I go?" He led her into the opening. "*Yallah!* Be quick."

Omm was relieved to discover that the passageway seemed free of debris. For the first few meters, she met no resistance but then heard strange sounds from deep below.

Was it Amenemhat telling her to clear off? She listened more closely. *No, whatever made this noise was of this world, not the pharaoh's.*

"Oh, dear." Omm laid as low as she could, palms and feet flat to the floor. To rise too soon or even have a foot in the way could mean pain, disease, and death. The roar grew closer, first like one loud scream, then hundreds of angry souls. Omm pressed her face closer to the stone and shielded her eyes.

A thousand black bats, awakened to the night sky, poured past her, tangling up in her hair and pressing against her back and feet. They meant her no harm. Their only goal, she knew, was to reach the night sky as quickly as possible, where a billion juicy insects were waiting. The stampede went on for several minutes, and once or twice a floundering bat banged into her ass or heel, bid her pardon, and flew on. When it finally grew quiet again, Omm exhaled and craned an ear.

"Bats?" Said screamed from above. "This is insane!" His voice echoed down the corridor.

"I'm almost there," she yelled back up.

"*Yallah, yallah!* Someone's coming! A black car," Said shouted back.

"Don't tell them you're with a friend. I'll be back in a jiffy." She turned her ear towards the bottom of the shaft and listened again. This time she heard a once-human voice apologizing for the rude welcome. Amenemhat no longer held enough power to keep them out but said that Omm was welcome to visit his chapel just ahead. Her toes met open space as she entered.

Sitting in the gloom, Omm reached out to find the false door exactly where she remembered it. The room felt empty, likely looted in antiquity. A memory surfaced—hers or Tiya, she could no longer tell. It was all a fading jumble—and she reached into the small space behind the altar. Her fingers met something smooth and cool, and she laughed. The necklace she had misplaced thirty-three hundred years ago. A tingle ran through her body as if Mehy was touching her in the same spots.

Dear Gods, she missed making love to him.

"It was a lovely gift," said the voice, weak, yet warm. "I've treasured it ever since. The only thing that was never taken from me."

"So happy it brought you comfort. Now, I wonder if I may ask a favor."

Omm explained her predicament and waited for a reply.

It came slowly, meekly.

"I am grateful for your company. No one has visited here in over four thousand floods. But what you ask goes against the gods."

"Not at all," Omm responded. "Seti himself has allowed my friends to pass."

Again, a long silence. "You're asking the wrong king. You know as well as I that I was craven, killed by my own for indecision, little mourned, and greatly forgotten. Which, after all this time, suits me well. To do what you ask would cause unwanted attention. The gods may realize I still exist and erase me for lingering while greater men do not."

She tried again to convince him but to no avail. "I wonder, then, might you at least peek into the past for me? Tell me where my friends are."

"I will, but the other side remains closed to travel."

Omm thanked him and began reciting an incantation. A vague glow spread across the altar, more shadows than light, but Omm could sense the change and knew something would soon appear.

"Figures standing in a circle, peering downward at a body," Amenemhat described. "They're in mourning now, on their knees."

It's what she feared. *The falcon has flown to heaven.* Seti is dead. That meant the first gate would soon open. Twelve short hours and everything would disappear forever. Jared would be slaughtered, Mehy would fade, and even if she somehow managed to find a replacement, be it Jared or someone else should he perish, Omm's vow would be useless. There would be no one left to venerate.

Amenemhat was equally alarmed by what he saw. "I should not have spied on a dying king. I'll be cursed for intruding." He retreated back into the darkness where he had cowered for so long. Omm felt the necklace in her hand, remembered how Mehy tenderly clasped it around her neck, how his lips met her forehead when it was at last secure. She thought about taking it with her as a romantic keepsake but then considered her lonely host. Instead, she placed it exactly where she had found it and crawled toward daylight.

When she reached the top, shouting kept her hidden behind a boulder of stone. Below, she heard the idling motor of one car and what sounded like the approach of another. A click of handcuffs. Demands in Arabic followed, muffled and sharp.

But Said's response came loudly, so it echoed across the desert. "Of course, I'm alone. I'm a licensed tour guide, just forgot my permit." A car door slammed, and both cars drove off. Then nothing but the whimpering of a nearby dog that sounded as if being slaughtered.

Omm considered her next move. She had none. No car, no Said, and blind as those bats flying overhead. Pain shot across her spine and into her legs, and she wondered if this was where it all would end.

"Bollocks!"

As long as she was still breathing, she owed it to Mehy and Jared to keep trying. She located her cane and, knowing her way north, started trekking in that direction. But after a few yards, her feet met something sharply metallic, like a washing machine dropped from the sky. She felt its edges and concluded that, indeed, it *was* a washing machine on the edge of the western desert. She moved past it, only to cut her fingers on what felt like a shattered TV screen, then nearly tripped over a snarl of electrical cords. Omm tried to make sense of the shift: from an ancient necropolis to a graveyard of modern appliances in a few wobbly steps. Wherever she was, she needed to feel her way out of this hellscape before she was cut to ribbons. Yet no matter which way she turned, a serrated obstacle barred her way. Something sharp slashed her arm, perhaps the spokes of a mangled Vespa. *Was this all the gods doing, to prevent her from accomplishing her goal? If so, she wouldn't be so easily defeated.* Omm bent over and searched for something to stem the flow of blood. Instead, she found a human foot, shoeless and hairy. She thought she might have stumbled onto a fresh grave—until it jolted at her touch and rose.

CHAPTER 26

Interview transcript *(badly damaged, partially recovered)*

Location: undetermined, purportedly a "palace overlooking Thebes"

Date: undetermined, director claims "1279 BC"

Interview Subject: **Ramses the Great**

Interviewers: **Kara Hawkins, Ali Mabrouk**

(Note: media drive in quality is poor, many portions untranscribable. Transcription services bear no responsibility for incomplete dialogue.)

Ali: You set up?

Kara: Check, check…what's the point of this again?

Ali: Same as ever. Give Jared and Derek more time.

Kara: But you heard him yourself. They're dead.

Ali: Yes, I heard, but why should we trust anything these guys say? Let's at least stay alive until Seti is dead too, and the gates open. Got nothing else to do *(coughing fit follows)* You okay?

Kara: I'll survive. You didn't have to do that back there, you know.

Ali: Wasn't gonna watch you drown. *(pause/media drive noise)* You look like you wish I hadn't.

Kara: Not sure. Either way, it didn't amount to much. Ramses lives, Jared's dead, and we're exactly where we were before. Just a few hours behind our crew.

(a bang, perhaps door opening, chairs being dragged)

Unnamed voice: He wants to know if thy be ready.

Kara: Hey, it's Nehi, the soda guy.

Nehi: I shall translate. Say anything against thy pharaoh or thy gods, as I am keen to slay.

(more noise, muttering off camera in foreign language)

Kara: Great. So, umm, just look at me—-not the camera, please… and er, why don't you say and spell your full name, so we have it for editing purposes.

Ramses: I will answer to the man behind you with the useless metal spear. The one who saved you from my hippos.

Kara: Uh no, you can't do that. He's the sound guy. Eye line will look all weird. Stare only at me.

Ramses: I do not like gazing directly at a woman. It's beneath me.

Kara: *(off mic)* And so are you to me. You're a lot taller in your statues.

(note: translation follows each question—all future foreign conversations cut for convenience)

Ramses: I am the Usermaatre Setepenre, Son of Re, King of Kings, Ruler of Upper and Lower Egypt, *(noise)* He Who Conquered the Lands of the Hittites, Canaan, and Nubia, also known as Ramses the Second.

Kara: Mind if I call you Ramses? *(noise)* Um, why are we here, on this private balcony overlooking Thebes? It's, er, pretty. What kind of flowers are those?

Ramses: I do not understand these questions.

Kara: *(off mic)* I told you I suck at this. Wish Jared was here, he knows how to break the ice. Tell me about Jared, what you did to him.

Ramses: I don't deal in such trivial matters. We are here to talk about me. Do so, or this ends.

Kara: *(off mic, low voice)* Can't think of one goddamn thing I wanna know about him. Mostly just want to stab him in the eye with my pliers.

Ali: Not just yet. Ask him something he can brag about. He seemed excited to talk about the hippo hunt. And smile. You can hate him again later.

Kara: I'm not sure I can. Murderous misogynistic bast *(noise)* Oww… *(louder)* Okay, I'll try. We watched you kill three hippos with your bare hands today. That was damn impressive. How'd you manage to pull that off, exactly, being just one guy and all?

Ramses: Only the son of the gods can slay the chaos of.. *(break in media)* I grabbed my harpoon and told my men to stand back *(noise)*. I dived in and slayed each in turn, one with bare hands. Only thing I do not understand is why you two released the beasts so early? This was the job of my vizier.

Kara: We were very excited to see you in action. Funny thing, though: When I was up close to them, I noticed that they had their legs tied together and their mouths sewed shut, so all they could really do was fall forward. How do you imagine that happened?

Ramses: I have no idea what *(noise)*.

Nehi: Ask another question of my lord.

Kara: Here's one: why did you erase your brother from history?

Ali: You're supposed to humor him.

Kara: C'mon, it's my first good question. It's the only reason we're freakin' here. Omm might wanna know.

Ramses: Prince Mehy?

Kara: Yeah, why are you so jealous of a dead man? Was he tall?

Ramses: I did nothing to erase my brother's *ka*. He was weak of flesh, sullied the bloodline, and was punished for it. The great good Amun spoke to me, told us where the mother was hiding. We killed her so *(media drive noise)* blood pure. And found you two as well. Cowering in an embalmer's shed.

Kara: Tiya is dead?

Ramses: She is.

Kara: And our friends? How did they…die?

Ramses: They have not yet but soon. They were just seen within Karnak.

Kara: *(pause)* Wait, they live? Your stooge over here told me otherwise.

Ramses: *(foreign language, untranslatable)* My vizier wanted to see your reaction. He doesn't seem to like you very much.

Kara: What a cruel thing to say. *(pause)* But Tiya?

Ramses: She has been sliced into several pieces. But each piece will be wrapped and buried together in the same tomb. For my brother's memory. It is not love I am against but allowing that love to interfere with one's duty. So she may live by his side in the Duat, but no longer able to meddle in the land of the living.

Kara: In that case, tell me about that freak rainstorm that destroyed his tomb. Seems a lowdown thing to do to your brother, who sounded like a pretty good guy.

Ramses: Storm? I conjured no storm, did nothing to wash away Mehy's name. I don't even know where his mummy is located. Like a wild hyena, he hid it from me. For all I know, he has none and has returned to sand… *(noise)* most ignoble of end for an Egyptian.

Kara: Wait, so you didn't ask the gods of the underworld to wipe out his name?

Ramses: These questions bore me and make no sense. *(media noise)* Why are we talking about Mehy? He is long dead, and on this very day my father Seti travels to the Field of Reeds. I will escort him to his tomb, perform the Opening of the Mouth and accept the Double Crown. Nothing is further from my mind than my brother's *ka*. Let him roam the underworld as he wishes. I reign above. *(pause)* Is that why you are here? To somehow restore his name? If so, you will soon follow Tiya in the Duat.

Ali: *(whisper)* Told you, you should have been nice.

Kara: Face it, Ali, even if Jared really is alive, we're not getting out of here. Think kissing his puckered ass is gonna save us now? I tried to kill him a little while ago.

Ali: I remember. Doesn't mean we should give up. Didn't you tell me earlier that something might present itself?

Kara: I was just feeling sorry for you. But if we do somehow survive, it won't be anything we say or do in this interview. Maybe a plague of locusts or something. Oh, that's a good question! Tell me, Ramses, ever hear of the Hebrews? Or a guy named Moses?

Ramses: They build my new palace in the north. And Moses is the name of one of my advisors there. Both are unworthy of discussion.

Kara: Just you wait, buddy.

Ali: Dear God, don't give him a head's up. You really do suck at this. Ask something that won't alter history.

Kara: Umm, let's see. They call you Ramses the Great. What did you do to deserve such a self-aggrandizing—

Ali: Kara…

Kara: Wonderful title?

Ramses: They do? It is not a moniker I bestowed on myself. It must be that I remain the greatest Egyptian to ever walk the land. No one has given more to our civilization than me. All culture, law, and love pour from my every act.

Ali: *Kalam fadi.*

Kara: Yo! Thought we were playing nice.

Ali: Bullshit is bullshit. And you're right. We're not getting out of here. *(closer to mic, now addressing Ramses)*. What on earth have you done for Egyptian culture besides building a bunch of monuments to yourself?

Ramses: Now, the man with the soft metal spear speaks. And who are you?

Ali: An Egyptian, just like you.

Ramses: *(laughter)* You? A descendant of the great civilization ancestor of the Nile? Another imposter latching on to the past because you have failed to achieve a fraction of what I have.

Ali: *(Arabic, untranslated, but sounding like more curse words)* Egypt hardly peaked with you. How about Hypatia, the philosopher and astronomer? Or Saladin, the Sultan of Egypt who crushed the Crusader invaders? Pasha Muhammed Ali, who brought the country into the modern age. Poet Ibn al-Farid, novelists Naguib Mahfouz and Nawal El Saadawi, Umm Kulthum, Nassar, Sadat, Mohamad Salah, Omar Freakin' Sharif...

Ramses: These names mean nothing.

Ali: Because by the time they shared their lives and talents you and your culture of slavery and misogyny and oppression was destroyed. You know who Ozymandias is?

Ramses: Another forgotten Egyptian?

Ali: Exactly. He's another name for you. One day, all this around us, this balcony, the temples, even your very name, will be forgotten. So much that when a man named Shelly happened upon your great statue, he'll write an ode to your memory. Like millions of others, I know it by heart. Like to hear it?

Ramses: I would be honored.

Ali: *I met a traveler from an antique land,*

Who said—

"Two vast and trunkless legs of stone

Stand in the desert. . . . Near them, on the sand,

Half sunk a shattered visage lies, whose frown,

And wrinkled lip, and sneer of cold command,

Tell that its sculptor well those passions read.

And on the pedestal, these words appear:

My name is Ozymandias, King of Kings;

Look on my Works, ye Mighty, and despair!

Nothing beside remains. Round the decay.

Of that colossal Wreck, boundless and bare.

The lone and level sands stretch far away."

Ramses: This audience is at an end. We will take your magic box and entomb it with my father, as was his wish. Then we will dump you both in the Great Swamp and unloose the crocodiles. We then will do the same with you two companions. For some reason, they have entered the Holy of Holies.

Kara: You short little assho- *(media drive noise)*

Ali: Wait, wait, I understand why we must suffer and die for our intrusions. But as an Egyptian I ask only one thing. We are here as guests of your father, who this very day is being celebrated and mourned. Let us complete our task with him and die in his company.

Ramses: What, have you mummied so you may travel the *Duat*?

Ali: No, let us be locked in, die slowly and horribly without food and water. Our magic box will be preserved for eternity, while our flesh will wither and rot. A message that crossing the mighty Ramses means an eternity of agony and anonymity. I am an Egyptian after all, and you said it yourself: there is no death more ignoble.

Ramses: So you are. What could be more fitting? Your bones will crumble in the shadows of my great father, while your *ka* wanders the gates of hell forever. So let it be written, so let it be done.

Kara: My god, he really said that? *(more noises off camera; recording abruptly ends)*

CHAPTER 27

Jared remained frozen atop the Holy of Holies, clutching the *Book of the Gates* like a mouse with a piece of cheese. Blinded by mummy gauze, he couldn't determine the source of the noises across the lake of mercury. Any second an arrow would find him. He inhaled one last time, tasted noxious mercury, and prepared himself. If nothing else, no one would say he didn't try. Imagine if the Great Derek Dees was in charge. They never would have gotten past the portal.

The echo of a far-off shuffle reached him, like someone stepping closer to the lake, and he expected searing pain to follow. But all that reached him was the bang of something heavy at his feet. Then Derek's voice, trembling but clear: "There's a wooden plank at your feet. About four inches across. Put one foot in front of the other, and slowly walk straight ahead."

"What's going on?" Jared didn't recognize his own voice, muffled and thin.

"Quickly."

"*The Book of Gates*?"

"Bring it."

Slipping the scroll down his shirt, Jared raised his hands for balance and inched his way forward. Mercury had no real odor, but it coated his mouth, as if he had been licking dirty coins. His feet felt like cotton and a pounding headache preyed on his balance. The fumes, he knew, had reached his central nervous system and his body was beginning to shut down. The only thing worse would be falling in. That close to the poison, his respiratory system would cease to function in seconds.

Jared took another step, then another, a tipsy acrobat on a tightrope. On his third step, something brushed against his neck and he jerked back in horror and his foot fell from the plank. He took a final breath and prepared to be swallowed up, but when his foot hit the lake, it stayed there. Only then did his 8th grade chemistry lessons come back in full: mercury was the world's only liquid that was never wet, and so dense you can stand on it. It's the fumes that kill. Slowly, he raised his foot back to the board.

"That thing you felt is mummy wrapping hanging from above," Derek said. "Duck down and you can clear it."

Jared was now lightheaded and nauseated and at a complete loss for which direction he was going. He turned sideways and stepped into open air. A large, sweaty hand—certainly not Derek's—grabbed him before he fell and pulled him to the safety of dry land.

The same stranger removed Jared's poisoned shoes and carried him up the stairs. The headache followed, but in a few moments, Jared regained his equilibrium and removed his linen. Below him, down by the pool, were the two priests he had seen coming in, tied up and muffled, but still alive. And beyond, a plank stretched across the metallic lake. Seeing it now, it was far smaller than he imagined it—no more than ten feet. A moment ago, it was an ocean.

Jared could finally identify his savior: Mentmose. Why exactly he came for them Jared didn't know—the warrior said he would not tread on sacred ground—but something must have given him second thoughts. At first, he considered the obvious: warriors never take no for an answer.

But then Derek explained. "I can't understand all of it, but I think he's saying Ramses' men have tracked us and are searching Karnak temple. We need to get out now."

The trio worked their way up the corridor, dipping beneath the razor-sharp wire, but were stopped at the gateway of the Holy of Holies by a chorus of shouts. None came from directly nearby, but somewhere closer to the entrance of Karnak, near the secret passage. Escaping that way was impossible.

"Come," Mentmose whispered and slipped down an alley that zig-zagged deeper into the temple. It seemed as if the entire complex was awake and in a state of panic; nervous priests and priestesses were scurrying about everywhere, and crowds of laborers ran by, holding items of all shapes and sizes; furniture, golden boxes, alabaster jars, statues of the gods and goddesses. It was like mass looting, yet all done with the utmost precision and care. Was the most sacred site of Seti being ransacked now that he was dead? Was Egypt in revolt?

The alley ended near a sacred pool where all the precious items were being stacked. A long caravan of wagons, piled high with treasure, formed a convoy to the front pylon. Only then did it dawn on Jared what he was witnessing. The grand procession for Seti's funeral. All this would be transported to his tomb in the Valley of the Kings for his journey into the afterlife. The amount of gold and jewels boggled his mind. Only King Tut's tomb goods had survived to the modern era. What he saw now dwarfed that minuscule treasure.

Working his way down the caravan, inspecting each chariot, was the High Priest of Karnak, identifiable by a leopard skin draping down his back. Behind him followed a scribe who ticked off every item on a long scroll dragging sand as they walked. When satisfied, they moved on to the next wagon.

As they drew near, the scribe glanced Jared's way and reacted in alarm. Two warriors picked up spears but, at the last minute, were halted by the high priest. Something seemed to be missing from one of the wagons, and given the choice of taking orders from a holy man or a lowly scribe, they retreated.

The scribe soon followed, and Jared recognized that this was their only chance. He picked up a large jug of wine and, hiding his face, walked along the convoy. Mentmose and Derek did the same. After placing the jugs inside the nearest chariot, they slipped to the other side, beyond sight, and worked their way back to the front. A means of escape had presented itself to Jared, and without any words exchanged, he could see that Mentmose had the same idea.

The Medjay stopped at a covered wagon and lifted the curtain to reveal a stack of stools and chairs gilded with the images of Seti consorting with the gods. He moved a few things around and nodded.

Jared looked into the wagon and understood. "Life, Prosperity, Health, Mentmose, and thank you." He tossed his bookbag in and crawled inside.

"Why would we hide in there?" Derek asked. "It's the pharaoh's treasure! You don't think they're going to keep a close eye on it?"

Jared had become so fully at ease in this world that it took him a moment to remember that Derek wasn't.

"Don't you see? It's all destined for his tomb."

As he said this, a realization struck Jared. While he was still afraid, it was solely from external threats, not internal ones. That was a monumental shift. Whatever happened from here, the old Jared Plummer was already dead.

"Exactly," Derek nearly shouted. "A goddamn *tomb.*"

Jared bit his tongue. Don't treat Derek as he would when the roles were reversed. "Just take a moment and think about it. Remind me where we need to be."

A light bulb flickered over the dimly lit host of *Ancient Encounters,* and he clambered inside.

Jared found a cavity beneath a table shaped like a lion. Derek made himself at home between two footstools glittering in gold. Once settled, Mentmose nodded again. Nothing more needed to be communicated, so he gave Jared a final glance, closed the curtain and disappeared.

Jared's extremities tingled from the awkward position he had to hold. But panic didn't take hold. He knew the first gate wouldn't open until the mummy was in the tomb, so for the moment, he wasn't racing against the twelve-hour clock. His thoughts turned to Kara. Would she be there waiting for them, or was she lying arm and arm with Lynette? Forget about Seti and Mehy, Ramses and Omm, Ali, and Derek. Only one person needed saving. The one who saw the real Jared long before all of them did. Everything from here on in was about bringing Kara home alive.

Once or twice a skittish minion peeked inside the wagon. But Derek and Jared were hidden deep, and eventually, the wheels began to turn. Jared wished he could peel back the curtain to witness their procession along the Avenue of the Sphinx: hundreds, probably thousands of Thebans must have been lined up to bid farewell to an era. Seti was already a middle-aged man when he took the reins of Egypt, but he ruled for at least a dozen years, long enough to leave his mark on those witnessing his great ascension. Trumpets trilled, and women wailed. A wave of roars rose and fell, one at the beginning of the procession and one at the end. Jared could only imagine the first was for Ramses, probably peacocking on his golden chariot, the second for the mummy of his father Seti, lying in state in his alabaster resurrection machine. The sharp smack of incense was everywhere, and once Derek sneezed so loud, both were sure the wheels would stop, and warriors would appear. But the din outside was thunderous, and the procession moved on.

Finally, they reached Seti's tomb, and the wagons were unloaded. Now, the hard part, and Derek knew it too.

"How are we gonna get from here to the burial chamber?"

"Not sure," Jared confessed. "Maybe, like before, we can pretend to be laborers and carry stuff in?"

"I'm guessing they keep close tabs on who can go in there," Derek said, and for once was right. No way were two commoners going to traipse into a royal tomb clutching a god-king's Canopic jars. Jared started riffling around the wagon, desperate for a solution, when a shriek from outside stopped him. Some violent attack was underway. He heard what sounded like arrows whizzing by, then the screams of men and the stench of burning wood. Jared risked a peek. Priests and warriors ran by the carriages, some armed, others with arms akimbo. At the rear of the procession, flaming arrows had ignited a wagon. The attackers seemed to be hiding somewhere in the cliffs above the valley.

"Now," Jared said.

"*Now?* In the middle of an ambush?"

"It's Mentmose."

The two leaped from the wagon, and Jared was now certain it was the Medjay slinging the arrows, as none struck anywhere near them. As they ran towards the cliffs, Jared noticed a high priest that had taken an arrow in the neck. Jared swiftly stole the dead man's gold slippers to replace the toxic sneakers left in the Holy of Holies. Derek picked up his fallen dagger.

Jared dared a quick glance to the cliffside, where the broad, powerful frame of the Nubian warrior was silhouetted by the glow of the city behind him. He raised an arm and shield to say goodbye, then disappeared over the crest, this time, Jared suspected, forever.

Inside, stone masons were frantically putting the finishing touches on several reliefs and silently watched as Jared and Derek ran by. Any one of them could have stopped the intruders, but they had more urgent matters. Seti was about to be buried, and if the tomb was not complete, their own funerals would swiftly follow.

The burial chamber was thankfully empty. Jared and Derek dashed to the secret door and sealed themselves in just before several priests lumbered into view, carrying the first of the royal treasure. Jared noticed with alarm that the door was not completely shut, and anyone who'd glance in their direction might notice the break. To pull it closed would only make noise, so he took the risk to see what was happening.

Soon, the chamber was stacked high with precious goods, and Ramses and his advisors entered the chamber. The new pharaoh walked ahead, solemnly clutching a long instrument shaped like the head of a serpent. After several priests raised the stiff mummy to an upright position, Ramses moved the instrument in front of his father's wrapped face. Jared had read about this ceremony, the Opening of the Mouth. The ancients believed the deceased would need the gift of speaking, seeing and hearing to survive the twelve gates and only a holy man or descendent could bestow it. Ramses began an incantation, and Jared understood every word.

My mouth is given back to me by Ramses,

With that chisel of metal.

I am traveling to the gods who dwell in the west of heaven,

Where I will yet live and speak again in the Field of Reeds.

Ramses bowed a final time, kissed the coffin, and made his way up the corridor. The entourage followed. The high priest blew out the oil lamps and was the last to exit. Derek wanted to get out immediately, but Jared stopped him.

"Wait until we hear the front door lock."

It was only in the silence that followed that Jared's thoughts returned to Kara and Ali. Whatever happened, they didn't make it back. Maybe killed in their sleep at the embalmers, maybe decapitated like Tiya as they fled. Or worse, what Ramses had threatened from the beginning. He stifled a sob.

Had I not thought only of myself, we would have made a silly show and gone home. I'd still be Jared the Gerbil, but Ali would be with his wife and boys, and Kara might start a new beginning with a new love. The trade-off, he realized, was not worth it. He no longer wanted great knowledge or power. He'd give it all back for Kara.

If Derek was also considering his fallen comrades, it didn't register. "For Christ's sake, how about now? I gotta piss like a camel."

"Yeah, it should be safe." They pushed open the door.

But then the clang of bolts. Someone had returned.

"What the hell?" Derek whimpered. "Ramses' men saw us come in. We're screwed, like Kara and Ali."

So he did think about his colleagues.

Heralded by torchlight, Nehi the vizier and two of his henchmen appeared in the burial chamber, each carrying something shiny and black. The production gear. Then, a familiar sound.

"Hands off me, you creep. Where am I gonna run?"

Kara came into view, then Ali, both being escorted by two burly guards. It was all Jared could do to stifle a scream of joy.

The two were bound and harshly chained to a wall.

"Chains? It's a sealed tomb," Kara said. "A bit over the top, don't you think, soda man?"

Jared suppressed sobs turned to a repressed laugh. Kara Hawkins didn't need some old reincarnated embalmer to survive. She could take care of herself.

Satisfied they were going nowhere, the vizier picked up a large clay jar of water and a plate of figs and dates and sat them down on the far side of the tomb.

"I'm told it can take a week to perish from thirst and hunger. I'll leave this here to remind thee of what hath been denied." A final thought occurred, and it seemed to amuse him. "I wonder what future explorers will make of thee if and when they breach this tomb. The parched bones of two criminals held fast to a wall, grasping for an empty jug eternally out of reach."

Then after a moment of reflection, Nehi walked toward Ali and Kara with a fixed stare.

Jared grabbed the dagger Derek had found and prepared to pounce. Kara had already died once in his mind. It wouldn't happen again.

But instead of doing them harm, the vizier moved past Ali and Kara to their film cases. He crudely dumped the gear onto the floor and filled them with all the gold and jewels that would fit. After handing them to his henchmen, he headed back up the corridor. When the door was locked at last, Jared and Derek crawled out of the secret compartment and freed their friends. The bear hugs and laughter echo was so loud it could have woken the dead.

It was only later that a thought occurred: everything that had transpired to this point was merely the Cold Open. The real show—traversing the twelve gates of the underworld and doing their best not to die—was about to begin. Cue theme music.

CALL SHEET

EPISODE 37: MAGICAL MISTRESS OF THE NILE

Shoot dates: Egypt April 3-9th

Sunset: 6 PM/ Sunrise 6 AM. Weather: Dark

DAY 4

Scene 1: Enter Gates of Hell 6 PM- 6 AM All scenes to be TBD

Scene 2: Return to land of the living 6 PM

Dinner: TBD

CHAPTER 28

The hairy foot was replaced by a calloused hand, and it guided Omm to what felt like a mound of worn tires. A voice, simple and gruff, ordered her to sit. Her instinct was the opposite, but where was a sightless lady going to escape to in a hellscape of angry appliances? She sat.

Omm could sense that the man was not alone, and nearby, someone was grilling meat. She waited for him to say more, but he seemed preoccupied with the other stranger, who had so far remained silent. After a moment, he said more gently than she had expected.

"Yes, it's done. Take it off the spit and have your share." Several minutes of unabashed chewing followed.

The duo didn't seem dangerous, but neither were they particularly welcoming. Omm decided she would sit a moment or two, collect herself and perhaps ask them the best way out of this wasteland. Then she heard the bray of a donkey. Whoever they were, they had transport. "Would that lovely creature happen to belong to either of you?"

The other voice asked for another piece of meat, and Omm realized it was a young girl.

"Not for sale," the man said.

"Heavens no, love, I wouldn't dream. I simply need a ride up there to the necropolis of Saqqara." Omm pointed behind her, not sure if that was still north.

It wasn't. "North is the other way." He paused, and Omm could only imagine he was studying her. "And it's too far for an old blind lady. What are you walking around here for, anyway? It is run by the Zabbaleen. They hate outsiders."

Omm remembered the term. Zabbaleen meant trash people, and the populace of Cairo relied on them to haul away garbage from their front doors. Surviving on the margins, without permanent homes, this community offered a vital service for millions of residents while never rising above poverty. They were also fiercely protective of their trade, and anyone attempting to steal from their trash would be met with resistance, sometimes violent.

"I've no interest in your crops," Omm calmly assured them, suspecting the donkey was hitched to a wagon of rubbish and knowing at last where she was: The Great Trash Dump, where refuse was illegally hauled after it was picked clean in Cairo. "I simply need to visit a few tombs." She realized this made her sound like a daft tourist who had wandered away from a tour group, certainly not someone under a severe time crunch to save a half-dozen people, including herself, from oblivion.

"You look bad," the man said. There was a sucking sound, and after taking her hand again, he laid a piece of grilled meat in it. Having not eaten since the morning, she gratefully accepted. It was gamey and slightly raw but deeply welcome.

"Lovely, what is it?"

"Dead."

He offered her more, but this time she refused, not out of disgust. She had consumed worse, but out of respect for what little they had.

"I will leave such delicious food for you and your daughter."

Another moment of chewing followed. The man was in no rush to do much of anything.

"She's not mine. I found her on the road. Helps me get stuff we can resell. We work our way up from Minya to Cairo."

"So, you're off to Cairo from here?"

Again, a long pause. "Yes."

"Then might I tag along?"

Both strangers stood, and it wasn't clear to Omm if they were leaving or simply searching for more goods.

"I can pay you. Quite handsomely."

Omm knew she didn't have a single Egyptian pound on her, and unless Said magically returned with his wallet, her promise would be broken. She wished she had hung on to the necklace she found in the last pyramid. That alone would make them immeasurably rich.

A yawning pause followed. The donkey brayed, and the wagon creaked. The girl clanged a few tin items together, perhaps tidying up the dishes. After a while, and with some annoyance, he responded.

"Well? You said you can pay, right?"

"Indeed I did."

"Then why are you still sitting down there? Mariam, help the nice lady into the wagon."

Omm squeezed onto the back, between bags overflowing with plastic bottles and broken electronics. The girl had kindly offered to give up her seat in the front, but Omm wouldn't hear of it. There were so few comforts in their world she wouldn't take that away. And Omm was used to discomfort. Indeed, she almost craved it. Last year, for her eightieth birthday, Said bought her a mattress, but after two days, she demanded he cart it away. It was too soft, too indolent. She needed to remain alert, and committed. The threadbare cot in her hut was more than suitable, even if a few springs had come loose and nicked her legs every now and again.

The cart owner's name, Omm learned, was Mahmoud. He had been a garbage person all his life in the City of the Dead, the medieval cemetery in Old Cairo. Once the finest Islamic mausoleums of their day, over the centuries, they instead became lodging for the poorest of Cairene. After his parents died, Mahmoud struggled to find his place. If it wasn't for the Zabbaleen, he would have surely followed his folks into the afterlife, but not being Coptic, he couldn't live among them. Instead, he was permitted to work the desert wastelands east of the Nile. But they were kind and often left him valuable goods he could claim as his own. The donkey was the first thing Mahmoud had ever purchased that he didn't eat or drink.

"As long as I have my animal and my cart," he proudly told Omm. "I have a home." Mahmoud impressed Omm. Like so many Egyptians she had met over the centuries, he persevered without complaint, regardless of the obstacles. There was a reason Egypt had lasted as long as it had. It wasn't the place that was eternal. It was the people.

As they bounced along a rutted road, Omm cursed her choice of transport. The donkey was in worse shape than she was and sometimes would stop in the road and shake uncontrollably. Mahmoud would set the reins down, tenderly caress its mane, and permit the creature to regain its senses. This often took several minutes. The little girl would use the time to leap from the cart and seek out mysterious items Omm could no longer see. Soon there was no room for her, and after a change of heart from Mahmoud, she accepted the invitation to join them upfront.

The child sat on her lap.

"Where do you come from?" Omm inquired.

The little girl remained as silent as a sphinx.

"She doesn't speak," Mahmoud said.

"Poor lamb. Mute?"

"She mumbles in her sleep. So perhaps she simply chooses not to."

Omm caressed the child's back. "Does she have a name?"

"I call her Mariam, after a woman I knew back in the City of the Dead. She used to work the trash mounds, separating syringes from the plastic. One time she stepped on an old needle and got very sick."

Omm thought of the many people in her own life who had passed. "A nice way to honor those we lost."

"Mariam didn't die. She is too tough for that," Mahmoud said with pride. "If this girl is to help me, she needs the same kind of strength." He gently urged his donkey forward. "I'm not even sure what town she's from. One time, when we passed an orphanage in Beni Suef she hid between bags. Wouldn't come out for miles."

"Poor dear, no family."

Mahmoud shrugged. "The only thing that matters is where you're going, not where you've been."

"Oh, I quite disagree," Omm responded wistfully. "We must never forget where we come from."

"That's a luxury. For me and her, it's a curse. Forgetting is best."

The cart inched slowly down a road worn deep from a million carts. After a few more stops to collect plastic chairs and tables, Omm lied that the faster they moved, the greater the payment. Mahmoud picked up the pace.

"Tell me when you see a giant pyramid built like a set of stairs. I'll just pop off there," Omm said.

"I see it now. How long has it stood there?" he asked.

Omm added up the years in her head. She loved recounting stories of the glorious past. "First pyramid in history. Built around 2650 BC as a ladder to the stars."

The donkey moved again, and Omm relaxed. She would soon be in the necropolis, and certainly, one of its original denizens would be welcoming. It wasn't until she heard the honk and screeches of a busy road that she grew worried.

"Excuse me, are we still going to the necropolis? They're all in the desert, you know."

"You said it's been there for thousands of years. Then waiting another hour or so shouldn't be a problem."

He got his donkey moving again.

Omm grew cross, knowing she had no right to be.

"But I'm in rather a hurry."

"So many people are. But today is Thursday, and the cart is full. Payday at the recycling plant."

Mariam screamed in delight, and Omm wanted to hop off, be free of these people. But when she tried, her legs wouldn't let her. They now appeared to be as useless as her eyes.

CHAPTER 29

Jared wouldn't let go of Kara for what seemed an eternity. She hugged him back and wiped away their collective tears with her scarf, now stained with blood, sweat, and hippo shit.

"They told me..." Kara said. "I thought... *Fuck.*" She gave him another hug.

"So did I."

Kara laughed. "You know some half-pint pharaoh's no match for me."

"Exactly what I said when I saw you turn that corner."

They leaned against the tomb wall and chatted softly while Ali and Derek swapped stories of how they got there.

"And then I realized if I tied mummy wrappings together..." Derek was explaining.

"I know why I thought you were dead," Kara said to Jared. "Some bastard told me. But why did you think the same of me?"

"When Tiya told you, you'd never see Lynette in the Field of Reed, I was worried you might... you know. Give up."

Kara blew her nose into her scarf. "Not gonna lie. I tried. Saw no purpose being here anymore and figured, hell, if death was coming anyways, I might as well go out with a bang. Have a good story to tell you and Lynette."

Jared smiled. "But you changed your mind? Good to hear."

"Not exactly. Ali changed it for me. He has strong arms. Thank him." She scrutinized her friend. "You look different. Taller. Satisfied. Almost smug." She smiled. "I know that look. Kinda like you're out and proud."

Jared blushed in a way that Kara had seen before. "I think I am."

"How? Yo. You didn't?" she whispered. "We're being chased by pharaoh's army and you found time to get laid?"

He remained silent, but his grin revealed all.

"Who? Not that hot warrior dude who looks like Djimon Hounsou?"

"Damn, he was fine..." Jared's smile faded as his thoughts turned to why he said goodbye to Mentmose. Part of it was to save her.

"Kara, listen, it's only going to get harder. I can see it. If we're going to get through this, I need you. Don't do anything stupid like that again." When she didn't seem convinced, he continued. "I rediscovered the person I used to be, maybe always was, but no longer saw. I'm asking you, as my dearest friend, to do the same."

Kara reached into her empty pockets. "I'd kill for a cigarette." She ran cool sand through her fingers instead. "The thing that kept me alive so long was my promise to you. Now that you've been resurrected, it won't happen again."

He reached into his bag and pulled out the lacquered box. "I kept this for you."

She took it lightly. "I knew you would." She sat it aside. "I think I'll leave it here for some archeologist to find three thousand years from now. You and I can visit her at the Met on a Sunday afternoon when we return." She raised her voice so the others could join the conversation. "So, let's see this stolen scroll of yours."

Jared unrolled the *Book of Gates* on the tomb floor and placed pebbles on either side so it wouldn't curl up.

"Can you make sense of any of this?" Ali asked, moving closer.

"Most of it, yes. This is the first gate right where we are standing," Jared said after locating the correct spot in the text. A few wavy lines with a boat on top. "And that's our boat."

Derek joined them. "We're in a dry desert tomb. You sure you're reading that right?"

"Here's the hieroglyph for a pharaoh," Jared pointed out. "This represents a solar barge that will transport Seti through the gates, so just stay close to him."

Nearby, Ali collected the film gear strewn across the burial chamber.

"The bastards could have left at least one case," he muttered. "How'd they expect us to carry it all?" He began shoving his sound gear into his pockets.

"They didn't, remember?" Kara dusted off her camera and flicked it on. "Okay, if this is it, let's gear up. Ali, clip a lav on Derek."

A few minutes later, they were a four-person film crew again.

"Check, check..." Derek said into his lavalier. "How do we start?"

Jared scratched his head. "Guess we wait until the first gate opens and follow Seti. Until then, catch your breath." He told Kara how they had come to acquire the scroll.

Ali retrieved the food and water left by the vizier—figs, dates, and chunks of roasted duck—and passed it around. "The call sheet did mention a 'light lunch'."

"What's the time, anyway?" Kara asked Derek. "As soon as something happens, set the timer for twelve hours."

Derek finally had something to offer. He got out his fancy underwater watch and held it tight in preparation, like a referee at a race track.

As he did this, Seti's alabaster sarcophagus began to radiate. Emerald images carved into the lid and sides, details of the *Book of Gates*, cast distorted men and monsters onto the ceiling. Then the entire coffin glowed. Inside they could see the outline of the pharaoh's reclining mummy.

The light grew brighter, so bright eyes were shielded, and Derek slipped beneath his fedora. Moving silhouettes appeared around the tomb and became flesh—eight wiry men in jackal masks. It wasn't clear to Jared if they had also been in hiding or had traveled from the world below.

Four of the men lifted the sarcophagus and transported it to a large boat that was moored in what appeared to be a misty river, where a moment ago, there was only mother rock. The boat was similar to the one Seti had traveled with on the Nile: fluted on either end, with a covered bench in the middle where the coffin could be cradled.

"The *Mesektet*, the night barque," Jared said, pointing to the boat and wavy lines on the scroll. "This will shepherd Seti through the hours of darkness."

Derek pressed a button on his watch. "6 PM on the dot. We're good until 6 AM. But how do we follow?"

The answer came soon enough. Another boat was moored nearby, not as long or as ornately built, but impressive just the same. The remaining jackal-faced sentries picked up oars and stepped inside, two up front, two in the rear.

"We tailgate," Jared said. "Remember what Tiya said. Our job is not to interfere in his journey, just to keep close and search for Mehy as we travel, record what we can. He's lost out there, and Seti wants us to bring him back into the world of the living. Do that for him, and he'll keep us safe."

Kara flicked on the onboard light and illuminated Derek, whose gaze remained fixed on the ground.

"Yo, Mr. Presenter."

"I know, I know. Present."

Nothing motivated Derek more than a spotlight. He slicked his hair back, checked his hat in the compact mirror and stepped onto the boat.

"Make way for the master of adventure," he announced, as did at the beginning of every episode.

Kara and Ali sat in the front, and turned their gear on Jared.

"Kara and I have been talking," Ali said. "We need to put you on camera. A host has to interview someone—and Derek barely speaks English, let alone a language 3,000 years dead."

"I'm the director, not a subject." Jared protested.

It had been a struggle enough to keep the team together and interpret the scroll. He had no desire to see every little screw-up captured on tape. Especially the Hall of Judgment, when his heart would be weighed against a feather to see if he was worthy to pass. He had done nothing but cower through his current life. If the gods played back the life and times of Jared Plummer, it would be plain for all to see. He'd be torn apart by a demon, and his crew would be lost forever within the Duat. All on camera for the gods to watch over and over.

"On this episode, we're all subjects," Ali said as he clipped a microphone onto Jared's collar.

As the boat left the dock, Derek turned to Jared, now in full presenter mode. "If we're traveling through the desert, why are we on a river?"

"The gates represent twelve hours of the nighttime sky," Jared explained. "It's part of their creation myth. When the earliest Egyptians looked up, they saw a giant bubble of blue water. Everything up there, the sun, the stars, the planets, sail across its surface in boats. In the evening, it's the same, they figured; you just can't see the water."

The river appeared a little wider than a stream at first, but as Seti's solar boat broke through the mist, features took on shape. The boats no longer seemed to be inside a hand-cut tomb but a glistening natural cavern. Mammoth stalactites clung to a ceiling so high it blended into black. A thin, eggshell haze coated the water and gave off a sulfuric odor as if something was rotting underneath. Seti's illuminated coffin acted as a beacon, but beyond that, there was no light source to tell the boatmen where they were going or what dangers lay ahead. Jared stole a peek at a ferryman standing next to him. His clothing and sandals were sewn of leather and cougar skin, and his face, it was now apparent, was not covered in a jackal's mask. He *was* a jackal from the neck up.

Ahead, the cave appeared to widen—no, open, like a door. Jared could glimpse natural light, but the sky was unnatural, the color of rust. The boats emerged into a denuded desert bisected by a tiny river, on either side broken statues of kings and queens. Some were buried to their chins, others sliced in half, their eyes fixed on something now out of reach. Ali repeated a final lines from 'Ozymandias.'

Round the decay of that colossal wreck, boundless and bare,

The lone and level sands stretch far away.

Strangest of all was the sun. It wasn't a sun at all but an enormous scarab beetle crawling over the cliffs and emitting an incandescent glow. Jared unrolled the scroll and recognized the hieroglyph for the sun god.

"That's Re, god of day," he whispered, out of respect for his presence. "Be prepared. As soon as Re dips over those mountains, the *Bakhu*, and his light disappears, we're in the Duat. He can no longer protect us until we sail through the hours of darkness and he rises again in the eastern cliffs."

"Who rules until then?" Derek asked.

Jared pointed to the image of a twisting snake on the scroll. "This guy. Apep."

"And he is...?"

"Lord of Chaos and the Eater of Souls."

"Ah, great." Derek looked to the camera as if to add a snarky comment, but words failed him.

Jared held up a hand to silence everyone as he peered into the placid river, seeing where Apep might be. This much he recalled: "Apep is banned from appearing above the horizon, anywhere the daylight can touch, so has not yet arrived. But I'm guessing he's close."

Re, still a scarab beetle, had halted his descent down the opposing cliff. His upper body now formed an orb that mimicked a setting sun.

Antennae wiggled, almost as if waving goodnight. A human-faced hawk landed on the bow of the boat, tilted its head in curiosity, and flew off muttering to itself. The sky bled from rust to red.

"Dear God, what the hell is that?" Kara asked, zooming on a large figure half up the mountain. There, almost camouflaged in the gloomy contours of the cliffs, was a monstrous serpent, his head eating its tail.

"Is that our Devourer of Souls?" Derek asked.

Jared only nodded. The thing was even bigger than he feared. The boatmen must have also been anxious. They dipped their oars deeper into the stream, increasing the speed and pulling closer to Seti's barque, which slowed as it approached a cave in the cliff.

Jared rolled up the scroll to keep it safe. He thought for a moment and then turned to his crew. The worst thing he could do was let them sit and tremble. Best keep them focused on what they were best at. Making a film. The show meant nothing to him by this point, but it did to them and made them feel worthy. "Seems a good place for a stand-up."

Kara tossed the camera on her shoulder and found her focus. "Rolling. Ali?"

"Speed."

A boom pole hovered over Derek, who appeared alarmed by the sudden attention like a kid caught daydreaming in class.

Jared moved behind the camera. "Okay, Derek, just tell us where we are and what our mission is."

"But I don't know the answer to either," he snapped. "This is all you're doing, remember."

"We're approaching the first gate. Pretend it's after a commercial break. A recap for your fans who are just tuning in."

STAND UP 4: ENTRANCE TO UNDERWORLD EXTERIOR: NIGHT

VIDEO: *Derek Dees standing on a boat.*

NARRATION: WELCOME BACK TO THIS VERY SPECIAL ANCIENT ENCOUNTERS. IF YOU'RE JUST JOINING ME, LET ME TELL YOU WHAT I'VE BEEN UP TO.

Derek moves towards the bow and for a wide shot.

SO FAR, I'VE BRAVED THE WORLD OF THE PHARAOHS, OUTWITTED RAMSES THE GREAT AND HIS BLOODTHIRSTY HENCHMEN, STOLEN A MAGICAL BOOK FROM THE HOLY OF HOLIES AND ELUDED HUNDREDS OF FLAMING ARROWS. NOW WITH THE SCROLL IN MY POSSESSION, I'M ABOUT TO SINGLE-HANDEDLY TRAVEL THE TWELVE GATES OF THE NIGHT AND SEARCH FOR MEHY, A PRINCE LOST TO TIME. IT'S MY PASSIONATE MISSION TO RETURN TO THIS LOST HERO TO THE WORLD ABOVE.

WHATEVER HAPPENS, REST ASSURED THAT THERE'S NO GATE THAT DEREK DEES CAN'T BREACH, NO CURSE TOO POWERFUL I WON'T OVERCOME, NO DEMON TOO EVIL I CAN'T—

"And cut," Jared shouted.

"I'm not done yet," Derek protested. "It was sounding good."

"A million flaming arrows?" Jared rolled his eyes. "Single-handedly travel the gates? I thought we were a team."

"It's my show. You guys are behind the scenes. That's the way it's always been."

"Two minutes ago, this was all my doing," Jared whispered into Kara's ear, but loud enough for all to hear. "Erase that crap, but shoot everything that happens from here on—even if someone breaks down in tears and begs you to power off. This time we're telling a real story."

Re continued his retreat. Only the tip of one antenna remained, and then everything succumbed to an eerie void. Seti's coffin, dimmer now but still glowing, acted as a beacon. After entering the cavern, it flickered like a restless spirit as it passed between rocky shores. Then, it, too, disappeared.

Abandoned to the dark, Jared could sense the boatmen stiffen. From the side of the barque, the lights on Ali's sound mixer went haywire: peaking and falling like a war zone. Below them, things were swimming, breathing, thumping against the bottom. Something chattered a few feet away. Kara leaned over to frame a shot but could see nothing beyond the fog in her lens created by nervous breathing.

"To hell with it," she said at last and flicked the onboard camera light on.

A misshapen face stared back, bloated and rotten. It smirked and continued chattering, but with a mouth full of water, its words were muddled. Suspecting that its message was not received, it tried to bite Kara in the arm.

Jared pulled her back and onto the floor of the boat.

"It should be apparent we stay inside the boat."

"Wha da fa? Who's out there?"

"Everything that wants to keep us from reaching paradise." Jared squinted ahead. "If that was the entrance to the underworld, that means the first gate is just ahead, beyond a long pointy corridor."

The river twisted towards a massive oval door, shut like the eyelid of the dead. On a high ledge stood a feline-faced creature. Not a house cat like the ones in Omm's hut, more like a lynx, clutching a trident and training her beady eyes on the intruders. At first, Jared thought it was a statue, but her head followed the direction of the boat. Below, fire licked at her claws.

"Hey, that's Am-heh," Ali said. "I remember her from my coloring book. They call her the Killer of Eternity." Seti's boat drew near, and a ferryman called out her name. Ali smiled when he heard it, pleased with his recollection. "To think that a circumcision gift would come in handy all these years later. Almost makes the pain of that day worth it." He considered his comment. "Almost."

Am-heh tapped her trident three times. The door rose from bottom to top, a single eye-opening with sharp, steely thorns for lashes. The two boats easily entered, but as soon as the gate blinked shut, titanic spikes emerged from the cave walls and slammed into the empty space above Seti's solar barque. Kara trained her light on one, which revealed them to be made of some shiny black stone, perhaps obsidian. A few contained the carcasses of those who had traveled no farther. The corpses wriggled, begging Seti for help, and Jared understood why. Anyone who entered the Duat was already dead and thus couldn't be killed again. An eternity of misery and pain.

As Jared's boat followed, more spikes were released, each closer than the last. One grazed the top of Ali's head as he stood to capture sound. He ducked to the safety of the boat before another emerged from the opposite end. Then, except for the echoed moans of the perpetually impaled, things grew quiet. Kara kept low but raised her viewfinder so they could all see the monitor. Nothing but empty walls.

One boatman rose to see what was ahead and yelped in pain as a spike pierced his shoulder. He tried to dislodge himself, but another one cut into his torso, and he hung there, suspended in space. The other ferryman tried to pull him down yet the boat was now moving on its own and they failed to reach him. From below the hull, the banging returned, louder and more insistent. Something was very keen to get inside.

The boat got caught in a tangle of weeds and one ferryman tried to unmoor the boat without standing. But the vessel held fast. Out of safe options, he stood and surveyed their landscape. He shouted something that Jared couldn't translate, more animal than human, which put the other two boatmen on guard.

They began frantically paddling as the water grew agitated, and a strange luster, emerald green, emanated from the depths.

"Could that be…?" Derek asked. Before he could finish his thought, the head of a gargantuan snake rose from the mist. "Apep?"

The lead boatman used his oar to smack it between the eyes, but only managed to make it cross. Apep's mouth opened wide and with a forked tongue, lassoed the ferryman and disappeared beneath the vessel. An oar bobbed to the surface, then a severed jackal head, frozen in a snarl.

"What does the scroll say?" Derek screamed. "Is there some spell to make it stop?"

With Jared's assistance, he unrolled the *Book*. His side of the papyrus trembled so badly that Ali had to help him hold it still.

"Oh shit," Jared said, pointing to what might have been a drawing of a bonfire. "Remain low."

The boat glided forward on its own, towards a narrow channel. Ahead, they could see Seti's boat had halted, hopefully at the entrance of the next gate.

Jared hazarded a glimpse behind him. Apep still followed, but when the boat reached through the narrows, it was too enormous to follow. Instead, it raised its head high and spat fire down the corridor. Jared felt the searing heat, but the boat somehow remained untouched. He felt along the floorboards, only then realizing that the ship was not made of wood but fused human bones.

The fire cooled, and the boat picked up pace. Darkness gave way to dim light, and a sudden breeze extinguished the remaining flames on the bow as they exited the mountain. Ahead, another gate loomed. This one rose above the river and swirled with mist. On a pedestal stood a goddess, mummified and clutching a staff. Seti's barque was awaiting Jared's, and as soon as it drew near, the mummy asked the pharaoh's boatmen something and waited for a reply.

Jared balanced his scroll between his knees. "Seti must name all the deities before entering the gate and what their powers are. If he forgets one, the door remains shut." The boatman called out a response, and the goddess tapped her staff. The door opened, and she turned to wood as if chiseled into the gate.

Before the gate could close, Jared stood and recited the same list of gods, not from just hearing them but from some religious text he had memorized as a young Egyptian boy. He could see himself squatting under a palm tree bending with dates, a dog by his side, and this time his father, stern and slender, listening in. Nearby a toddler, maybe his brother, played with the dog's tail. When Hori got two gods confused, his father handed him a slate and a chunk of lime. "Write it down and try again."

Jared glanced over at Kara, who was no longer filming. Instead, she was breathing heavily and seemed deeply shaken.

"I think he's gone for now," Jared comforted her. "You can relax."

Kara slowly nodded. She peered over the bow. "Only now am I grateful that Lynette couldn't be out there with all those rotting bodies. What a fool I was to wanna find her in a place like this."

The Second Gate remained open, and the boat sailed through. "Only eleven more to go," Jared sighed as he plucked the scroll from Derek's trembling hands and rolled it back up.

CHAPTER 30

A crystalline lake spread beyond end, so reflective it seemed as if Seti's boat, far ahead, had become two, the second traveling upside down. Then a heavy fog rolled in, and both faded from view.

As faces melted into the mist, no one did much but catch their breath. Ali checked the gash on his head, an inch from the one he received at the embalmers. The brim of Derek's fedora smoldered, and Jared reached over the boat to cup water and put it out. Remember the molten monsters of the last gate, he reconsidered and instead just stomped on the hat. He glimpsed Derek's tears but decided not to notice. Instead, he returned to the bizarre image on the scroll: a swirl of circles and a group of wrapped figures seated between trees or shrubs painted red. At first, he could make no sense of it. He closed his eyes and tried to access the past. An image flickered to life, something on an amulet he was placing between mummy wrappings. "Uh-oh."

"That's the best you can offer?" Derek's nerves were close to bursting. "What does it mean?"

"A fiery lake full of the unembalmed, I think."

"Is that bad?"

"In the Duat, it's the worst."

"And this?" Ali pointed below to a fish-headed woman holding onto a long cord, with the mummies pulling in the opposite direction. "Looks like a game of tug of war."

"I think it is," Jared said with a prick of recollection. "We need to find the rope."

Nothing was visible in the glassy water except a flat, undisturbed surface that cruelly reflected their troubled expressions. The oarsmen moved forward, but strangely, their efforts failed to produce a single ripple. It was like gliding across a mirror.

Ali pointed off the starboard side to what appeared to be something floating just ahead. At first, it looked like a long snake, and the boatmen halted. But then the lump took on detail. A long chunky cord of hemp floating loosely in the water. Kara tried to reach out for it but pulled back with a scream.

"What's wrong?" Jared asked.

Kara touched her palms, where welts had emerged. Her eyes were bloodshot, her forehead drenched in sweat. She picked up Derek's thermos of water and doused her face. "That lake is boiling."

A giggle from the back made Jared turn. Derek was staring into the water and grinning ear to ear. Had he finally gone insane?

"You good, man?"

The giggles continued.

"My first audition," Derek said. "I beat them all. Best looking, and I knew the job was mine as soon as I walked in." He beamed with joy.

"Say what?" Kara yelled. "You're thinking about that now, you arrogant little..." Her final word trailed off as something in the water caught her attention.

Jared consulted the scroll, but it was now aided by his own experiences. Embalmers often wove snatches of the *Book of the Dead* into the linens of their mummies. This way, should their tomb be destroyed, the dead traveler still had a backup plan to get through the Duat. This body of water was always mentioned as one of the most difficult challenges to overcome. "The Lake of Memories. All our best moments, our desires. Every rush of pride, every triumph, every kiss, every orgasm. It's a test for the dead."

"How do we get across?" Ali asked.

"We need that rope, fast."

Ali's face was now flush, not from heat but from some powerful memory. "How is my seeing my son's birth, a test?" He looked again and beamed with joy. "I need to see them now."

"The goal of the deceased is to reach the Field of Reeds, not be delayed by their old selves.' Jared said. "This water contains all the things that they left, still longed to be at the moment of death. The desire to dive in will be strong. If you do, you'll boil, and your body and soul will disappear."

"So, what's up with the cord?" Kara asked.

"That fish-headed goddess will help keep the rope taut. But only we can overcome our desires to remain in a past that no longer exists."

"But we *do* exist," Kara reminded him. "We ain't dead, remember?"

"If you're in the Duat, by their logic, you're dead. Just unembalmed. And have no right to be here."

They approached the rope. "We need to get that fast," Jared said to the oarsmen, who nodded in understanding. One managed to raise the cord a few inches before his wooden oar burst into flames.

"Find something that won't burn," Jared said.

Instinctively, everyone turned to Ali, whose face was moist with memory. He turned on Jared. "What the hell did you bring us for? So, I die and leave my children without a father, my wife a widow?"

"We won't die," Jared said calmly. "We just need that rope. Can you get it?"

Ali glanced at the cord, which was beginning to drift. He removed the microphone from his boom pole and, resting it on his shoulder like a harpoon, nudged it under the hemp and raised it. The boom's black paint melted away, and a silver sticker that warned "Property of Zamalek Rentals, Cairo Egypt" went up in a spark, but the metal underneath held. The rope, still smoking, was plopped across the bow of the boat. Now that it was hovering above the water line, it stretched beyond sight.

"Let it cool," Jared said. "Then we grab hold and pull. Wherever it takes us is where we're supposed to be."

Jared held on tight and tried to avert his eyes, but as it was only water that lay ahead, a jumble of memories surfaced. The first was a fresh one from ancient Egypt, deeply calming—a teenage boy, a bit older than he saw a few minutes ago, now sat by a pond, hunched over a scroll, scribbling away, while a bullfrog sat on a nearby lily pad and croaked. The boy picked up the frog, studied its underbelly, and went on scribbling. An older woman approached from behind, and Jared recognized her from his memory along the Nile.

His mother said warmly, "Hori, put that down and fetch water. Why are you forever studying every living thing in this garden?"

He placed the frog on a log and rose, and she tousled his hair as he passed. A flood of loss overcame him for a loving face long forgotten until now. How dare he ever let her slip from his memory? After all she had done. This time he would cling harder, never forgetting. The image faded, and others surfaced: seeing his first mummy, his younger brother. Hori was fascinated and, when no one was looking, ran his hand along the cool linen, noting how his arms were wrapped tightly to the body and how the death mask was strapped on with two thin beads of silver. He touched his brother's face. It was cool, silent, as smooth as hardened wax. Rather than recoil, Hori was transfixed. This was all that was left of his sibling, and he wanted only to honor and preserve him forever. Then, more memories swirled. Joining other boys in a stuffy windowless building but growing bored by religion lessons. Instead, he examined a dead sand viper he had picked up on the street, noting how its bones exquisitely joined its head, then glancing at another young man sitting nearby who shared the same fascination. His face was warm and beautiful, and in a flash, he saw the same man as old, still sitting next to Hori, their bare feet linked, toes casually playing with each other. Finally, as if one ancient expression of love was intimately linked to another a hundred lifetimes later, he settled in on his life as Jared Plummer. He walked through an Arabesque gate—*dear god, another gate?*—but this one was calming and delicately carved. He recognized it with a smile: the Alhambra in Granada, Spain. He had traveled there to assist in an episode highlighting 'The Haunted Castles of Andalusia.' While sitting by a trickling fountain, fact-checking a script, another man joined him. Young, warm, eyes radiating deep affection. Carlos, the local fixer.

On the job, Jared had always managed to keep his urges buried, but with Carlos, that proved impossible. The attraction was too ideal, too intense. Carlos had a long, lean swimmer's body, his skin tanned and glowing, his cheekbones high, his green eyes the center of any universe he might have found himself in. He was the perfect blend of masculine and feminine beauty. But more than that, he was wildly intelligent and witty, asking questions about the script few others had ever bothered. Carlos picked up on whatever subject made Jared's voice rise with excitement and became fully engaged—something Jared thought only he ever did. Carlos made his first move on Jared while the two were combing the city, looking for places to shoot stand-ups. In the middle of the Plaza de Espana, he took Jared by the shoulder, brushed away wind-blown hair, and kissed him in front of an Austrian tour group. It was so outrageously romantic that a fanny-packed couple raised their gelatos in celebration and snapped a picture. And that night, when Jared finally took Carlos into his body and their eyes locked onto each other until they both climaxed, it was obvious Carlos was The One.

Jared's memory lingered on the last days of the shoot and was one of the finest in his life. The two had been making breathless love for two weeks, and Jared couldn't wait for the work day to end so they could be alone again. Carlos knew of an intimate little Moroccan restaurant high in the hills of old Grenada and was keen to arrive before sunset. That was soon. As he sat next to Carlos, Jared felt their body heat mingling. An electrifying shiver coursed through him. Jared had certainly been with men before—strangers in bars and on apps that he could later delete. But defying his own rule about touching another man in public, Jared reached out and caressed Carlos's palm. Even here, in this dead lake of memories years later, Jared could feel his warm, sun-kissed skin; he drank in Carlos' cologne, which he had been searching for ever since that final, terrible day.

Dear God, how I miss him. I was handed a gift from the gods and threw it away.

Jared gazed directly into the Lake of Memories, his resolve defeated. He couldn't help himself. The feelings were too inviting, his face too overcome with pleasure. He wanted to jump in and sit on that shaded fountain at the Alhambra forever. But then he remembered he was here on a mission, and that was to make sure Kara loved again. Ali watched his children grow, and Derek became the genuine star he wanted so badly to be. And he would create new memories to share with Carlos.

He allowed them a final moment of bliss. Kara was grinning, Ali wept in joy, Derek was smirking, no doubt at some event where he bested everyone around them. He had never seen them so collectively happy.

Is true joy only possible in retrospect, when it's been smoothed of context and glimpsed in isolation?

Whatever the answer, everyone had lost their resolve to get across the lake. Even the oarsmen barely gripped the rope. The boat listed to one side as Derek and Ali were peering off the same side, the hemp abandoned at their feet.

It was time to bring them back, or they'd be lost forever. "Everybody! Pull!" Jared screamed.

Derek rubbed his eyes and grabbed the rope tight, disturbed by something he had seen. He put full effort into pulling the cord, and the solar boat jerked forward. Ali erased a tear and did the same, and then Kara, her face dripping with sweat, the sunburn on her face and hands now cut open and bleeding. The boat picked up speed.

A mild, unexpected breeze blew across Jared's face, and he could smell safety ahead, rich and verdant. The mist had lifted, and they were approaching a swampy island bursting with lotuses. Framing it was a gargantuan gate. As they passed under it, the crew marveled at its construction. The pyramid-shaped doorway appeared to be cut from enormous trees and studded with rubies, emeralds, and other precious stones. At the top sat a striking figure munching on a lotus blossom. He was short and green, with a pendulous belly and drooping breasts. An ibis perched casually on his head.

"Hapi, lord of the marshes," Ali said with relief as they sailed beneath. "A benevolent god, at least that's the way I colored him."

Seti's solar barque was harbored among the irises, the boatmen apparently waiting for them to catch up. Behind them, on a hill, the fish-faced goddess was holding the other end of the cord. When Jared's boat was safely through the gate, she let go and dived into the water. The rope became root and blended into tangled earth.

The other crew members rubbed bloodshot eyes and took stock of their surroundings. The allure of cherished memories still held them fast, and they remained too vulnerable to speak. Instead, they stared into the middle distance, a mask of loss marring their expression as faces and voices, now just fragile feelings, fragmented and faded.

As they pushed through the marshlands, Jared saw what, at first glimpse, looked like gray-shelled turtles floating among the stalks. But as he drew closer, one of the shells stood up, and two human eyes stared back. Soon, hundreds of human heads poked up from the muck. Blanched and bloated, each remained grotesquely alive. Some blinked, and one scratched her head where a weevil had been burrowing a hole. But as the boat approached, they all slunk down again as if it was some other party they were expecting. Only the top of their heads remained above water, perhaps so they could be spotted by whomever they were awaiting.

"This is in the scroll—a bunch of round things coming out of the water, but I couldn't make sense of it," Jared said as he moved to the center of the boat. More and more eyes appeared in the swamp. "Maybe the Forgotten Ones. The millions who died in the Nile, swept away in floods, eaten by crocodiles, drowned when mothers turned their heads. None had a proper burial, their names and bodies lost for all time."

"Why are they here?" Kara asked, zooming in as one of the heads drifted closer.

"The Nile is sacred. Without it, Egypt wouldn't exist. Osiris says that any who succumb to its power will be remembered in the Duat."

A few drew near, as if understanding his words and desperate to be seen. Some were old, others no more than infants.

Jared pointed to the riverbank, where Hapi's minions were clearing space in a field of wheat with golden scythes. "I guess they await their turn."

The minions plucked a body out of the water, a gaunt woman whose half-eaten midsection ended at the ribcage. With great respect, they laid her on a wooden plank and walked her to a fresh hole. A smile crossed her face as she was lowered and a handful of raven soil tossed on top. Ripe wheat sprung up, and soon, there was no trace of a grave at all. Hapi's minions returned to the marshlands and reached for another, this time a baby still bundled in swaddling. So tiny, he was carried to his grave in the palm of a single hand.

The boat reached the shore. One of the minions bridged it to dry land with one of the wooden planks, being mindful not to disturb the colony of heads poking from the water. The crew made their way to a grassy pasture. Reed mats had been arranged, and Jared stretched out on one, fighting fatigue. Above, the sky, neither dark nor light, cast a weak shadow that blended into the grass below. As they sat, wiping beads from their brows, Hapi brought a basket of figs and bowls of crisp, cool water.

"Is it okay?" Derek asked.

Jared grabbed a fig and nodded. "Should be. This is now the fifth gate, a sort of way station." The minions arrived with freshly baked bread, but knowing where the wheat came from, everyone avoided it. The *Book of the Gates* was unfurled, and Jared studied it. "Weird. There seems to be some sort of town up ahead, on dry land and away from the gates. Never heard about this before."

"Who'd choose to live here?" Ali asked. "Halfway through the gates of hell."

"No idea. Even the words on the script are written lightly, as if barely there."

Jared nibbled on a fig and stretched his legs, happy that, for the moment anyway, all were safe.

Surprising everyone, Derek rose with a start. "Well then, why are you all sitting there like a bunch of gay-ass sissies? Get your camera and let's go see if our prince is there. That's our job, right?"

He traipsed off down a hill.

"What suddenly got into him?" Ali asked in surprise.

"Would it be wrong to just kill him?" Kara half-joked, while Jared groaned. "We're in hell, after all. Save him a trip later."

After a sigh, Jared stood. Derek was no friend, but a promise was a promise. Everyone makes it out alive.

"Ah, shit, come on. He'll only piss off some demons by trying to give 'em Derek Dees swag."

CHAPTER 31

At the crest of the hill, the crew let out a collective gasp. Below, the field dipped to a sprawling town, where hundreds of forms came and went, some fully visible, others flickering like an old black-and-white TV. Yet one thing was strangely missing: noise. Not one voice, not one scrape of the grindstone, not one counteroffer in the marketplace.

"Yo, director, what does your magic scroll say about that?" Kara asked.

There were so many people passing through and blurring into one another that it almost seemed like one pulsating life force, not individual souls. Many were dressed like everyday denizens of the Nile, but others wore colorful wool fabrics or feather plums in their headdresses.

"Not sure. But according to the *Book of the Dead*," Jared recalled, "anyone who ever passed through Ancient Egypt, in any life and any form, is allowed passage here."

He could see Kara scanning faces, obviously looking for Lynette, but he knew she wouldn't be here. This was only for those who followed the ancient gods, were invited into the Duat, and for reasons unknown, gave up along the way. As far as he knew, that didn't include Lynette Tannenbaum, who never showed any real love or interest in Egyptian mythology, let alone the Torah. He wondered briefly if he'd see his ancient mother or brother, but also knew they wouldn't be here. Not only did they have the strength to survive the Weighing of the Heart, he made sure they were flawlessly embalmed after they died so the gods would embrace them.

The crew watched as phantoms drifted past, some silently calling out hello to each other, others blithely dipping through those around them. Many had faded to the barest of forms, more smudges than people. A few appeared absolutely feral, tribesmen from the earliest days of civilization, while others dressed in medieval Islamic garb or even blue jeans and T-shirts. One had a still camera around his neck and clutched a *Lonely Planet.*

"So all these people, no matter when and where they were born, came here after they died?"

"Egypt meant something to them. Reincarnation, maybe, or just obsession. But I guess they were afraid to confront the next gate and make it to paradise." As Jared said this, he wondered if one day this was his destiny, linked to some past, he couldn't find peace with and was unable to move beyond it. A lifetime of wandering in place, afraid to take a leap of faith. Part of it, he had to admit, held a certain charm.

How easy life would be. A world free of confrontation.

The village resembled a normal Egyptian town. Low-rise mud brick houses and tiny stone temples were linked by unclogged canals and manicured footpaths free of wear and tear. But up close, it proved to be as ill-defined as those who dwelled within. Houses were papyrus thin, opaque enough to expose those living within, who mostly sat staring. An indeterminate market spread out in the center of town; stalls lined the perimeter, and peddlers pushed wagons bereft of goods. Yet not one sound escaped their lips. Not one cloud of dust was disturbed by their shuffling feet. Above, a shining sun offered mild heat but little light, as if the entire place was under a protective dome. The town was a pantomime of what life was like in the world above. No one showed interest in the four intruders or, quite possibly, simply couldn't see them as they existed in another realm.

"Does this place have a name?" Derek asked Jared when the camera found him.

Jared sounded out the hieroglyphs. "*Shu-yet Ni-wt*," he said. "Shadowtown."

A girl no older than six or seven, skin marble white and dressed not in ancient garb but in a tattered blouse, drew closer. A yellowed bandage circled her head. She looked more like something out of *Angela's Ashes* than pharaonic Egypt. But unlike the others, she appeared to take notice of the crew. A look of surprise spread across her face when she saw Jared.

"Well, blimey, I thought you'd be taller." Her accent was pure Dickensian.

"You see us? You know us?" Jared asked as Kara zoomed in for a close-up.

"Of course, Omm mentioned you, said I should say hello should you come 'round. You bein' my replacement 'n all."

"Replacement?" Jared asked.

"You're Jared, right? Takin' over for Omm, I hear." Then she remembered something and pantomimed a lock and key over the mouth. "Was supposed to be a secret."

Jared halted in shock. So that's what Omm meant during their first call when she said, "I can show you things you've only dreamt about, and if you like them, make them last forever."

She expected me to take her place? Who said I wanted to? Or…do I? A life bereft of fear or disease, where all I had to do was watch over an ancient tomb as I gently grew old.

He was about to ask her to explain herself, but Derek jumped in first. "You're saying you know Omm?"

The girl went silent as if the question was a puzzle. At last, something sparkled in her eyes. "Ah, yes. I was Omm, or rather I suppose, she was me. I daresay it's all a terrible muddle by this point."

Derek stepped closer and offered a practiced smile. "You're Dorothy Kershaw, the *real* Dorothy Kershaw?"

"Was that my name? We don't need them in Shadowtown. No one ever asks questions here."

Derek was now in full-fledged host mode and at his best. "Well then, may I be the first?"

Ali stretched a boom pole over the little girl's head, mindful not to brush her bandage. "Speed."

Dorothy: How exciting. What's all this for, then?

Derek: For a film we're making. You remember those of course.

Dorothy: Do I?

Derek: You know, umm, Charlie Chaplin, Buster Keaton… Jared, when did she give up the ghost again?

Jared: Escapes me—a freakin' long time ago.

Derek: *A Trip to the Moon? Train Entering the Station*?

Dorothy: Afraid no bells are ringing.

Derek: Never mind. We're searching for Prince Mehy, Son of Seti. Have you seen him?

Dorothy: The Crown Prince? Whyever would he linger in Shadowtown?

Derek: It seems good enough for you, why not him?

Dorothy: That's just daft. He has the power of the gods and kings helping him onward. A big coffin and a roomy solar boat. *(whispering)* Friends in high places, as it were. Most of us didn't have anyone. We were on our own when we arrived. Many, like me, were not even mummified, which means we'd never get past the next few gates anyway, so why bother?

Derek: So Mehy is relaxing in heaven, and you're wandering Shadowtown in the same clothes you were buried in. Seems a bit unfair. Tell me, how did you feel about Omm taking over your body, thrusting you out?

Dorothy: I don't think that's how it happened. Did it?

Derek: As Omm told me herself, you fell on your head, and when you died, she invaded your body or something.

Dorothy: Not Omm, silly, you mean Tiya.

Derek: Right, Tiya.

Dorothy: She didn't take it. That'd be awfully rude. I gave it to her, you see.

Derek: But why?

Dorothy: I just fancied coming here, I suppose. My present existence bored me. It was a bit dull and jog-trotty. London weather, you know. And I had bandy legs and dodgy eyes, didn't much fancy where things were going. And she seemed keen to use my *ka* for other purposes. A fair swap.

Derek: You like it here, then?

Dorothy: It's grand.

Derek: Mind showing us around?

Dorothy: My pleasure. But fair warning, residents will only see if they're not afraid of you. We've no place for fear here.

Derek: Fascinating.

Jared: Derek, we don't have time for a tour right now, especially if Mehy isn't here. We need to move on. But one final question for you, Dorothy. Why do you see us when no one else does?

Dorothy: I can only imagine I'm not afraid of you. *(pause)* Not sure why. You all look quite terrifying. Except for that hat. It's funny.

Jared: Were you sent to tell us something? Does Tiya or Omm have a message?

Dorothy: Yes, that's it.

Derek: What is it?

Dorothy: From Tiya, now that you mention.

Derek: Tiya, who's dead?

Dorothy: Look around, love. Most of us are.

Derek: Fair enough. What did she say?

Dorothy: I'm afraid it's gone soft again. Can't recall. It was ever so important, though, that I remember.

Jared: Do think, please. We're in a hurry. Was it about the gates?

Dorothy: Yes, that was it! The gates.

Jared: What exactly?

Dorothy: Have you nicked a book of some sort?

Jared: *(noise, microphone scratching)* This? The *Book of Gates*?

Dorothy: Must be.

Jared: Well?

Dorothy: Sorry?

Jared: What about the *Book of Gates*?

Dorothy: Tiya said to get rid of it. Quickly.

Jared: Get rid of it? She said that?

Dorothy: Quite sternly.

Jared: Did she say why?

Dorothy: She did indeed.

(pause)

Jared: And?

Dorothy: Come again?

Jared: I'm curious to know why she said to chuck the book?

Dorothy: Ah. If you arrive at the Hall of Judgment with that stolen artifact, the gods will be most displeased. You'll be gobbled up by Ammit, Eater of Hearts.

Jared: Wait, we're to be judged as well? Thought we could slip by behind Seti.

Dorothy: No one slips by the scales, silly. Then we'd have heaps of undesirables running about, ruining it for the honorable ones. A bit like Liverpool. *Eww.*

Jared: Certainly, we're an exception? Honored guests?

Dorothy: I can't imagine. More like intruders, I dare say. Best take it up with management.

Derek: Is that the only message? Anything more?

Dorothy: That's not enough? Seems rather a lot. *(pause)* Right. She did say it would be a pity if I ran into you at all. I recall that bit.

Derek: And why's that?

Dorothy: Because I'm afraid she doesn't need you anymore. Said that Mehy should not be saved, and it would have been best if you had not come at all. You'll only muck things up.

Derek: She told you all that?

Dorothy: I think so. To be honest, I've completely forgotten what I've just said. *(pause)* Tell me, have any of you a tin of Fray Bentos Steak and Kidney Pie?

Derek: Fresh out.

Dorothy: I do miss those.

Derek: Would you care for a baseball cap with *Ancient Encounters* on it?

Dorothy: *Eww.*

Jared: Wait, come back! What did she mean about me being a replacement? Or how we survive the Hall of Judgment? You can tell me, I won't say anything!

Derek: Who cares, Jared? The rest seems more pressing. She said we shouldn't have come? Dorothy, are you sure?

Dorothy: *(faintly)* Possibly. She said the whole thing was a dreadful blunder, and she'd feel just awful if you all got stuck here for nothing. Ta!

At the docks, the oarsmen were nervously awaiting the crew, and they jumped into the boat before they could make any sense of what they just heard.

"Rewind the footage," Jared demanded, too nervous to sit. "Let's be sure she said what we think she said. The accent was thick."

Kara laid the camera on her lap, and the player whirled to life. When she peered into the viewfinder, he could only muster a *Wha da fa*?!

"So we *did* hear it wrong?" Jared asked hopefully.

"No freakin' clue." She held the monitor up so they could view the playback. Derek and Jared were the only things on the screen. No

Dorothy Kershaw, not one figure or house from the *Shuyet* had been captured. It was two men talking to a fallow field.

A terrifying thought occurred to Kara. She hurriedly rewound the footage. When they saw the Nile bodies and, further back, the spikey cave, there was a collective exhale.

"It's only this place the camera couldn't capture," Kara concluded. "A world of delusion."

"So then everything she said wasn't real either," Jared said with visible relief. "Maybe the whole thing was a trick? The book, the weighing of the heart..."

"But what if it's not?" Derek turned on Jared, his voice trembling. "What if they've been playing us all along? I told you stealing that book was stupid, Plummer. What was I thinking, letting you lead me in there?"

Jared had no response. For the first time, Derek might have been right. What the hell *was* he thinking of stealing from the gods and then entering their domain? As if they wouldn't know. He was doomed. They all were.

The current pulled them silently along, the river beneath them a mossy green. The team slipped deep into their own thoughts, unsure what to do but wait and see what lay ahead.

Kara touched the welts on her forehead, remembered something, and moved closer to Jared. Her tone was soft and intimate. "So, what did you see in the lake of memories?"

The question took Jared by surprise, and he struggled to formulate a lie. "Nothing much, silly stuff from childhood. Why?"

"I happened to catch sight of you. Haven't seen you that happy since Seville."

Jared nervously glanced behind him to make sure that Derek and Ali were not listening. Both stared off the side of the boat, enveloped in private thought. Just to be safe, Jared lowered his voice to a conspiratorial whisper.

"Yes, I thought of Carlos. But that's ancient history."

"Funny you using that expression here," Kara joked, trying to coax her friend to reveal more.

The quip failed to elicit a laugh, so she tried a different tack.

"We were only in Spain a year ago. His number is still in your phone."

Jared was about to insist they'd talk about it later, but a voice from behind didn't give him a chance.

"You talking about Carlos? That swishy fixer guy?" Derek asked, not as deep in thought as Jared had hoped. "*That* explains it. I knew something was off about you." The host shook his head and glanced at Ali for some sort of mutual distaste, but the sound man only peered back in confusion. "We shoulda saw it a mile away, buddy," Derek explained. "Our director here's a queer."

Jared's face glowed molten red. One of his greatest fears had come to pass, and at a moment when he was finally beginning to gain control of his feelings and actions. Now, complete emasculation would surely follow. He threw Kara an angry stare for outing him but, too terrified to communicate anything more, looked at the river ahead as the boat pushed through an embankment of orchids. Even these delicate, gentle flowers seemed to be judging him, seeing him in a critical new light. Jared had come so far, only to be exposed as a liar, thief, and fraud. With nowhere safe to turn, he placed the *Book of Gates* across his lap and studied it in minute detail. His fingers traced the edges: tattered, frayed, and brittle, as venerable as time itself. Inside, arcane hieroglyphs only he could read revealed their secrets.

The most prized artifact in Egyptian history, and here it is in the hands of Jared Plummer, the nobody kid from Kansas. Yes, I stole it, but only to save my friends. I risked everything to claim it, to take charge and make the most out of a bad situation. Now, I'm gonna be defeated because some guy I work with, some pompous clown who thinks only of himself, doesn't approve of who I'm attracted to? Who has the audacity to judge me for whom I love and value? With everything that's unfolded, all that I've faced, this is what I feared for so long?

Jared carefully rolled the scroll back up and turned to Kara, his angry stare replaced with a relieved smile, like someone who had just survived a crash landing without a scratch:

"Yes, of course, I thought of Carlos," he said loudly. "I thought about how much I love him, miss his touch. The last time we made love." Then the smile waned. "Mostly, I thought about our last words."

Carlos had offered him everything he desired in a lover and friend and had lifted Jared to new heights in a few short weeks. And what did Jared the Gerbil do with the gift? True to form, he abandoned it the moment it got too real, the moment he weighed his desires against the fleeting opinion of others. And the Pool of Memories called him out on it, reminding him how he had let two people down instead of one. It could have been wonderful. Carlos had never been to New York, and after the show wrapped, he suggested a New Year's trip over to spend it together. But it wasn't until they were in a cab to the airport and Jared had still not offered his address or phone number that the penny finally dropped. Carlos was shocked and hurt, asking if all he had been was a meaningless hotel hook-up, a dirty secret not worthy to share with Jared's friends and family. They rode the rest of the way in aching silence, and when Carlos leaned over for a goodbye kiss, Jared jerked away. A day hadn't gone by since where Jared didn't regret that repulsive act, hating himself for how wholly devastated Carlos looked. How would that look on the Scales of Justice? A million times since that ride, Jared thought about calling, apologizing, wondering if he'd be forgiven. And a million times, he never did. Because that would mean coming out and facing himself.

"You guys were great together," Kara said, aware of what Jared was reliving and revealing publicly for the first time. "You know he was the one."

"He was. And if we make it out of here, I'll tell him that personally."

Another word reached them from behind, but it wasn't Derek's. "Who exactly are we talking about?" Ali asked.

There was a pause before Jared turned around and looked both his crew members in the eye. "An old boyfriend. Someone I should have loved far better than I did."

Ali smiled warmly, unaffected by the proclamation. "*Malesh.* No matter, like Kara said, we ain't dead yet."

Jared's attention shifted to Derek. The host clearly wanted to say something, no doubt hurtful, but still seeking the ugliest words possible. As Jared waited, one thing became certain—he didn't give a toss as to what those words would be. The "host," he now realized, was the opposite: a parasite feeding off the lifeblood of others. But his attacks could no longer do damage, could no longer get under Jared's skin. The two maintained eye contact until Derek, flinching first, pointed to the scroll.

"So, you gonna read that thing and tell us what's next? It's not like we have all night."

Jared returned to the book as Kara scooted closer, ostensibly for a better look. Instead, she squeezed his arm and gave him a peck on the cheek. "There, didn't I tell you it would be easy? And don't you feel wonderful?"

"Like I'm floating on air," Jared said, his eyes still lined with tears, both from memories of Carlos and how an enormous anchor had been lifted with such ease. He said nothing more because there was nothing more that needed to be said.

A metallic bang at the crew's feet snapped them back to the crisis at hand. One of the minions had placed a golden scythe in the boat.

Ali raised it and squinted at the approaching gate ahead, black and fathomless.

"*Allah ya'een.* What do those minions know that we don't?"

CHAPTER 32

As the donkey cart at last approached the necropolis of Saqqara, Omm sought voices coming from the many tombs that peppered the desert. Yet the only sound that reached her was the wail of Mahmoud's beast as it brayed and dug its hooves into the sand. The message seemed obvious: it had no intention of shepherding some old coot up a steep hill to a sunbaked ruin.

"We'll rest here for the night," Mahmoud said, and then, nothing more.

Omm tried to jump off the cart, but her legs still refused to budge. With every passing moment, her link to Tiya faded, and whatever afflictions had been kept at bay had returned in full.

Mahmoud could see that Omm was ailing. He helped her down from the wagon and pulled something else from the cart after moving her to a nearby rock. It squeaked as it approached, and it wasn't until she was guided into it that she recognized what it was. An old swiveling office chair, one wheel lost and replaced with what felt like a worn tennis ball.

"Where to?" Mahmoud asked.

"The nearest tomb, if you'd be so kind."

Ahead lay a row of rectangular tombs with sloped sides and flat roofs. These were called *mastabas*, Arabic for 'bench' and popular with the elite in the earliest dynasties of Egypt. As they approached the first and largest, Omm heard a faint voice echoing from within. *So there is a false door.* But as they approached, a wizened man in a gallabiyah halted their advance.

"Ticket, ticket," he muttered in English.

"I haven't time, love, lives are at stake," Omm answered in flawless Arabic. "I must get inside and talk to the owner. She's expecting me."

The man shifted to his native tongue. "If I let you in without a ticket, all those behind you will expect the same. Then the Antiquities inspector will get word, and guess who will be out of a job?" The voices Omm was hearing from inside the tomb were no longer talking but screaming. Something awful was unfolding, possibly to Jared and his friends, and if she didn't get in there soon, they might be silenced forever. "I can come round with the money in a few days. Someone in there needs help straightaway."

"One hundred Egyptian pounds. Only sixty if Egyptian."

"Oh, but I am."

The guard laughed. "One hundred, I think."

Omm bridled at the insult and was keen to tell him so. But inside, more screams brought her to the edge of despair. Being thwarted by her own crumbling body was an obstacle she had long expected. But coming so far to be defeated by an entrance fee of one hundred pounds, about six US dollars, was simply unacceptable. Mehy would never forgive her. And Jared and his friends would spend eternity getting torn to shreds every night by Apep.

"You should be ashamed of yourself, talking to an old blind woman like that." Mahmoud reached into his waistcoat and pulled out the soiled stack of bills that he had just received at the recycling center. The one Omm begged him not to go to, and the only money the three of them possessed. "That's two hundred and fifty. Two Egyptians and one foreigner. You owe us thirty change."

Omm listened as Mahmoud handed the guard all of his earnings, and they were counted out. She wanted to protest, but too much was at stake. Instead, with a bowed head, she thanked him. "Shukran."

"Afwan," Mahmoud said mildly. "I always knew you had nothing. Otherwise, why put your trust in two Zabbaleen? Why not hire a taxi?" He called to Mariam, and the two followed her in. "She has never seen the inside of a tomb. Consider it her first holiday."

Mahmoud pushed the busted office chair into the tomb. A series of rooms linked by a labyrinthian hallway led to a cramped burial chamber. Omm again heard terrible cries coming from some place beyond the walls, terror echoing across centuries. Running her hand along the wall told Omm that the tomb had been badly damaged in the ancient past and repurposed many times since. Still, enough of the original wall must have survived, as she could sense someone was waiting on the other side.

"Get me closer to the wall, love," Omm said to Mahmoud. Once the squeaking stopped, Omm lowered her head and summoned the owner. She heard sandstorms rising and falling, a million suns buzzing bright and melting away. Mariam and Mahmoud drew near and placed their hands on the chair for support, presumably seeing all that was unfolding but saying nothing. Perhaps they assumed all ancient tombs did this, having never been in one.

Time shuttered and stopped. Omm turned to Mahmoud. "What do you see?"

"A sad lady dressed for a funeral."

"Lovely, is she the one doing the screaming?"

Mahmoud waited a moment before answering. "No, that's coming from behind her. I see men on horseback with silly silver hats and black beards chasing people down. A bald man just took a saber in the belly. This is heaven? This is what happens when you die and are buried?"

The woman spoke hurriedly for a few moments until Omm shook her head grimly. "Persians," she informed Mahmoud, who had not asked. "She welcomes us in, calling us fools for wanting to visit. But her offer is of no help. I'm afraid it can't travel back any further than this."

Mahmoud only sniffled, at ease with all Omm was sharing. "Looks plenty old to me. How far do you want to go back?"

"It's not me that needs to go back. It's my friend Jared needs to come forward. He's in 1279 BC, you see, and this one only goes back to the 6th century BC."

"Poor Jared," Mahmoud remarked without irony and was then distracted by what sounded like someone being slaughtered on the other side. "Who are they? Seems nasty."

"The army of King Cambyses. Conquered Egypt and killed everyone they could. Not a great time to go poking about. This kind Persian lady suggested I try a few doors down. It's older, pharaonic. And according to her, someone there is expecting us."

Mahmoud wiped his nose, saying nothing. In time, the office chair squeaked to life as they exited the tomb. Outside, someone was waiting. "There you are! Why are you in a broken office chair?"

Omm clapped her hand in delight. "Dear God, I've missed you!"

"And I you," Said replied. "I would have caught up sooner, but the inspector's computer was pre-pharaonic. Kept crashing, or they would have seen my Tourist Guide certificate." He reached down and gave her a hug. "I've been looking for you in every tomb between here and Abydos. Are you okay? Who are your friends? And what's kept you?"

"Let's just say I've not been at my best. And the transportation has been spotty."

"No luck? We only have—" he glanced at his watch. *2.46 AM.* "Less than four hours."

"I'll tell you on the way to the tomb three down. Seems that's the one we need. But first, a word with Mahmoud. Is he still here?"

"I am," came a voice from not far away.

"Thank you for the loan of one hundred and sixty pounds. I must repay your generosity," Omm added. "Have you ever heard of the Lost Army of Cambyses? They belonged to the awful king responsible for all you just saw in there. Ruled cruelly, killed many, but the gods finally fought back."

Mahmoud was barely listening. He had just seen a tomb containing some ancient war. Hearing about another was likely of no interest.

"On a sunny morning in 542 BC," Omm said, hoping he was still listening, "he led an army of fifty thousand Persians into the desert from this very spot. Was off to attack the temple of Amun but never made it."

"Why?"

"A sandstorm swallowed them to the man. Treasure hunters have been searching ever since. Herodotus spoke of it. Silver swords, jeweled helmets, golden shields, all still cling to their bones. The dying merchant in there just told me where they fell." She let that image sink in a moment but the two had yet to catch on. "Mariam, dear, fetch me some pen and paper." The little girl presented what felt like a tattered school notebook and the nub of a crayon.

"Now, pay attention." Omm made a purple X. "This is the little rise we are standing on. Beyond the ruins, due west, there's a dry riverbed." Omm drew a red line with two wiggles. Mahmoud and Mariam remained confused and even Said was unsure where Omm was going with this. "Everybody understand? Now, just past an old monastery half buried in sand, you'll note that the ground dips." Omm's eyes closed as she recalled the chatty Persian woman's words. "Dig there and you'll find the entire army down the belt buckle."

Mahmoud glanced at the drawing and only snorted. "I like stories, but people like us aren't meant to find treasure."

"Nonsense. That's exactly who should find it. Consider yourself repaid in full."

Said pushed her down the cobbled street. "You know I have money in my wallet. Could have just paid them back."

"This is far lovelier. Think they'll bother to look?"

Said stopped pushing long enough to glance behind them. "They're already on the desert road. The little girl is holding your drawing up the horizon."

They approached the next *mastaba* and new voices emerged from within. Unlike the Persian tomb, which reverberated with horrid cries and screams, this one presented a completely different vibe. Inside, they heard peals of laughter and the clink of glasses. A raucous party was in full swing.

CHAPTER 33

As they sailed nearer the serpent's lair, Jared unrolled the *Book of Gates* and tried not to dwell on Dorothy's warning to toss it before it was too late. He'd be lost without it, and holding made him the leader by default. It was a good feeling and one he had no desire to relinquish.

"Damn, that's some freaky shit," Kara said as she caught a glimpse of the papyrus. "What do you make of it?"

Jared hunched over for a closer view. "Well, this is a snake-shaped table lined with mummies, then on the top, men holding tridents in one hand, a long snake in the other."

"Which means?"

The scroll was rolled up and carefully placed at Jared's side. "Best I can glean is that Apep is waiting, in some awful form or other."

Kara began filming again as the boat meandered toward the mountain, the riverbank weedy and ill-defined. In the center, a perfectly round tunnel plunged into the rock. On rippled ridges, watching them approach, were hundreds of baboons, baring fangs and scratching themselves. A few copulated with each other. Another swung low and tried to steal the golden scythe from Ali's hand, but he saw it coming and sliced the animal's hand clear off. It didn't scream, just retreated up the mountain and made a noise that resembled a laugh. Now keeping their distance, the baboons began pissing and tossing feces. A glob hit Derek on the head, but he didn't flinch. He was somewhere else, consumed by thoughts and, as usual, unwilling to help. As the boat skirted the cliff, Jared noticed that all the baboons now sported erections.

The largest, silver-backed and boasting a huge phallus, awaited them at the door. "Babi, son of Osiris," Ali informed them. "My coloring book didn't include the erection. Might have been cruel considering it was a circumcision gift."

Ali stood up and repeated the gatekeeper's name. The door parted, and the oarsmen glided the vessel into the tunnel. The crew laid flat, but no spikes sprang from the wall, and no blast of fire roared down the cave. Ahead, the pharaoh's solar barque illuminated the water like a floating Chinese lantern, letting them know they were on the right path. A foul odor of charred meat made Jared close to retching. From the side of the boat came random thumps, inanimate but heavy, but this time no one dared peak off the side for a better view. Instead, Kara flicked on her camera from the safety of the vessel, and they watched through the viewfinder. The water was choked with mummies, distorted, slimy, and misshaped. Some retained golden death masks. Others appeared to have melted into stubs. "These travelers didn't make it past Apep," Jared surmised. "He must have swallowed and dissolved them, then spat them out."

Despite what lay ahead, the tunnel was long and gloomy, and each fell into their roles as documentary filmmakers. Kara put a fresh drive into the camera and began filming, and Ali raised his boom pole to capture the strange ambient noise. Only Derek, with no script to follow or subject to interview, remained at a loss. He glanced off the side of the boat, fiddling with his hat.

"Derek, wanna help me interpret the scroll?" Jared asked, not because he thought the host could in any way aid him but because something fundamental had changed in their relationship. After the ease and honesty in which he hooked up with Mentmose, Jared felt unimaginably free of the burden he had been carrying around for so long. He reflected on it now, not with guilt or shame, but with the joy of two men who had found each other—if only for a brief moment. Then, calling Derek out on his hate neutered any lingering fear he had harbored. Jared had told everyone not only that he was gay, but that he believed he was reborn from ancient times. Instead of derision, it was clear they looked to him as their leader and protector. He had done so not by pretending he was someone else but by embracing the person he always was. Derek, by contrast, appeared defeated and small, a feeling Jared knew all too well. For the first time in their working relationship, he felt empathy for his boss.

"Love to, Plummer." Derek smiled and brought his toenail light close to the scroll. "Hey man, I really am sorry. Had I known…"

"About what?"

"You know what you are. I wouldn't have used all those words. Would have, I dunno…"

"Treated me with a little respect?"

"Yeah." He said no more.

"And '*what I am*? Like I'm some other species?"

"No, not that. Just I'm good-looking, you know that. Guys hit on me all the time, and it's…"

"For Christ's sake Derek. One, you ain't my type, not by a long shot. And two, we've got more important things to think about than your fragile masculinity."

As if on cue, something banged on the bottom of the boat. A moment later, another thump, this one more insistent. Jared tumbled to the side, and it took Derek's fast reaction to keep him from falling into the water. From the mist rose an opened hole framed by twin fangs as big as the boat.

The lead ferryman swung into action. He slammed his oar into the creature's eye and it wept with blood. But when he tried for the other one, Apep was prepared. Its forked tongue curled around the oar and tossed it aside. A stream of acidic venom ignited the boatman's hairy snout. Before he could stamp it out, Apep's tongue yanked him deep into its mouth. Then the god of the underworld slunk backwards and disappeared below a lily pad of mummies.

Everyone knew he wasn't gone. From the front of the boat a clog of corpses rose in the murky water as Apep swam underneath. Some fifty feet later, it ended with a tail and a band of shredded skin that stretched back to the boat.

The crew manned the four cardinal directions, searching for disturbances on the water. Only one oarsman remained but the current was gentle and the vessel sailed through the murk tunnel without effort. Ahead, as they drew near the Eighth Gate, Seti's glowing coffin was no longer visible, but little fires, curiously spaced like torches, guided the way. Jared wasn't sure what the source of the fuel was until they passed one: linen-clad mummies that had drifted onto the rocks had become dry enough to burn.

A splashing sound echoed from behind, but it was too dark to pinpoint the source. The putrid odor returned, so ripe Jared could almost *see* it. But nothing advanced. Still, he knew Apep was near, lying in wait.

As always, Kara never stopped filming and was eager for the best shot possible. She cautiously crept to the stern of the boat. At first, nothing could be seen but odd bits of detritus. Something moved, and she moved back for a wide shot. A thick reptilian trunk, skin diamond-shaped like a cobra, slowly rose from the muck. It seemed twice as big as before. Steam billowed from his nostrils, and his mouth dropped open, almost to the size of the cave itself.

Apep lurched forward and engulfed the entire vessel. The air grew rank and warm, gooey substance dripped from above. Eclipsed in darkness, everyone's screams became one. The boat remained afloat but now in stomach acid and deep within the bowels of the beast. Walls contracted, and panic took root. The cast and crew of *Ancient Encounters* would soon be squeezed to death.

Jared sliced at Apep's belly with the dagger they had found on the way into Seti's tomb. Ali used his boom pole to prevent the walls from shrinking further. The first was as effective as a needle, the second a toothpick. The pliers from Kara's utility belt proved even worse. Constricting walls meet heads and hands.

Only Derek, standing right behind Jared, remained frozen. But then, with a sudden jerk, he grabbed hold of the scythe. He sliced it into the flesh above their heads using all his strength. Blood rained down, and the creature writhed back and forth. It was too dark to see the depth of the incision, and Apep kept moving forward.

"Deeper!" Jared shouted to Derek as he grabbed hold of the other end. Together they plunged the blade deeper into the serpent, this time striking bone. More acid rained down, and the snake writhed frantically, rocking the boat from side to side.

Another incision followed, this one so cruel it pierced the outer skin and Jared and Derek hung from the scythe, bodies suspended. Ali grabbed both men by the waist, rocking them back and forth and slicing the snake from front to back. Air billowed in. Apep let out a terrible hiss and dipped beneath the waterline, perhaps in hopes of drowning the parasites in its belly. But as it descended, the cut to its body was so wide the boat remained afloat and undamaged.

"Is that it?" Kara asked. "Did we kill it?"

"For this journey, yes," Jared said, scanning the water. "Apep is a demon, so it never really dies. The goal is to injure it deeply enough that it lets us pass, at least for the night."

"For the night?" Kara said with alarm. "I thought twelve hours, and we're out of here."

"If any of the gates remain closed to us, we start over at the first one as soon as the sun sets again." But for this evening, it seemed as if Apep had been vanquished. Surprised it had happened so swiftly, Jared took stock: everyone was accounted for. Ali and Kara had moved away from the edge of the barque and seemed unharmed. Derek's right cheek was raw and splattered by stomach acid: he'd no longer be the pretty boy, but he seemed fine. In fact, it almost looked like he was *smiling.*

The water remained still, suggesting Apep was indeed gone. "There's a light ahead," Jared said, "which means we're coming to another gate." He picked up the book, still smoldering and began reciting spells. The words now came easily to him.

Jared felt the scroll's weight, its immense power. It had transformed him into a leader, both in how he retrieved it and in how only he could decipher its meaning. Abandoning it now could erase all he had accomplished, and, if little Dorothy was lying, it could hasten their doom. How would he traverse the gates without it, using only his limited wits and fragmented memories to survive? He'd revert to being Jared Plummer again, the terrified kid who wouldn't step over a *Free Willy* lunchbox.

He held it in his hand, and Kara watched from behind the lens, an opinion frozen on her tongue. She knew what Jared did. This had to be his decision. She wouldn't say anything, but through the whirling camera, she was at least communicating one thing: everyone was watching, waiting to see what he would do. This was Jared's moment.

A narrow cavern pocked with cavities closed in on them. Before the rest of the crew could protest, and before he could talk himself out of it, Jared placed the scroll on a ledge.

The camera zoomed into a close up of the ledge just in time to capture a shriveled hand as it emerged from the rock and snatched the book away.

CHAPTER 34

To Jared's relief, no god or goddess watched over the next gate. Indeed, it seemed like it had been abandoned eons ago. The foundations were cracked, the paint faded, and one side of the door was missing. Beyond, soaring cliffs drew so close the boat scraped against a translucent rock that crumbled at the touch. The place was desolate and uninviting, but Jared remained confident. The book had given him strength, yet he realized he no longer needed it. Instead, an inner voice was impelling him forward.

Seti's boat had sailed far ahead and out of view, obscured by translucent hoodoos that crumbled as they passed. Jared picked up a smooth and brittle chunk that had fallen into the boat. Its identity was unmistakable: pure natron salt. A substance that was once more valuable than gold. Ancient memories flooded his senses, and he instinctively knew where they were.

"The Eight Gate," he announced. "A place where those not fully mummified get trapped." When he was a royal embalmer, it was the hour of the night he feared the most—not for himself, but for those who put themselves in his care. If he failed in his duty to preserve the body, the dead would get stuck here and curse him the rest of their days, which were literally endless.

"I thought all Egyptians were mummified," Derek said to the camera after Jared explained. He no longer acted like a sulking child but *almost* the rugged adventurer he was hired to play. A red welt of acid that ran from cheek to jaw lent him an air of credibility.

Jared moved in closer, happy for once to act as an interviewee. On this subject, he truly was an expert. "No one can enter the Duat without a mummy, but that doesn't mean it's always a good one. Some can't afford embalming but are still wrapped and placed into coffins hoping they won't get noticed. Others spend a lifetime of savings only to be cheated. Natron is expensive, and removing organs and moisture is time-consuming. Embalmers know this, and once you're dead and wrapped, some unscrupulous ones figure.

"Who's going to complain?"

Jared remembered one embalmer who wrapped up a dead cat rather than mummified an infant and sold it to grieving parents. When he was found out, he himself joined the child in the afterlife. And like the child, he entered the Duat with his organs intact and blood still clotted in his veins. The agony must have been unimaginable.

The river shrank to a stream, and the boat ran aground. Jared peered over a dune. The river resurfaced down below, where he spied the very tip of a gate.

"From here, we walk," he said as they hopped out, and the oarsmen lifted the vessel above their snouts. As the crew descended, they began passing bodies. At first, they just seemed like more corpses—there had been so many—but these were alive and writhing in pain. Their skin was flaky, their faces chapped and burnt. Hungrily they gazed at the travelers, clutching throats and licking the air with gray tongues.

"What have they done wrong to deserve such a fate?" Ali asked as one limply grabbed his foot. He easily kicked it away.

"The Duat was not created for those with flesh and blood," Jared said, his lost knowledge pouring back, the forfeit of the book, for the moment, of no concern. "Thus, these people are eternally dying of thirst."

As they made their way down a narrow canyon, the half-dead stumbled to their feet and slowly followed. Those that couldn't stand crawled, but each seemed to have the same goal, catch up to the crew.

"I'm guessing they smell the moisture in our bodies."

The few became dozens, then hundreds of parched souls eager to slake their thirst. Yet they were so weak none could gain ground. Down below, where the stream picked up again, the four boatmen were waiting.

"I don't get it. There's enough water in the river for everyone," Derek said, genuinely confused.

"This is a land of salt. To drink that will only cause more agony." As they reached the summit of a rolling dune, they noticed that the gate was guarded by a demon. He appeared a little different from the hundreds of writhing bodies behind them, except he was at least five times their size.

"For fuck's sake, now what?" Kara said when she saw him. "I'm starting to sour on your Egyptian underworld, gotta admit."

The art of embalming came easily to Jared, but the tangled mythology behind it was always of less interest and escaped him now. Suddenly aware that he didn't have all the answers after all, Jared turned to Ali. "Any idea? I'm at a loss."

"I do remember some big giant god in my coloring book but can't place his name. I think they drew him with fangs, though. Started with a K." He sighed. "Or an S..." Ali let out a frustrated groan. "Shit, it was twenty years ago. Never thought I'd be quizzed as an adult."

They ducked behind a dune. "Try to remember. We gotta know who it is and how to appease him."

Ali wracked his memory. When he was young, like most Egyptian boys, he loved the ancient gods. He had action figures of the most popular ones, and Saturday morning cartoons showed them battling evil to save the wholesome but hapless villagers of the Nile. But as in all childhood escapes, it soon became uncool to wallow in the ancient past. That was for grandparents, scholars, and tourists with fanny packs and floppy hats. Instead, like most boys, he dumped his trading cards for soccer balls. "Does it matter?" Ali said, drawing a blank. "He looks pretty listless."

"If he's in the Eight Gate, he's someone to fear," Jared said. "Must have something to do with all these poor souls."

Ali wrinkled his forehead, and a chill ran through him. "Khufi, must be the demon Khufi."

"What do you recall?" Derek asked.

"I was more interested in coloring than context, but this one really scared me. Was said to be one of the most dangerous of all gatekeepers. The challenge of this hour was not getting in but getting out. Which I guess is why it's the exit he's guarding."

Khufi slumped along the exit, half standing, half squatting. He watched the boatmen draw near but didn't move.

"I think you're confusing your gatekeepers. I see no fangs, and he's so lazy he can't even stand," Kara noted through her camera lens. "We just sail on by." She zoomed in as one of the oarsmen approached Khufi, perhaps to ask permission to cross. As he did, the demon violently leaped from the gate and pinned him to the sand. After a sniff of his neck, Khufi opened a blackened mouth and bit deeply into his jackal-headed throat, hungrily slurping the juices. Before the other boatmen could react, Khufi did the same to them. Three were held fast by powerful arms, and their fluids drained in a matter of seconds. Only the fourth found time to escape up the dune toward the crew's safety.

"Right," Jared said, the memory flooding back. "Khufi..." He should have been better prepared.

Why didn't I wait to dump that book until just before the Ninth Gate?

Khufi wiped his lips and watched the oarsman go—he had more than enough to satisfy his hunger for the time being. He didn't eat the flesh but simply tossed the corpses aside when they were drained of liquid. Belly swollen, the demon returned to his outpost, a spring in his step and a ruby complexion on his cheeks. He sniffed the air, gazed at where the crew was hiding, and grinned. A boisterous burp was quickly followed by a snore.

The gate, little more than a sandstone post and lintel, reminded Jared of the scant foundations of a once mighty city. On either side was nothing but raw, undulating desert. "Can we just walk around?" Kara asked.

Jared shook his head. "The next hour can only be reached by crossing through. To walk around only means wandering deeper into the wastelands."

"The goal at every gate is to humor the gods, to give them peace," Ali noted. "Something that satisfies them enough to let us pass, right?"

"Correct," Jared said, "but I'm not sacrificing any of us to save the others."

"What if we donate blood? I do it all the time for the Red Crescent." He took a penknife from his pocket. "A peace offering. I'll cut myself. You be ready to stem the flow after we get a pint or two."

Jared took the knife from Ali's hand. "You saw how much that thing needs. No way a pint's gonna fill him up." They dipped further behind the shade of a dune and watched as Khufi leaned against a gatepost, licked his fingers, and stared off into the desert. His eyes kept fluttering shut.

The crew, themselves parched and exhausted, soon followed suit. "Don't fall asleep," Jared warned them with a yawn. "Or you'll only end up like the others."

He dipped his head to a far dune, where the army of the half-dead continued their snail-like advance. Their teeth chattered in anticipation.

But the crew soon succumbed. They had battled pharaohs, snakes, spikes, and an endless onslaught of the dead for over eight hours. Jared glanced at Derek's watch.

3.17 AM. Less than three hours to go.

He stared at Khufi, waiting for a sign he had drifted off, and soon he, too, struggled to stay awake. Familiar memories bubbled to the surface…

A grand palace with a soaring pylon, painted purple and gold, rises before the royal embalmer Hori. Forked flags snap above a tower manned by leather-clad warriors. On either side loom statues of the great pharaoh Ahmose, who has reunited the tribes to repel the invading Hyksos. A final battle has raged in the fields outside Memphis for nearly a week, and the Egyptians seem close to defeating the enemy. Until tragedy strikes.

The populous must not know, or they will lose hope. Hori darts between the palace gates, staring at the ground to avoid raising the alarm. A glistening dagger hangs from a sash, still wet from his work at the mortuary temple. At the end of the twisting alleys, two saturnine guards await him and open a wooden door. At the top of the stairs, a blood-splattered soldier in full regalia, Ahmose's top general, anxiously awaits him. His eyes travel to the corner, where the young pharaoh, his head violently cut open, is propped against the wall. A carpet of blood spreads beneath him. Nearby lies Nefertari, his consort and queen. She holds his royal crown, sliced down the middle where the ax made contact, and fights back tears. She brushes flies away from her husband's open skull.

"How long has he been dead?" Hori asks.

"Nearly two days," the general admits, eyes downcast.

"So long?" Hori snaps.

"It was difficult to get him off the battlefield and smuggle him here. Many died trying."

"I'm aware of that," Hori snaps and bends in front of the dead king. "You should have brought him sooner. First, I need to dry him out to halt the decay, remove the organs. Go collect natron." The general bows and leaves.

Hori moves forward, and after a silent apology to the wailing queen, he takes his dagger and deeply rips the king's chest wide open, from rib cage to belly, and removes the rotting organs. Then he reaches for a basket of natron.

Jared now realized that these images were never threats but signs to help him prepare for danger. He thought back to the falling statue during the storm on their first day. All this time, someone was hoping he'd *react,* not recoil. Perhaps Hori himself. But why, exactly, he had no idea.

Jared opened his eyes and saw that the unembalmed were now only a few feet away. He listened for Khufi's snore. Brusquely, he shook his sleeping crew.

"Derek, where's your bag?"

The host groggily handed it to him and rolled over.

"Wake up! Everyone!"

Jared began tossing the contents of the bag onto the sand. Out popped T-shirts, a baseball cap, a script, a *Hollywood Reporter,* but not what he was searching for.

"The sewing kit? Where's your sewing kit?"

Now everyone was awake and gazing at Jared with alarm. He had finally lost it.

"Da-fa?" Kara rubbed her eyes and remembered where they were.

"Where is it?" Jared repeated urgently, and Derek moved forward and unzipped a concealed inside pocket. "Here, but—"

Jared grabbed the needle and thread and surveyed his surroundings. Only sand. Then he saw the boat at the bottom of the dune and remembered. Chunks of natron had fallen inside. That'll have to be enough.

He rose.

"Okay, listen. If it's peace Khufi wants, I know how to give it to him." Indeed, he had been preparing for it his entire life. Jared glanced around and picked up Derek's Indiana Jones hat. "This might do." He pointed to the demon and pantomiming for the boatman so everyone understood. "We sneak up on him while he's sleeping. You all grab an arm or leg and pin him down. I'll do the rest."

Khufi rested on his back and snored, mouth agape and face encrusted with blood. The bodies of the three drained oarsmen lay nearby, their jackal hair matted and falling off. Once at the boat, Jared flipped the hat upside down and filled it with natron. Some of it was in clumps, and this he crumbled into a powder. "Everyone grab as much as you can carry."

The demon was asleep, but it didn't appear deep. He scratched his nose, licked his lips, and sniffed. The mouth relaxed, and the snoring returned. Jared raised a hand to beckon his crew forward. The sun was at their backs, and long shadows cast stripes across Khufi's swollen body. Khufi swatted at one and shifted. His eyes opened briefly, and Jared was shocked to see they still contained eyeballs, shriveled and useless. No one even bothered to remove his eyes, the first step in embalming, as they rot the fastest. The pain must have been overwhelming. Jared could smell the demon's wretched breath and see the rot hanging from his body. He knew by the aroma alone that what he was about to do was going to hurt like hell—but only for a while. Afterward, it would bring eternal comfort. In one hand was the hat, the other the needle and thread. Silently, Jared brought them to the demon's lips. As he reached out for the demon's nose, it sniffed the air and cracked open one shrunken eye.

"Now!"

Jared squeezed the demon's nostrils shut until it gasped for air and then poured the salt into its mouth. The hole was enormous, and it took a fedora's worth of natron before it filled. Khufi coughed, and salt dribbled down his cheeks. He tried to rise, but five people were now standing on his limbs. Jared knew they were no match, so he acted fast. He ripped the eyes out, poured salt into Khufi's open sockets, and packed them tight with his elbow. He reached for the needle, but it slipped from his fingers and into the sand.

"Where did it go?" he screamed to Ali, who was sitting on the demon's chest.

Ali saw something sparkle and picked it up with his toes. "I can't hold him much longer."

Jared brought the needle and thread to the creature's mouth. He pierced one lip and then the other. Khufi screamed, and half the salt came out, but the oarsman filled it back up. To Jared's relief, the lips were brittle, and the needle made fast work sewing them shut. He moved to the nostrils. After Ali used his thumbs to pack them with natron, Jared sewed them up several times and then left the needle dangling.

Khufi was now writhing violently, tossing Derek off his leg and attempting to stand. Jared took the boatman's dagger and plunged it into Khufi's chest, from rib cage to groin. The organs were still there, final proof that poor Khufi was a shoddy mummification victim. Liver, intestine, and heart were removed, and the space filled with fistfuls of natron. The kicking quivered and stopped. The color drained from Khufi's flesh, his face went slack, and his stitched mouth relaxed. Etched on it was an eternal, peaceful grin.

Behind them, the half-dead army halted in confusion when they saw what had happened to their jailer. The team returned the solar boat to the water and quickly traveled through the gate. On the other side lay another world, tropical, humid, and drizzling with mist. A majestic waterfall bisected a shaded grove of palms. Behind the boat, the half-dead crawled through. But they no longer were in pursuit. Instead, they exhaled deeply and disappeared under the bubbling brook, mouths agape. Jared wanted to join them, to wash off the millennia of salt that caked his body. But the clock was ticking, and they still had three gates to traverse before sunrise. And the next one, the infamous Ninth Gate, was where all his insecurities, fears, and failings would finally be exposed and judged. Nothing he had so far encountered, not Khufi, Apep, or even the Holy of Holies, terrified him more. No one—Kara, Ali, or even Hori—could help him now. He would be judged solely on his *ka*, and if he had used it wisely. He didn't need a heart and feather to know which way the scale would tip.

CHAPTER 35

A dozen bearded mummies surrounded a gate composed of flame. Above them hung the heads of horned animals—mastodons, aurochs, and other megafauna that no longer existed. This reminded any traveler that the Ninth Gate was older than time and civilization and had welcomed millions of souls through its door. Most, like these prehistoric beasts, never made it any further.

One of the mummies, after consulting a long scroll that stretched a hundred feet, led Jared's boat into a magnificent chamber, grand and opulent. The vessel came to rest at a golden pier below nine obsidian steps. On each stair hovered a god, some with bird faces, others with the eyes and ears of a rabbit. One had two snake heads, each facing the opposite direction. A creature with bulging eyes, protruding tongue and a lion's mane danced in anticipation of what was to come.

"Where the hell are we?" Derek asked.

"Exactly," thought Jared, "we're in hell." He tried to keep his outside voice firm and strong. "The Hall of Judgment, where Osiris rules."

"And what happens here again?"

Jared recited a quote he had long ago committed to memory:

"Man survives after death, and his deeds are laid before him in a heap. For the man who reaches them without doing evil, he will abide there as a god, roaming free like the lords of time. If not, darkness and oblivion swallow him forever."

At the top of the ghats was the God of the Dead, emerald-skinned and sitting on a throne of amber. He wore the double crown and clutched a crook and flail, symbols of kingship. This was clearly his domain. On his left, Ibis-headed Thoth consulted a brittle papyrus. An enormous gold scale, empty now and evenly weighted, towered to his right. And peeking from behind it was the demon Jared feared above all others. A beast with the head of a crocodile, the upper body of a leopard and the rear end of a rhinoceros, saliva dribbling from her mouth. It looked down at the arriving visitors and bared her fangs. Ammit, the Gobbler of Souls. Jared's only hope was that, despite what little Dorothy said, if Seti passed without incident, then his guest would be permitted to follow.

The pharaoh's barque was tethered to a plankway, where jackal-faced Anubis, God of Mummification, awaited. The boatmen stepped aside to let several deities lift the sarcophagus and walk it up the stairs. Once laid on a bench, Anubis approached the coffin, and the lid was removed. A few words were spoken, or at least Jared assumed they were words, they sounded more canine than human. But it clearly was some incantation, as the other gods responded in kind, some chirping like birds, others growling like leopards. A scarab-faced one merely clicked. The coffin radiated, and Seti sat upright on his own, still wrapped in linen and hidden under a dazzling death mask. A gecko goddess offered cool refreshments.

Anubis moved closer and, after barking something that sent everyone to their knees, tore Seti's linens open and plunged his fist deep into the pharaoh's chest. He rifled around for a short while, looking for Seti's heart, the only organ left in the body for just this occasion. The king remained passive, unbothered by the intrusion, and Jared understood why: the king was fully mummified and could feel no pain, so this must be some symbolic ritual performed for the gods.

A final goddess joined them, a huge ostrich feather bursting from her crown. Ma'at plucked a white feather from her headdress and placed it on one of the scales. If it was lighter than her feather—free of weakness, indolence, and evil—the soul would be allowed to move through the final gates and into the Field of Reeds. If the heart was even slightly heavier, Ammit stood nearby, eager to devour it whole. Without a heart, the person's soul would cease to exist, which in Egypt was death without hope of return.

Anubis carefully laid Seti's heart on the other scale. It dropped for a second, rose, and dropped again. A long string of drool fell from Ammit's jaw as she took a step closer, her sharp nails echoing across the floor. She licked her chops and prepared to pounce. Thoth scrutinized the scale and scribbled something on the scroll. No one stirred; every god remained immobile as if etched onto a wall. In the boat, the only sound was the incongruous hum of the camera.

Back and forth, the scale wobbled—feather, heart, feather, heart, the shifts less and less perceptible until it finally creaked to a halt. Thoth grew close, his beak hanging over the feather as he measured and put quill to papyrus. It seemed as if the heart was ever-so-slightly lower, but then, another subtle shift and it rose to just above the feather. Satisfied at last, Thoth noted his final judgment and walked it over to Osiris. The God of the Underworld nodded and said something that didn't reach Jared's boat.

Ammit slumped in disappointment while Ma'at placed the feather back into her headdress. The heart was returned to Seti's body, linens instantly healed over the hole, and bearded mummies raised the coffin and returned to the solar boat. Seti would continue onto Paradise. While the outcome was never in any real doubt, Jared trembled at the discovery that even the great Pharaoh Seti Mery-en-ptah, "He of the God Seth,

Beloved of Ptah," just barely survived the scales. If forced to climb the stairs, "Jared Plummer, Producer of *Ancient Encounters with Derek Dees,* Episode 37," faced swift annihilation.

There was a moment of calm as the gods began chatting, and Seti's solar boat pushed back from the pier. Jared stayed small and hoped both vessels would soon be on their way, but, as he feared, Anubis now stood in front of his boat, demanding they disembark. Anubis said something in a canine growl, and when no one reacted, said it again in lucid English. "Which of you is captain of this vessel?"

For the first time since they began their journey, Jared wished it wasn't him. For a moment, he hoped that Derek might try to salvage his bruised ego by raising his hand. But the host only lowered his hat over his eyes and remained invisible. Even if he did step forward, Jared wouldn't let him disembark. Not only had he pleaded to lead the team, but his main goal was to make sure his crew survived the night. Derek's *ka* would face certain death.

With a start, Kara rose. "I am," she announced.

"Then follow me to the scale," Anubis announced.

For one brief moment of flight, Jared was about to let her go until his strength returned. He also stood. "Stay in the boat. This is my journey."

He stepped forward, but Kara barred his way.

"Don't try being a hero again so fast. You got us out of the last gate. My turn. I can handle these old dead gods." She looked up at Anubis, who snarled. "If I don't, hey, it's been one helluva shoot. Water my plants when you get back to Brooklyn. And tell that hot barista at the *Hungry Ghost* cafe I'm sorry I never called her back."

Jared blocked her way. "You promised me you wouldn't try anything stupid again. I know their world and customs. Just make sure you get everyone out of here if I don't make it." Behind them, a noise in the boat drew their attention. Derek was hiding behind Ali as if he was a shield. "Even Derek."

Before she could protest, Jared stepped onto the obsidian stairs and followed Anubis to the top. When no one stopped them, Kara and Ali followed, filming everything they could.

Anubis scrutinized Jared from head to toe and looked confused more than anything else. "Who is this little man who wishes to pass the Ninth Gate?"

"I am Jared Wade Plummer." He wasn't sure why he added his middle name. A longer title sounded more regal, he guessed.

"And from where do you hail?"

"15 Melvin Drive, Junction City, Kansas." Realizing that sounded provincial, Jared quickly amended it. "But now I live in Bedford Stuyvesant, Brooklyn." It was the fanciest thing he could think of.

What might have been a smile crossed the God of the Dead's face. He reached down and gave Ammit a warm pat on her head. "This shan't take long at all."

Interview transcript *(partially recovered)*

Location: Hall of Judgment

Date: Ninth Hour of the *Duat*

Subject: **Jared Plummer**

Interviewers: **Osiris and Anubis** *(Gods of the Underworld and the Dead, respectively)*

(transcriber's note: great damage to tape. Company holds no responsibility for poor quality of recording or gaps in interviews)

Osiris: We will speak in the language of our travelers. You have followed Seti into the Duat. If his heart was not lighter than *(media noise)* all be gobbled up by Ammit for trespassing. But he has proven that his ma'at is in harmony *(noise)* .... So as long as the leader's ka is in balance, the boat shall join Seti's. Is the pantheon in agreement?

Various voices, barks, growls, unable to translate. Tape cuts out for almost a minute, but sounds appear to be mostly ambient noise.

Anubis will first retrieve your heart. Best hold on to something tight.

(unidentified clanks, plunging, rifling, ending with a sucking sound)

Anubis: I am God of Embalming and the Afterlife and... *(slurping noises)* Down, girl! All in due time. Tell me Jared, how does a man of such lowly birth and stature, who is neither born from the black soil of the Nile, nor embalmed, come to sit in judgment before this exalted pantheon?

Jared: By invitation.

Anubis: I don't recall inviting you here, nor, if I may, ask our Lord: Osiris, did you invite this heathen to sully your realm, to make a mockery of all it stands for?

Osiris: I did not. But let the traveler answer for himself, do not judge before the facts are known. His heart will reveal all.

Anubis: Apologies, my Lord. Jared, we will now display moments of your life that surfaced both in the Lake of Memories and in your head while in the Duat. *(noise, shuffle)* Do keep your distance.

Kara: Sorry, dude.

Anubis: Before your trial, we glimpsed Seti's exalted memories. Subduing the Hittites, building the temple Abydos in celebration of the gods, bringing peace and prosperity to the two lands. In short, he has bravely led his people and his gods, and his memories prove him to be proud and at peace with his earthly accomplishments. When I look at you, I first see... can't make sense of it. An aluminum box with an image of a whale, with food inside, and a crying girl.

Jared: That was one image years ago. I was just a kid.

Anubis: Yet it's a theme that seemed to follow you the rest of your days. Explain this one: a man, a child really, half your size, pushes you over in front of a group of others. Equally small, it appears. You knew you could conquer him. Yet you chose to remain on the ground while others laughed.

Jared: You're speaking of things I did as a young child before I knew myself. Certainly, being bullied as a kid doesn't disqualify one from entering the Field of Heaven. Blessed are the meek, don't they say?

Anubis: Do they? Certainly not here. *(noise)* It is not childhood fear alone we examine, but how you dealt with that as you grew. A *ka* is the most valuable entity in existence, gifted by the gods, but to use it more than once, it must be earned. Otherwise, it can and should be taken away.

Jared: There are other things, great things, that I have done in past lives that should—

Anubis: Those lives are not on trial. They have come and gone. Only Jared Plummer is on trial. You mention a place called Brooklyn. For almost a year, a homeless man has lived outside your apartment there, slowly starving and freezing, and while you want every day to help, instead, you don't even offer him eye contact, thinking it's safer not to get involved. Can you tell me what happened to this man? Do not lie. We will know.

Jared: *(pause)* He froze to death.

Anubis: So he did.

Jared: I wasn't the only one who ignored him. New York is a city of ten million.

Anubis: And as I said, they are not on trial. Only you are presumptuous enough to challenge the Ninth Gate. *(flicker of sounds, inaudible)* Here is another image, even more telling: a young man sits crying in an airport parking lot after you deny both he and you what you promised: love and support. What *ka* would do such a thing, both to itself and someone it loves?

Jared: It's true I've been a coward. Especially with the man at the airport. But can you see a more recent image, when I said goodbye to another lover?

Anubis: Ah, only the other day. A Medjay guard of the Sacred Valley. A man who loved you, and, I presume, you him. So once again, you run rather than face yourself?

Jared: Like your boss Osiris says, rather than presume, why don't you let me talk?

Osiris: Agreed. Anubis do not prejudge. Go on…

Jared: I said goodbye to Mentmose so that I may undo the wrong I did to the first man.

Anubis: One act of strength isn't enough. Letting a man freeze in the street is not the act of a man who deserves a place in the Field of Reeds.

Jared: Am I any different from the millions of others who pass through here? Are you saying every mummy given permission to cross was selfless and strong in all things? It's not only me who looks the other way. The slums of Thebes are full of needy people being ignored. I've seen them myself. Seti ruled them until today, and Ramses does now. But I have been to the future, where both their bodies lie in state, still venerated and remembered. Are you suggesting neither of them ever hurt another soul?

Anubis: Again, they are not—

Jared: On trial, I know. But they have been, and will be, and you look the other way. What about you and this pantheon behind you? Your devoted worshippers die of hunger, disease, and war and are put to the whip to build self-centered monuments to you, all while they're not even offered passage here. Rich men break into your tombs and steal your treasures, yet still get fancy burials, and EZ passes through the Duat because they can afford it. I know because, at one time, I embalmed them. Wrapped them in jewels to bribe the gatekeepers. For the right price, they're able to slip by unchallenged. Why are my actions crimes when yours go unpunished?

Anubis: The gods are not to be judged.

Jared: Perhaps they should be. I've hurt a few dozen, mostly myself. You've ignored and dismissed millions. It's why, in my day, you're remembered only in children's coloring books. You failed to protect your people, and in time, they walked away. Found better gods. And your world crumbled.

Anubis: Sacrilege.

Osiris: It's a fair defense. You just accused Seti of the same thing, failing to raise his people from the mud, but allowed him in the end to pass through the gate because he had the correct amulets. And the boy is not wrong when he says that one day, we will all be forgotten. We cannot blame others for that.

Anubis: *(shuffle)* Stand back, I said.

Kara: I need a close-up. You look kinda nervous.

Anubis: Jared Wade Plummer, not all who come here are worthy of a Second Life of immortality. What have you accomplished that will outlive you?

Jared: My work *(noise)* As you see by my colleagues here, I document the world around me so future generations can know of the great men and women who walked this earth. *(more noise)*

Anubis: And that explains your interest in *(pause, as if consulting something)* Big Foot, UFOs, a broom closet in a Scottish chapel? And a 'Chupacabra'? What is that exactly?

Jared: A goat-sucking dog in Mexico *(media drive noise).*

Anubis: And this is your gift to mankind?

Jared: Don't forget the story I am now capturing.

Anubis: I have not. And that is what will surely spell your doom.

Osiris: It is not you who decides, Anubis. If he is doomed, Ma'at's feather will tell us. Simply ask the questions so the pantheon knows the facts.

Anubis: My humble apologies, Lord. We simply have not had a traveler quite like this one in some time. Tell me about the *Book of Gates.*

Jared: *(pause)* What do you want to know?

Anubis: First, inform us where it is and how you sullied the Holy of Holies to steal it.

Jared: I no longer have it.

Anubis: One of the most sacred texts of the underworld, and you've misplaced it?

Jared: Not misplaced... I... gave it back.

Anubis: Who said it was yours to take?

Jared: I needed to… Tiya… *(media drive noise)* it's a long story.

Anubis: Luckily for us all, the Duat exists for all time. If you miss the rising of the sun, you can traverse the gates again tomorrow from the beginning, and we will continue for all time if necessary.

Jared: I was chosen, I am told, by the gods, to perform a task. At great risk to my current *ka*, and those of my crew, I traveled here for the express purpose of saving Prince Mehy's *ka*. His father invited me, and if you hadn't let Tiya be cut down, I would not have been forced to act as I did.

Anubis: I know nothing of this.

Jared: Did you not tell me you were omnipotent and could see everything? How did you drop the ball on this? Seems you're already slipping into oblivion.

Kara: Wait, say that again. I lost focus for a minute.

Jared: Seems you're already slipping into oblivion.

Anubis: Watch your tongue. Both of you.

Osiris: If this is true, we must know about it. Go on, Jared.

Jared: I also, without embalming or any amulets for protection, crossed through eight gates, and gave the Demon Khufi the peace you refused him when he was poorly mummified. And I did it not for glory, but so one of your own, and my crew, would live again. Surely that makes up for the *Free Willy* lunchbox?

Anubis: I believe none of it. I see no proof of such valor.

Jared: If I may, will you permit my crew to approach?

Anubis: No, only you are on trial.

Osiris: I see no harm in it. Allowed.

Jared: Kara, rewind the footage. Hook up the monitor. *(a moment or two of noise, the whirling of a camera)* Can everyone see? Good. Wait, Ali, crank the volume.

Ali: Cranked.

(Snippets of audio sound from a camera, jumbled)

"Get them safely home to Omm, I'll do it myself…"

"Derek, hand me your sewing kit. I have an idea…"

"Stay in the boat, this was my doing, my journey."

Osiris: Admirable, but all this you have done in the last few hours? Why then, Jared Plummer, did you waste so many years before?

Jared: I was only awaiting the chance to use my gifts properly.

Anubis: A few acts of strength do not a *ka* make.

Osiris: Now it's time to mention who he was. He has already passed this way one million, two thousand and four hundred sunsets ago, as Hori, Royal Embalmer to the great king Ahmose, who conquered the Hyksos invaders and returned Egypt to the gods. He served the court well and allowed many other royals to pass through here without damage. It was why, Jared Plummer of 15 Melvin Drive, we were so hard on you. How far you had fallen.

Anubis: I still think it's not enough.

Osiris: I think you care more for your pet Ammit's hunger than you do justice. Jared, do you have any final words before we place your heart on the scale?

Jared: I was asked to perform a great task, and it's true, I may not have been the perfect person for it. Yet, as you had a hand in creating them, you know humans can change when put to the test. I stand before you, both me and my crew still alive, while Apep lies in pieces and the *Book of Gates* returned, unharmed, to its rightful owners. From here, I have two missions: restore the name of Prince Mehy, who all agree is worthy. And make sure my friends return to their world unharmed. How many who pass through here can claim that?

Osiris: Ma'at, place your ostrich feather on the scale.

(The sound of a plucked feather is followed by the squeak of a scale. Then a plunging sound, wet and deep)

Kara*:* *(off camera)* Whoa, you okay?

Jared: Yeah, doesn't hurt.

Kara: They just took your freakin' heart out of your chest.

Jared: I'm fully aware of that.

(For a long moment, nothing is heard but Jared's anxious breath. Then more squeaking, and the sound of something licking its chops)

Anubis: As I suspected, the heart sinks. The man is condemned. Ammit, the heart belongs to you.

(more squeaking)

Osiris: Give it time to stop, as you did Seti.

(more heavy breathing and tiny squeaking)

Kara: *(off camera)* Thank fuckin' god. *(quieter)* Gods, I mean...

Anubis: Forgive my impatience, Lord. Judgment is done. Ammit must wait another day.

Oasis: Jared, return your barque. Re will soon return over the horizon. In honor of your good deeds, you may skip Ten and Eleven and move to the final gate. The consul has ended. We return to our tongues as we call the next soul, Nehi, former Vizier of Thebes, killed by bandits for a box of gold.

A sour-faced Nehi climbed the stairs and seemed surprised to see Kara and Ali standing next to the scale, videotaping his approach. He surely must have wondered how these intruders, whom he personally chained to a tomb wall to die an agonizing death, were here capturing his final judgment.

"Ask him why he stole all that sacred gold from Seti's tomb," Kara called out to Anubis. "Seems like a big no-no, right?"

Before Nehi could defend himself, the God of the Dead led him to the scale.

"Hang on one sec guys, I wanna get this on tape."

Kara returned for a close-up as Nehi's heart plummeted to the floor.

"Wait, girl," she said as she got on her knees.

"Okay, action!" she yelled as the Gobbler pounced.

CHAPTER 36

As they pushed back from the dock, Kara hadn't felt this proud of her friend in ages. Jared had finally proved himself, as she always knew he could, and it was all on tape. She gave him a long hug. "Never doubted you for a second, boss. You can use this footage for your next job interview."

In a blur, two gates passed them by, one with a hissing pit of vipers, another with a very disappointed-looking goddess holding a flaming trident.

"Guess they gotta wait for the next tour," Kara said with a wave.

Eventually, the boat slowed as it entered a meandering river, free of molten heads and monster serpents. For the first time in hours, Kara flicked the camera off. She needed a break from the viewfinder to take in the world around her and reflect on what she had left behind. Lynette's box of ashes, yes, but something more. She didn't know what or why yet, but she didn't feel quite as defensive or angry. Even Derek looked benign.

Seeing her make eye contact, Derek nudged closer. "Will the gods judge me next?"

Kara shrugged. The fate of Derek Dees, a fake adventurer, was of little importance.

"How should I know? Ask Jared. You can see he knows a shit more than us."

Derek looked towards Jared, who was fast asleep.

"Good," Kara sighed. "He's earned it. Give him a few."

She was about to cut Derek down to size, tell him he wasn't half the man that Jared was, but realized she'd get no satisfaction from it. Instead, why not humor him just this once?

"We're out of the Hall of Truth. I think you're okay."

"But I'm just like that Nehi guy you called out," Derek whispered. "A tomb raider. I have made a name robbing treasures and plundering sacred places." His voice lowered an octave. "You won't rat me out too, will you?"

So that's why he was talking to her. "You've never stolen a relic or broken into a chamber that hadn't already been looted long ago. You'll be fine."

Derek protested. "But I'm Derek Dees, the modern-day Belzoni. Millions of people call me that, all over the world."

Kara wanted to laugh, remind him that Derek Dees wasn't even his real name. It was Derek DeMarino, and unlike his hero Giovanni Belzoni, he wasn't born in the rugged hills of 18th century Italy but Sherman Oaks, California, a stone's throw from the Galleria Mall on Ventura Blvd.

"I've worked with you on, like, what, fifteen shows? When have you desecrated a mummy? Erased someone's name? You've done nothing but pretend."

The words were meant to soothe, but, as Kara knew better than anyone, what she thought and how it came it sounded in words was rarely the same thing.

"You're right," Derek said, slipping out of his fedora. "I'm a joke and a fraud."

Without his crown, Derek appeared small and sad, an unloved jester. Kara tried a new tack. Take a page out of Jared's playbook. Be… nice.

"Hey, you're a performer, an excellent one," she said. "We all know you're just playing a part for entertainment's sake. Nothing evil about that. Hell, gladiators did the same."

It was a poor analogy, as gladiators fought wild tigers, and each other, to the death, but as neither knew much about history, the comparison landed.

Derek peered off the side as the boat moved through a thicket of wild ferns. He reached out and grabbed a leaf, and twirled it in his hand.

"You asked Jared, but never me what I saw in the Lake of Memories."

Kara sighed. To be honest, she didn't give a rat's ass. Whatever it was, it was likely self-congratulatory.

"That daytime Emmy you're always talking about?"

Derek shook his head. "What I saw was me looking into that water, pulling that rope."

What looked like a gate appeared on the horizon, and Kara wanted to grab her camera and hide. But another minute wouldn't hurt. "See, then, you're no fraud. That means you were strong enough to focus on the present. Exactly what the book said we should do. Attaboy."

"No, that's just it. My proudest memory, it turns out, was the one I was living at the moment. I was finally being what I only pretended to be: an adventurer. Where do you think I got the strength to attack that snake-thing?"

"That was impressive," Kara said, and meant it. Derek was ready to cut Apep with the golden scythe even before she was. "But whataya saying, exactly?"

"I'm saying I'm tired of coasting on your scenes and Jared's script and blaming you when I look bad." His voice almost cracked. "I've made a decision about something, and I wanna tell you first. Jared can't know yet. He'd say no. If we get out of here alive, I'm not—"

The boat hit a tangle of weeds and lurched to a stop. Jared awoke with a start. Beyond a corbelled door lay a verdant landscape of wheat, palms bursting with fruit, and on a faraway hill, a city gleaming in the sun.

"Is it?" Ali asked, yanking the headphones from his ears. "The Field of Reeds?"

"I think it is," Jared said with a laugh. "How on earth did I fall asleep?"

"You gave that last gate your heart and soul—well, almost," Ali said. "I can only imagine you were exhausted."

Derek stood to survey the landscape. "One more gate, and we're outta here?"

"Yep," Jared said with a smile. "As long as this last gatekeeper gives us no problem and Omm's still standing by at the false door, we should be home within the hour."

Kara put the camera back to her eye and got ready. Her thoughts turned to home, a place she never much cared for until now.

CHAPTER 37

As Said wheeled her office chair into the tomb, Omm reached her hands out and caressed the decorated walls. She could no longer see them, of course, but the merest brush brought vivid images into view. "Oh, I know this place! I was here once with Mehy. It's special. I should have known this would be the one."

Said stopped pushing the chair and seemed to be looking around. "What's so unique about this one? Seems like a typical Old Kingdom mastaba. Bunch of royal hangers-on partying forever in the afterlife."

Omm ran her bony fingers along a door jamb. "Look more closely." She waited for his response.

"Oh, so *this* is the one? The lovers' tomb of Khnumhotep and Niankhkhnum."

Omm never met the denizens of this tomb, they lived a thousand years before Tiya did, but their story always filled her with glee. "Overseers of the Manicurists of the Palace of the King. Reputed to be the oldest same-sex tomb in history."

Said took a long drag of his cigarette and laughed. "I've also heard, from so-called learned men, they could have been brothers or Siamese twins."

"Modern scholarship," Omm sniffed, "is often just another name for bigotry and intolerance. Can you find the painting of two men nose to nose and arms around each other's waists?"

"I'm looking at it now."

"When was the last time you held your brother Adly like that?"

Said squeaked her deeper into the tomb, where they both knew the false door would be. "Oh, love was so much simpler back then," Omm sighed. "Unless you fell for a crown prince. Then things could get rather thorny."

The tomb was crafted with immense joy—each wall a celebration: grand feasts and parades, intimate scenes of fishing and cooking, and everywhere open affection between the two men, from holding hands to sharing some private joke only they could hear. In the very last room were twin false doors, one for each *ka*. A painting of the couple kissing in a solar boat appeared between them, but where two statues once rested, only empty niches remained.

"Can you feel anything?" Said asked.

"I can. Someone is on the other side. Mind the door for tourists while I try to get their attention." Chants reverberated through the small space, and within no time, both doors swirled. Said acted as Omm's eyes, describing everything he saw. First, several men, not thieves, it seemed, but archeologists ("Same bloody thing," Omm remarked), ripped twin statues off the wall and left, and then, further back in time, sand rolled in. Nothing happened for a long spell, which was most likely why the tomb was so well preserved, until a group of mourners brought in a sarcophagus and sat it next to one already in place. They kissed both coffins, and one priest remarked how lovely it was that the boys were back together. A jug of wine was shared, a few songs played, and after flowers were laid, they blew out the lamps and left the lovers in peace.

A moment later, two men were standing in front of the door on the right. The first was jowly and short, the other lean and tall. But nothing else about them seemed ill-matched. They dressed exactly alike, in shimmering amber silk robes, fingernails impeccably polished, and their hands linked like newlyweds, four and half millennia after their deaths. If this wasn't a love match, nothing in history was.

"About time," said the larger one. "I'm Niankhkhnum. It's a mouthful, I know, so call me Nian."

"And I'm Khnum," the other said. "Why did you waste your time on all those other people? Those selfish pyramid kings and that depressing Persian lady. Moan, moan, moan...You should have come straight here."

"Yes," Omm confessed. "The reception has been frosty."

"Imagine what it's like to have them as neighbors," Nian said. "We didn't care for their type when we were alive. And here we are, sharing eternity with them."

"You know about us?" Omm asked with surprise.

With Tiya dead, she had no idea how anyone could communicate with her friends on the other side.

"We do. The entire necropolis has been chattering about you, saying how presumptuous it was for you to visit, disturbing their Second Life to ask them to save a band of traveling minstrels."

"Since you know who they are, are you still willing to help?" Omm pleaded. "We've precious little time, if it's not too late already."

"It would be our joy," Khnum said. "As soon as we heard about your plight, Nian scoured the Field of Reeds to find out more."

Nian raised a finger to add something. "Your Jared has just survived the scale of justice. So few of us have. My own father never made it."

"Homophobic old boar," Khnum muttered.

"Indeed. And Jared's one of the tribe, I hear." He gave Khnum's hand a tender squeeze, perhaps telling him to mind his manners. "Or was in past lives."

Khnum rolled his eyes. "You know how it works. Once a member, always a member. He's still gay. And we must help him."

Omm considered the situation. "Can you get word to them not to return to Abydos but to come here?"

"We can try," Khnum said. "Nian will go. His mummy's held up much better than mine. While you wait, would you and your friend care for something to eat? We were just sitting down to supper. Use this door. Nian's was badly damaged in an earthquake. It squeaks, and no longer shuts properly."

Omm held out her hand to Said, who lifted her and guided her through the gate. A grand feast was underway, with musicians, dancers, and tables of guests of every gender, color, and size. For Said, the fabled sights and smells from a time he had spoken about every day for decades come to life at last. What he saw now was no longer a timeworn story, and he had no need to fill in the blanks on the wall with easy jokes to keep tourists entertained. What enveloped him now was the real thing, and as Khnum offered him a seat at a banquet table, he burst into tears of joy.

"Tonight it's mountain lion and poached ibis egg in a goose fat deduction," Khnum said with pride. "But first, a glass of date wine? Imported from Troy." Khnum pointed to two beautiful men at the end of the table, arm in arm. "Achilles, Patroclus, I'd like you to meet Said and Omm. They're awaiting friends from the underworld."

CHAPTER 38

As they sailed near, the final gate appeared to be one of reprieve, free of challenges and bloodthirsty demons. The weakest souls never made it that far, and those that did and were not swallowed up by Ammit, had, like Jared's crew, found renewed strength to carry on. The boat meandered along a babbling stream arched in vines. Animals large and small peered out from the mangroves, but none approached. Ahead, fluttering in and out of the canopy, lay a vast grassland bathed in golden light.

"That's the Field of Reeds," Jared announced, now fully awake.

He wanted to relive his experience in the Hall of Records, savoring his victory, but not yet. One more gatekeeper to go. After all he had just accomplished, he expected to make short work of him.

Ahead lay a lake carpeted by a tangle of vines. It would have been impossible for Seti's boat to cut through the weeds if it wasn't for the wizened old man who stood at the front of the pharaoh's boat. He reached into a sack and tossed what appeared to be beetles into the water. As he did, the bugs ate the vines to form a path. Seti's barque glided to the other side, where another gate loomed and where the water seemed to end for good. The wizened man gave a farmer's blow of snot and retreated to the other side. Behind him, the carpet of vines returned.

Soon, Jared's boat arrived at a little wooden gate, where the old man was waiting. He gave the group a disgusted glare and spat at their approach.

"Who's this old coot?" Derek sighed. "I thought we got a free pass after your big speech back there."

"The Divine Ferryman Hraf-hef," Ali said. "'He Who Looks Backwards and Behind'. He's the last god in my book. I never even bothered coloring him in. He seemed so grotty. By this point, I wanted to go out and play."

"I agree," Kara said after zooming in. "He doesn't seem that… impressive."

"He's not," Ali said. "Perpetually foul, always grumbling about the old days when he was still alive."

"What do we need to do for him to open the lock for us?" Derek asked. "Give him a bath?"

"I think you just make him smile, feel good about himself," Ali said. "I remember they used his likeness in a series of burger commercials when I was a kid. Only the Paradise Meal and side of fries would bring a grin."

The boat pulled closer, and Hraf-hef regarded them as if they were rabid dogs begging for handouts. "Don't even think I'm going to take you sorry-looking creatures across. Lord knows how you got this far." His entire body was encased in dirt, as if he'd been standing in that very spot for centuries, never bothering to change clothes, wash, or even rest. Matted hair reached his knees. His nails were at least two inches long and curled in an explosion of directions. One sandal was missing, the other broken.

"I'll try first," Ali whispered.

He greeted Hraf-hef with a warm smile and inquired about his health.

The gatekeeper scratched his beard, and something large and crusty, perhaps a dead dragonfly, fell out.

"That's the best you can do? Bland pleasantries? You know nothing of respect." He considered his own observation. "No one does. It's a lost art on all the lame souls who wash up on my shore."

Ali smiled again. "Forgive me." He stood and bowed. "I've seen you on TV. Burger Time. You're famous!" Ali hunted for a scrap of paper and found the script. "Could I get your autograph?"

This seemed to have the opposite effect on Hraf-hef. "How dare you mention that? Never asked me for permission. Never thanked me, never even gave me a damn Paradise Meal for stealing my identity. I've been forgotten by everyone."

Jared was reminded of his Great Uncle Roger, whom his dad forced him to visit in the retirement home when Jared was young. He was miserable about everything; the world had let him down and no amount of happy talk from his family would lighten his load. Each visit lasted no more than fifteen minutes and even that was pure misery. In fact, come to think of it, Jared had met lots of people just like Hraf-hef in his years as a documentary filmmaker, people who believed they had unjustly failed to receive the credit they richly deserved. And if his time as a researcher and booker had taught him anything, it was that the only way to get someone to open up was simply to show personal interest. Give them a platform to talk, to be the center of attention, to feel important again.

"Let me try." Jared moved forward. "We've come all the way from the next world to talk to you, set the record straight so it's never forgotten." He glanced at Kara who, true to form, was already filming. They once did the same thing to a crazy old hermit who lived in a foxhole on Iwo Jima, convinced World War II was still raging. (That he was born and raised in El Salvador made it even stranger.) After a bit of videotaping and a few celebratory questions, he packed his bags and went home.

But Hraf-hef wasn't so easily fooled. "You don't care about anything other than getting across this lake. Just pretending, like all you TV types do." He spat again, much closer. "I know why you're here. Steal my beetles. Talking to you is the last thing I would do."

"Beetles?" Derek asked with genuine curiosity.

"That's all you took away from his statement, Derek?" Kara snapped. "Beetles?"

"No, it's true," Jared continued. "I'd love to hear your story. I'm sure it deserves to be told."

"Blaah," Hraf-hef spat. "Obsequious little toad."

"Let me try," Kara said.

Jared raised an arm to stop her. "In all due respect, we both agree interviewing people, especially ones like him, is not your strong point."

"He's just a grumpy, lonely man. Needs some tough love, that's all," Kara said. "Do you know what this is?" She approached the encrusted gatekeeper and pointed to her camera. "This will capture your voice and your image so I can take it back with me and tell the world what a great man you are." She flipped the viewfinder to show Hraf-hef his image.

This gave the ferryman a start. "What soul-sucking trick is this?"

"No trick. Turn this on, and I can record for everyone all you have done, all that the world owes you. But, I'm thinkin' you have no real story to tell."

"What do you mean by that?"

"I mean, look at you. You're a hot mess. Blaming everyone but yourself for your troubles. No way someone like you could have power. Certainly not to cross this final gate to paradise." She videotaped him. "You're just an old has-been with a sack of bugs. I think the burger people got it wrong. I think you're bluffing."

"You do, huh? And who are you?"

"I'm a soul catcher. I take this box back to my world where your story lives. If you decide instead to sit there like roadkill, well, that's all you'll ever be."

Hraf-hef considered this. "No one cares about my story." Then he thought some more. "Ah, it's another ruse to get across."

"You think I'd be standing here, holding this heavy thing to my face, if I thought you didn't have a story?" This line she stole from Jared, but this time truly believed it. This guy was no ogre, just angry and alone, and had been wallowing in his misery for way too long. Like she had done for Derek a few minutes earlier, was it so hard to hear him out, no matter how foolish he may appear? No harm in being nice. Now and then.

"You didn't even know I existed until this gate, probably," he grumbled.

"Meh, stop feeling sorry for yourself. Look, we even brought gifts," Kara said to a sharp glare from Jared. *What gifts?*

"Derek, hand me that bag you made after killing that elephant in Zambia."

Jared raised an eyebrow: they both knew Derek bought it at a fancy leather store in the Dubai Airport. Jared still had the discarded receipt on his refrigerator, and it had become a running joke. But when Derek handed it over, Kara thanked him with a smile.

Was it so tough to let him pretend a little bit if it made him feel important?

After opening the bag, Kara produced an *Ancient Encounters* T-shirt and ball cap.

"Dear god," Jared whispered. "Swag? The last hour of hell, and that's the best we can do?"

"For you," she said cheerily. "Unless, of course, you'd rather sit here and sulk."

The man did his best not to mirror her smile. "What game are you playing? It's laced with poison."

Kara flipped off her commando cap and placed it on her own head. She turned to Ali, who was now holding the camera. "Frame me in this shot, and I'll kill you." She moved closer. "Poison-free. Try it on, if you dare."

"I'd never…" Hraf-hef said as he plopped it on top of his matted hair. A few spiders crawled free. "How does it fit?"

"Dude, it's so you. And there's more." Kara moved closer with a T-shirt and demonstrated how to put it on. "Very few of these ever made, but this one I brought just for you." The ferryman slipped into it. Flies and weevils scattered. It was the strangest billboard for *Ancient Encounters* the crew had ever seen. Ali zoomed in and suppressed a grin.

"Does it look okay?" Hraf-hef asked. "Not too tight in the belly?"

"Sexy as hell. Now I can see you must have really been someone special."

"About time someone noticed." He pointed to the camera and rubbed drool from his lip. "What you want to know?"

"Tell me about your life before you came here," Kara asked. "Bet you were some big cheese to get a job like this."

"No, you don't want to hear about that…" the ferryman said, and then launched into a supremely boring tale that involved an ox that had fallen into a well, a heap of stolen laundry and someone named Hepset, which could have been either the beast or the owner of the laundry, it was never made clear. He wasn't even bragging anymore, just wanted to talk.

"Fascinating," Kara lied as Hraf-hef opened the lock up and let the water drain. "Whatever did Hepset think of that?"

"That's the funny part," the sentry said before launching into another rambling tale that wasn't the least bit funny. Even following the narrative for follow-up questions was difficult, as Hraf-hef had few teeth and many of the words were slurred.

"After you," Kara said as Hraf-hef hopped into the boat and started chucking beetles. The lake opened up and the solar boat sailed across. Before they knew it, they were standing on the far shore, the boat somehow anchored and docked. From the other side, Hraf-hef waved back with his baseball cap, then plopped it on and admired it in his new mirror.

Jared gave Kara a bear kiss. "Didn't think you had it in you, kiddo."

"Learned from the best."

On the shore, a large cow approached. That it was standing on two legs and was only bovine from the head up barely registered to Jared. He had seen so many mind-bending hybrids that it had become commonplace. Between her curved horns rested an orange disk radiating like the sun. He didn't need Ali's help identifying this prime deity.

"Hathor," he said aloud so the deity could hear. "The mother goddess who gives birth to Re every morning. We are honored."

Hathor welcomed them with a tip of the horns, giving them tacit permission to enter.

"Is that it?" Kara asked. "We're in?"

"Yes," Hathor answered in English. "You have all done well." They expected more, but she only moved on, munching some grass.

The crew gazed around, collectively amazed that they had actually reached their destination. Ali looked at Derek and shook his head approvingly. Kara took Jared by the hand and squeezed it tight. "Congratulations Mr. Director, one hell of a first shoot. Talk about trial by fire."

The group busted up laughing. Jared had never felt so proud.

He turned to Derek. "*So...* what did I promise?"

Derek knew both the question and the answer. "You were right. Best episode ever."

A sumptuous field of ripened wheat awaited them. In the distance, shrubs bursting with citrus and acacia trees offered inviting shade. Streams rambled in between, the trickle of water creating a lush soundtrack.

People sat along the banks sipping wine, bouncing children, sleeping, laughing and making love. Beyond, perfectly preserved homes crested over rolling hills. It appeared to Jared like a romanticized version of ancient Egypt, something from a Disney film, but with a few notable exceptions: absolutely no one was working the fields, chiseling tombs or erecting monuments to someone else.

A woman approached, young and striking. So much had happened in the last few hours, and the feeling of accomplishment was so overwhelming that it took Jared a few seconds to recognize her.

"Tiya?"

"I didn't think you'd make it." She seemed more worried about their arrival than pleased. "In fact, I'm shocked you did."

Jared could only imagine she was still in mourning. "We never saw Mehy on the way," Jared said. "I'm sorry."

"I know. Everything has changed, and the prince is, well, it's best you speak to him yourself." She turned and started up the hill. "He's going to be angry when he sees you've made it after everything he did to stop you."

CHAPTER 39

"That's why I was killed at the Hippo's Jaw," Tiya explained as they walked down a shaded path. "I no longer had his protection; he no longer wanted me to safeguard his name."

"So he had you *decapitated?*" Derek asked, camera whirling. "Your boyfriend?"

"Not personally, no." They approached a little footbridge festooned with lilies. "I was to be killed a short while later anyway after Ramses took the crown. Mehy merely allowed things to speed up." Tiya pointed to a mud brick house on a nearby hill. "He can explain it better than I. I'm still struggling with it." She turned to Jared. "Perhaps you can change his mind. Only you have the power to keep things as they were."

"Me, how?" Jared asked, but Tiya had moved forward. The crew followed closely behind, yet, in spite of Tiya's tone, he was strangely in no hurry. He had led his crew through the gates and deserved a moment to himself to take in the cool, fragrant air. It wafted across his skin, and it was as if every follicle, every single atom in his body, was alert and tingling.

How strange to feel so fully alive in the afterlife.

Whatever happened next—with Mehy, the film, the strange dreams, the offer of replacing Omm—none felt beyond his comprehension or capabilities. One way or the other, he'd figure it out.

On the far end of the footbridge, Jared noticed an old man sitting alone in the reeds, lost in thought. Although facing the other way, something about his bearing, his intensity, felt deeply familiar. He wore a tunic splattered in mud but paid it no mind. A bullfrog hopped closer, and the man gently picked it up to examine its underbelly. He must have sensed Jared's stare and turned around with a casual grin as if Jared had simply walked away for a moment and was now returning. Jared knew exactly who the man was and approached.

Hori silently offered him a seat on the soft earth next to him. "I am still fascinated by how all the muscles come together," he said. "How it all holds so perfectly, so easy to take apart and rebuild." Hori let the frog go and said nothing more.

"Why?" Jared asked.

"Because you were stuck, and although a long time has passed, you're still me. I knew you could do with a little help."

Jared dipped his finger into the cool water and watched tadpoles scatter. "I've been dreaming of you, of the things you saw and did since I was a boy. But only since I arrived in Egypt did they become so..." he searched for the right word, "Insistent."

"It wasn't my place, I know. I'm not Jared. You are. But I knew what Omm and Tiya were going to ask of you."

"You mean coming here and saving Mehy?"

"No, that you did and did well. It's not your coming I was trying to prevent, but your staying."

Jared suddenly understood everything. It was Hori reaching out all this time, giving him the strength to face his true self. And once found, not to forfeit it. But now he had a million more questions to ask. Before he could, another old man, the one from his memory in the stuffy school room when he and Hori were playing footsie, approached.

"Hori, you'll catch your death down there," he said in a warmly chiding tone that suggested that he had uttered this same phrase a million times before.

All the funnier considering where they were. The man reached out and helped Hori stand.

"Just look at you, love. We'll have to get you cleaned before supper."

Hand in hand, they started down the trail. Before he turned a corner, the older man glanced back at Jared and nodded goodbye.

"He's really not supposed to be talking to you. But he couldn't bear to watch you disappear. Now, do as he says and go home to your own loved ones. Keep your *ka* strong so you may pass it on when it's your time to join us here."

He and Hori walked beyond a grove of papyri. Before they disappeared, Hori turned around one last time and waved. Then he flickered between stalks as was gone.

Jared caught up with the rest of the crew, who had gathered in front of a house on the hill.

"Our trying to save his name was precisely what upset him," Tiya said as she approached the front door. "It wasn't Ramses who washed away his tomb. It was his own request to Tefnut, goddess of moisture."

On the terrace flapped a loose canopy. Tiya called up, and Mehy appeared: not quite the Harlequin Romance image Omm had described in her memoirs, but a young, good-looking man with thick eyebrows and a long, bent nose similar to his father's.

He waved them up.

"It's easier if he tells you the rest."

Tiya led them through a simple dwelling consisting of a mud brick bench, a well-worn carpet and a few wicker baskets packed with loaves and vegetables. In the back room, Jared could hear the braying of a donkey and the quacking of a goose. A staircase, each cracked step of slightly different size, led to the roof. Jared couldn't believe the Crown Prince of Egypt lived here; this was little more than a laborer's hut.

On the terrace, Mehy acknowledged the crew with a polite smile and offered them a place on a pillowed mat. A fresh vat of beer lay under the awning, and he collected several bowls. Kara trained the camera on him. He frowned but didn't stop her. After nodding for them all to drink, he spoke at last.

"Tiya must have told you that I do not approve of any of this. Had I been consulted before you stepped through the door, I would have stopped you."

Jared was about to ask why, but Derek, who had found his voice after losing it within the gates, beat him to it.

"Why would you do that?"

"As you have all heard, my death was brutal." The prince turned to Tiya. "For you, my father, and certainly myself. I had become vain, assuming all that Seti had planned for me on the walls of his temple, preserved in the scrolls in the Hall of Records, would come to pass. One slice to my belly changed all that. I can still recall my last thoughts as I lay dying in that terrible tent so far from home. For my father, who would be so disappointed, to my brother who would be so gleeful, to you, Tiya, who would be truly heartbroken." He took a sip. "But mostly, I must confess with embarrassment, I grieved for myself. It meant I would never achieve immortal greatness."

"That has been my mission for centuries," Tiya said. "Have I not done enough?"

"Quite the contrary. I survived as long as I did because of your devotion." Mehy said as he took her hand. "But I've come to see that in doing so, I've robbed you of your own path. Your only purpose was to feed my ego. To keep the embers lit for something that should have been snuffed out long ago. That's not love. How happy have you truly been, in life after life, doing only that?"

"Your love has given me purpose. My own feelings are of little consequence."

"It would have been so much better if you simply came here, and we could share paradise together in full. But your *ka* was always splintered, returning to the world above and never here with me. And for what? To keep my name alive in a dark tomb no one knew about? I denied you paradise to serve my own vanity."

"You did not force me to do anything. You asked, and I agreed. It's how it's always been. To me, that's true love." She looked at Jared. "And must continue to be."

Kara's lens moved in for a close-up, and Jared followed.

"Why now," he asked. "After all this time?"

Mehy fixed his eyes on Jared. "It had much to do with you. Tiya told me you had been chosen to replace Omm. She explained that you were a perfect candidate because you were, if I may speak candidly, weak and discontent. Like all the others."

"That's always been the way," Tiya said. "Find someone with a connection to our world, someone who might gladly swap places for their own sense of peace."

Mehy studied Jared's face. "Had they even asked you if it's what you wanted?"

Jared shook his head. "No, but I figured it out on my own."

"There once was a time when there was no need to deceive someone into accepting. It would have been an honor to appease our gods and keep a king's spirit alive." Mehy filled up Ali's bowl. "But that was long ago, and both the gods and our way of life have faded away so much that it takes, as you wisely told the gods, the help of a coloring book to remember them."

Jared was surprised by all the attention but no longer afraid of it.

"I'm grateful I came, whatever the reason."

Kara had a question of her own. "We did all you asked, with great skill, as you say. Bully for us," she said, her tone rather surprisingly sharp. "I personally have other people in my life I would have braved the afterlife for instead of you, but you promised that we could make the most amazing documentary of all time. We've spent twelve hellish hours doing just that. You're not gonna renege on that promise just because you had a belated blast of modesty? Decided to live and die like the rest of us?"

Mehy raised his hands in the air. "You've proven your devotion to both my father and Tiya. It's why I'm letting you film me now. Capture anything you choose; ask any question you want. Not to revive my name, but to celebrate Tiya's. If there is a purer display of love in all of history, I've yet to come across it. After forfeiting so much, she should live forever through your film, not me."

Tiya seemed unready to let go just yet. "Seti arranged all this for you, so that his son may live forever. As long as that pact with the gods remains, it is up to him and Omm's replacement to decide what happens next."

"Easy enough. I will speak to my father," Mehy said with a dismissive wave.

Tiya turned to Jared. "But that's only half the pact. It's only fair to formally ask you: do you wish to replace Omm at Abydos, to keep Mehy's name eternal? With it comes a charmed life under the protection of the gods and an open window to this world. And Mentmose, I know, is waiting." She shrugged before continuing, as if the best part of her offer had been vocalized and the rest was merely contractual. "Or would you rather return to your life as it existed before you were called here?"

Jared asked for a refill before giving them his answer. Not because he needed time to think, but because the beer was good. Even before meeting himself along the canal, he had made up his mind.

CHAPTER 40

For Kara, the Field of Reeds was as beautiful as she could have hoped. The breeze, the sun, and the faces were all calm and soothing. It was a place she had not dipped her toes into for a long time. And it gave her comfort to know, as sublime as it was, she was still alive in it, not dead. There would be time enough for that later. She had done all she could for Lynette, and when it was obvious she could no more, leaving her ashes in the tomb, a place built to be protected and venerated for eternity, was by far the greatest gift. That she never saw Lynette face to face... *well, who does?* Her grief was just as palpable, but no longer did she blame herself for what transpired. Death, she now saw, wasn't just a burial but also a resurrection. One day they'd kiss again.

Jared and Ali were packing up the gear on the boat, and Derek was weirdly off picking flowers or something. She had a few moments to get some B roll, and on top of the hill seemed the perfect spot. A huge olive tree sparkled in the breeze, shimmering from green to silver depending on which side of the leaves were facing her. A great place to get wide shots.

But as she reached the crest, she realized she was not alone. A beautiful woman in a peacock dress was resting against its trunk, waiting for her.

Finally, after two endless years, the tears ran like the Nile, and for a long time, they said nothing. Lynette held Kara's hand, and she hers. Then, finally, Kara managed a single word. "How?"

"Not sure," Lynette said with a smile. "I was in heaven with my grandparents at a Bowie show. Some cat-headed gods appeared and asked if I wanted to visit you."

"They did?"

"Seems they were impressed. Said you traveled the underworld looking for a lost love, at great risk to yourself." Lynette thought of something else and giggled. "They also told me you charmed some selfish old gatekeeper to get into paradise." She moved in closer. "How'd my baby do that? It's not like you suck up to a crabby old man."

Kara traced the curve of Lynette's knee. "He was only sad and lonely. Guess I could relate."

She wanted to tell Lynette everything that happened to her, how she got there, and where she had left her ashes but then realized none of it mattered. She did it all for one burning purpose. To hold Lynette again. And here she was.

Kara drew in tight and wrapped her arm around Lynette's back. They held each other tight, more closely than they ever had before. Little things she had forgotten about Lynette. The tiny mole on her neck, the fact she never trimmed her cuticles, the tender curve of her collar bone, and her crooked smile came roaring back like a love poem.

Together they watched the sky start to change colors and the breeze pick up.

"Finally, you join me at the end of a work trip," she said, and Lynette giggled again.

Kara knew it was time. And they both also knew Kara wouldn't be staying, or swapping places, or demanding Lynette be reborn. This is how things worked since the world's very first death, and the vast expanse of time spread out in front of them now seemed only like a minute. They would meet again under a tree just like this one, and Kara would hold Lynette tight through eternity.

Until then, Kara Hawkins had things to do. Get Jared and crew home safe, finish this film, and maybe, just maybe, love again. She wanted to ask Lynette if that would be all right. She turned to her, and Lynette smiled, her approval already given.

From the bottom of the hill, Kara's name was being called. Tiya was telling them it was time to go. She nestled into Lynette's embrace one last time and inhaled. There was still a faint aroma of her favorite perfume on her neck, the one they bought together the day they were engaged, the one she sprinkled on her before she was sent to the morgue. She kissed it and stood. When she reached down to collect her camera and cap, Lynette was already gone.

Kara walked down the hill, where Jared was watching and waiting. Hand in hand, they made their way to the boat.

On the dock were several new faces, starting with four fresh jackal-headed men who had taken up oars. Also joining them was a tall, rather jolly-looking Egyptian wearing an emerald silk robe and sparkling rings. He welcomed the crew with a jug of wine. "Hello, I'm Nian. You'll be returning through my false door. It's an honor to serve you." He handed them silver goblets and filled each with palm wine. "From Troy, you know. Achilles brought it special."

Jared pulled Kara aside. "You okay?"

"Never better," she sniffed, then looked at all the gear. "You call this packin', Ali? Gimme a break. Let's count it all one more time."

Only Derek was slow to return. He meandered the shoreline, muttering to himself. When at last he approached, he called to Tiya, and the two walked off. Jared couldn't hear what was shared. The host was probably asking for some selfies he could use when he returned, for he surely would be famous: the only TV presenter who traveled to the past for adventure. This film would change all of their lives forever, and for Derek Dees, his dreams would come true: a movie and a book deal at the very least.

Tiya and Derek returned.

"You sure?" she asked him as they approached the pier.

"Completely."

They shared an unexpected hug as they boarded the boat.

"I'll guide you personally to the last gate. Omm knows nothing of what's happened here with the prince," Tiya said and then whispered something to the lead boatman. "Everyone on board and holding on tight?" Tiya asked the crew. "This last gate is safe but may be the strangest yet."

"*Imshi!* Let's go," Ali said. "Everyone is hugging people but me."

Mehy, now joined by his father Seti, waved goodbye from the shore. Everyone waved back but Kara, who kept her gaze on the solitary olive tree on the hill, flickering silver and green in the breeze.

CHAPTER 41

Five final gatekeepers stood watch atop an earthen pyramid. They held shiny, rounded stars that resembled sand dollars high above their heads. At the last twinkle of night a trap door opened. Inside the body of an enormous naked woman, radiating cobalt blue and slathered in stars, arched over the solar boat like the Milky Way. Nut, Goddess of the Night. The vessel sailed between thighs, pendulous breasts and towards her upside-down eyes. The oarsmen steered toward Nut's mouth, which, in Jared's mind, seemed like a terrible idea. But she opened it wide to accept the solar barque. As they passed between ruby lips, the stars glittered one last time, and ahead, a faint blush of orange peaked over a foreign cityscape. They were back in the Sun God Re's domain. Another day had begun.

But their terminus was not the Temple of Seti, where they had begun their journey. They were instead inside a cramped tomb, much smaller than Abydos. The crumbling Step Pyramid of Djoser loomed over the horizon and Jared sighed in relief. It may not be their point of departure, but Saqqara was a ruin, which meant that they were no longer in ancient times. He scanned the necropolis for Omm but she was nowhere to be seen.

"Um, Tiya, I think the boatmen's compass is off," Ali said, raising a finger to a group of men arriving on horseback.

As the party drew near, it was clear their dress was not 21st century. They wore thick blue uniforms, made of wool and held fast by bronze buttons. Hats like upturned banana boats, similar to those worn by Napoleon, capped their heads, and sabers hung from belted waistcoats. A few of them reached the tomb, but instead of paying the crew any mind, they began measuring and sketching the walls.

"They got the time wrong," Jared cried to Nian. "These are French epigraphers. Tell them they need to travel forward another two centuries."

Nian translated this to the boatmen, and their response made his eyes go wide. He bowed to Derek and stepped aside.

"Must say I am impressed. This appears to be your stop."

Derek dusted off his Indiana Jones hat. With a raised chin, he walked towards the false door.

"Derek! Stop! This is not our time," Jared said.

"Not yours, perhaps. But it's mine."

"Gimme a break," Kara screamed from behind the lens. "We're about to return safely home, and you wanna play-act Belzoni one last time? Get your perfumed butt back in the boat."

"I'm not coming with you."

"Derek?" Jared raised his voice, as one might to an errant child. He had no more time for the host's selfish theatrics. "I'm not leaving anyone behind, you know that."

"I don't want to play at being an explorer. I want to be one. Now I can be the most infamous one who ever lived. That's what I was trying to tell Kara earlier. The Great Giovanni Belzoni died somewhere along the Niger River in 1821, right? His body was never found."

"So?"

"So, I look the same. Well, my teeth are better, and I've got to be twenty pounds lighter. But I've been dressing the part for ages."

"You're going to give up your career just as it's about to explode?" Jared stood as if to stop him. "To die of dysentery like Belzoni?"

Derek shook the bottle of Cipro he retrieved from his bag. "I'll take one to a lab, invent more. Finish what Belzoni couldn't." He looked at Tiya and smiled. "And keep everything in Egypt where it belongs."

"Wait a minute," Kara said, "if you go off to live another life, what happens when we return to New York and tell them the host vanished? Hell, what happens to *Ancient Encounters with Derek Dees*, with us getting these jobs, making this film?"

Derek waved away the question. "If I never existed, they'd only hire someone more qualified."

"Like who?"

"How about *Ancient Encounters with Jared Plummer*? Has an authentic ring to it."

"Now *that* I'd watch," Ali said.

"Are you certain about this? There's no coming back." Jared looked at Tiya. "Is there?"

"Unless someone returns to collect him, his decision is forever."

Kara blew on her camera lens and gave it a wipe. "Yo. Don't look at me."

"Wouldn't expect you to. You've got better things to do." Derek ran a finger through his curly locks. He was about to put on his fedora but instead handed it to Jared. "For the new host. Where I'm going, they haven't been invented yet. You told me that on a shoot once."

He approached the door.

"Think I'll start by finding the Rosetta Stone before those French pansies—eh, epigraphers, sorry—do. Stop it from ending up in some European museum." Derek glanced around at his crew members.

"Thanks for one hell of a show. Sorry, I was kind of a jerk there at first. Plummer, you're by far the best producer I've ever worked with."

He stepped through the door, and the men on horseback approached.

With wide-eyed amazement, they watched him go.

"Allah help him," Ali said. "He won't last the night."

Jared was grinning. "I think he'll manage just fine."

It seems they had him all wrong. Perhaps Derek, like Jared, was always an adventurer, and it just took the right episode to bring out his best.

Jared giggled. "All this time, maybe it really was my script that was to blame."

The door faded shut, and after a bit of leapfrogging back in time, they landed in a much earlier era. Outside, the Step Pyramid gleamed as new. "Why are we going back again instead of forward?"

"We need to collect Omm and Said," Tiya said. "Seems they were invited to a dinner party in 2396 BC."

Beyond the false door, a grand banquet table was stacked with fish, meat, and several amphorae of wine. On one side, Said grinned, appearing rather tipsy, and across from him, a finely dressed Egyptian regaled him with stories.

"Ah," the fashionable man said when he noticed the new guests. "You've returned. I'm Khumun, and you're just in time for honey cakes and tiger nut sweets." He kissed Nian. "How was the journey? The leg didn't act up?"

"Not at all. It was fun to be on the road again."

Khumun raised a glass to Jared. "So, you're the Great Plummer? It's a privilege for you to feast at our table. Please."

Only then did Jared notice Omm sitting on the other end of the table. She was smiling, but her gaze was off, as if not fully there.

"She's lost her connection to me and Mehy," Tiya said. "And she doesn't yet know what he's decided. I need to tell her."

Tiya walked over to Omm and held her hand. Omm grinned widely at the recognition but then grew confused when she realized she and Tiya must never be seen together.

"It's against the rules," she said. "What's happened? Have we failed?"

Tiya whispered something in Omm's ear. At first, her eyes teared up in shock, then sadness, but slowly, a smile broke through. Finally, she exhaled deeply, as if she'd been holding her breath for eons.

Tiya beckoned Jared. "She wants to have a word."

"Jared, you're back!" Omm reached out for him, her hands rough but inviting.

"Are you okay?" is all he could ask.

"I'm grand." She ripped off a piece of goat from the tray in front of her. "We have a long journey back to Abydos, loves, so eat up, and then we cross over to our world. We'll chat along the way."

More wine was poured, and the crew recounted their journey to their hosts.

"You actually tried to kill Ramses the Great and then got an interview with him?" Nian marveled after Kara told her tale. "The most interesting visitors we've had in four thousand years." He unsealed another amphora. "This one is from a small batch made in 15th-century Orleans. Quite strong. Rumored to have given Joan of Arc strange dreams." He thought for a moment and whispered something to Khumun before continuing. "You know, our door is always open."

He pointed to the false door behind them.

"For what?" Ali asked. "Why on earth would we come back here?"

"Well, that film you created will surely make you all famous. They'll be begging for a sequel. And about time we have a famous gay traveler to tell our tales, don't you agree, Nian?"

"They called us Siamese twins! I certainly do." He turned to Jared. "Perhaps since you've had a glance around, you can set the records straight with that camera of yours. But not just Egypt. Who else do we know that could use a fresh look?"

Khimn thought for a moment. "Well, for a start, sad old Emperor Hadrian and his boy Antinous. Pity how that ended. Or those poor nameless lovers of Pompeii. And Alexander the Great and young Bagoas, they got that all wrong too." He raised a glass to his guest at the far end of the table. "Too many to name, really. Achilles, would you and Patroclus be open to showing them around Troy? Some lovely clubs there—well, until you burned them all down."

Achilles took his lips off Patroclus just long enough to answer. "Be delighted," he said with a distracted wave.

"So, only gay dudes deserve to have the records put straight?" Kara asked. "Doesn't seem like all that much has changed after all."

"You remind me of Sappho." Khumun laughed. "She was always going on about the same thing. I'll take you to Lesbos and introduce you to her personally."

"Enticing offer," Jared said, genuinely intrigued. "But we'd need Tiya or Omm to open the door. And their job is done."

Tiya's eyes went wide as she remembered something. "Oh, it nearly slipped my mind with all that's happened. You don't need us anymore. You have the power to do it yourself. Seti and the gods were most appreciative of what you did. They wanted to reward you in some way."

Jared considered this and giggled. "Tell me more about Alexander and Bagoas. Were they really as hot as the history books, and Mary Renault suggested?"

"Oh my, you don't know the half of it…" Nian began as more wine was poured.

CHAPTER 42

As sun and smog engulfed the motorway, Jared headed south back to Abydos, not keen on driving but beyond Omm, the only one still awake. She nodded approvingly.

"You really did splendidly. I knew you could pull it off."

"Are you disappointed I didn't agree to replace you?"

"I'm not now that I know what Mehy wanted. Better you live, and he dies."

Jared beamed with pride. "Turns out I used to be an embalmer for the royal court."

"I thought perhaps a scribe, but embalmer makes sense too."

A truck behind him honked for him to move faster, but Jared ignored it.

There's more than one lane. Let him go at his pace. I'll go at mine.

"If I didn't have those memories, we never would have made it through."

"Nonsense. One can never fully rely on past experiences. You survived because you're Jared Plummer, not some ancient mortician."

Omm wanted to say more but winced and massaged her heart.

Jared knew she didn't have much longer. "Are you ready to join him?" he asked.

"I am, love. Once the shock wore off, I was surprisingly relieved. It's been a long and satisfying journey, and it gave my life a purpose that I wouldn't have had otherwise. But it's a tremendous release to know my responsibilities are at an end. I'm knackered, I must admit." Outside, the Western desert glowed in the soft morning light. "Tell me, is the Field of Reeds beautiful?"

"It is."

"I'm so very keen to see it." Her voice was weaker now. "I wonder, considering past experiences, if you wouldn't mind doing me a final favor before you pack off. I'd be eternally grateful." She moved closer and in a raspy but determined voice, spelled out her request.

A few hours later, the van pulled up to their hotel in the village of El Araba, near the temple of Seti.

"Shall I take you to your house, Omm?" Jared asked but got no reply.

He gently shook her but knew she wouldn't respond.

"What's wrong?" Said asked as he opened the car door.

"She's gone."

Omm gazed ahead, hands crossed on her chest, a slight grin on her face.

Said's eyes brimmed with tears.

"I'm surprised she made it this far, but she was determined to get you all home safely."

They carried her body to her hut, where her legion of cats and dogs and the rest of the village were pacing. Loving tales were told, songs were sung, and a collective cry echoed across the desert. From darkened cliffs, unseen animals howled. To Jared, it registered as more raw and real than the one he witnessed for the pharaoh Seti all those millions of evenings ago. While the others went home to wash the twelve gates of hell from their hair and slip into clothes not slathered in serpent, Jared couldn't be bothered. He had a mission that he had to see through, and how he looked was far less important than how his 'client' did.

"She had a last request that may detain me a bit," Jared told Kara and Ali when they joined him in the temple. "You can go back to Cairo if you want, but Said, I'll need your assistance."

When he explained what he had to do, all agreed to help. Ali was so intrigued he even said goodbye to his kids and hung up the phone.

"*Ma'lesh.* What's one more day?" he told them.

Omm, aka Dorothy Kershaw, aka Bentreshyt, aka Tiya, and so many other souls, was buried, as requested, in Mehy's hidden tomb deep within the Osireion. Modern graves in ancient sites were illegal, as they were protected by the Supreme Council of Antiquities, so they did it in secret after the sun went down. What little remained of Mehy's mummy had already been reassembled by Said, shrouded in Omm's bed sheets and laid in his coffin. But Omm's body, thanks to Jared's promise, was fully embalmed so she would be prepared for the Twelve Gates. Normally the process took weeks, a luxury they didn't have. But recalling how he saved both the pharaoh Ahmose and the Demon Khufi, he removed Omm's organs and placed them in Canopic jars, in this case, Nescafe coffee tins. Her insides were packed tightly with natron that Omm had collected over the years for this very purpose. Finally, using her old floral dresses, Jared wrapped and placed her in the tomb next to her lover of thirty-three centuries. As a final gesture, Said slid her fuzzy green slippers onto her feet.

On the wall, in a space not destroyed by the storm, Jared wrote out, in large hieroglyphic letters, "Tiya and Mehy, reunited at last." This way, should someone stumble upon the crypt in the future, at least their names and their love for each other would prevail.

The hole in the floor was sealed, and the altar moved over the entrance. On the way out of the Osireion, in the submerged passage, stones were dislodged, so turbid water rose another foot, obscuring the entrance even further. Outside, everyone—crew and villagers alike—promised never to reveal the secret.

The crew returned to the hotel to get the last of the gear.

"Give me ten minutes for one last look around," Jared said, still unshaven and unbathed.

From the shade of the temple of Seti, Jared scanned the courtyard and reflected on all that happened. Everything seemed exactly as it did when he arrived, except Omm was no longer its gatekeeper. For the first time, the place seemed like what others had long called it. A ruin, nothing but a jumble of blanched and battered stones.

"It's like no trace is left from her time here at all," he confessed to Said, who walked alongside him.

"What makes you say that?" Said responded with surprise. "Her name may not appear on any temple wall, but her presence envelopes this place. I'll certainly never forget her. Nor will the villagers."

Jared thought of Mehy and Hori, and beautiful Mentmose, now three thousand years dead. "Stone remains, but we pass through like a breeze. For a while, we'll be remembered, talked about, until there comes a day when someone will utter our name for the last time. Our footprints are erased by the wind and sand."

"For most perhaps, but not you." Said began walking towards the temple. "You've left your mark. One that will puzzle historians for ages to come."

"What's that?"

"Come."

They plunged into the darkest recess of Seti's temple to a corridor Jared had walked before. Then, it seemed badly eroded, the walls bare of inscriptions. Now, it was alive with sumptuous carvings, many so well preserved they appeared new.

"How long has—"

"It's always been here, but that big rainstorm washed away plaster put up by early Christians, probably to hide the pagan symbols underneath."

Said produced a flashlight and sought out a busy relief some five feet up.

At first, Jared could make no sense of what he saw. Along a column showcasing Seti's journey through the underworld—the Opening of the Mouth, the Scale of Truth, his arrival in the Field of Reeds—was one strange panel. The dead king was lying in his solar boat and trailing behind in a smaller vessel were what looked like warriors in close pursuit. One brandished a thick spear, another, a female dressed like a warrior, wore a blocky face mask held to the eyes.

"I don't understand," Jared said. "I never saw that down there."

Said moved the flashlight closer, and details came into sharper relief. The spear was a boom pole, the face mask a camera, the warrior Kara. Behind them sat two men, one in a fedora and holding a scythe, the other pointing as if beckoning the boat forward.

"Won't that confuse the hell out of Egyptologists when they stumble across it?" Said laughed.

Jared chuckled too. "It's like the most historically unsound of my shows come to life. But why would Ramses carve us into the wall?"

"This mortuary temple was for his father, a god-king, and you were part of his journey into the Duat. That makes it sacred." Jared considered the implications. If it had always been here, did that mean this was all preordained, and it was no coincidence that he came here at exactly this time? The storm, Omm, the dreams, were they all part of some grand design? Jared shrugged and let it go. He thought about all those silly episodes of *Ancient Encounters* and decided not to dwell on it. *If we solved all of life's mysteries, what fun would the journey be?*

From down the corridor, a familiar voice.

"Yo, Plummer," Kara shouted. "Ali's back on the phone talking, loudly, to his family about the most boring, inane things. Right now, he's discussing which beans are best for *foul medames.* Can we hit the freakin' road already? I wanna get home."

"Coming!" Jared called back. "What will you do from here?" he asked Said, knowing this was goodbye.

Said shrugged. "Same as always. Give tours. But I think I'll add Omm's shed to the itinerary. Every great myth needs to be told and retold or it's lost to time."

The two men embraced, and Jared hurried down the hall and into the courtyard. The van was idling, a local driver behind the wheel. Jared was grateful he didn't have a jackal's face. Kara was counting cases and Ali was still on the phone to his children. "Yes, the black beans are so much better." He shook his head. "Oh, we're about to move. Wait until you see the treasures I got from ancient Egypt."

Jared looked on worried—had Ali been stealing as he went? But he smiled when he saw the plastic bags at his feet. A bunch of cheap plaster heads and sphinxes were bought at the local souvenir stand in the village. A King Tut piggy bank that looked more like Michael Jackson.

Ali saw him peeking. "You'd think I'd give my boys priceless relics? They'd only be destroyed before sundown."

Jared turned to Seti's temple one last time. A tour bus had arrived, and Said was stepping over the lazy dog to greet them. A gaggle of hefty Russians waddled off and complained of the heat. Jared slid into the back seat. For a moment, he thought he saw Omm standing in the shadows of the hypostyle hall, but it was only a trick of the eye. Or was it? He leaned back and was asleep before he got an answer. For the first time in ages, he didn't dream.

Seven almost disturbingly uneventful hours later, the crew arrived in downtown Cairo. Ali's wife and children were waiting for him in Tahrir Square. He hugged them tight, insanely so, and with tears in his eyes until his wife asked if he was okay.

"It's just been so damn long," he said and hugged her again.

"It's been since Monday. Today is Thursday." She ran a finger along the gash in his forehead. "What happened down there?"

"I'll tell you along the way." He rubbed the heads of his boys and handed them their gifts. "Ancient loot from the land of the pharaohs." One boy pulled out a plaster bust of Ramses and seemed overjoyed. "You know, the real Ramses was a very tiny man."

Ali hugged Jared and Kara. "That sure beats any other show I've worked on. Call me next time you need a sound guy. I'd love to see Saladin beat the snot out of Richard the Lionhearted." His mobile rang. "Yes, speaking... *What?* Really, oh wow. That's huge news… *la, la*, sorry, I'm not free."

"What was all of that?" Jared asked when he hung up. "Your eyes went wide."

"Yes, big discovery out in the desert. Seems some Zabbaleen, an old trash picker and a little girl, found the Lost Army of Cambyses. Thousands of bodies were all decked out in gold. That was Al Jazeera TV, wanted to know if I'm free to do sound."

"Amazing. You're going, right?"

"No way, I have two boys who I haven't seen in a thousand years, and it's Couscous Thursday. Plus, I've seen enough ancient corpses to last several lifetimes."

He took his youngest by the hand and slid into his car. His phone, Jared noticed, had disappeared.

Jared and Kara continued on to Cairo Airport. Near the entrance, they passed a billboard for the Grand Egyptian Museum featuring images of the Rosetta Stone, the bust of Nefertiti, and the alabaster sarcophagus of Seti the 1st. All part of the famous 'Belzoni Collection.'

"Well, I'll be damned," Kara said with a laugh. "The asshat did it."

When they arrived at international check-in, Jared stopped in front of the Iberia Airlines ticket counter.

"I knew it," Kara said with a smile. "I'm flyin' solo."

Jared grinned back. "Go back to New York, get the footage transcribed. Watch the editors like a hawk so they get the story right. Then, maybe go see Caterina, that cute barista."

"Funny thing," Kara said. "I texted her this morning. We're meeting for dinner on Monday." She studied her best friend's face. "I'm sure he'll be delighted to see you again. But… you know… what if he…"

"Isn't? I dunno. Been flying by the seat of my pants for thousands of years. Why stop now?"

Only the squeak of the crosstown Seville bus let Jared know that he was still alive and not back in 'Shadow Town.' His story at an end, he glanced worriedly at Carlos, who had fallen silent.

Carlos mindlessly fiddled with his tourist brochures, the dung beetle that had been listening along to Jared's tale gone with the afternoon sun. Eager bus passengers pushed past, one of them the desk clerk who had shot Jared a look of disgust when he barged into Carlos' office.

"Estas bien?" she asked her colleague, tossing Jared another evil glance.

"Si," Carlos said with a wave. "Gracias, Maria." Finally, he met Jared's stare. "It's not like you to lie, but come on, ancient Egypt… mummies… serpents… being chased by Ramses the Great?"

"It's a lot to take in, I know," Jared sighed. "Saying it aloud, I must admit I'm not sure I believe it all myself."

"Do you have any proof this happened, and it's not just sunstroke?"

"Well, I do have episode 37 of *Ancient Encounters with Derek Dees*. About 50 hours of raw footage." He forced a smile. "How's that?"

Carlos could no longer suppress a smirk. "I never cared for that stupid show. You know how TV people make shit up." Before Jared could counter, he held up a hand. "I'm joking." He rose with a start, surprising Jared, who could only imagine this is where he said his final, bitter goodbye. "Come," Carlos commanded, "let's get you some clothes that don't smell like the Bog of Eternal Stench." When they passed a trash bin, Carlos dumped the brochures and took Jared's hand. "Just one question. This Mentmose guy you hooked up with. Like, *how* hot are we are talking?"

Jared giggled and held his boyfriend's hand tighter than he had ever dared. There wasn't a chance in hell he'd ever let go again.

ACKNOWLEDGMENT

There are far too many people to thank for this novel's existence—starting with my husband Carl, who lived the adventure with me, even when he had far better things to do in the modern world, and my dear family, friends and fellow writers who read draft after draft (after freakin' draft), and the Egyptologists, editors and experts who gave their time and talents so generously as I tried to get it right.

Most of all, thank you for taking this journey with me, and stay tuned for the further adventures of Jared Plummer and the cast of *Ancient Encounters*. (After shooting the 'greatest documentary in the history of humankind', you don't think you've heard the last of them, do you?)

ABOUT THE AUTHOR

Neil Laird is a multiple Emmy-nominated director of historical films for Discovery, BBC, PBS, National Geographic and many other networks. He has produced over 100 programs around the globe that feature crumbling Egyptian tombs, lost Mayan cities and mysterious shipwrecks at the bottom of the sea. But to his continued disappointment, he has yet to stumble upon a time machine to see these things when they were shiny and new. This book, the first in a series, aims to remedy that grave injustice.

A FINAL REQUEST

If you enjoyed this book, please let the world know by showering the eternal internet skies with a bunch of stars on Amazon and other review sites, and visit neillaird.com where the portal to the ancient past is always open.

Printed in Great Britain
by Amazon

41587894R00219